DEATH'S LONG SHADOW

A HARRY BROCK MYSTERY

DEATH'S LONG SHADOW

KINLEY ROBY

FIVE STAR
A part of Gale, Cengage Learning

GALE
CENGAGE Learning™

Detroit • New York • San Francisco • New Haven, Conn • Waterville, Maine • London

GALE
CENGAGE Learning"

LIBRARY OF CONGRESS CATALOGING-IN-PUBLICATION DATA

Roby, Kinley E.
  Death's long shadow : a Harry Brock mystery / Kinley Roby. —
1st ed.
    p. cm.
  ISBN-13: 978-1-4328-2535-5 (hardcover)
  ISBN-10: 1-4328-2535-6 (hardcover)
  1. Brock, Harry (Fictitious character : Roby)—Fiction. 2. Private
investigators—Florida—Fiction. 3. Murder—Investigation—Fiction. I. Title.
PS3618.O3385D445 2011
813'.6—dc23   2011024997

First Edition. First Printing: October 2011.
Published in 2011 in conjunction with Tekno Books and Ed Gorman.

Printed in the United States of America
1 2 3 4 5 6 7 15 14 13 12 11

For Linn and Chris

"Somewhere out beyond our ideas of right doing and wrong doing, There is a field. I'll meet you there."

Rumi

1

"The trail narrows just beyond the brook," Harry said, waving a moth away from the lamp.

"I know the place," Tucker put in, passing Harry the jug of plum brandy. "Were you ever at The Oaks?"

"Getting invitations to ten-million-dollar horse farms," Harry said, amused at the idea, "is a little above a private investigator's social grade."

Tucker laughed.

"I was out there a few times years ago," he said, "and I remember that part of the trail—I believe they call them rides—because I came on a panther having a drink in the creek. He decided I didn't look edible, so I'm still here talking with you."

The two men were holding down a pair of bentwood rockers on Tucker's unscreened back stoop. The last of the light had drained out of the sky; on the small table between them a kerosene lamp, enclosing the stoop in a soft yellow glow, spilled their shadows into the encroaching darkness.

"That's where Brandon Pike hit the wire," Harry said. "His horse must have been going full out because, according to Jim Snyder, Pike's head was sliced off as clean as if it had been done with a sword."

Harry, deeply tanned, of medium height and stocky build, with close-cropped hair liberally sprinkled with silver, got out of his rocker and filled Tucker's glass, then set the jug on the floor between them.

"I wonder if Brandon got what he wanted?" Tucker asked in a quiet voice, staring out into the darkness of the forest that crowded within a few dozen yards of the stoop.

Harry looked at his friend and gave a short laugh before noticing he wasn't joking. Then he went back to sipping his brandy, thinking about Tucker's question, and listening to the dense spring piping of colony frogs, backed up by a full string symphony of insects, fiddling and rasping in the tangle of trees and vines that in Southwest Florida is more jungle than woods.

"You're not suggesting he committed suicide?" Harry asked.

"You said Jim told you the horse must have been going at a full gallop," Tucker said, standing up to stretch.

A short, thin man with a lively, weathered face remarkably free of wrinkles, given his advanced years, and a fringe of wispy white hair above his ears, he was dressed in a long-sleeved, collarless white shirt buttoned at the wrists, a pair of time-faded overalls, and well-oiled work boots. Beside his chair lay a straw hat. In all the years Harry had known him, he had never seen the old farmer dressed any other way.

"The earth near the brook was soft." Harry said. "Jim and Hodges and their crime scene people measured the horse's stride at about eleven feet where it went under the wire. It was really stretched out. It would be an odd way to commit suicide."

"Neither of us thinks this was suicide," Tucker said impatiently, easing back into his chair and picking up his glass, "but do you recall Ellen Blevitt's piece in the *Avola Banner* last year? It came out two or three months after Brandon had his heart attack."

"Not in any detail," Harry replied. "I do recall Pike sued the *Banner* over it."

"He did, but he and the *Banner* found common ground, as they say, and kept it out of court," Tucker said. "My point is that she claimed Brandon was ignoring the advice Fred

Bascomb, his cardiologist, had given him when Brandon came out of the hospital. She quoted Bascomb as having told him that, if he expected to stay alive, he was going to have to give up cigars, jumping out of airplanes, racing cars, and acting like a damned fool."

"Casting pearls before swine," Harry said sardonically.

"Well," Tucker said with a chuckle, "you always were able to control your enthusiasm for Brandon Pike. Do you know who found him?"

"Tyce Yellen, his stable manager. Is there any truth to the rumors about Yellen and Holly Pike?"

"It's hard to know," Tucker said. "Holly must be twenty years younger than Brandon, and no one would accuse her of putting off until tomorrow what she could throw her legs around today. Did Jim say anything about the horse Brandon was riding when he was killed?"

"That comment about Holly Pike's not like you!" Harry exclaimed in surprise.

"Well," Tucker said defensively, "I guess I think she's had a lot to do with Brandon's behaving the way he did in recent years. What about that horse?"

"Jim did mention Tyce had tied a saddled chestnut stallion to a young post oak near the trail and warned everyone to stay away from the animal. Tyce was driving a Jeep so I assume Pike had been riding the horse."

"Jack!" Tucker said, shaking his head. "Ellen got it right. Brandon was living harder than ever. His riding that red devil is proof positive."

"Of his living hard?"

"That he was trying to kill himself."

"If that's so, he got unexpected help," Harry said, "and if I was Jim, I'd start thinking about Tyce."

Tucker seemed to have drifted off, but after a moment he

said, "Do you remember that trial, oh, three years ago, I think, Brandon hit a man on Orchard Street in Avola and was charged with vehicular homicide?"

"The man's name was Henry Jackson," Harry said. "The trial created quite a stir for a month or so."

"That's it, and Jackson's blood alcohol content was so high no one could figure out how he ever managed to walk into the street in front of Brandon."

"Hadn't Pike been drinking, too?" Harry asked.

"He had, but, as I remember, his BAC was 0.06," Tucker said, "which didn't make the DUI level, but he was charged under the impairment of normal faculties portion of the law. It didn't stick, though. Witnesses said Jackson staggered out from behind a parked SUV right in front of Brandon's BMW, and that Brandon jumped out of the car, took one look at Jackson, pulled out his cell phone, and called 911."

"That blew away the impaired faculties charge," Harry said, "but wasn't there a civil suit filed right after that? I don't recall the outcome."

Tucker tested his drink again and set his glass down with a deep sigh of satisfaction. "If I should get to heaven and find there's no plum brandy, I'm going to try the other place."

Harry laughed, then said, "Wasn't there a wrongful death suit filed against Pike? It bothers me a little the way I'm forgetting things."

"It's age," Tucker said with a mischievous grin. "As for the lawsuit, the judge dismissed it. I never did know the grounds."

They sat without talking for a while. Then Harry asked Tucker how he came to know so much about the Pikes.

"At one time, Brandon's father Zebulon and I were good friends," Tucker explained. "Then in 1940, Zebulon got so worked up over Hitler, he joined the Royal Canadian Air Force, was shot down over the Channel, and had the good luck to be

saved. While he was mending, he fell in love with his nurse
Elspeth Mortimer and married her. She was the only child of
an English arms manufacturer and the heiress to a fortune."

Tucker rocked for a few moments then went on.

"Zebulon and I stayed in touch over the years, but by the
time he found his way back here, bringing Elspeth and their son
Brandon with him, we had gone different ways. He bought The
Oaks and went into business, then took up breeding horses. He
died of a heart attack in, let's see—1966, the year I moved onto
Bartram's Hammock."

"You've been out here over forty years!"

"So I have, and you've been here twenty-five."

"Time passes," Harry said, not liking the thought. "What
happened to his wife?"

"Moved back to England and left Brandon to run The Oaks.
She died a few years ago."

"Then I arrived and ruined your peace and privacy," Harry
replied, hearing the melancholy note that had crept into Tucker's
voice and wanting to lighten his mood.

Two dark shadows detached themselves from the larger darkness of the trees and moved silently toward the stoop.

"It's Oh, Brother! and Sanchez," Harry said, standing up to
greet the tall black mule and big blue tic hound that walked
into the light.

"We've talked right past their suppertime," Tucker said with a
laugh. "Will you stay and eat?"

"No," Harry said, grasping the hound's head and giving it a
good shake, which pleased the dog so much that he bared all
his teeth, giving Harry his best smile. "The work I came here to
escape is still waiting for me."

He straightened up and stroked the mule's glistening neck
while Oh, Brother! pushed his nose into Harry's chest and blew
softly in welcome.

"Let me know if you hear anything more about Brandon's murder," Tucker said, picking up their glasses and the brandy jug and turning toward the kitchen door. "Oh, Brother! and Sanchez will see you home if you want the company."

"I'll settle for their walking me to the end of your driveway. The moon's up enough for me to see snakes on the road. I think it's more likely that you'll get any news before I do, but I do wonder why Brandon was killed."

Tucker turned back, looking reflective.

"Brandon Pike could be a trial, no mistake, but he was a good man in many ways. And Tequesta County won't find a replacement for him anytime soon. He was generous to a fault, never turned his back on anyone needing help."

"You're right. I didn't like him," Harry said, feeling less than generous, "but I agree with you—he quietly gave a lot of his time and money to the kind of causes that helped a lot of people but don't get a lot of attention. That daycare center he built for the farm worker community in northeast Avola is thriving."

"Well," Tucker said, sounding sad but resigned, "he's beyond all that now."

"Yes," Harry said, stepping off the stoop with the two animals turning to accompany him, "and it's clear from what's happened that somebody wanted him dead. I'd give a lot to know who that is."

"Professional interest?" Tucker asked.

"Sounds right, but I also think people who cut off other people's heads ought to be restrained."

2

The white sand track where Harry took leave of Sanchez and Oh, Brother! was the only road on Bartram's Hammock. It ran from a narrow hump-backed bridge, connecting County Road 19 to Bartram's Hammock, past Harry's house, past Tucker's farm road, ending in a cypress swamp that formed part of the Stickpen Preserve, a huge watershed protection area administered by the state.

Bartram's Hammock, Harry's home and refuge, was a heavily wooded, slightly higher piece of land in the midst of the swamp, and one of the places the Indians favored for their settlements because hammocks had sweet, fresh water and, thanks to the heavy growth of hardwood trees, were about ten degrees cooler in the summer than the surrounding oven, fired by the Florida sun.

Harry loved walking on the Hammock day or night, although, given the fact that several varieties of poisonous snakes— rattlesnakes and cottonmouths being the largest—called Florida home, it made sense not to be walking at night. The warm sand road attracted the coldblooded critters once the sun set, making the trek risky unless there was moonlight enough to see where you were stepping, especially if, like Harry, you were wearing shorts and sandals.

But tonight the moon was up, making silver tracks on the slow-flowing Puc Puggy Creek, which ran beside the road all the way to the bridge, glowing in the haze and floating over the creek's floodplain. Harry went his way, savoring the aftertaste of the brandy as well as the sights and sounds of the night.

Leaving the road and crossing what he called his lawn but what was chiefly white sand and sunburned bunch grass, Harry was pulling open the screen door when one of his barn owls ghosted around the corner of the lanai and sailed, pale and silent, over the lawn, pitching down suddenly and snatching a cotton rat out of the ferns at the edge of the woods. The rat screeched once before the owl struck its victim with its beak and rose soundlessly on its powerful wings, beating its way back to the barn.

Harry was not sentimental about the death of animals. He had been a game warden in Maine before coming to Florida and was, as well as being a private investigator, a warden employed by the state to protect Bartram's Hammock from poachers and monitor the health of the animals living on the Hammock. And while he did not subscribe to the "nature red in tooth and claw" theory of how ecosystems function, he was adjusted to the fact that predators killed their prey and ate them. But in this instance, possibly because of the gruesome nature of Brandon Pike's murder, he experienced a sudden revulsion against the intrusion of violence into the quiet moonlit beauty and peace of the night.

Harry stood and watched the silent killer moving purposely toward the barn and its six young owls. Perhaps because of the suddenness of the owl's attack, the rat's scream, and the brutal efficiency of the owl's killing strike had jumped his adrenaline flow. For a moment, gripping the handle of the screen door, his mind suddenly flooded with the figure of a man, leaned forward in the saddle, the powerful horse straining under him, snatched backward as the wire sliced into his neck, the head spinning away, the body still thrashing as it slammed into the ground, and the stallion thundering on, riderless.

The ringing of his house phone shattered the hellish vision, but smoking fragments of it were still falling through the ruins of his peace of mind as he picked up the phone.

"Mr. Brock?" a deep but clearly feminine voice asked.

"Yes," Harry answered.

"My name is Holly Pike, Brandon Pike's widow. You may recognize his name."

Maryland, Harry thought, listening to her voice.

"My condolences, Mrs. Pike. You've suffered a terrible loss."

"Thank you, Mr. Brock. That's very kind of you."

She paused, and Harry wondered briefly, not liking his reaction, whether the hesitation was natural or orchestrated.

"A few minutes ago I spoke with Mr. LaBeau. I believe you and he are neighbors."

"He's a close friend," Harry said and waited.

"A gentleman," she replied.

"That too," Harry agreed, wondering how long this was going to go on.

"You must forgive me, Mr. Brock, for hesitating this way," she said, strain coloring her voice. "I'm usually much more straightforward. Brandon's death seems to have undone me somewhat."

"I'm sure it has," Harry said. "Take your time."

"Thank you. That's New England I hear, isn't it?"

"Maine, although it's been some time since I left there."

"Yes, well, it's stuck to you the way Maryland has stuck to me. I'm not in any hurry to lose it either. As long as I can still hear it, I know something of me is left."

"It's a lovely accent," Harry said. "I like it very much."

My God, he thought, why am I making small talk with this woman who's just lost her husband?

"I want to hire you," she said. "There, I've said it."

"To do what?" he asked, laying aside his plantation hat.

17

"I'm not quite sure," she said. "No, that's not true. I want to talk to you. When I've done that, I think I'll know just what it is I need from you."

"And you can't give me any idea of what that need might be?"

"Ah, I was afraid you'd stick on that."

Harry was surprised to find himself liking this woman, which was unusual because, as a rule, he didn't connect well on the phone with people he was meeting for the first time. In addition, it wasn't much of a reach to think she might have had a hand in killing her husband. Often, the killer in such cases was someone in the victim's family.

"I'm not so much stuck as puzzled."

"In another moment or two, I'm going to start feeling like a fool, Mr. Brock."

"That would be premature," Harry said, suddenly making up his mind. "I'll listen to you, talk to you, do whatever I can to help. How's that?"

"That would be very kind of you. Please tell me your fee."

"I don't charge for listening, only doing," he said. "But I do have a favor to ask."

"Yes?"

"Please call me Harry because a long time ago during a trial in which I was being tried for murder, a judge and a prosecuting attorney insisted on calling me Mr. Brock. Hearing the name brings it all back."

"Harry it will be," she said, then added wryly, "I hope you were acquitted."

"Mrs. Pike is in the conservatory," the Vietnamese butler said after Harry gave him his name. "Please follow me."

He followed the man, flanked by a pair of Rottweilers almost as big as Shetland ponies, whose alert attention kept Harry walking as close to the butler as he could get without actually stepping on his heels. They passed through a great many rooms with shining, dark floors, overstuffed furniture, and bright paintings on the walls. It seemed to Harry a very long time before they stepped into an octagonal room, constructed largely of glass and full of hanging plants and the morning sun, where Holly Pike awaited them.

She was dressed in jodhpurs, a white blouse, and riding boots. Her honey-colored hair was cut short and styled to set off a lean, handsome face that reflected its years and became her. Her large, hazel eyes were clear, and the smudges under them registered frankly, Harry thought, the pain of the past few days—or was it years? The question interested him because she interested him.

"Thank you, Thahn," she said with a quiet smile to the butler. "Leave Nip and Tuck with me. I want them to become accustomed to our visitor."

Thahn inclined his head and left as silently as he had arrived, and the dogs, taking their cue from their mistress, relaxed and began to wag their stubby tails.

"Let's get this out of the way, Harry," she said in a businesslike voice. "Nip, Tuck, come here. This is Harry. Shake hands."

To Harry's surprise, they did, and when the ceremony was over, flopped down on the flagstone floor, apparently losing all interest in him.

"There," she said, "now you are safe as houses. They know you belong here and will protect you the way they protect me. It takes awhile to get used to them, but once that's behind you, they are very comforting."

"I'm not quite there yet," Harry said, provoking a laugh. "Before we begin, I want to apologize for springing that reference to my trial on you. I haven't mentioned it in a very long time, and there was no need of my doing it with you."

"I assume you were acquitted," she replied, a smile tugging at the corners of her mouth.

"Yes, but aside from keeping me out of jail, it didn't do me much good."

"How so?"

"Well, the state decided the trial had ruined my usefulness as a warden and fired me. My wife was so furious with me for having gotten myself arrested that she left me and took our two children with her."

"How wretched! What had you done to set her off like that, or was it the cherry on the sundae?"

"Are you sure you want to hear this?" Harry asked. "It's not what you'd call edifying."

"Start out and see what happens."

"I know what happens. I came on a man dressing out a deer he had shot after the season was closed. When he saw me, he grabbed his rifle and began shooting at me. When he nicked my left arm, I fired at him, planning to take him down but not kill him. The bullet hit bone, splintered, and a fragment struck his heart."

"Bad beginning, Harry, semi-bad ending."

"You could say that, but it's still with me."

She stood looking at him, her thumbs hooked into her jodhpur pockets. Harry found it hard to guess what she was thinking.

"True, but I suppose time will bring changes."

"For better or worse."

She nodded.

"Can you ride a horse?" she asked.

"Not in the sense you probably mean."

"I don't expect you to gallop," she said.

"Certainly not . . ."

Harry stopped just in time to prevent himself saying, ". . . on this farm."

But he could see by the stricken look on her face that she had already finished the sentence.

"I'm sorry," he began, but she shook her head.

"Don't be," she said. "There are miles of rides on this estate. And you've just alerted me to the possibility that there may be wires strung across some of them."

She paused to give Harry a watery smile.

"I don't think anyone but you has considered that possibility. Thank you. Now, if I promise to put you on a horse that would rather miss a meal than run, will you go out with me?"

The horse that Harry found himself on was an old, gray mare, calm as sunlight on still water.

As they ambled out of the stable, Harry said, "If nobody tells me that she ain't what she used to be, I think I can stand the embarrassment."

"I kept my word," Holly said with a laugh. "Let's try to pick up the pace a little."

She was mounted on a dark bay hunter, whose arched neck and sideways skitter told Harry it was itching to find a high fence.

"What's her name?"

"Sueño."

"Oh, good," Harry said. "Sleep."

"Some of our horses have Spanish names because at one time many of our staff were Hispanic," she told him. "In Zebulon's time, I gather it became something of a tradition at The Oaks."

"Except for Tyce Yellen," Harry said.

"Yes, Brandon made changes when he inherited. Our manager is from eastern Tennessee, I think."

Harry gave her several points for the ease with which she dealt with his fairly obvious probe.

By this time they were moving at a sedate trot that soon got them away from the stables and onto a wide and winding dirt track that finally brought them to a gate with a punch key lock, which Holly negotiated without getting off her horse. Harry walked the mare through the gate into a wide pasture dotted with clumps of oaks, feeling like an elderly gentlemen, possibly convalescent.

"Now I can talk," Holly said, having ridden up beside him, the gate safely closed. "Are you ready to listen?"

"I think so," Harry said, not yet having found a seat that was comfortable.

She looked at him critically.

"Rest your weight evenly in the saddle," she told him in a brisk voice. "Sit up straight, let your legs hang loosely, let your feet rest lightly in the stirrups, don't let your toes point in or out, and hold your reins a little lower than your navel. Good. Now relax."

"That's only six things to keep in mind while I'm listening," Harry said, already feeling more comfortable.

"If you become a horseman," Holly said cheerfully, "you'll spend the rest of your life trying to master those simple things, along with a few more."

She rode beside him for a few minutes, watching and making occasional suggestions.

"Good," she said. "If you get tired, say so, and we'll stop to let you rest."

I'll die in this damned saddle first, Harry told himself while smiling at her and trying to keep his toes straight, convinced he looked as ridiculous as Governor Dukakis with his head sticking out of that tank.

"Do you remember my mentioning the fact that most of our

staff was Hispanic?" Holly asked, emerging from a period of silence.

Harry said he did.

"Well, that fact has a central place in what I'm going to tell you," she said, "and everything I'm going to say now is absolutely confidential. Are we agreed?"

"Am I employed by you to hear these facts?"

"Why are you asking me this?" Holly did not sound pleased.

"Because if I am, whatever you say to me, providing you don't confess to having committed a crime or your intent to commit one, is legally protected as confidential information."

"We haven't signed anything," she said, obviously confused.

"Can you reach over here and shake my hand?" he asked while reaching out his right hand and keeping his eyes fixed between the mare's ears for balance.

She laughed. He felt his face burn. Then he felt her grip his hand.

"Okay," he said. "Go ahead."

"Don't fall off," she told him.

"Cruel," he said. "Very cruel."

"It's true," she said, laughter still in her voice, "but I don't feel bad."

"Tell me your story."

3

She did, and when she finished, she said, "Let's dismount and walk the horses for a while," dropping lightly to the ground in a single smooth movement.

Harry's dismount resembled the flailings of a man falling off a roof, but he managed to land on his feet. Holly and the horses watched with interest.

"I see we're going into the woods," Harry said, urgently wanting to distract them. "Walking is a good idea."

"Yes," Holly said, "your remark about the possibility of there being more wire has stayed with me."

In Southwest Florida, areas of scattered slash pine and low-growing saw palmetto are called upland forest. Woods of this sort are usually dry, and a foot or so higher than the surrounding swamps, providing the pines with what they need—plenty of sunlight and water not too deep for their shallow root system to tap into.

"Rattlesnake country," Harry said.

"Oh, yes," Holly said. "The place is stiff with them. Are you afraid of snakes?"

"No," he said, walking with his hand on his mare's neck, the reins hanging loosely in his left hand.

"She likes you," Holly said with an indulgent smile.

"How do you know?" Harry asked.

"She's walking with you, not being led. High marks to you."

"Tucker's mule always walks with me like this," Harry said.

"I've heard that animal all but talks," she said.

"Tucker talks with him all the time," Harry said with a chuckle. "When I talk to him, half the time I think he knows what I'm saying. Half the time I think I'm nuts.

"But so far," he continued more seriously, "I haven't heard anything to make me think you need my services. Have I missed something?"

A large pileated woodpecker rocketed off the side of a pine to their right with an ear-splitting cackle and shot across the ride in front of them. The mare stopped and cocked her ears, but the bay used the event as an excuse to stand on his hind legs and squeal in protest. Harry looked up at all that horse over his and Holly's heads and caught his breath, but Holly added her free hand to the one on the reins and unceremoniously pulled him down with a sharp, "Stand!"

Having done what he wanted to do, the horse dropped back to earth and snorted with satisfaction.

"He expected to be run this morning," Holly said, rubbing his nose affectionately, then turning her back on him and resuming their walk. "No, you haven't. I've been holding back that part. I think I'm getting cold feet."

The sun had climbed and bent its rays a little more directly on them while they had been walking, and Harry was beginning to miss his hat. Holly showed no signs of discomfort, however, so Harry said nothing and waited for her to go on, although finding it increasingly difficult not to ask what was troubling her.

"Well, I'm not going to be happy with myself no matter what I do," she said, leaving Harry uncertain whether she was talking to him or herself.

"I'd like to help here, but I don't see how I can," he said as sympathetically as he could, having no idea where she was trying to go with the conversation.

"No, you can't," Holly said, "but I guess I'd better get on with it. There's one family whose members have lived here from the beginning. Their name is Cruz. Brandon's father had a child by Alejandra Cruz very soon after their arrival from England. Understandably, it widened the rift that had been building between Zebulon and Elspeth over Brandon's education and the move to this country."

Plus rocks in the bed, Harry thought.

"Is that why after his death, Elspeth returned to England?" he asked.

"It probably helped."

Harry waited for her to go on. When she didn't, his curiosity piqued, he asked what happened to the mother, expecting to be told she was bought off and sent away.

Holly gave a low and humorless laugh.

"Did you know there's a second entrance to The Oaks?" she asked by way of an answer.

"No," Harry said, "should I?"

She didn't answer that question either, and if she thought it a little sharp, she gave no indication. In a few minutes they emerged from the pine woods and encountered another gate.

"Let's ride again, shall we?" she said, turning to rub the bay's nose again. "Scotsman needs to stretch his legs."

"Sure," Harry said, trying to sound cheerful about the prospect.

"We have Black Angus in this pasture," Holly said, having dealt with the gate. "They were Brandon's pet project. I prefer horses. I wouldn't walk through this pasture on a bet."

"I can see why," Harry said. "I think there's just about time for us to get back through that gate."

The cattle were bunched about fifty yards to their right and had stopped grazing to stare at them, their ears fanned out; but it was not the cows that worried Harry, although they did not look very friendly. It was the herd bull that held his attention, a mountainous beast with a brass ring glinting in his nose and a massive head and equally massive horns. He was trotting toward them, dewlap swinging, and Harry didn't think he was coming over to shake hands like Nip and Tuck.

"That's Thor," Holly said calmly, moving up beside Harry and watching the bull with interest. "It's an odd thing. As long as we're on horseback, he won't bother us. Brandon got him doing this by giving him a sack of grain for a treat when he came into the pasture, to check on his pets. Some pets," she added disdainfully. "The cows are stupid and meaner than Thor is."

The bull was now only a few yards from them and had stopped to toss his head and rumble at them, drool hanging from his mouth. Harry did not like his looks.

"Ugly beast," she said, setting the bay in motion. "Let's go."

Harry managed to pull the mare's head up from the grass, and seeing the bay trotting away, she followed. To Harry's great relief, the bull went back to grazing.

"Ride toward that clump of palms," Holly called over her shoulder. "I'm going to give Scotsman his head for a while."

Turning, she leaned forward, loosening the reins. Scotsman gathered himself and was away like a rocket, flinging clots of earth behind him. By the time the mare had carried Harry to the stand of Canary Island palms, Holly and Scotsman had thundered around a wide circle and finished their race workout with a canter around the trees. Sueño appeared unimpressed with the show. The bay was still prancing, and Harry noticed that the ride had put some color back in Holly's face.

"He's a showoff," Holly said with a laugh as the horse reared a little, snorting with pleasure, "but I love his spirit. I've never known him to refuse a fence. He's a real Pegasus."

Then she pulled Scotsman into a gentle trot and led them

around the trees and on toward the fence. The mare took her time about catching up, but when she had, Holly pointed to a small cluster of buildings a few hundred yards beyond the fence. Harry noticed that much of the land surrounding the buildings was under cultivation. The house itself was surrounded by a stunning display of trees, all in pink and white bloom.

"Oleanders are beautiful," Harry said.

"It's called Oleander Farm," Holly said. "Zebulon built the place for Alejandra Cruz when she became pregnant and put her in it with a sixty-year lease," Holly said. "So the farm belongs to The Oaks, but its entrance is off Fullington Road."

Harry had never heard of it.

"You can't reach the place from here," he said, wondering why the fence wasn't gated.

"You noticed," Holly said, giving him a sour smile. "Actually there's a ride from The Oaks, but Brandon was the only one who used it. He rode over to see the family fairly often. He always came back threatening to widen the ride, but he never did."

"His father also visited?"

"From what Brandon told me, he went nearly every day," she said.

"Is Alejandra still there?" he asked, listening to the click of the electric fence.

"No. She died about fifteen years ago. She had three children, Clarissa, the oldest, then Felipe and Miguel."

"The children are Zebulon's?"

"Yes. Of course they are no longer children. Clarissa is in her fifties."

"She was about Brandon's age," Harry said.

"A few years younger," Holly said quickly as if she wished to move on.

Harry noticed a little stiffness in her voice.

"Married?"

"Divorced."

"Do you know her?"

"Not in the biblical sense, but I see her from time to time. She's beautiful, but she's also a cold, proud bitch who doesn't like me and shows it."

Harry smiled. "Why did Felipe leave the farm?" he asked.

"I think there was some trouble with Brandon and his mother, but I don't know."

"Does Clarissa run the farm?"

"No, Miguel's the farmer. He earned a degree in agriculture from the University of Florida. Since his grandmother's death, he has devoted himself to the farm."

"The lease is about to run out," Harry said in a matter-of-fact voice, testing the water.

"Two or three years."

"Is he aware of that?"

"He has to be."

"Was it your husband's intention to renew it?"

"I don't know," she told him, but Harry found himself doubting her answer without knowing why.

"Are you going to renew it?" he asked her.

She pulled the bay around sharply.

"We're going back to the house," she said, "because I have something to show you."

"Damn!" Holly said when she saw a man opening the pasture gate and kicked Scotsman into a gallop.

The herd had wandered away and was grazing along the edge of the woods. Harry managed to urge Sueño into a gentle run, but she soberly kept two hooves on the ground throughout the little race. When Harry caught up with Holly, the man was standing at her stirrup and Holly was bent over, speaking intently.

She broke off the conversation when Harry was close enough to hear what they were saying.

"This is Tyce Yellen, our manager," she told him.

Yellen, a lightly built, sun-darkened man with black hair, deep-set dark eyes, and a receding hairline, reached up and shook Harry's hand. Like Holly, he was dressed in riding breeches and boots, but Harry saw that a Jeep was parked outside the gate. Despite his slimness, Yellen had a horseman's grip, and when Harry got his hand back, he knew it had been shaken.

"Then I should just go ahead as usual," Yellen said, resuming his conversation with Holly, who did not look pleased with whatever had passed between them.

"Yes, for God's sake," she said. "Manage the gate for us."

The steel in her voice surprised Harry. She did not sound as if she was talking to her lover.

Holly did not speak to him on their ride back, but, Harry concluded, whatever had made her angry had not been resolved in her brief conversation with Yellen. Once their mounts had been turned over to a groom, she led him back into the house at a sharp clip where they were greeted by Nip and Tuck, who would not let Harry through the front door until their noses had confirmed the judgment of their eyes.

"Follow me," she told Harry when the ceremony was over.

She unlocked a large ornate door off the main hall and led Harry into what he guessed had been Brandon's study, a large, high-ceilinged room overlooking lawns, horse pastures, and a dark line of woods in the distance.

"Have a seat," she said, pointing at the dark cherry table with four high-backed chairs around it before crossing the room to a wall safe.

Harry pulled out one of the chairs, thinking a little sourly that she was accustomed to ordering people around, and sat down.

"Read these," she said, dropping in front of him a bundle of envelopes tied with a black ribbon. "When you're done, we'll talk."

When he had finished the last letter, Harry leaned back in the chair and blew out his breath in troubled astonishment as he stared at the stack of papers. They had all been written in longhand on Oleander Farm letterhead. He had no idea what to say.

Holly had scarcely moved the entire time he was reading, standing, still as a statue and as inscrutable, beside one of the study's floor-to-ceiling windows. Gathering his courage, he forced himself onto his feet and asked, "How long have you known about this?"

"Since yesterday," Holly said, turning and coming to the table. "I found them in his wall safe. Whether or not that was intended, I can't say. Tyce brought me Brandon's keys and his wallet. He thought it best not to leave them. The key to Brandon's desk was in the wallet. The combination to the safe was in his desk."

He decided to let the comment about Brandon's intending to have her find the letters and the rest pass, but he intended to remember what she had said and the coldness of her voice as she was saying it. And he intended to remember that Yellen had technically committed a crime by ransacking the body before the police arrived and retrieving the keys and the wallet.

"I'm sorry you had to find out . . . under these circumstances," he said, thinking there weren't any circumstances where such knowledge could be anything but devastating.

"Thank you," she said. "I may be in shock, but I don't seem to find it all that surprising or awful."

She put her hands on the back of one of the chairs and suddenly rocked it hard, slamming it into the table and then releasing it to hug herself tightly as if she was cold.

Not angry either, Harry thought.

"I've known for a long time—I knew before his heart attack that something was wrong," she said in a rush of words. "I may have known it even before we were married and suppressed it."

"You have only Clarissa's letters to him—and I gather not all that were written," Harry said. "Perhaps . . ."

"No! Stop!" she said vehemently. "I know you want to be kind, but don't try to make it anything other than it is. Of course he loved her, you do not say the things she says in those letters to someone who does not love you at least as much as you love him."

"But she married," Harry said, still trying to find something to ameliorate what was in the letters.

"So did he!" Holly said in a loud voice, flinging open her arms as though she were casting something from her. "And what does that signify?"

Harry saw she was no longer making any effort to conceal her anger. Her back had straightened, her eyes were blazing, her voice was hard, and blood had suffused her face. He was still struggling to answer her question when she answered for him.

"Let me tell you what it signifies," she went on in a ringing voice. "She broke faith, she was fleeing, running away, betraying her love and his as well."

Her voice grew more condemnatory.

"Betraying the one thing that could—if anything could have—saved them."

Harry stared at her in surprise. She had gone in a direction he had not anticipated. Was she defending their affair and condemning Clarissa and Brandon for not being true to one another? He had expected her to heap burning coals on them.

Didn't she see that Brandon's marrying her was a breach of faith with her as well as with Clarissa? For a moment he thought of pointing it out to her, saw where that might lead, and quickly changed the subject.

"This must have been going on for years under her mother's nose," he said. "Are there any children?"

"No, thank God," Holly said, throwing up her hands.

"Living this close, why did she have to write to him?"

"Brandon was frequently away on business, often for weeks at a time."

"Did he write to her?"

Holly shrugged, obviously annoyed by the question. Harry dropped the subject.

"Have you spoken with her since Brandon's death?" he asked.

"Yes. As soon as I was able to do anything after being told, I called her."

"Who told you?"

"Tyce. He called the police, then came up here, told me Brandon had been killed in a riding accident, and stayed with me until he heard the sirens. Then he went out to meet the police."

Holly's voice trailed off.

"Was that when you called Clarissa?" Harry asked.

"Yes. I told her there had been an accident and that Brandon was dead. She didn't say anything, only groaned as if she were dying and then began sobbing and hung up. I wasn't surprised. I expected her to be very upset. She'd known Brandon all of her life, and he had known her since he was a child. Of course, when I called her, I didn't know the rest."

Once again Harry was not sure he believed her, but he left it.

"No," he said. "Did you call her brothers?"

She shook her head as if dismissing the question.

"My God, Harry," she broke out, "how wretched, how utterly wretched."

Harry was unsure what exactly she thought was wretched, or what contribution she had made to it.

4

"Then you're working for her," Jim said, spinning his pen on the yellow notepad in front of him.

He was a tall, rawboned man with short, pale hair and large ears that tended to turn red when he was upset. He had moved to Avola from the mountains of eastern Tennessee and sounded it.

"It looks that way," Harry answered.

"I still don't see what she wants you to do," Hodges said, "unless it's to hold her hand through the worst of it."

Sergeant Frank Hodges was a head shorter than the Captain and about twice his circumference with a round, red, smiling face that had backwoods Florida written all over it, but Harry had learned there wasn't much about people and being a lawman that Hodges didn't know.

"You mean the investigation into Brandon's death," Harry said.

"It's a good beginning," Hodges replied, his belt creaking as he shifted his weight on the folding black metal chair that passed for furniture in the Sheriff Department's offices.

The budget crunch had become so breathtaking that Hodges said he expected any day now to be assigned a tin cup and told to go downtown and stand on the corner of 41st and Sweet Gum, to beg for spare change.

"How is Mrs. Pike holding up?" Jim asked, dropping his feet off the corner of the desk.

"It's hard to tell," Harry said. "She's a strong woman, but she's taken a direct hit and shows it. You spoke with her, didn't you?"

"Barely," Jim said. "She was holding on when I talked with her, but I didn't think much if anything of what I said registered. I didn't try questioning her."

"Was Tyce Yellen with her?"

Jim shook his head.

"Interesting thing about Yellen," Hodges said. "He comes from the same part of Tennessee as the Captain. I didn't take to him all that much, but sometimes a situation like that skews things enough to make a first impression suspect."

"Well," Jim said, "he seemed all right to me. He kept his head, found the horse, called us, told Mrs. Pike, and answered my questions."

"Do you have a time of death?" Harry asked, hoping to head off a long wrangle between Jim and Hodges over first impressions at a crime scene.

In some ways, Harry thought, the two were like an old married couple arguing over whether Uncle Freeman was or wasn't an alcoholic, an argument that had no resolution, which was what made it so attractive.

"Kathleen is thinking, subject to revision," Jim said, "it was about seven A.M."

Kathleen Towers was the county medical examiner and Jim's fiancée. They had been engaged so long that their friends had given up asking when they were going to be married. Harry and Hodges occasionally gave Jim a nudge altar-wise, but without effect beyond making Jim's ears flare up.

"Yellen called it in a little after eleven," Hodges added, anticipating Harry's next question.

"Then they'd been lying out there four hours, give or take," Harry said in surprise and a little irritation. "Hadn't anyone missed him?"

"What do you mean, *they?*" Jim demanded.

"The head and the body," Harry said, which started Hodges laughing.

"I don't see what's funny," Jim protested.

"No, you wouldn't," Hodges gasped. Addressing Harry, he said, "You could of said, 'Hadn't anyone missed *them?*' "

That set him off again until his eyes began to water, and he had to stop laughing to blow his nose.

"Sometimes, Frank," Jim said, "I worry about your mind."

"It's such a small thing, I wouldn't bother about it," Hodges said, wiping his eyes.

That made Harry laugh and even Jim grinned.

"The groom," he said, turning to Harry, "who saddled the stallion that morning, backed up what Yellen told me," Jim said. "It seems Pike was often away from the house for long periods of time."

"Didn't sound right to me," Hodges said. "And it still doesn't."

"It would have had to be a fairly general conspiracy if killing Pike involved the grooms," Harry said, thinking of Holly Pike, Brandon, and Clarissa Cruz.

"We'll know a lot more once I have the medical examiner's report in hand and begin questioning the people involved," Jim said.

Harry got to his feet.

"We still don't know what you're doing for Holly Pike," Hodges said, "and you're not getting away until we do."

"I'm not sure what or for how long," Harry said, "but I agree with you, Frank, for the moment at least, I think she does want me to talk to and possibly to help her think about what's happened to her."

"Doesn't she have any women friends?" Hodges demanded.

"Maybe," Harry said, "but from what I've seen of her, I doubt she would want to talk to them about this."

"Well, try to prepare her for what's coming," Jim said seriously, rubbing his head with his hand as he always did when he was thinking hard. "This is the eye of the storm. First the death, then this."

He paused, lost in his own thought.

"Then we start turning over her life with a dung fork," Hodges said, finishing Jim's sentence.

"And not only hers," Jim added.

"Definitely not," Harry agreed, mentally adding Yellen, Clarissa, and her brothers to the list of those coming under scrutiny.

"Does the name Clarissa Cruz mean anything to you?" Harry asked.

"Only that in Spanish Clarissa is the diminutive of Clara," Soñadora told him. "Why do you ask?"

"Then you don't know her?"

"Of course I know her, but that was not what you asked me."

"Do you know you're looking particularly fetching this morning?" Harry asked.

They were on a narrow footbridge that arched over Fiddler's Pass. To their left beyond a thicket of sea grapes and sea oats lay a wide, white beach. To their right was a stand of coconut palms and beyond them, the tile roofs of half a dozen three-story beach houses, empty at this time of year. In front of them lay the Gulf, streaked with intense shades of green and blue, dotted with white caps kicked up by the morning wind. At their backs, the sun had found them and the bridge. Beneath their feet, the tide was running inland swiftly in a churning green and white surge.

"I hope so," she said, suppressing a smile. "This ridiculous outfit cost me a fortune."

"Let me see. I haven't looked carefully," he lied, taking her hands and stepping back so that he could see her at arms' length.

She was wearing a crimson, short-sleeved blouse, forest green shorts and matching sandals. Dropping one of her hands, he lifted the other and slowly turned her around. She was not quite his height, with heavy, shining black hair, caught back in a silver clasp, that swung gracefully as she turned.

"You are making me very embarrassed," she said sternly when she was facing him again, but Harry saw that her black eyes were dancing with pleasure, not anger, and she was blushing, a sure sign with her that she was pleased.

Before she could protest, he drew her against him and kissed her. Putting her arms around his neck, she pressed her body against his.

"It frightens me, Harry," she said softly when their lips slid away from one another.

"What frightens you?" he asked, rocking her gently in his arms.

"This," she said, leaning back to stare at him.

"I love you," he said.

"And I love you," she said with sudden intensity, "and that is what frightens me."

"How can loving me frighten you?" he asked.

"It is not loving you that frightens me," she said. "It is my history."

Although they had known one another for years, they had only recently become lovers, and Harry, when he was away from her, still had trouble believing it had happened.

He kissed her again and said, "All of that is over, past. You are safe here."

"What if someone should see us?" she said, laughing and hugging him.

"You're still safe. There is nothing to be afraid of."

"*¡Idiota!*" she cried, her face flaming as she threw herself against him and clasped him to her, then said quietly, "there is always something to fear."

The fact she had called him an idiot in Spanish assured him that she had recovered from her fright and was ready to enjoy her life again, but the shadows in that life, as she had just demonstrated, were never far away.

She had been born in Guatemala, the daughter of Paulus Jogues, a Dutch priest, and a Mayan Indian woman when the liberation theology movement in Central America and the Guatemalan government's murderous assaults against the nation's Indian people were gaining momentum. Her mother and the rest of her family were slaughtered in a death squad attack on her village. The priest paid for her care and kept close watch of her until she was thirteen and then sent her away to school without telling her that he was her father, a fact she had discovered only after she had met Harry.

Her life during her early years had been dominated by danger, struggle, work, and loneliness. Established in this country as an undocumented alien, she had contracted a loveless marriage and fell out of that more broken and lonely than ever.

"How do you happen to know Clarissa Cruz?" he asked as they were leaving the bridge.

"Through *Salvamento*," she said. "Oleander Farm has been one of our safehouses for several years now."

Salvamento was the name of the organization she had founded shortly after coming to Southwest Florida. Dedicated to the tasks of providing shelter and aid to women in need of help and to locating and rescuing enslaved men and women caught in the coils of human trafficking, *Salvamento* had, because of Soñadora's and a handful of undocumented women's unremitting efforts, grown into a powerful organization of minority women, many now documented and all on their way to becoming citizens. *Salvamento* had a headquarters building in Avola with a large staff of workers, safehouses, and connections with many Anglo organizations in Tequesta County.

"What can you tell me about her?" he asked.

"Why are you interested in Clarissa Cruz?" she demanded.

"It has to do with some work I've taken on," he said.

He had not wanted to tell her anything about the Pike affair. Both of his marriages had gone to pieces because of his refusal to change jobs, and with Soñadora he was determined to keep his personal life separated from his professional activities. At least, that had been the plan; but, of course, the plan was his, not Soñadora's.

"You know about Brandon Pike's murder," he said, compromising a little.

"Yes," she said in a way that made it clear that she expected to hear more.

"Well," he added, "his widow has hired me to help her deal with some issues connected with her husband's death. I don't expect to be there more than a week or two."

He opened the Rover's door and stood aside to let her get in. Instead, she planted her fists on her hips and waited.

"What?" he asked.

"You are working for Holly Pike. What does this have to do with the lovely Latina Clarissa Cruz?"

"I've never seen her," he said, hoping he had found an exit. "Is she really lovely?"

"Mucho notable."

"Striking? That's a surprise. She's in her late fifties, lives on a farm . . ."

"And very, very proud. About your age," Soñadora said. "You live in the woods. She is a registered broker and manages the Avola branch of Silversmith Brokerage . . ."

"Okay," Harry said, recognizing defeat when it was glaring at

41

him, "I got off to a bad start there. Now, let's just kick off our sandals, take a walk on the beach, and work this out."

"No bullshit."

"When did you start saying *bullshit?*" Harry demanded, shocked.

"Don't look so startled," she said, laughing. "It is a common word nowadays."

"Not when you say it," he retorted. "It doesn't sound right."

"When I think of what we have been doing together," she replied, stepping out of her sandals, "the word *bullshit* seems very innocent."

Harry tossed their sandals into the Rover and said, "Innocence and guilt have nothing to do with making love."

"If you say so. How does Clarissa come into the murder of Brandon Pike?"

"Clarissa's mother worked for Zebulon Pike, Brandon's father," Harry said as they crossed the warm, white sand to water's edge and stood with their feet in the gently breaking waves. "Then he built for her the farmhouse where Clarissa now lives. Clarissa and Brandon were brought up together. Clarissa and her brothers are close to the Pike family but not exactly part of it."

That sounded lame to Harry and far from honest, but it was all he was prepared to tell her about the tangled web in which the Pikes and Cruzes were caught.

"Until you mentioned Silversmith Brokerage, I had no idea Clarissa Cruz had ever done anything but run that farmhouse with her mother. No," he said, correcting himself. "Holly told me she had been married."

Another delicate subject, Harry reminded himself, planning to hurry on.

"*Holly!*" she said loudly, the waves foaming around her ankles. "Not *Mrs. Pike!* I see your relationship is coming along by jumps and leaps."

"Leaps and bounds," he said, thinking how beautiful she was with the wind lifting her hair and filling it with sunlight.

"What?"

"The expression is not *jumps and leaps;* it's *leaps and bounds.*"

"Are you sleeping with her?"

"Stop showing off and tell me about Clarissa Cruz," he said.

Except for the occasional runner and stray person with a string bag collecting shells that passed them, they had the beach to themselves.

"There is little to say," Soñadora told him after watching a flock of dark skimmers flash past, flying in perfect formation as their bills sliced the water. "She has been very generous to *Salvamento.* For the rest, she is a haughty, dignified, and, I would say, very private woman. What happened to her marriage?"

"I don't know. From what Mrs. Pike told me, I gather it didn't last very long."

"She is, I think, a little sad. There is something in her eyes. She does not often smile," Soñadora said. "Are you going to talk with her?"

"Perhaps," Harry said. "I have to find out first just what Holly wants from me."

"Because we are hooked up," she said, "you are treating me with disdain."

Harry gave a shout of laughter.

"Where did you hear that phrase?" he asked.

"The younger women at *Salvamento* talk freely of hooking up."

"Okay," Harry said, "but for people your age and station in life, perhaps it would be better to speak of us as lovers. What do you think?"

"I think whatever you call us, no name is enough."

5

That afternoon Harry returned to The Oaks, and this time Nip and Tuck met him as soon as he stepped down from the Rover, allowed him to stroke their heads briefly, shook hands with him, and then led him with great formality and dignity around the house to where Holly was sitting on a wooden bench under a spreading live oak on the west lawn.

Stepping out of the blazing sun into the tree's deep shade left Harry partially blind for a few moments, but when he could see Holly, he noticed at once that she had been sitting with neither book nor work to distract her and wondered if the pain of Brandon's death had deepened. However, she stood up with her usual athletic grace and welcomed him.

"I saw you coming up the drive," she said, "and sent Nip and Tuck to fetch you. Did they behave themselves?"

"Impeccably," Harry said, dropping a hand onto Nip's head.

Tuck crowded in for his share of attention, nearly knocking Harry off his feet, bringing a short laugh from Holly. Recovering his balance, Harry stroked Tuck's head, restoring harmony.

"Join me on the bench," Holly said after telling the dogs to lie down, which they did, throwing themselves full-length onto the grass as if they had been shot.

She was wearing a blue sundress and white sandals, an outfit that Harry thought softened her appearance significantly, and although he liked the effect, he also thought it made her look much more vulnerable.

"How are you feeling?" he asked, sitting down beside her.

"It comes in waves," she said, clasping her hands between her knees for a moment, then leaning back against the tree. "I was in the house earlier, and one of them nearly carried me away. That's why I'm out here."

"I could go away," Harry said, starting to get up.

"No. No," she said, putting a restraining hand on his arm. "Please, no. I'm all right. Besides, talking with you will help."

"Are you just being brave?" he asked, his concern growing despite her protest.

"Harry, don't go all funny on me. I'm okay."

There was no help for it. Harry had to laugh. "I'm sorry, but I don't think I know what it means to go 'all funny.' "

"Neither do I, but I know it when I see it, and it makes me angry."

"All right, no going funny. Want to talk some business?"

"Yes, I do, but you go first."

"It starts with a question. Have you told Jim Snyder about your husband's relationship with Clarissa Cruz?"

"Absolutely not. What would be gained by telling the police that?"

She was glaring at Harry with obvious anger.

"Either everything or nothing."

"This is no time to be cryptic."

Harry remembered how she had talked to Tyce Yellen and thought she was sounding much the same now. Whether she was newly widowed or not, he didn't like it. He took a moment to make some extra space for her and tightened the leash on his temper.

"At this point in the investigation," he said, "everyone con-nected with your husband is a potential suspect."

"Including me."

"Yes, and including Clarissa Cruz and her two brothers."

"And Tyce."

"Without a doubt."

"But what possible motive would Clarissa have for killing Brandon?" she demanded in a dismissive voice. "She's been in love with him for God knows how many years, and it would appear that much of that time she's been sleeping with him. If she had decided to kill someone, it would have been me."

Her face was drained of color, and just as Harry thought she was about to launch into another attack, she suddenly burst into tears that carried her with them.

"Oh, shit!" she wailed and, leaping to her feet, ran, stumbling and weeping toward the house, pursued by Nip and Tuck.

But she was scarcely out of the shade of the tree before she slowed to a walk and then sank onto the grass in a miserable heap, sobbing helplessly. Harry jumped up and started toward her, but Nip and Tuck, standing over the prostrate woman, growled at him menacingly.

Harry stopped and backed up a few steps. The dogs stopped growling.

"Holly," Harry said. "I can't come any closer. Are you all right? Is there anything I can do?"

There was no response, but a few moments later she pushed herself into a sitting position and, fishing in her skirt pockets, found a tissue and blew her nose. When she had staunched the flow of tears, she stood up.

"It's all right," she said, "Don't look so worried. When it comes, there's nothing I can do but hang on until it's over."

She grabbed both dogs by their collars and gave them a shake. She might as well have tried to shake a pair of stone lions. "Shame on you for growling at Harry," she said.

Settling herself on the bench again, she said in a stiff voice, "You were going to explain to me why I should tell Captain Snyder about Brandon and Clarissa."

46

"It comes down to motive," Harry said, sitting down beside her. "After establishing that, it becomes a question of means and opportunity."

"This sounds more like an introduction to police procedure than an explanation."

"To understand the explanation," Harry said, "you need to understand how Jim and his people go about deciding whom to arrest."

He stopped because he knew that at some point he was going to have to ask her if she and Tyce Yellen were lovers, and he didn't want her to set the dogs on him, which, he thought, was a possible outcome of his asking the question.

"Why aren't you talking?" she demanded.

"As soon as the medical examiner gives Jim and the State Attorney the autopsy report," he said, "the investigation will open in earnest. You and Tyce Yellen will probably be the first people they question."

"Why?"

She was sitting very straight, partially turned toward Harry but not looking at him.

"I think you can guess."

"They will assume Tyce and I are lovers."

"Right. But more importantly, sooner or later they're going to discover the real nature of the relationship between Clarissa and your husband. If you haven't told them, do you see the problem?"

"Can they gain access to Brandon's papers?"

"Almost certainly."

"I could burn the letters."

"Don't even think of it," Harry said without hesitation. "At least one other person knows about those letters. Your husband may have written to her, and she may have kept them. Even if she didn't, from the content of her letters, their relationship will

47

become clear."

"You're suggesting," Holly said, giving Harry her full attention, "that if I don't tell them about Brandon and Clarissa, they'll assume I suppressed the information because my knowing about the relationship would be a motive for murdering Brandon."

"Yes. Lying to the police in your situation would be like putting a poisonous snake in a dark room you have to walk through every day. Sooner or later, you'll step on it, and it will bite you."

She made a harsh sound that might have been a laugh and brought the dogs' heads up off the grass.

"I'm not in an enviable position," she said.

"No, but remember that if you had no part in the murder, truth is your best friend."

"I'll think about it. Now I have something to say."

She stood up and, pushing her hands into her skirt pockets, began walking back and forth in front of Harry, frowning at the ground. Harry stood up and she stopped pacing.

"Harry," she said calmly and in a clear voice, devoid of self-pity, "I thought so before and now, having listened to you, I'm certain that Tyce and I are going to be charged with killing Brandon."

Harry started to say that it was too soon to be certain about who would be charged, but she stopped him.

"There's something you have to know," she said with a rueful smile. "I'm two months pregnant. Brandon's not the father. We stopped sleeping together after his heart attack."

Harry was startled by the revelation and struggled for a suitable response.

"Are you happy about it?" he asked.

"Very," she answered with a trace of defiance.

"Then congratulations," he said, feeling it was now safe to go on and also finding himself thinking again about the way she had treated Yellen that day in the pasture. "Is Tyce the father?" Harry asked.

"No," she said firmly, "and I'm not going to discuss it."

"But you just said . . ."

"And *you* said that whoever was investigating the murder would assume Tyce and I are lovers until I proved we weren't."

"All right," Harry said.

"I think you've got it wrong," she said with sudden defiance. "I think that if our relationship is crucial to their case, they're going to have to prove we are."

"I warn you," Harry replied. "If you are, they will."

She shrugged.

"I have something else that worries me much more," Holly said. "I want you to find out what, if anything, Clarissa Cruz is hiding regarding the lease. I'm certain she's hiding something."

"You must already know far more about her and her brothers than I do," Harry said, pushed back on his heels by the request.

"I know almost nothing about any of them," she said. "Except for our annual Christmas party, Clarissa hasn't been in The Oaks since Brandon and I were married. I haven't seen Felipe for years."

"Why not?"

"As I told you," she said, flushing but meeting Harry's gaze squarely, "she doesn't like me. And Brandon made it clear that except for business dealings, he had very little to do with the family and wanted it kept that way."

"Why now? Haven't you got enough on your plate?" Harry asked, thinking that the water he was wading into had suddenly grown deeper and murkier, a development that made him uneasy.

"Somebody killed Brandon. It wasn't me, and it wasn't Tyce," she said, anger still darkening her face. Then, seemingly dragged away from that thought, added, "Clarissa and Miguel are two people living on what is now my land. They have the same father as Brandon. Aside from the lease, I have no idea what the legal arrangements are concerning that damned farm, and I don't want to demean myself by asking the lawyers to do it for me."

"You want me to do it."

"Yes."

Holly paused to breathe and pace, her arms locked across her breasts in that defensive posture Harry had seen her assume before. He decided to say something about Brandon's death, thinking that she had veered away from it.

"Holly," he said as gently as he could, "you have Brandon's death to deal with. If you want me to, I'll find out what I can about the lease and other arrangements with the Cruzes. You can tell your lawyers to cooperate with me, but even then what I can do is limited. And remember, the sheriff's people are going to be all over the Cruzes as soon as they know about Clarissa and Brandon."

Harry paused, giving her time to absorb what he had said and respond if she wanted to. When she merely nodded, he went on.

"There's one more thing: Do you think Clarissa killed Brandon?"

"I'm not concerned with the police," she said with a dismissive gesture as if she was shooing away a fly.

"First, I think she may hate me enough to want me dead, but I don't think she killed Brandon or had him killed. Her letters make it clear she loved him. I know very little about her brothers, and it's too late now for me to mend the breach between us, even if I wanted to, which I don't."

"I guess you could try," Harry said in a voice wholly lacking in conviction.

She glared at him.

"I can see it," she said with a false smile. "It would go

something like this, 'Hi, Clarissa, this is Holly Pike. I know you've been shagging my husband, your half brother, since he began wearing pants with a fly, but, hey, we can get beyond that. Let's do lunch.' "

"Sounds right," he said, allowing himself to laugh. "Now, are you up to answering some more questions on another less fraught subject?"

"Ask away," she said, looking more relaxed.

"About three years ago, Brandon ran over and killed Henry Jackson."

"Oh, God," she said, "Are you going to drag me through that again?"

"I'm sorry, Holly, but it may be important."

"So you say. But I can't imagine how it could possibly have anything to do Brandon's death."

"Perhaps it doesn't. The problem is that we won't know unless I take a good look at it. To do that, I'll need your help."

"What do you want to know?"

"I've read the *Avola Banner* accounts," Harry said quickly before she could change her mind, "and I think I understand pretty well how Judge Kline handled the charges of vehicular homicide while driving under the influence with his normal faculties impaired."

"The witnesses testified that Jackson walked right out in front of Brandon," Holly said with some irritation.

"Yes," Harry said. "I know that and also that Brandon's actions after the accident made it clear that his mental and physical faculties were functioning normally."

"Then I don't see . . . ?"

"Wait!" Harry said. "There was another trial, a civil trial. Do you recall that?"

"Of course," she responded, irritation morphing into disgust. "Rosalee Franklin, claiming to be Henry's wife, brought a

51

wrongful death suit against Brandon. Our lawyers presented the judge with evidence that destroyed her case and ended the proceedings."

"I found out that much from the *Banner*, but aside from giving the woman's name as Rosalee Franklin, the paper gave no details."

"Sit down," she told him, dropping to the bench herself. "This will take a couple of minutes."

Harry joined her, thinking how remarkable it was that she could drag herself back from grief so quickly. She was, he realized, a very strong woman.

"It's a sad story really," Holly began, "but I didn't think so then. At the time I wanted to wring her neck."

"You said Rosalee Franklin *claimed* to be Jackson's wife," Harry said, wanting to be sure he understood her.

Holly made a wry face.

"Her suit claimed they had been married eight years. She also said Henry was the father of three of her children. But it was proven that they had only lived together intermittently, and that he had never contributed to the children's upkeep. Rosalee's mother lived with her and cared for the children while Rosalee earned minimum wages cleaning houses for the Scrub-A-Dub company."

"Were they actually married?" Harry asked, anticipating where the story was going.

"She had no proof of it and said she had kept her own name when they were married," Holly said, shaking her head. "What was evident was that she was miserably poor. Our lawyers established that for the past three years she had been sharing her bed with another man who had a drinking problem that made it impossible for him to keep a job. In all, she had five children and was obviously pregnant when she appeared in court."

"Was she mentally impaired?" Harry asked.

"Who knows? Whenever the judge asked her a question, her lawyer told her what to say."

"How old was she then?"

"Late twenties and she looked forty. The whole thing was very sad, really. I wanted Brandon to give her money, but the lawyers threw a fit and said if he did that he would be admitting that she had a valid case and that a smart attorney could bring it back to bite him."

Holly gave a deep sigh, and Harry nodded, feeling like sighing too.

"There's two more things," Harry said. "First, I'm going to have to interview all the grooms. Do I have your permission?"

"Yes."

"Will you tell Yellen that?"

"Yes."

"Second. You will have to give Brandon's lawyers your written permission for me to find out from them what Brandon's arrangements are concerning Oleander Farm. Will you do that very soon?"

"Do you have a computer in your head?" Holly asked.

"No," Harry replied, "but I have a voice recorder and a very small and fast camera. Then there's one more thing. Promise me you'll call Jim. Tell him about Brandon and Clarissa."

She agreed.

And Harry, seeing it was all he was going to get from her, decided it was enough.

6

The Rover's global positioning system located Fullington Road and led Harry through an undeveloped section of the county he seldom visited. He was no friend of large-scale development or the creation of subdivision housing and gated associations. However, the overall effect of the tedious succession of swamps, sandy pine barrens, and saw palmetto jungles dotted with ragged cabbage palms, all under the surveillance of a sinking sun and monotonously circling turkey vultures drifting on the unfailing updrafts and bringing the watchers news of death, made Harry think more kindly of bulldozers, giant earth movers, drainage ditches, cinder blocks, cement trucks, and gangs of the underpaid undocumented, toiling in the heat.

The faithful guidance system eventually took him to a narrow, paved road, marked by a white wooden shield suspended from the arm of a black iron post with the name OLEANDER FARM painted on it in bold, green letters.

"Congratulations, you found us," the woman said when Harry stepped out of the Rover. "I am Clarissa Cruz."

She was tall and stately with thick black hair streaked with silver. Even in the fading light of late afternoon, Harry could see that her dark eyes were dimmed with sadness. He paused a moment to study her, recalling for an instant the passion in those letters. She was dressed, clearly in mourning, in a black skirt with a black belt and a long-sleeved black blouse. A light black lace mantilla covered her head and fell loosely over her shoulders.

"I'm Harry Brock, Ms. Cruz," he said, shaking hands. "Modern technology brought me here, although perhaps I could have found it on my own."

"I'm sure you could," she said with a slight smile. "Come in. The breeze may be dying but not the heat."

As he followed her up the wide flagstone path, bordered by shoulder-high plumbago shrubs in full bloom, Harry saw that distance had diminished the house when he first saw it with Holly from the pasture. Seen from its front walk, the cream-colored stucco building with its tall windows was large, even imposing. Zebulon Pike had built an impressive home for his mistress.

"This is a beautiful house, and the gardens are wonderful," he said without exaggeration.

Indeed, the entire front area of the house was a riot of color.

"Thank you," she said, opening the front door and stepping through it. "Like your finding your way here, I can claim no credit for it. My son Miguel designed the gardens, and our farm crew cares for them. I walk along the paths and admire the results."

The dark, cool, red-tiled room into which Clarissa led them was richly furnished with dark leather sofas and Mexican chairs, tables, lamps, and rugs. A huge stone fireplace occupied a third of one wall. Like the woman waiting for him to sit down, Harry thought, it was austere and a little daunting. He was having trouble imagining her in a brokerage office.

"Will you have coffee," she asked, "or, perhaps, something stronger?"

"Coffee would be fine," he said.

Once seated opposite him in a heavy, leather cushioned chair across an equally dark and heavy coffee table, she rang a small silver bell that she picked up from the table.

A young woman, dressed in a black uniform with a white apron, came silently into the room. Clarissa spoke to her in Spanish, and she vanished as silently as she had come. Somewhere deeper in the house Harry heard the sonorous tones of a clock striking six o'clock.

"It may be presumptuous of me," Harry said, "but I want to offer you my condolences. This must be a very difficult time for you. I understand you have known Mr. Pike all of your life."

"Thank you, Mr. Brock," she replied. "Yes, Brandon and I grew up together. His death has been a severe blow." She hesitated, then appeared to gather herself. "The manner of his going is indescribably terrible. That vicious trap could have caught anyone riding on that track."

"Do you doubt that it was intended for Mr. Pike?" Harry asked.

"How is anyone to know? Mrs. Pike and Mr. Yellen occasionally used that trail, or so I'm told."

Harry caught the addendum and wondered if its purpose was to underline her separation from the Pike household. The maid returned, carrying a silver tray with cups and saucers and a silver coffee service. Clarissa poured. Harry was not surprised to find it was excellent. Clarissa left hers untouched.

"The device was so vicious that I can't begin to imagine the mind that conceived it," she said, evidently concluding her thought.

"It certainly suggests malice," Harry said, "but I'm afraid the sheriff's people haven't been working on the case long enough to find who might have hated Mr. Pike badly enough to kill him."

"No, I suppose not," Clarissa replied. "You said you had been hired by Ho . . . Mrs. Pike."

"That's right."

"Why?"

Harry noted that her voice had hardened perceptibly.

"First, let me say that you're probably not going to be satisfied with my answer," he told her.

Now that he had met her, he was aware that nothing but as much truth as he could reveal would even keep her in the room with him.

"You've probably already guessed that Mrs. Pike is in a very exposed position," he said.

He waited for Clarissa to indicate whether she agreed or not. When she made no response beyond indicating that she was waiting for him to continue, he did.

"What I'm going to say in no way reflects what I consider to be the facts of the case. Is that clear?"

"Let's find out," she replied with a shadowy smile.

"All right. She's about twenty years younger than her late husband . . ."

"Twenty-four," Clarissa said, her voice expressionless.

"Mr. Pike has not been in very good health for several years," he went on, having acknowledged the correction. "The Pikes' farm manager is a man only a few years older than Mrs. Pike. She takes an active interest in the horses and their management, and she and Yellen ride together frequently. All told, they spend a fair amount of time together."

"And the police will have already made them their first objects of interest," Clarissa said with increased animation. "But what does this have to do with why you're here?"

"Most of those who watch local television or read the *Avola Banner* will be less generous in their response than you," Harry told her. "My job, as I see it, is to make sure the law doesn't come to the same conclusion if another would be the right one. Given the extreme budget constraints of the Sheriff's Department and the political pressures on the State Attorney's Office coming from Tallahassee, there'll be a strong tailwind pushing them toward early arrests and quick convictions."

"I repeat: Why are you here?"

Harry thought he had learned enough in the last half hour about this imperious woman, now watching him with hawklike intensity, to risk being honest.

"I want you and your brothers to help me understand as fully as I can your relationship with the Pikes."

"Because you see my brothers and me as possibly being involved in Brandon's murder?" she demanded with a surprising vehemence.

Harry wondered if she had slipped in calling Holly and Brandon by their last name or was it deliberate, to let him know that they had a significant stake in Pike's death or, perhaps, the consequences of his dying. Which? He would have to think about that later, but at this moment there was something looking out of Clarissa's dark eyes that made the hair on his neck stir.

"No," Harry said, "but if you have any thoughts about who might have killed Brandon Pike or why, I'd be more than glad to hear them."

"I'm disappointed in you, Mr. Brock," she said with a fleeting twitch of her lips that might have been either a smile or a sneer. "If you did not think we might be involved, you would not be here."

"And if you had not wanted to know what I knew about that involvement, Ms. Cruz, would you have agreed to see me?"

The standoff was broken when a young man strode into the room, scowling fiercely. Harry saw at once that he bore a striking but darker and slighter resemblance to Brandon Pike.

"Miguel," Clarissa said in a return of her pleasant voice, "this is Mr. Harry Brock . . ."

"I know who he is," Miguel said, ignoring Harry, who had

risen as well. "What the hell is he doing here?"

Unfazed by the younger man's hostility, Clarissa asked him if he would like a cup of coffee. When he refused, she smiled at Harry and said, "Please sit down. Excuse me for a moment. Miguel, come with me, please."

To Harry's surprise, Miguel without protest followed his sister out of the room. A heavy door slammed. The exchange, whatever it was, was brief, and Clarissa returned unruffled.

"I'm sure this coffee is cold," she said before she sat down. "Would you like more?"

Harry declined.

"About Miguel," she said, frowning slightly, "I apologize for his behavior. Brandon's death has upset him."

"I understand that he runs the farm," Harry said, thinking that *furious* would have described his emotional state more accurately and wondering what he was angry about.

"After graduating from college, he came back and gradually took over the task from Felipe and me. I must say," she added with a genuine smile, "he is much better at it than we were."

Harry thought he saw something of a proud mother in her smile and suspected that she had played a major role in guiding Miguel's life, even when his mother was alive.

"Does Felipe live here?" Harry asked.

"No," she replied with a discernible chilling of her mood. "He's an electrical engineer, married and living in North Carolina. He has four children, two in college, two in secondary school. His wife works, and we see very little of them."

That's that, Harry thought, noting the sharper edge in her voice.

"And Miguel is not married?"

"Perhaps to the farm," she said wryly.

"Will Brandon Pike's death affect that?" Harry asked, hoping the question was sufficiently oblique to elicit an answer.

"I don't want to go there, Mr. Brock," Clarissa said firmly.

Harry nodded.

"And your response to my earlier question about your relationship with the Pikes?"

"The same."

"You have been very gracious and generous with your time," Harry told her, getting to his feet. "At some point, I would like to talk with Miguel. Will that be possible? I had the feeling that some, perhaps a great deal, of his anger was directed at me."

"Miguel is a very private person," she said thoughtfully, walking with him to the door. "I can't help you there. Besides," she said as if expecting the statement to clarify everything. "We have lived a long time in the shadow of The Oaks. Any disturbance there has its echo here."

And then opening the door on the heat of the evening, she said, "Goodbye, Mr. Brock. I wish you well with your investigations."

The thick mahogany door swung shut with a heavy sound that had for Harry the weight of finality. He left Oleander Farm with his head swimming with impressions, many contradictory. Whatever he had expected to find, it was not the composed, elegant, silently grieving woman with flawless manners who had taken him into her house, poured him coffee, and dismissed him when she was done with him, the woman who, if her letters were to be believed, had been the passionate mistress of her half brother for thirty years, interrupted only briefly—if it had been interrupted—by a disastrous marriage.

And what was he to make of Miguel's anger? What had Clarissa wanted from him? Had she gotten it? What had he learned from her? Nothing, certainly, that would indicate she was in any way involved in Brandon Pike's murder. He drove home wondering if his frustration was the result of having asked the wrong questions.

That night as he was finishing his dinner, the phone rang. It was Jesse.

"I thought you were in Australia!" Harry said.

"I was, but we finished our work sooner than expected. Unfortunately, it bore out our expectations. The coral is dying. The inhabitants of the reefs are declining in health and numbers. The situation stinks, but that's how it is."

"Same off the Keys," Harry said, "and it's too soon to tell if the efforts to halt the die-off are working."

"Look, Harry," Jesse broke in, "I've been talking with Minna. She's worried about K."

K was the name that, over her protests, Jesse and his sister Minna had started calling their mother when they'd left for college. Harry had adopted Jesse and Minna when he'd married Katherine. Their brother Thornton, Katherine and Harry's son, just entering the ninth grade, lived under a fatwa against calling her anything but *Ma.*

Katherine had divorced Harry the year Thornton was born because he'd refused to give up being a private investigator; being married to a man who lived perpetually with the risk of being killed had been more than she could endure. Fortunately or unfortunately for Harry, living apart and having other relationships had failed to break the emotional bonds he had forged with her.

"What's wrong?" Harry asked, trying not to sound alarmed.

"Minna's not sure," Jesse said. "You know, don't you, that K lost her job when Ridland's went into Chapter 13?"

"Yes, but that was six months ago. The last time I talked with her, she said she wasn't in any hurry to look for another job in property management but that she had offers and wasn't worried. How recently have you seen her?"

Jesse was a doctoral student in the MIT/Woods Hole Oceanographic Institution Joint Program. He now spent most of his time at the Woods Hole site on Cape Cod when he was not working somewhere at sea on a research project.

"Christmas, and that was a flying visit. I'm working seven twenty-four," he replied. "We come back from our fieldwork with a ton of data, and everybody on Earth wants it in a form they can use, especially the resident gurus. It's why I'm bothering you. There's no way I can get away from the Cape just now."

"You're not bothering me," Harry said. "How's your own research going?"

The question was more than a question. Unable to fully grasp what Jesse was actually doing in his research, he worried whenever he thought about it that he was constantly being taken away from it to go haring off to poke around on the Great Barrier Reef in the company of tiger sharks or dive into the icy Kuro-Shiyo Current.

"Harry, stop worrying. I'm not falling behind with the writing. Actually, I'm ahead of schedule. Anyway, time's not a problem."

"I don't believe it, but tell me more about your mother. Minna must have said something."

"When did K ever tell you anything that she thought might worry you?" Jesse asked.

It was a very odd experience, Harry reflected, to have your children speak to you the way you must have once spoken to them when they were trying your patience.

"Only the times when she was preparing me for burial," Harry said.

Jesse laughed.

"Well, Minna's growing more like her every day," he said.

"Getting information out of her is like wringing water from a rock."

"I'll call," Harry said, "and thanks for the heads-up."

He had tried to sound cheerful, but he was already in the grips of a clammy-handed foreboding.

7

Harry glanced at his watch. It was seven-thirty. Minna should be home, he thought, knowing that if she was, it would be safe to call because if Katherine could avoid answering the phone, she would. He tried very hard not to compare Minna and Jesse, who had fallen in love with the natural world when he was a very small child and by the time he was seven, spent most of his time outdoors, carrying an aquarium net, a jar of water for specimens, and a magnifying glass. That love was matched by a shining intelligence that had taken him everywhere he had wanted to go.

Minna was bright enough, but she had still not caught fire. An attractive young woman, she was, in that respect, clearly her mother's daughter; but where Katherine was decisive, direct, and assertive, Minna was not, with the result that, convinced she was unprepared, she had insisted on taking a year in a local community college before applying to a university. She also insisted on working, something she had done when she could all through high school.

Harry made the call.

The voice that answered was almost the exact duplicate of Katherine's.

"Minna."

"Hi, little girl," Harry said.

"I'm taller than you are, and in any race you want to name, you'd eat my dust."

Minna had been too young when her father had died to remember him, and Harry had come to fill that role. She loved her mother, but she adored Harry. The feeling was too strong for her to express in any way other than by pretending the opposite.

"Is that any way to talk to your father?"

"You're not my father."

"Do you think you'll ever amount to anything?"

"Probably not. What do you want?"

"Can you talk?"

"Give me a minute. I'll take this upstairs."

"I've had a call from Jesse," Harry said when she came on the line again.

"Did he tell you about K?"

"A little. It didn't make a lot of sense."

Harry heard the bed creak as she threw herself onto it, as she had been doing all her life when she wanted to talk seriously about anything.

"Something's wrong with her, Harry, but she refuses to see her doctor."

"Symptoms?" Harry asked.

"She's losing weight. She's morose. She flies off the handle and scares poor Thornton about to death," Minna said with a short laugh. "I tell him that, considering the way she used to chew out Jesse and me, he doesn't know he's born. But until now the spoiled darling has refused to believe his gentle, loving mother could ever have been harsh."

"Is she looking for another job?"

"She's had several offers but turned them all down."

"Is this a physical thing, do you think?"

"Maybe. As I said, she's losing weight, but that may just be because she's not eating enough to keep a chickadee singing."

"How long has this been going on?"

"About a month, I'd say. And before you ask, yes, it might be menopause."

The possibility hadn't occurred to him because the thought of Katherine being old enough to have that happen was entirely unacceptable to him.

"I've got a suggestion, Harry," Minna continued, and he could hear the hesitation in her voice. "Call her and ask her to come to the Hammock for a visit. You two haven't seen one another for a while. I think a change might be what she needs."

Harry was not about to tell Minna about Soñadora or that this was not the time for him to have Katherine arrive for an extended stay.

"Harry," Minna said, breaking the silence, "you're the only person she'll talk to. You know I'm right."

"What are the chances she'll say yes?" he asked.

"Probably not great, at least not at first. You know how she is. If she was hanging off a burning building, she'd turn down the first offer of a ladder."

Harry laughed. The patient impatience in Minna's voice spoke volumes about her relationship with her mother. He listened and sighed inwardly. Soñadora or no Soñadora, Jesse and Minna were not going to let him off the hook. More to the point, if Katherine needed him, he had no choice but to help any way he could.

"This is going to take teamwork," Harry said. "Shall I talk to Thornton or will you?"

"I'll talk to him. He's terrified of me. Years of torment have crushed his spirit."

"Ha!" Harry said. "You've spoiled him worse than his mother has."

"Maybe. He's a lamb, you know, and always has been. The only bad thing is that the older he gets, the more he looks like you."

"Lucky kid. You deal with Thornton. I'll talk to Jesse. After three days of concerted psychological pressure just short of water boarding, I think there's a thirty-five percent chance she'll say yes when I call and ask her. How are things with you?"

"I got three As and an A-minus this quarter," she said.

"I know I'm supposed to say, 'Not bad for a dummy,' but I'm going to spoil your day by telling you I'm proud of my skinny daughter."

"Skinny! I cause traffic accidents just crossing the street," she cried.

"Don't tell me that! And remember, I'm calling your mother on Thursday."

She hung up laughing, and Harry had a fairly bad few minutes thinking of the years he had missed of her and her two brothers' company. Then he shook off the old and threadbare self-pity and called Jesse, who promised to call Katherine as soon as they were done talking and that he'd call her twice more before Thursday.

His first thought on hanging up was that parents had little or no chance once their children had decided on a course of action. Next, he thought it likely that she wouldn't come. There was a flicker of hope in that second reflection because then he wouldn't have to explain to Soñadora why Katherine was coming to stay with him.

The following morning, Harry called Tyce Yellen and asked him if Holly had told him he was going to talk with the grooms.

"She told me," Tyce said sourly, "and you'll be wasting your time. These men don't know anything about the Pikes or me, for that matter. And it's also certain that none of them killed Brandon."

"You're probably right," Harry said, determined not to quarrel with Yellen, "but it has to be done. How do you want to arrange the times for me to talk to them?"

"Let me talk to Elijah Blue. He's the head groom. Then, I'll get back to you."

"I'd like to get this done right away and have it over with."

"I'll call you back within the hour."

He did, and Harry drove to The Oaks that afternoon. In the east, brilliant white thunderheads were piling up over the Everglades, climbing almost as fast as the temperature. When Harry got out of the Rover, the swelling and subsiding din from the locusts and the cicadas in the oaks, throbbing over his head, momentarily took his mind off the upcoming interviews.

"I arranged to have Elijah talk with you first," Yellen said a little stiffly, greeting him outside Barn One. As he had been the first time Harry saw him, he was dressed in an immaculate white jersey and jodhpurs, his boots polished to a gleaming shine. After Harry thanked him, he pointed into the shadows of the stable. "You can use my office," he said. "It's halfway down the corridor, next to the tack room. Elijah's there now.

"Don't let him intimidate you," he told Harry with a grin. "He will if you let him. In the last few months his disposition has taken a turn for the worse, but it's mostly style. Another thing, he's smarter than he lets on. Don't underestimate him. He'll send in the others when you're done with him. Questions?"

"I don't think so," Harry said, finding he was beginning to like Yellen. "I appreciate your help."

Harry stepped into the stable, surprised to find it much cooler and fresher-smelling than he had expected. The corridor ran the length of the building between roomy box stalls, the top half of whose outer walls were hinged and propped open. The openings were fitted with wooden bars, to prevent the horses from putting their heads outside, and wooden bars separated the stalls, allowing the wind to pass through the stable. The horses not in the pastures or the paddocks had their heads thrust into the corridor, waiting for something interesting to happen.

One of them nickered at him, and Harry recognized Sueño, the gray mare he had ridden on his first visit to The Oaks.

"Hello, girl," he said, stopping to stroke her neck.

She pushed her nose into his chest and blew gently, welcoming his attentions.

"I wish you could meet Oh, Brother!" Harry said. "I think you'd like one another."

"Down here," someone called in a heavy, commanding voice.

Harry turned away from the horse and saw a large, broad figure silhouetted against the light.

Yellen's office was small and meagerly lighted by a single, double-sashed window, open and screened. Standing straddle-legged in front of the desk, Elijah gave Harry the impression of pretty well filling the room. Harry paused for a moment and studied the big man, who was no youngster. Nearly bald, what remained of his cropped hair was steel gray. He had the battered and scarred face and the thick, sloped shoulders of an old boxer. Bracing himself, Harry stepped forward, gave his name, and extended his hand. Elijah did not take it.

Instead, scowling down on Harry, he demanded in a deep growl, "Whachou wan with me?"

Harry waited a moment, returning the big man's stare. Then he said, "You know why we're here, Blue. If you're not going to talk with me, I'll make of note of that, pass it along to Mrs. Pike and the State Attorney's Office. Do what you want, but this might not be the best time to bring to everyone's attention your unwillingness to cooperate in this investigation."

"Who said anything about not cooperating?" Elijah grumbled.

"Then sit down, and let's get on with this."

Listening to the answers to his questions, Harry quickly decided Yellen was right about Elijah. He was an intelligent and observant man. Once some of Elijah's history with The Oaks was established, Harry closed his notebook and said, "What do you think happened here?"

"You might as well call me Elijah," he said, shifting his weight on the old straight-backed chair where he was seated, making it creak dangerously.

"All right," Harry said. "I'm Harry."

"I don't think I've got a clear idea to give you," the big man said, leaning his elbows on his knees. "Aside from the possibilities that there's some connection to his business or that there's a killing fool loose, I don't know what to tell you." He paused, scowled at his hands, and said, "A man like Brandon Pike gonna make some enemies."

He paused, giving his attention to the squeals of the stallion in his paddock in front of the stable, then continued. Apparently satisfied with what he'd heard, he said, "Nothing wrong there," bringing his attention back to Harry. "But one thing is certain. Whoever strung that wire wanted somebody dead."

"Not necessarily Brandon Pike?" Harry asked.

"There's three people ride that path, although he was generally the first one of the day."

"Then the odds are, assuming this someone wanted Brandon dead, by stringing that wire the night before, he was going to get his man," Harry said, watching Elijah closely.

"That would be my guess," Elijah said.

"One more question. Brandon was found at eleven o'clock. Why wasn't someone looking for him sooner?"

Elijah hesitated before answering; his answer, when it came, sounded straightforward.

"This is off the record, okay? You know where he was going on those rides?" Elijah asked.

"To Oleander Farm."

"Then you know why no one went looking for him."

Harry wondered how much Blue knew about that relationship but decided not to ask and only nodded. He and Elijah parted on good terms, and Harry's sessions with the six undergrooms went uneventfully. None of them knew where Brandon was going that morning, only that he frequently took long rides.

Three days later, after mustering all his courage, Harry called Katherine. To his mingled pleasure and dread, she accepted at once.

"I'll come, Harry," she said, "but if I become a nuisance, you've got to promise you'll throw me out. Is that understood?"

"Absolutely. I doubt you'll last two days."

"And I'm only staying a week."

"Don't forget what will happen to you if you return home that soon."

Katherine groaned.

"You don't know what I've been through the past three days. And from my own children! I also see your hand in this. There's nothing wrong with me, you know. I'm perfectly all right."

"Of course you are," Harry said, "but come anyway. I haven't had anyone to fight with since you were last here."

"All right, but you'll only have yourself to blame." She paused. "Are you seeing anyone?"

"Are you?"

"You are. That's all right, Harry. We're grown-ups. Right?"

Harry thought she was and said so, although he still retained doubts about himself.

When they finished talking, he was assailed by a mixture of feelings, involving the way talking with Katherine made him feel as if they had never separated, followed by the discomfort of knowing that they had. Those feelings, though painful, were familiar, but now he had the additional confusion arising from his involvement with Soñadora and his uncertainty as to how

71

best to explain Katherine's visit.

It's going to be all right, he assured himself while cleaning up after breakfast before leaving for The Oaks. I'm sure she'll understand.

"I've just learned you're having a talk with Tyce and I'm not included," Holly said, arriving at the door just after Thahn opened it.

Nip and Tuck nearly knocked him down, pressing forward to be greeted first.

"Stand!" Holly commanded.

Based on the tone of her opening statement, Harry wasn't sure whether she was speaking to the dogs or him. The dogs whined but backed away to let Harry step across the threshold. Thahn vanished, smiling.

"That's right," Harry said. "Are you taking Scotsman out for a spin?"

Holly was wearing her riding habit—booted and spurred, Harry thought with amusement—but he had to admit that she wore it as if she belonged in it, riding crop and all.

"You're not talking to Tyce without me," she said with finality, color rising in her face.

Harry took a moment to be certain that the fight-or-flight juice had drained out of his system. Then he said, "I may as well not talk to him at all if you're going to be there."

"Do you mean he's going to lie with me present?" she demanded.

"Yes. He may be able to tell me his name and what he had for breakfast with something approaching truthfulness, but if you've been urging him to lose weight and he ate a muffin, you'll never hear it."

"He's thin as a rail," she said, her grip on the crop loosening a little.

"Good for him," Harry said a bit more sharply than he had intended.

He was a little sensitive about the waistline issue. He had already gone over several times in his mind what Katherine was going to say when she saw him.

Holly cocked her head slightly.

"Now who's showing some edge?" she said with a smirky grin, and when Harry made no response, she asked, "why do you want to talk to him at all?"

"Because everyone connected with your husband has a story about what happened to him, why it happened, their role in it, what part you played in it. I want to hear them all."

Then, because he could see that Holly was listening closely to what he was saying, he decided to say some more.

"A crime like this is a collection of stories. If the right questions are asked of enough people and we're lucky, in the end we will find the story that gives us the truth—or enough of it anyway to reveal who killed Brandon."

"And why he was killed?"

"Possibly," Harry agreed, "but motives are almost never simple, never fully revealed, and never fully understood."

"Not even by the one who commits the crime?" Holly said.

"No, but juries have to make do with what they're given. Are you planning to ride alone?"

"All the rides have been swept," she replied, and he became aware that something had upset her. "The police drove over them after Tyce had ridden them himself."

Harry was still concerned about her riding alone, but before he could ask what had disturbed her, he was interrupted by the sound of boots on the crushed gravel walk. He turned to see Yellen, also dressed in jodhpurs, coming toward them.

"I'll have Thahn take you to the red room," Holly said tersely. She left without greeting Yellen. By the time he and Harry had finished shaking hands and exchanging comments on the blazing day, Thahn returned to lead them to a large sitting room dominated by a large oriental rug that had dark red in its design.

"Were you and Mrs. Pike going to ride this morning?" Harry asked as they settled themselves in dark leather chairs that looked out over the grounds.

"If she waits for me," Yellen said a bit sourly, as if he didn't expect she would. "I've told her it's not particularly intelligent to be riding alone, even with Nip and Tuck with her."

"No," Harry agreed. "Have the police talked with you yet?"

"Only to ask about why I was in a Jeep instead of on a horse when I found Brandon, but I expect they'll be along soon, now that the medical examiner's report is in."

"Have you had a report?"

"No. Neither has Mrs. Pike. Captain Snyder did call to say there were no surprises. I expect he wanted to spare her the details as much as he could."

"None of this can be very easy for you," Harry said.

"How do you mean?"

"Being the object of police scrutiny."

Yellen, sprawled in his chair, the picture of either indifference or profound resignation—Harry wasn't sure which—waved away the suggestion.

"I didn't kill him. Why should I worry?"

"When the police have you in their sights, it's always smart to worry," Harry said, moving toward the questions he wanted to ask.

Yellen bent forward and tugged at one of his boots, then brushed some dust off the polished leather.

"You're thinking that they assume that Holly and I are lovers and that we cooked up a scheme to get rid of Brandon," he said dismissively.

"It would be my first thought. Why not theirs?" Harry replied and then continued without pausing for an answer to his question. "Is there anyone on the staff or connected with The Oaks in some other way who might want to harm you?"

It took Yellen a few frowning moments to answer.

"I really don't know anyone here well enough to have quarreled with them." He paused before adding, "Over time I've fired a few people for incompetence, petty theft, various derelictions, but that's about it."

"How well do you know Clarissa, Felipe, and Miguel Cruz?"

"Part of what I do, or did, was make quarterly reports to Brandon on the general condition of the farm. The lease calls for him to maintain certain things like access roads and culverts, ditches, original fences, the frame, cladding, roofs, and chimneys of the house."

Yellen shoved out his feet and leaned back in the chair.

"Brandon was a stickler for maintaining the property. If I said the window frames on the south side of the building needed painting, he would tell me to get it done. If I didn't have a crew there within a week, I would hear about it."

"You must have gotten to know Miguel over time," Harry said. "His sister told me he's been running the farm for several years. What's your impression of him?"

"He's a hard worker," Yellen answered, "and as dedicated to that farm as he would be if he owned it. Felipe was gone by the time I came, and although I've talked with Clarissa occasionally, I can't say I know her all that well. She's not an easy woman to know."

When Harry went on to ask if he had any idea what would happen when the lease ran out, he could see that Yellen didn't like the question.

"You'll have to ask Holly."

"Brandon never talked with you about it?"

"I can't imagine he'd want any changes made," Yellen said, his voice increasingly sour.

Harry thought he'd have one more go before dropping the subject.

"Doesn't it seem strange to you that Clarissa and Miguel, especially Miguel, would put all of the effort that's gone into making that farm what it is, knowing that it would never be theirs and that they could lose it when the lease expired?"

"I hadn't thought about it," Yellen said.

"Of course, it's not your business," Harry said. "Thanks for talking with me; although it's none of *my* business, when Jim Snyder's people come to question you, I advise you to tell them the truth. You're not a good enough liar not to."

"Are you suggesting I'm lying?" Tyce said, bridling.

"What kind of manager would you be never to have thought about the lease on Oleander Farm?" Harry asked. "It's coming up for renewal in two years. Even if you did not discuss the matter with Brandon, you must have broached it with Holly."

Yellen scowled and flung himself around his chair, his face coloring.

"The Cruzes were not a subject you 'broached' with Pike," he said stiffly, "not if you wanted to keep your job. From what I've picked up since coming here, I think Brandon's father Zeb Pike built the place for a mistress, Clarissa and Miguel's mother. Whether he was their father, I don't know, but it seems likely."

"What does Holly say about that?"

"Christ, Brock! Do you think I'd have mentioned that to her?"

"I thought she might have said something to you about it. It's hard to believe a story like that wouldn't have reached her."

Yellen made a disparaging sound and leaned his elbows on his knees.

"Maybe it has, but if it has, she never mentioned it to me."

Stranger and stranger, Harry thought. Of course, he couldn't be certain, but he was almost certain that Yellen was telling him the truth.

8

Harry got home to find Sanchez standing on the lanai steps. He was wearing the green bandanna he had picked out that morning, but there was no note in it, which was Tucker's usual way of communicating with Harry.

"Come in," Harry said, pulling open the lanai door. "You look thirsty. Have you been waiting long?"

Harry got his answer from the way Sanchez pitched into his water bowl. The fact the dog had not gone across the road to the creek to drink suggested to Harry that he was feeling under pressure, a conclusion that was strengthened when he refused a Milk Bone and went back onto the lanai and pushed through the door. Once outside, he ran to the Rover and turned to bark at Harry.

"I'm coming!" Harry said, growing increasingly worried.

They found Tucker in the orchard, lying on his side, unconscious, next to one of his lemon trees with his tripod ladder lying across him and Oh, Brother! standing over him. Dropping to his knees, Harry pressed a finger against Tucker's throat and, to his relief, felt a pulse.

Lifting the ladder off the old farmer, he carefully began turning him onto his back, his relief vanishing after one look at the bloody gash in Tucker's scalp and the awkward position of his left arm bent under him. Harry stopped turning him.

Pulling out his cell, he dialed 911.

"He's stable, but that's as far as I'd go," the large, red-haired woman in a blue jump suit with CAROL on her name tag told him fifteen minutes later in a take-charge voice while her two helpers had stored Tucker in the ambulance. "Probable concussion, broken left humerus, possible fracture of radius and ulna." She paused, pulling a blue cloth out of her pocket to wipe the sweat off her face, then added, "and I don't like his heart."

"Awhile back he was treated for congestive heart failure," Harry told her.

"Sounds right," she said, slapping him on the shoulder, making him stagger a little, before she climbed into the ambulance. "We'll do what we can for him," she called loudly and yanked the doors shut as the ambulance lurched out of the orchard.

Followed by Sanchez and Oh, Brother!, Harry carried the ladder back to the barn and hung it on its pegs. After making sure that Oh, Brother!'s hay rack was full and the bubbler clean and working, he hurried to the hen run to check their water, then on to the house, where he filled Sanchez's food and water dishes and set them on the stoop floor.

"That's it," Harry told them. "I've got some things to do, then I'll go to the hospital. Tucker's going to be all right. He'll be home before you know it."

That last bit of encouragement was for himself as well as for the animals because he wasn't at all sure Tucker was going to be all right. His two companions walked him to the Rover. Harry stopped to pat and stroke them and assure them he would be back before dark, and drove away, aware of a sharp drop in his spirits as he left them.

Tucker was not all right.

"We got the head wound sutured, and the arm bones set," Bradley Post, Tucker's doctor, told Harry, "and he was looking good to go when his heart began to quit on him."

Harry and Post were sitting in the waiting room. Post, a dark-haired man with a permanent five o'clock shadow, was still in his green OR scrubs and obviously weary. He sat with his elbows on his knees, rubbing a hand over his face now and then as if he had been walking through spider webs.

"Did you lose him?" Harry asked in alarm.

"No, no!" Post said, rallying a little. "But his heart is troubling me."

"Is he going to be all right?"

Post pushed himself to his feet. "I'll know more in three days. We're going to keep him pretty quiet until then."

He shook hands quickly with Harry, who had gotten up with him, and said, "Come in if you want, but I don't think you'll get much conversation out of him."

Harry called Jim, who had known Tucker almost as long as Harry, and told him what had happened.

"Awful news," Jim said. "I guess we'll just have to keep track of him and hope for the best."

"If you and I both drop in every day," Harry said, "they'll know we're watching."

"Right. Anything to report on Mrs. Pike?"

"No. Have you begun your interrogations?"

"We're beginning today," Jim said, not sounding happy. "I wish I thought it was going to help."

After closing with Jim, Harry called Soñadora at *Salvamento*, sure she would want to know that Tucker had been hurt and possibly also because he wanted an excuse to hear her voice, although he didn't allow himself to admit it.

"I'm in town," he said. "Tucker fell off his tripod ladder, and I've just come from the hospital. He broke two bones in his left arm, and those have been set. But Bradley Post says his heart isn't strong enough for them to make any predictions."

"How awful," Soñadora said. "I can get away for an hour. Are you too upset to eat?"

"No. How about The Blue Duck?"

"Do they have a grouper sandwich?"

"They do, and the restaurant's on the Seminole River. We can eat under canvas and enjoy the breeze."

The deck of the restaurant extended over the river and boats on the way to and returning from the Gulf slipped past The Blue Duck sedately, the sailboats with bare poles swaying. The deep water diesels, their brass work gleaming, rumbling softly, wallowed by like sleepy giants.

"What's going to happen if they cannot stabilize his heart?" she asked when they were seated.

"I've been trying not to think about that," Harry replied.

"But you must. How would he live without his animals and his plants around him?"

"Exactly, but Post thinks that in a few days they'll know more. If he makes it for three days, the prospects for recovery brighten."

"I hope he is right. I want to ask you about Clarissa Cruz, but perhaps you would prefer to talk some more about Tucker?"

"In all honesty, I think I've said enough. Talking about it only makes me feel bad."

Also, he had noticed that Soñadora, while genuinely concerned, seemed to be having trouble keeping her mind on what he was saying.

"Then you must wait," she said. "Have you talked with Clarissa?"

"I met her. We talked. She was gracious and as elegant as you said, but she told me very little. Miguel came into the room while we were talking, but he was too angry to say more to me than, 'I know who he is,' when his sister tried to introduce me. Have you ever met him?"

"Once. Clarissa introduced him. He was polite but brusque, insisted on speaking English when I addressed him in Spanish, and left us to greet a man I spoke with very briefly later in the evening. I remember he worked for Brandon Pike."

"Were you at Oleander Farm?" Harry asked in surprise.

"Yes. About three months ago, Clarissa gave a party to raise money for *Salvamento.*"

"The man you met, was his name Tyce Yellen?" Harry asked.

"Yes," Soñadora said. "How did you guess?"

"He manages the horses at The Oaks," Harry replied, wondering why Yellen would be at a *Salvamento* fundraising event. "Is he a supporter of *Salvamento?*"

"I don't think so," Soñadora replied. "I don't think he knew anyone there except Miguel and Clarissa, who appeared to avoid him. When Miguel came back after speaking with him, he and his sister exchanged some quiet but obviously angry words about it."

Harry was thinking about what Soñadora had just told him when the waitress arrived to take their order. After ordering, Soñadora fell silent and was staring at the water and the passing boats as if she had stopped seeing them.

"What was the color of that Boston Whaler that just went by?" he asked.

"What?" she said.

"You were a long way away," he said with a smile. "Is anything wrong?"

"Not really," she replied.

"That won't wash," he told her.

"Wash what?"

"Wash away whatever it is that isn't bothering you."

She stared at him for a moment in silence, then said, "When

I went to Guatemala to see my father just before he died, I met a young priest who had come from Quebec to try to reestablish the church. Do you remember my mentioning him?"

Harry said he did, but refrained from adding that with Pierre this and Pierre that, he had heard altogether too much about him. On more than one occasion, her enthusiasm for the dedication, devotion, and intelligence of this young hero had set the green devils dancing in his head.

"He has written to me," she said, glancing at Harry quickly, then looking away.

"Okay," Harry said as if she had just laid a dead frog on the table.

"You might show some interest," she said sharply.

"*Might* is the operative word," Harry said, forcing out a smile. "What did he say?"

"Probably nothing that would interest you," she snapped.

"We're in just about up to our pockets, and I'm ready to negotiate a truce. How about you?"

When she's angry, those eyes would score diamonds, he thought, staring at her with admiration.

"I do not approve of the Catholic Church," she said defiantly. "They abandoned their congregations to the death squads. My father and a few others stayed. Many who stayed were killed. Pierre Robichaud is, of course, a Catholic priest. But from what I saw, he will also follow in my father's footsteps in his dedication to the people."

"I'm glad," Harry said. Then unwisely added, "But I think you've mentioned Pierre's breathtaking qualities of kindness, consideration, and dedication before."

"Sarcastic brute!" she burst out. "Why are you being so mean?"

Will I ever learn? he asked himself and got no comforting answer.

"I'm sorry," he said. "Please tell me what he said that's upset you. I really want to know."

It was true. He did want to know. He just didn't want to know any more than he absolutely had to about Pierre the Perfect.

"This is the last chance," she warned him.

"Okay," he said, stifling ironic addenda massing on the borders of his control.

"Diphtheria has appeared in some of the remote villages. Of course, very few of the people have been inoculated. Pierre is only just beginning to master the basics of Quiche," she said. "As a result, he is dependent on a translator to communicate because those who live in the remote hamlets usually speak very little Spanish and no English."

"I'm surprised they talk to him at all, considering what they've been through," Harry said.

"They are patient, forgiving, and hospitable," she said, "but they are also deeply suspicious of those who cannot speak directly to them."

"And as a result," Harry said, "when he talks about inoculating the children, he runs into a wall."

"Yes. He is very concerned and feeling overwhelmed."

She paused and looked away again, lost once more to him. Harry wondered what she seeing.

"The area Pierre has to serve is larger even than Tequesta County, and there are few roads," she said at last, returning with a sigh. "People used to walk sometimes for days to reach my father's clinic, which is now Pierre's clinic."

"Aside from the fact that people are falling ill, which is bad enough, what's worrying you about this situation?" he asked, wondering if she was seeing in this young priest her father when she was a child.

"There is so much to be done," she said with sudden

intensity, "and so few to do it."

Before he could say, "And it's all your responsibility," their food came, sparing them both. Her mood gradually lightened, but Harry was not deceived. He would now have to share her with a priest in Guatemala as well as with *Salvamento,* which until very recently had been the center of her life.

While waiting to hear more about Tucker's condition, Harry decided to have another talk with Yellen. He found the manager in the stables, watching Jack being brushed and curried. The stallion was held with two heavy leather straps fastened to the walls and snapped into his halter rings. Harry had heard the animal squealing and trampling as he approached the long, low building.

"Don't go any closer to him than I am," Yellen warned as the big chestnut reared and plunged, eyes rolling malevolently.

Up and down the gangway, horses had stopped eating, poking their heads out of their stalls to watch the show.

"What's wrong with him?" Harry said, as the grooms, two middle-aged black men, struggled with no apparent fear with the leads, trying to settle the stallion enough to keep all four of his feet on the floor, and dodging his flying hooves.

Yellen laughed.

"Nothing, really. He's not actually trying to kill anyone. He's just performing for us, but he's still dangerous."

When the horse grew tired of rearing, striking, and kicking, one of the grooms put a feed bag on him. Then he and the other groom got to work with brushes and curry combs.

"What brings you out here?" Yellen asked, leading Harry away from the stallion.

"Did you go to a fundraiser a while ago at the Cruzes?" Harry asked.

"I'd forgotten that fundraiser until you asked about it," Yellen told Harry, his puzzled look clearing. "I don't really know why I was there aside from helping to fill up the room."

"Did Clarissa invite you?" Harry asked.

"No, it was Miguel. When he called to ask me to come, he said his sister had made his acting as host a matter of family honor and would I help out by adding to the head count. Why do you ask?"

"From what you said about the Cruzes the last time we talked, I had the impression that you hardly knew them."

"You were right. Of course, Miguel and I talk about the crops, the rotations, the flowers, that sort of thing," Yellen said.

"How do you and Clarissa get along?" Harry asked, recalling what Soñadora had told him about her reaction to seeing Yellen at the fundraiser.

"I don't know her well enough to say. She's civil. I seldom see her to speak to. Most of my business is with Miguel."

"Did she or Miguel ever talk to you about Brandon?"

Yellen frowned, whether in anger or puzzlement Harry couldn't say; the expression vanished as quickly as it had come.

"Not that I recall."

Harry felt something soft nudge his back. Turning, he found himself looking into two very large dark eyes. The next nudge was against his stomach and more insistent.

"Sueño!" Harry said in surprise, reaching out to stroke her neck.

"You two know each other?" Yellen asked with a grin.

"Yes," Harry said, putting his left arm around her gray head and continuing to stroke her neck and scratch behind an ear.

"Well, she certainly likes you," Yellen said. "I'm impressed. She's a particular old girl."

"She was very patient with me the day I rode her," Harry said, pleased by her attention. "She's well named, I guess."

After a moment, the two men moved on, walking slowly back

toward the stallion and the men working on him.

"Why do you suppose Miguel never mentioned Brandon or the lease or the fact that he was at risk of losing everything when the lease ended?" Harry asked, trying to make the question as casual as possible.

"No idea," Yellen said and then, suddenly, "watch him!"

The grooms leaped away just as Jack kicked through the places where they been standing a moment before.

"Get that nose nag off him!" Yellen said as the horse rose up, pawing the air. "Get him into his stall!"

The grooms led the stallion, dancing, into his stall, turned him, and unsnapped the leads from his halter. Harry caught his breath when Jack reared and struck right and left, quick as a snake. The strikes fell short only because both men had jumped away from the horse as soon as they unsnapped the leads.

"Get out of there!" Yellen said, moving quickly into the stall and grabbing Jack's halter.

With a loud squeal, Jack threw up his head at the restraint, lifting Yellen into the air. Yellen let go of the horse and leaped back as soon as his feet touched the floor, then dodged out of the stall. The two grooms slammed and bolted the door shut and stepped back, just escaping the animal's teeth.

"My God!" Harry said, his adrenaline pumping as Jack swung his head back with another squeal and began kicking the sides of his stall with both hind feet with a sound like howitzers firing. "That animal will kill someone one of these days."

"Scary, isn't he," Yellen said with a grin.

Harry couldn't understand why neither Yellen nor the two grooms seemed at all concerned by what had just happened and said so, still rattled.

"He's about average to work with for a stallion of his age," Yellen told Harry when the grooms had left.

Harry must have looked doubtful because Yellen tried again.

"Stallions are difficult," he said. "They're big, powerful, and aggressive. It's their nature. What Jack ought to be doing is chivvying a dozen mares around on a mountain somewhere and fighting off wolves and the competition. Instead, when one of us is not riding him, between servicing mares to support this outfit, he's either here in his box or out in a paddock, bored out of his shoes."

"Does Holly ride him?" Harry asked.

"Against my advice," Yellen said. "If he got wind of a mare in heat, she'd never be able to control him."

"And you ride him."

"He needs a lot of exercise," Yellen said, looking admiringly at the stallion that now was standing with his head out in the gangway, his ears cocked, looking calm as a summer morning. "You have no idea of his strength and speed. It's like riding the wind."

"I can believe it," Harry said. Then, hoping to slip under Yellen's guard, he said, "How long are you going to stick with your story that you and Miguel never talked about either Brandon or the lease?"

Until that moment, Yellen had seemed relaxed and comfortable, but Harry's question changed things.

"I know Holly hired you to 'protect' her and me," the manager said, clearly angry, "but I'm not going to put up with being cross-examined by you or anyone else."

"Tyce, wait . . ."

"No, you wait. I didn't kill Brandon Pike, and I don't need protection."

With that he strode off, leaving Harry to stare after him and wonder whom he was protecting and why.

9

Harry, increasingly puzzled by Yellen's unwillingness to talk about the Cruzes, gave Sueño a final pat and went in search of Holly, who met him at the door with Nip and Tuck crowding past her to greet him.

"Whoa!" she said sternly, grabbing a handful of Tuck's hide to regain her balance. "Wait your turn."

The two dogs sat down, their tongues lolling in happy expectation.

"Come in, Harry," she said. "God, it's like living with a team of oxen. Okay, say hello."

Harry braced himself as the two dogs sprang to their feet and shoved their heads into his stomach. Braced or not, Harry was almost pushed out the door by their enthusiasm.

"Have you talked with Jim's people yet?" he asked, having survived the civilities.

The dogs now had him between them and were leaning against him contentedly, making sure he was not going to leave them.

"Yes, for nearly two hours," she said with a frown, "and I gather they're coming back for another session, although I don't know what there is left to ask. Would you like some coffee? Let him go."

"No, thanks," he said, studying her for signs of stress but seeing instead a woman in a pink sundress and sandals with her hair drawn back in a gold clasp, apparently at ease with herself.

He wondered if she was past those paroxysms of anguish that she'd been enduring the last time he'd seen her.

"How are you feeling?" he asked.

"I'm a lot better, knock on wood."

They went deeper into the house, and Holly steered them into a room that Harry guessed from the pastels was Holly's study.

"Out," she said as Nip and Tuck trotted forward to claim the rug in front of the fireplace.

"We could have used them for ottomans," Harry said, settling into one of the two chairs facing one another across the fireplace.

"No," she said. "Since Brandon's death, they seem to think they have to be everywhere. It's all I can do to keep them out of my bed."

Harry opened his mouth to say, "Smart dogs," then shut it very quickly.

"What?" she asked.

She was still standing, looking down at him with a slight smile. There was no doubt, he thought, *she's a beautiful woman.*

"Nothing," he said.

"Answer the question."

"I refuse on the grounds it might incriminate me."

"Ah-ha!" she said with a bright laugh.

Harry was pleased by her shift of mood and wondered what could have caused it.

"Please sit down. I want to talk to you."

"Talking can wait," she said. "You have no idea how good it makes me feel to have you look at me that way."

"I wasn't!" Harry protested. "I insist . . ."

"Harry, you were, and if you weren't, don't tell me."

"Actually, I was. I was thinking how good you looked."

"Well," she said, "that's a start, and if you're a knocked-up widow, you have to settle for what you can get."

"Beautiful, wealthy widows, pregnant or not, seeking attention," Harry replied, "usually find it."

She was grinning by now.

"How do you think I got into this condition?" she asked.

"I hope with a lot of shouting, sweat, and pleasure," he answered, determined to hold up his end.

"In my dreams," she said in a sudden shift in mood. "What do you want to talk about?"

"You and Tyce Yellen."

"We've already done this," she answered, giving him a cold stare.

Harry shook his head.

"I want to talk about you, then about Yellen. What kinds of questions did Jim's people ask you?"

Holly dropped into her chair with a groan.

"They began by asking where I was and what I was doing that morning and ended by pressing me hard about Brandon's and my relationship."

"Where were you?" Harry asked.

"I got up somewhere between five and six because that's when Brandon wakes up. We had breakfast together, read the papers, and shared our plans for the day."

"And they were?"

"I had a golf date at eight-thirty with three women friends from the club and a three o'clock meeting with the Featherstone Action Committee. Between the two I had hoped to have some lunch, get in a ride, and get my feet up for half an hour. That's what I did."

The Featherstone Group, Harry knew, was a charitable organization, made up of fifty wealthy women in Tequesta County, who gave money anonymously to organizations and enterprises they thought worthy of support. Soñadora had recently told Harry that *Salvamento* had received a very large sum of money and assumed it had come from Featherstone.

"It is wonderful for *Salvamento* and the people it helps," she had told him, "but that much money makes me very nervous. Also, it takes a lot of time and hard work to manage it properly. I fear it will change us."

"Hire someone to look after it," Harry had said, only realizing later that he had not been listening.

"What about Brandon?" Harry asked, bringing his mind back to the task at hand.

"He was rather vague," she said a bit stiffly. "I gathered he had some sort of business meeting in the afternoon."

"Did anyone call you to ask why he didn't show up?"

"No, I assume they called his office or the office called them."

"Is there someone at the office I could talk to?"

"Emily Bradshaw is the person I depend on."

"Is there a company name?"

"Pike Enterprises," she said. "They're in the book and online."

Harry was surprised by how detached she sounded.

"Did you talk with him much about business?"

"Only about the farm. He kept his other affairs to himself and didn't respond to questions about them."

"Did you send Yellen to look for your husband?" Harry asked, wondering if she had used the word *affairs* deliberately—if so, her expression gave nothing away.

"No. I didn't see him that morning until he came here to tell me what had happened."

"Did you go for a ride?"

"Yes, and Elijah saddled Scotsman for me and walked him and gave him a good wash when I came home because I had ridden him hard."

"Had something upset you?"

"No. I had been playing golf with three nincompoops and

forced to listen to them talk about restaurants and shopping for an hour and a half," she said spiritedly, rustling around in her chair as if just thinking of them made her want to jump up and run. "Giving Scotsman his head for half an hour and going over a few gates made me feel human again."

"As opposed to not going over," Harry said, shaken by the prospect of being on Scotsman as he thundered toward a five-barred gate. "How long can you go on doing it?"

His comment seemed to restore her good humor because she grinned and said, "As long as I know what a stirrup is."

"I mean pregnant," Harry said.

She shrugged and leaned back in her chair, somewhat less cheerful.

"If I were to ride Sueño, I could probably have the baby in the saddle, but I shouldn't be jumping any more gates, and I'm not riding Jack."

"Still riding alone?"

"Sometimes. And don't scold me. What do you want to ask about Tyce?"

"Hold that a bit. Has anyone told you that there can't be a cremation or a committal until the Tequesta County Medical Examiner issues her report and either Harley Dillard, the district attorney, or Sheriff Fisher signs a release, allowing you to go ahead with whatever arrangements you've decided on?"

"Yes, Snyder explained it all to me," Holly said quietly.

"There's nothing stopping you from having a memorial service without Brandon's body present if that's what you want," Harry added.

"I know. It's good of you to tell me these things," she said, clasping her hands tightly, "but let's move on."

"All right. One more thing before I get to Yellen. What are the estate's lawyers telling you about the will and getting access to it and the rest of his papers?"

"You're wondering if something unexpected has turned up," she said.

"That and whether Brandon left instructions for Oleander."

"Basically," she told him, frowning, "all they've said is that I'm not to worry about the costs accumulating for running the business, the stud, and The Oaks."

"What about the will?" he asked. "There must be one."

She sighed.

"Brisket, Shriver, Polyphemus, and Thrale is a large firm. I work with a Josie Holmes, a junior partner," Holly said, sounding, Harry thought, dispirited. "She tells me not to worry, that there is a will, but there is still work to be done before we're ready to go through probate."

That startled Harry, and he asked, "What does your lawyer say about that?"

"Lawyer? I've got that whole firm working for me. They'd better be for the money they're getting," Holly replied.

Harry hesitated. Giving Holly Pike legal advice wasn't in his job description, and while he doubted that Brisket et al. were scamming Holly, the longer the lead-up to probate, the more money they made. Also, they were Brandon's estate lawyers, not hers, and he suspected that one of the senior partners was making decisions about the estate that Holly should be making or at least be made aware of.

"You need a lawyer," he told her. "Brisket and company were hired to look after your husband's interests. They're still doing it. Your interests are not their primary concern."

Holly was quiet for a few moments, then she said, "I've been thinking it was odd I wasn't working directly with Gus Shriver. He and Brandon have known one another for years. I think you're right. I should have my own lawyer."

"I can recommend Jeff Smolkin," Harry said. "He's smart and absolutely reliable."

"Can he run with the wolves?" she asked with a smile.

"Leader of the pack," Harry assured her.

She lost her smile, and Harry was reminded that her self-confidence came and went.

"I hope he'll take me," she said.

Harry took out his cell, dialed, and spoke with someone. After a brief wait, he thanked the person he had been speaking with and turned to Holly with a smile.

"Call and make an appointment," he told her. Then, seeing the sadness shadowing her face, he said gently, "You're going to be fine, you know."

"You," she said and shook her head again. "What do you want to ask me about Tyce?"

"I found out that he recently went to a fundraising event thrown by Clarissa Cruz," Harry said, deciding not to inquire into the *You*. "Yellen told me during our first talk that he knew little or nothing about the Cruzes. Miguel called him and asked him to swell the progress, so to speak. When I asked him, just before coming to see you, if he was going to go on telling me that Miguel had never mentioned either Brandon or the lease, he got very hot under the collar and said he wouldn't be cross-examined by me or anyone else."

"Why should he be?" she asked.

Harry didn't miss the hostility but decided to ignore it.

"You're changing the subject. Why is Yellen lying to me?"

"Ask him."

"What were you and he quarrelling about that day you took me to look at Oleander Farm?"

"That's none of your business."

Harry tried once more. "Do you have any idea why Clarissa would be upset by Yellen's presence at her fundraiser?"

"I have no idea."

Harry got up and said, "I'm leaving. I won't send in a bill

because I haven't done enough to warrant one. Good luck and I mean that."

He had almost reached the door when Holly said sharply, "Nip, Tuck, hold."

The two dogs, stumpy tails wagging, jumped to their feet and filled the door.

"You're not quitting, much less leaving," Holly said with a complacent smile when Harry looked back at her.

"Interesting situation," Harry said, stroking the dogs' heads.

"Harry, please come back and sit down."

"I don't see how this is going to help," Harry said, deciding to indulge her and dropping back into his chair.

"Why do you want to leave me?" she asked.

"Because you won't answer my questions."

"No, not those that don't have anything to do with Brandon's death."

"What would you say if you were saddling a horse and I said you were doing it all wrong?" he asked.

"But you wouldn't because you don't know the first thing about saddling a horse."

"And you don't know the first thing about how to conduct an investigation."

They looked at each other, still being polite but on Harry's part, at least, only with some effort.

"What are you saying?" she demanded.

"First, no fair setting Nip and Tuck on me if you don't like what you hear."

"Okay," she said, her expression looking less stormy.

Then she giggled. Harry had never heard her giggle before, and looking at her made it difficult for him to remember he was supposed to be angry.

"There are only three reasons why you would refuse to answer my questions," he said, trying for a stern expression and expecting an explosion—"arrogance, stupidity, or because you have something to hide."

She was sitting with her knees together, staring at her hands folded on her lap, looking somber again. The silence lengthened.

"Tell me what use to you my answering that last question could be," she finally replied, looking up at him unhappily.

Harry could simply not form any fixed idea of who this woman was, and it bothered him. At this moment, she looked lonely and very vulnerable. A few minutes ago, before she'd giggled, she had sounded singularly unpleasant. Snapping at Yellen, she had sounded harsh and bad tempered, and weeping on the grass, she had appeared to be a woman broken in spirit. He took a deep breath and began.

"You and Yellen are the focus of the Sheriff Department's investigation into the death of your husband," he said as gently as he could and still make his point. "They're turning over stones in the creek looking for any reason at all for you and Yellen to have killed him."

"They already think they have it," she said dismissively, looking away from him. "They think we're lovers."

"The child's not his," Harry said, "and it's not Brandon's." When she said nothing, he continued, "Then that motive is useless. You can prove through the child's DNA that someone else is the father."

"I suppose so," she said, sounding cornered.

"And what are you going to tell them when they ask about your being pregnant?"

"That I never met him. So much for the sweat and pleasure."

"Jesus," Harry breathed, dropping back in his chair, staring at her in frustration.

"No," she said, "wrong again."

The next day Harry met Katherine at the airport. Standing at the arrival gate, still nervous after all these years, he watched her walking up the gangway toward him with the same unselfconscious, swinging stride that was one of the things he had loved and still loved about her. Her hair, which had once been dark gold, was now a silver gray, worn stylishly short and, Harry noted, although she was slimmer than when he last saw her, she still had her figure and looked fit.

They stood for a moment, looking almost shyly at one another. Then they embraced and clung to one another for perhaps longer than they had intended, kissed on the mouth instead of the cheeks, and broke away somewhat flustered.

"You look great," Harry said.

Katherine, regaining her composure faster than Harry, smiled and said, "You look as if you've been eating well."

Harry smiled back, staring into those brilliant, green eyes, lost as always in them, impervious to the jibe.

"You grow more beautiful with every passing year," he said.

People were pushing around them, but neither of them seemed to notice.

"You are a shameless flatterer," she told him, putting a hand against his face.

It must have been done unconsciously because a moment later she snatched it away and blushed.

"I speak only the truth," he told her, stealing another kiss, which was unplanned. "All right!" he said a little too loudly, trying to restore calm to his insides. "I guess we should go."

"I guess we should," she said, mocking him, but letting him take her bag.

"The way the kids talked, I expected to see you come off the plane in a wheelchair," Harry said when he had cleared the parking gate.

"I think Minna just wanted me out of the house," Katherine answered with some irritation. "I can't say that I blame her."

"Are you and she getting across one another?" Harry asked, trying to discover how she was feeling about herself.

Katherine had always been at ease with her body, which gave her a natural grace, but she had never been at ease with her mind. Stealing glances at her as they left the airport, he saw that the worry lines around her eyes had deepened and, their greetings over, her infrequent smiles were brief and lacking conviction.

"Not really," Katherine replied. "I've just been a little short-tempered."

She gave a low, deprecating laugh that Harry read as an attempt to make light of her comment, but he persisted.

"That's not like you," he said. "You're usually calm as a morning lake or going after someone full bore. I wouldn't, of course, be speaking from personal experience. We never quarreled."

She appeared to be watching Southwest Florida unroll outside her window as he spoke.

"That's right," she said.

Harry waited.

A moment later, her head snapped around and she said, her green eyes blazing, "What are you saying, Harry Brock? Are you crazy? Our fights scared birds out of the trees and brought in the buzzards, expecting a feast."

"I just wanted to see if you were listening," Harry said with affected innocence. "You weren't. What were you thinking of?"

"Nothing," she said emphatically. "Just plain nothing."

"Now who's fibbing?" he asked. "But never mind that," he added quickly, deciding there would be plenty of time to find out what was eating at her. "I want to tell you about Tucker."

10

Two days later, Post called to say Tucker could go home.

"I think he's got a genie hidden inside him somewhere," Post grumbled. "His heart needs watching, but there's no reason for him not to go home."

Harry and Katherine picked up her rental car and then drove to the hospital. Bradley Post was finally convinced that he was sufficiently mobile to take care of himself but insisted Harry take along the cane and an aluminum walker Tucker had refused when he was discharged.

"When I'm tired, I'll sit down," he said indignantly as he walked to the waiting Rover. "And you can give that cane to somebody who needs it."

"I think I hear cheering," Harry said, holding the door for Tucker as he got slowly into the Rover's front seat, with Katherine giving him a hand up whether he wanted it or not.

"Where's it coming from?" Tucker demanded, settling himself in the seat.

"From inside the hospital. I heard it when the orderly went back inside with the empty wheelchair."

"The main thing is to leave an impression," Tucker said complacently. "Otherwise, we blow away like smoke. Let's get me home."

Katherine, who was putting the cane and the walker into the back of the Rover, broke down laughing, which delighted Harry, who had not heard her laugh since she got off the plane.

The extended greeting Sanchez and Oh, Brother! gave Tucker began before the old farmer could get out of the Rover, causing some difficulties, particularly when the mule got his head inside the cab and pushed Tucker into Harry. Then in the melee, he stepped on Sanchez's foot while the dog was trying to clamber onto the seat with Tucker, causing the dog to begin howling. Everything then had to stop while Tucker and Katherine comforted and petted him.

At the back stoop, the group was met by a large tortoise shell female cat with an extremely bushy tail pointing straight up and two larger editions of herself. Harry, Sanchez, and Oh, Brother! gave her plenty of space, but Tucker caught Katherine by the hand and led her forward.

"Katherine," he said in a formal voice, "I want to introduce you to Jane Bunting."

"Hello, Jane Bunting," Katherine said, bending down to stroke her.

"Watch out!" Harry said in alarm. "She'll rip your arm off."

Oh, Brother! gave a snort of concern and Sanchez barked sharply.

"Nonsense," Katherine said and went ahead and stroked the big cat, who lifted her head to accept Katherine's hand and purred loudly.

"And these are her son and daughter Frederica and Aurelius."

"How lovely," Katherine responded, stroking each of them in turn while Jane Bunting and Tucker looked on proudly.

Harry, Oh, Brother!, and Sanchez glanced at one another in astonishment.

"If I hadn't seen it, I wouldn't have believed it," Harry said. "The first time I tried to pick her up, she ripped my shirt to pieces and there was blood all over Tucker's kitchen."

"That was just a misunderstanding," Tucker said. "Come in,

I'm ready to get off this leg."

"Who's the father?" Katherine asked. "He must have been a big cat."

"We don't talk about that," Tucker said in a low voice, leaning toward Katherine. "We suspect it's a bobcat, but it's a sensitive subject with Jane Bunting. I gather in her circle bobcats are considered déclassé."

"I see," Katherine said, looking back at Harry with a straight face.

Harry was enjoying the exchange because he knew that, like him, Katherine wasn't sure where belief and disbelief began and ended. Also like him, she took what he told her at face value and enjoyed it, trying not to laugh. While she stroked the cats, Harry looked at the oversized kittens and noticed, to his surprise, that both had tufts of erect hair on the tips of their ears.

They went inside where Tucker insisted on making tea before sitting down for a few minutes to drink it and catch up with Katherine's life since last seeing her. That done, Katherine persuaded him to take a rest.

"The leg's stiff and the arm's sore," he admitted, "but I can't say it hurts all that much, although Bradley Post gave me a handful of pain pills, each one strong enough to knock Oh, Brother! off his feet."

They were sitting on the stoop, and Harry had begun to talk about the Brandon Pike investigation when his cell rang.

"I've got some bad news, Harry," Holly said. "Tyce has been seriously injured. The doctors don't know whether he'll live or not."

"Was it an automobile accident?"

"No. It was Jack. No one seems to know what happened."

"Where are you?"

"Home. I've just come back from the hospital."

"Has anyone called the Sheriff's Department?"

"Someone in Emergency Admissions said she would report it."

"Where did the attack take place?"

"Elijah and I found him in the stable's gangway in front of Jack's stall. Jack was standing over Tyce when we came in. He bolted at the sight of us, and I sent Elijah to find help and get him back into either a paddock or his stall. Then I called 911 and asked for an ambulance."

"Try not to let anyone near where Tyce was found. I'll be there as soon as I can."

"What is it?" Katherine asked as Harry was getting up.

"Tyce Yellen has been badly hurt by that damned stallion Brandon thought so much of," Harry said. "Holly says the doctors aren't sure they can save him."

"Jack's got a reputation for mayhem," Tucker said. "Brandon's grooms were always getting nipped or knocked into next week, but this is the first I've heard of his trying to kill a man."

"Do you have to do something?" Katherine asked.

"Yes. I'm going to talk with Holly and take a look at the place where she and Elijah found Yellen."

"Why?" asked Katherine.

"Because from what I've seen of Jack," Harry said slowly, "I think he's quite capable of killing someone, but as Tucker's just said, he's never seriously hurt anyone. Add to that the fact the men working with him don't seem frightened of him makes me think it's possible it wasn't the horse that attacked Tyce. Are you going to stay here?"

"There's no need of that," Tucker said. "Go with Harry. I'm probably going to lie down for a while anyway."

"Do you mind if I don't go?" Katherine asked Harry. "I want to make some calls, and this would be a good time to do it."

"All right, and when I'm back we can come over and see how

you're getting on," Harry told Tucker.

"Don't worry about me," Tucker said. "I'll be fine."

"We'll check just the same," Katherine said, following Harry off the stoop.

"Here's where Elijah and I found him," Holly said, standing with her fists on her hips, staring down at the blood-soaked patch of floor at their feet.

"As far as you know, you and Elijah were the first people to see him," Harry said, looking around them at the gangway, stretching out the length of the stable to the two sets of double doors, all open now, and at the box stalls, mostly empty because the mares that occupied them had been let out into their paddocks.

"As far as I know," she said with a sigh, turning away from the stained floor. "God, how I hate this!"

Her outburst sounded so general that Harry felt he had to ask what she meant.

"What do you think I mean?" she demanded in an angry voice.

"We can come back to that," he said. "Where's Jack?"

"He's in Barn Two. Elijah and his men couldn't get him in here," she said, suddenly deflated. "I suppose it was the smell of the blood."

"Has anyone examined him?"

"He's not hurt."

"That's not what I mean. Has he got blood on his hooves and legs?"

She went pale, and for a moment Harry thought she might faint; he put out a hand to steady her.

"Don't," she said. "I'm all right."

"Let's go outside," Harry said. "I could use some fresh air."

"I hadn't thought of that," she said in a weak voice when

they were in the sunshine.

"Let's look at him," Harry said, looking at the scattering of similarly shaped outbuildings around them.

"This way," she said, taking out her cell. "I'll ask Elijah to meet us there with some help."

When Harry and Holly reached the stable, Elijah was waiting for them with two younger men.

"What do you want with Jack?" he asked Holly in a heavy voice after shaking hands with Harry.

Harry was surprised by the sullen note in Elijah's voice.

"We need to get him into the light, Elijah," she said as they all went down the gangway to the box stall where the stallion was pawing and whinnying.

"He's still worked up," Elijah told her, "but we can try. We had a little trouble getting him in here, but let's see."

Harry decided that what he had heard in Elijah's voice was not sullenness but remoteness, as if he was speaking to them from a distance.

"Be careful," she said as the three men let themselves into the stall.

To Harry's surprise, the horse came along quietly, snorting occasionally and dancing a little as he was led out of the stable.

"Will he let me examine his hooves and legs?" Harry asked Elijah, who was holding Jack by his halter. The other two men held him, one on each side, with leads snapped into his halter rings.

"Come up here with me," Elijah said, "so he can smell you. You might speak to him, and then stroke his head."

With serious misgivings, Harry moved in beside Elijah, standing for a moment while the big horse looked at him.

Then to Harry's surprise, he lowered his head and let Harry stroke his nose, his ears staying cocked with interest.

"You would have made a horseman, Harry," Holly said. "I

thought he'd try to bite your head off."

"Now's the time to do your looking," Elijah told Harry. "Move around slowly, but keep it short."

Still speaking to the animal, Harry bent over and began examining the stallion's hooves and legs, watched with apparent interest by the horse. In a few minutes, he had worked his way around Jack and finally, giving him a parting pat on the shoulder, stepped away from him, relieved as well as puzzled.

"Elijah," Harry said, "has he been washed or brushed since you found Yellen?"

"No," Elijah said. "He's just as he was."

"You two better have a look," Harry said.

Elijah and Holly moved slowly around Jack. Holly even picked up one of his front feet and studied the hoof.

"See any blood?" Harry asked.

Both shook their heads.

"Then we agree. Holly, I suggest you ask the vet to take a closer look and run some tests. Also, have two of the grooms stay with Jack until the vet gets here."

"But how is it possible?" Holly demanded. "You saw that floor. He couldn't have trampled Tyce like that without having bloodied his hooves."

"Nobody's gone near Jack since we put him in that stall," Elijah said with finality. "I was working on that mare with the cracked hoof. Tyrone and Duncan here been with those two new mares getting ready to foal. There's only the three of us up here at the stables. Buster, Steven, Watson, and Carlyle are checking the fences."

"I'll call Heather Parkinson. What's the farrier's name, Elijah?"

"Calvin Hudson."

"Call him as soon as I tell you when we can expect Parkinson," she told Elijah. "We're going to pull Jack's shoes and give

106

them to the vet. If there's the slightest chance that Jack didn't trample Tyce, we've got to know it."

"Those shoes are going to be valuable evidence," Harry said. "What I suggest is to start keeping a chain of custody on them."

"What's that?" Elijah asked.

"It's a written record the police keep of physical evidence from the time it's found until it's introduced in court as evidence by either the prosecution or the defense."

"How would it work here?" Holly asked.

"It can begin with Elijah writing down that the shoes the farrier removed were the same ones Jack was wearing when he found Yellen. The farrier will say he removed the shoes and gave them to the vet. Then Heather will say she took them from the farrier and write down what she did with them. The record has to say who had the shoes, what was done with them, and give the time and place when they changed hands. Every transfer will be signed and dated by both people."

"Would you be willing to sign such a paper, Elijah?" Holly asked.

"If it would help Jack, I'll do it gladly."

"Then you don't think he trampled Yellen?"

"No, Mr. Brock, I don't."

11

"My report from the hospital," Jim said grimly, "said a man working for the Brandon Stud had been injured by a horse."

Harry had stopped at Jim's office on his way home from The Oaks and found Hodges with him.

"That's what Holly Pike told me," Harry replied. "She and Elijah Blue, the head groom, found Yellen. It was only after I went out there and asked if anyone had seen any blood on the stallion that the three of us actually examined him and agreed that he was clean."

Then he told Jim about telling Holly to have Jack examined by the vet and his shoes removed.

"I don't want those horse's shoes taken out of that barn," Jim said. "Will you call her and tell her that?"

Harry made the call, and passed on Jim's request. Holly said she would have the farrier put the shoes in a plastic bag, but Harry told her to put each shoe in a separate bag and enclose a tag saying which foot it came from.

"Okay," she said. "Elijah and I are with Jack, waiting for Heather Parkinson and the farrier, who are on their way. Why are you with the sheriff?"

"The sooner he knows it may not have been Jack who attacked Yellen the better. Any word from the hospital?"

"No. They're saying his condition is critical."

"I'm sorry. How are you?"

"It helps having things to do," she said.

When Harry hung up, he repeated what she had said about Yellen's condition.

"Be a big help to us if he lived," Hodges put in, trying to frown and not quite making it.

Harry suppressed a flinch and nodded, but Jim said, "That's not funny, Frank. You ought not to joke about a man's death."

"Who's joking?" Hodges demanded, his big face getting red. "I was being serious."

"That's even worse," Jim insisted.

"Maybe your crime scene people ought to get out there just in case," Harry said, hoping to stop the wrangling.

"I was going to say that before Frank started up," Jim said, looking offended as a wet hen.

"I still don't see what's wrong with telling the truth," Hodges countered, still deep in justification and offended virtue.

"No, you wouldn't," Jim replied.

"There's another thing that needs saying," Hodges put in loudly, "and it's this. If Yellen dies, and wasn't killed by that stallion, it looks to me as if Holly Pike's been doing some tidying up."

"How seriously are you looking at Holly and Yellen?" Harry asked, assuming they were looking very seriously but taking advantage of the moment to test his thinking.

"We look at everyone of interest seriously," Jim said. "You know that."

"And it's not as though we had a room full of people with motive, means, and opportunity," Hodges said with a loud laugh.

That started Jim finding fault with Hodges again.

"What about Felipe?" Harry asked.

"He's been in his office or his house every day but Sundays for the past month," Jim said. "Based on the tape and the phone call, I'd say he's put his mother and brother and whatever life he had at the Oleander pretty much behind him."

"Okay," Harry said. "I'm going home. Katherine's waiting for me."

"You give her my best," Jim said, brightening. "How long is she staying?"

"Long enough for you two to see her," Harry told them, opening the door.

"Tell her I'll bring her some of the wife's rhubarb pie when I come," Hodges added.

Jim had once been in love with Katherine, and Harry had never forgotten how close he had come to losing her. He still couldn't see Jim's ears redden at the mention of her name without feeling a twinge of jealousy.

"Why didn't you tell Soñadora I was coming to stay with you?" Katherine asked by way of greeting as he walked into the kitchen.

She was rolling out pastry dough and kept on with her task. Her voice told Harry all he needed to know about how she was feeling. Regarding his relationship with Soñadora, he had a choice among several untruths, which he had been working on ever since Katherine had agreed to the visit. Now they all seemed pathetically inadequate. "I forgot," made a feeble showing. "I was planning to," was even lamer.

"I gather she called," Harry said.

"No, I called her and said, 'Soñadora, did Harry tell you I was going to spend a few days with him on the Hammock?' "

"Cowardice," he said, abandoning his post under enemy fire.

Still holding the rolling pin, Katherine turned around. Her expression was not one bright with warmth and approval.

"By not telling her," she said, "you have left that woman thinking that you and I are sleeping together."

"Katherine," Harry said, groping for sincerity, "I never said any such thing."

"You and she are in a sexual relationship," Katherine said sternly in a voice that made Harry feel as if he had been caught flashing a fourth-grade class.

"I wouldn't go so far . . ."

"Don't be ridiculous, Harry," she said and actually stamped her foot. "She comes out here, and you make love to her in our . . . your bed, and you go to sleep in one another's arms, and . . . excuse me."

Katherine stalked out of the room and up the stairs. A door slammed, followed by silence. Harry liked his kitchen. It was his favorite room in the house; but now, standing in it, he felt as if he was on a treeless island in the center of a cold, gray sea. Looking around, he saw no boat. He thought about her slip of the tongue concerning the bed and felt an icy wind begin to blow. This went on for a while; then Katherine came back down the stairs.

"Harry," she said, coming into the kitchen. "I'm sorry. This is my fault. I shouldn't have come here. I'll leave tomorrow, but I'm afraid I've already done some damage. Soñadora sounded seriously upset."

He saw that she had been crying and knew how hurt she had to be to give way to tears. She was one of the most stoical women he had ever known.

"It's my fault, not yours," he said, angry with himself, "and you haven't damaged anything."

"But how can I stay?"

"I'll show you," he said.

Before she could stop him, he put his arms around her and said, "Now, put your arms around me."

"Harry," she said.

"Do it."

"You are hopeless," she said and did what he asked. "Now what?"

111

"We're going to hug one another. On the count of three. Three."

They hugged, and, very slowly, Harry felt the rigidity leaving her body.

"Why are we doing this?" she asked in a slightly unsteady voice.

"We're practicing," he said and held her a little closer.

"What are we practicing?"

"Remembering who we are."

They were about the same height, and she pressed her face against his.

"Who are we, Harry?" she asked.

"Two people who used to love each other."

"Do you still love me?"

"I'm still in love with you. Does that count?"

"Yes."

Harry closed his eyes and took a chance.

"Do you still love me?"

"Sometimes."

Harry laughed. The kitchen became the kitchen again.

"Then you're not leaving tomorrow?"

"Not if you still want me to stay."

"I do, very much. And by the way, last night you slept in our bed. Mine is new."

Just at that moment, he thought of Soñadora again and felt his joy drain away.

"The new one is good too," she said to Harry the next morning when he woke to find her leaning on her elbow, watching him.

"Better," he said, rolling toward her.

"I can't decide," she countered, easing closer to him.

"Let's try again, to help you make up your mind," he said, sliding a hand over her hip.

"Oh, good," she said, "but I'm feeling a little odd."

"I think I know the cure for that," he told her.

Things went very well down the home stretch through the photo finish. They were slowing to a winded trot when Katherine suddenly pitched off him with a groan, clapped a hand over her mouth, ran for the bathroom, and vomited.

"God, Harry, I'm sorry," she said when she could speak again.

She flushed the toilet and was struggling to her feet by the time he got there.

"Are you all right?" he asked, helping her to find her balance.

She appeared to be unsteady on her feet, and he half supported her to the wash basin where she splashed water over her face, then rinsed her mouth. She was very pale, and her body felt cold. He grabbed his bathrobe off its hook and threw it over her shoulders.

"I'm good," she said, wiping her face and hands. "Please, don't fuss over me."

"Are you pregnant?" he asked her to cover his concern.

"I haven't had a period for a while," she said, starting for the bed but veering toward a window.

Harry got her to the bed where she paused uncertainly.

"I'm still dizzy," she said in a fading voice and fainted.

Harry caught her and tumbled her onto the bed, rolled her onto her back, then, kneeling on the bed, lifted her head and shoulders enough to ease her head onto a pillow. He was pulling the bedding over her when she regained consciousness.

"I must be really out of practice," she said feebly.

"I never claimed to be a whiz as a lover, but this is the first time I've made you throw up," he said, looking down at her and trying to mask his worry.

"It's happened a few times lately," she said, freeing a hand from the covers and wiping her face. "The good news is that it goes as quickly as it comes. I'm already feeling better."

Harry had to admit that her color had returned and her voice was strong and steady.

"Are you sure you're feeling okay?" he demanded.

"Move," she told him.

He leaned back and she sat up.

"Aside from a slight headache, I'm fine," she said and wiped her face again, this time with both hands.

"Is there something on your face?" he asked. "Can I bring a face cloth?"

"No, it's nothing. Come here."

She held out her arms. When he reached her, she pulled him down on top of her, pressing her face against his.

"It was wonderful, Harry," she said seriously. "I know I'm wicked, but I don't care, and I'm starving."

She insisted on making breakfast, and while they were eating, Harry asked if she still had a headache. She said it was almost gone, but Harry wondered. She had never liked to admit that she was ill. Minna thought something was wrong. Had he just seen evidence of it? Possibly, he thought; but as for her saying she had been missing her periods, that could have been an extension of his joke about her being pregnant.

While eating and thinking about her health, he was pushing away an unwelcome question: Why had she pulled off her nightgown and jumped into his bed last night without any discussion, with no mention of Soñadora? It kept returning despite his efforts, forcing him, finally, to admit that it was completely unlike her and because it was so unlike her, troubling. As for that, why hadn't he told Soñadora that Katherine was coming? He fled from that question the way a fox flees the hounds.

He thought of Katherine's nausea and dizziness again two hours later while they were driving to see Tucker. Was it possible that this illness, if it was an illness, had anything to do with her willingness to sleep with him? If the answer was *yes*, how could he justify his actions? How could he answer, he asked himself, without knowing whether or not she really was ill? With that, he hastily turned his mind to other things.

Later, on his way to see Emily Bradshaw at Pike Enterprises, he called Jim about the attack on Tyce Yellen, during which he learned that two C.I.D. officers had already talked with Holly and Elijah without learning anything useful. Following that conversation, he called Soñadora. She was less disturbed than he had expected, but his initial relief was short-lived.

"I'm sorry to hear that Katherine has not been well," she said, "and I realize that you must still have feelings for her. It is only natural. She is the mother of your children. I hope coming back to the Hammock will help."

"I should have told you," Harry said, "and I'm sorry I didn't."

"Yes, you should have done that, but I'm not surprised that you didn't," Soñadora continued in a quiet, rational voice that offended Harry. "You keep things in separate boxes and try not to open two of them at the same time. I think this was a time when the one with me in it and the one with Katherine in it should have been opened together."

"It really doesn't have anything to do with boxes," Harry insisted, huffed by the metaphor.

"I'm afraid it does, and someone is waiting to speak with me, Harry," she said. "Goodbye."

Well, what did you expect? he asked himself. Tears? Recrimination? Perhaps some sign that she gave a damn?

He did not have time to brood over his rebuff because he was already approaching the Pike Enterprises building on Flagler Street, but a part of his mind went on insisting, while another part refused to confront it, that what he was doing with Katherine and Soñadora was building a fire in which he was likely to burn.

Like many of the older buildings in downtown Avola, it was designed to fit in among the other red-tiled roofs and pastel stucco walls of the low buildings surrounding it. Stepping out of the Rover into the palm-shaded parking area, Harry paused to listen to the soft rattle of the trees, whose fronds were stirring in the onshore breeze, and to enjoy the sun-speckled quiet. In his somewhat bruised state, he thought Avola had not improved in the years since these places were built.

The *Olde Avola* mood deserted him as soon as he entered the sanely air-conditioned and marble-floored elegance of the lobby hidden behind the modest, varnished entrance door and its polished brass plate, tastefully engraved with the company name.

A smiling young woman in a red and gold sari rose from behind her desk at his entrance and said, "May I help you?"

Harry thought his shorts, sandals, and Tommy Bahama shirt probably signaled that he was lost, but he gave her his name and said Emily Bradshaw was expecting him, and her slightly hesitant expression relaxed into a smile.

Bradshaw was waiting for him on the turkey runner outside the elevator.

"Nice to meet you," she said, shaking Harry's hand.

He surprised himself with the thought that they might have been in kindergarten together. She was short, trim, with dark hair and gold-flecked brown eyes and dressed in a navy suit and white blouse.

"Do you think we've ever met?" he asked as they went into her office after passing through a somewhat crowded outer office where two secretaries were working the phones, their eyes glued to their computer monitors. Bradshaw occupied a corner office with two west-facing windows providing views of the Gulf, which told Harry she was very far up on the administrative food chain.

"Possibly in grammar school," she said, settling them in leather chairs, matching a mahogany desk swept clean of everything other than a closed silver laptop. "Were you born in Red Bluff, California?"

"Rumford, Maine," he said and then laughed with her.

"I can still hear it," she told him. "I like it."

"Thank you. I can't place yours."

"What is it called now? Mid-Atlantic? Something like that. How can I help you?"

"How much do you know about the lease arrangements Brandon had with Clarissa Cruz, regarding Oleander?"

"Not much, and although I know you're helping Mrs. Pike deal with the ghastly death of Mr. Pike, I'm not comfortable discussing his business dealings with you."

Harry took out his cell phone and punched in a number. Holly answered. Harry spoke briefly and passed it to Bradshaw.

"It's Mrs. Pike," he said.

"Excuse me," Bradshaw said a bit stiffly and left the room, closing the door behind her.

"I've been asked or told to cooperate with you," she said flatly when she returned two minutes later and handed him his phone.

She was no longer smiling.

Someone has had her toes stepped on, Harry concluded.

"I'm sorry if this is making you uncomfortable," Harry said, "but the situation regarding that lease is beyond anomalous."

Bradshaw sat down and said nothing.

"It may have a direct connection with Mr. Pike's death," Harry continued, deciding to ignore Bradshaw's state of mind. "Have you read the lease?"

Bradshaw sighed and pushed herself abruptly back in her

chair and crossed her legs and folded her arms, still avoiding his gaze.

"Of course I have," she snapped. "Our lawyers have looked at it. There's nothing *anomalous* about it."

"The lease may be simplicity itself," he said, "but the situation it embraces isn't. Clarissa Cruz and her two brothers, Felipe and Miguel, grew up on Oleander. Clarissa, except for a brief absence, and Miguel have lived there all their lives. Felipe left home some years ago. Miguel has poured years of labor into the place. He's made it a successful and very beautiful farm. Also, his gardens are beautiful. The lease is due to expire in two years. What's wrong with that picture?"

"Are you being insolent?" she asked, fixing Harry with a steely look.

"Absolutely not," he responded but gave no ground. "I think it is practically impossible that Brandon Pike would have left the Cruz family exposed to the possibility of being evicted from Oleander in the event of his death."

"Where is this leading?" Bradshaw asked coldly.

"Most immediately to you and me sitting in this room," Harry replied.

"And from here where?"

"Have you talked with anyone from the Assistant District Attorney's Office yet?"

"Despite Mrs. Pike's *directive,*" she said as though speaking through clenched teeth, "I wouldn't dream of answering that question without consulting our legal department. Do you understand my position?"

"Of course I do," Harry said, a response that seemed to calm her.

"Let's try this," he said. "If Mr. Pike had kept a document in this office giving the Cruz family the right to go on occupying

Oleander beyond the time stated in the lease, would you know about it?"

"That's very difficult to say," she replied, unwinding from her coiled position and looking at him again, her hands folded on her lap. "He conducted very little business that did not involve me, and increasingly since his illness he expected me to deal with everything but company policy decisions. He especially left me to deal with the people coming to him with complaints, questions, or requests."

"Did he ever talk with you about Clarissa Cruz or Oleander?" Harry asked.

She shook her head. "Very rarely and usually about work being done on the property. He occasionally said what you did earlier that Miguel was managing the farm very well. I don't recall his ever mentioning Clarissa Cruz or Felipe."

"How long were you with Mr. Pike?"

"Past tense," she said with a catch in her voice. "You know I still expect to see him come through that door."

She stared for a while at the door Harry assumed opened into Pike's private office, then said, "Fifteen years."

"Have you or anyone else gone through whatever papers he may have kept in there?" Harry asked quietly.

"No," she said. "There's very little in the office besides a desk and some chairs and his horse pictures. He talked on the phone a lot and signed papers I took in, but he dictated his letters, and I did the rest."

"There's no safe?"

She shook her head.

"I think the police will want to examine the room," Harry said, standing up. "This must all be very hard for you. I'm sorry."

"Thank you," she said. "It's probably silly of me, but I find I miss him terribly."

"I'm sure you do," Harry said, "and there's nothing the least bit silly about it."

An hour later, Harry and Holly with Nip and Tuck on point were walking from the house up the avenue of oaks to the stable through the blazing afternoon heat and the high, pulsing fiddling of the cicadas and the locusts. The Oaks was at least two miles from the Gulf, and the breeze blowing in from the water had lost its blue-green freshness long before reaching them, but it was still welcome.

"Then Heather found none of Tyce's blood on Jack's shoes?" Holly asked as they stepped out of the shade of the oaks into the full heat of the sun drenching the open space in front of Barn One and passed through a small, glittering rabble of dark zebra wing butterflies, flickering together in the brilliant light. Nip and Tuck made a few half-hearted leaps, snapping at the butterflies, and then gave up.

"Jim said her report to him found no human blood on any of his legs or shoes, except for a trace on the caulks of the front right shoe, which most likely came from his standing on the smeared area of the floor where Yellen was lying."

"It's established then," Holly asked, "that Jack didn't attack Tyce?"

"I think so," he said, "but the shoes have gone to the police labs to be tested again. That always takes time."

They stepped out of the sun into the welcome shade of Barn One. The central section of the stable had been sealed off with yellow crime scene tape, and all the horses had been housed in the other three stables, a situation that had, according to Holly, deeply offended Elijah, who was standing in for Yellen.

"Any news on Yellen?" Harry asked as they stepped into the welcome shade.

"He's still unconscious," Holly said. "I went in this morning and sat with him awhile. He's still wrapped up like a mummy. His injuries must be terrible."

"Has he been conscious at all?" Harry asked.

She shook her head.

"What's to be done, Harry?" she asked, folding her arms tightly, her shoulder slightly hunched.

Harry knew she was not cold.

"I'm sure Jim Snyder and his people are either already beginning the search or will begin it as soon as they have all the reports in hand."

"Everything takes so long," she said with a slight shudder, "everything but the violence, which seems to happen in an instant."

Harry wanted to say that whoever attacked Yellen hadn't done that amount of damage in an instant, but he saw no point in making her feel worse than she felt already.

"What is Jeff Smolkin telling you about the will?" he asked, hoping to ease her mind.

"A bright spot," she said, releasing herself and pulling her shoulders down. "The probate process begins tomorrow."

"Have you seen the will?"

"Yes, Jeff took me into Josie's office yesterday and together we took a preliminary look at it."

"And?"

"There's nothing surprising, except for one thing."

She seemed to drift off.

"Holly?" Harry asked.

She looked at him as if surprised by his voice.

"There's nothing there about Oleander," she said at last, seeming to have trouble conveying the information.

"Is there anything in the safe in his study?" Harry asked, recalling the letters from Clarissa.

"No. I've read every piece of paper in there, and some I wish

I'd never read," she said harshly.

"Then unless there's a document somewhere else," Harry said, "but, as I've told you already, Emily Bradshaw is quite sure there is no document in the Pike Associates office referring to Oleander. If something isn't found, the lease is just going to run out, and you'll have to decide what to do about it."

"I know, and the prospect is making me ill," Holly admitted. "Why did Brandon do it?"

She stared at Harry as if he had the answer.

"It's so cruel!" she burst out, breaking through his silence, "to me, to Clarissa and Miguel. What could he have been thinking of to leave us all hanging like this? And now Tyce! What could he have done to deserve such treatment? What did Brandon do?"

There was something in her voice that brought the lounging dogs to their feet, staring at her in sudden alertness and growling deep in their chests to tell her they were there. Their hyper-vigilance kept Harry from putting an arm around Holly.

"You're right," he said as calmly as he could. "It is cruel, all of it, and, at least for us at this moment, it makes no sense."

She pressed her hands against the sides of her face as if she was holding her head on, and Harry thought that, in a way, she may have been doing just that because when she spoke, her voice was calmer, steadier. Nip and Tuck relaxed.

"Will we ever know why this has happened, why it's still happening?" she asked. "Could this ever make sense? I don't see how."

"Have you ever read Eliot?" he asked, making another attempt to explain what was happening and to distract her at the same time.

"Yes, years ago. I read a lot of him. Why do you ask? What does it have to do with what's happening here?"

"I think he has been where you are," Harry said, then added,

"I mean where you are mentally. Shall I go on?"

"I don't see that it matters one way or another," she said with a shrug. "I don't see that anything matters. Nothing can be changed."

"That's the point," Harry said.

They were both leaning on a stall gate, staring into its dark and empty interior.

"In Eliot's 'Fragment of an Agon,' " Harry began bravely, "Sweeney tells a story about a man who killed a girl and kept her in a bathtub, preserved in a gallon of Lysol. He kept her there, Sweeney says, for 'a couple of months.' During that time, the man gradually lost his capacity to distinguish between reality and unreality, his ability to tell who is alive and who is dead. And another of the characters asks Sweeney what the man did all that time, and Sweeney says, '. . . he took in the milk and he paid the rent.' "

"You've lost me," Holly said, sounding impatient.

"Having the dead girl in the bathtub caused the man's world to stop making sense," Harry said, "and he was reduced to mundane activities that had no meaning. Isn't that what you meant a moment or two ago?"

Holly looked at him with a flicker of interest replacing the mask of bitterness on her face.

"Yes," she said quietly, "I suppose it is. My world has stopped making sense."

"With the passing of time, it will make sense again, but probably not in quite the same way."

Holly looked at him with a wry expression.

"Are you trying to make me feel better?" she asked.

"Maybe."

"You're really weird, do you know that?"

"Do you feel better?"

"Not really."

"Then . . ."

"Don't tell me! I'll just have to go on taking in the milk and paying the rent."

"I'm afraid so."

"Thanks a lot."

"You're welcome, and there's one more thing you can do."

"What's that, read more Eliot?"

"No. Help me find out who's doing this."

12

"It's official," Jim said. "The doctors who are working on Yellen have finally agreed after bringing Kathleen, I mean the medical examiner, into their deliberations that Yellen's wounds were inflicted by a person, wielding some kind of heavy object at least three inches wide, and not by a horse. Also, by some miracle, we have the lab reports back on the horseshoes, and only one has a trace of human blood on it."

"Baseball bat," Hodges said.

"Could be," Harry said, "and Heather Parkinson confirmed what Holly, Elijah, and I concluded. There were no traces of blood on Jack's hooves or legs,"

"With the medical examiner, the doctors, and the vet all in agreement," Hodges said, his mouth half full of one of Katherine's homemade jelly donuts, "even the State Attorney is going to agree that we've got another murder on our hands."

The three men were sitting on Harry's lanai, enjoying the early morning sun, with coffee and donuts within reach. Jim and Hodges were not only glowing from having seen Katherine again, they were profoundly grateful they were not obliged to drink Harry's coffee, which Hodges once said tasted like paint remover.

"How could you know how paint remover tastes?" Jim had demanded.

"I had spilled some on my hand while scraping a blind I planned to repaint," Hodges said earnestly. "Then didn't I go ahead and skin my thumb with the scraper, and before I thought, I stuck my thumb in my mouth. I expected I was done for, but the worst thing that happened, which was bad enough, was that for a week nothing I ate tasted like it was supposed to."

Harry, touchy as he was about his coffee, had been so diverted by Hodge's story he'd forgotten to be offended. Also, Katherine had been ill when she woke up, but except for a slight headache, which was wearing off by the time Jim and Hodges arrived, she claimed to be fully recovered.

"I expect that whoever attacked Yellen opened Jack's box stall," Harry said, "hoping the stallion would trample Yellen or at least be blamed for doing it."

"You'd think it would most likely have been someone working on the farm," Jim said.

"And someone Yellen knew," Hodges added, reaching for another donut. "He was taken down in the middle of that walkway, but after seeing Yellen in the hospital, it would be hard to say if there'd been a struggle."

"We've overlooked something," Harry put in. "Holly said she and Elijah found Yellen."

"That's what she told us," Jim said. "What have we overlooked?"

"Nip and Tuck," Harry said, his mind moving ahead of his tongue.

"The dogs," Hodges said, pausing to speak before taking another bite of the donut.

"They're always with her when she's out of the house," Harry said.

"So the attack must have taken place while Mrs. Pike was in the house," Jim said.

"Unless it was the Pike woman swinging that bat or whatever it was," Hodges said. "In that case the dogs would have sat and watched."

"Right," Harry said, flinching away from the possibility, "but I don't think Holly attacked Yellen. I just can't see her doing it."

"Someone did it," Hodges insisted.

Harry let it go.

"As for the timing," he said, "I wonder if any of the surgeons who worked on him could tell us when the wounds were inflicted?"

"Well, we'll ask them," Jim replied. "The C.I.D. report says Yellen was found at about 8:30 A.M. The ambulance arrived at 8:55, and Yellen was admitted to the hospital at 9:40."

"Come to think of it," Hodges said, "I didn't see anything in the report saying what time the crew shows up for work out there."

"Harry?" Jim asked.

"I don't know, but Holly told me that while Brandon was alive she got up at five or a little after to eat breakfast with him. I take it he rode most mornings, so I imagine the stable crew came in early. Elijah can tell us if they still do."

"Odd one of the detectives didn't ask him," Hodges added. "Mrs. Pike says she didn't leave the house that morning until Elijah came to get her, to ask something about one of the mares."

"I wonder why he didn't take the problem to Yellen?" Jim asked.

No one had an answer, but Harry suggested asking Elijah again. Jim got up, and Hodges reluctantly left the plate of donuts. Katherine came out of the kitchen to say goodbye and urge them to come back soon.

"And say hello to Kathleen for me," she told Jim, giving him a farewell hug.

Harry managed to keep smiling.

"You're still jealous of him, aren't you?" she asked Harry as they stood on the grass, waving the cruiser out of the yard.

"Yes," Harry said, feeling happy and foolish at the same time.

"Good," she told him crisply, reconfiguring the moment. "It will give me something pleasant to think of when you're out with Soñadora."

Harry decided to visit Tyce Yellen, knowing the man was still unconscious but wanting to make the gesture. Driving to the hospital, he found the sting of Katherine's comment was keeping him company. He had made no response to it, and she'd marched into the house, letting the lanai door slam behind her. It was true, he admitted, he was sleeping—or had been—with Soñadora. He seemed now to be sleeping also with Katherine, who until now had made no mention of Soñadora after that early outburst.

What do I feel about this? he asked himself and found his answer breaking up in his brain like fried connections; from the wreckage he salvaged the disturbing thought that something was definitely wrong. What that something was he resolutely left unexplored.

Holly had been right, Harry thought, staring at the silent figure in the bed. He does look like a mummy. Yellen's head and face were swathed in bandages, his arms, encased in new-style casts, resting on the outside of the sheet to accommodate a gathering of IVs and other devices registering with green blinks and graphs on the assembled monitors at the head of his bed.

A solitary gray metal chair stood empty beside the bed, and Harry took it. Once seated, he began to wonder what, if anything, Yellen had done that had led to his lying here, hanging onto life by a thread. More to the point, what sense of being wronged could have driven his attacker to this degree of savagery, not once, probably, but twice? Increasingly it seemed to Harry that whoever killed Brandon had also attacked Yellen.

Speculating about the killer's identity proved useless, and, gradually, Harry's mind grew quieter. For several minutes he sat, simply keeping the still figure in the bed company. The click of heels on the floor behind him jerked him out of his vigil. Turning, he saw Miguel Cruz entering the room, dressed in denims, western boots, and a white T-shirt.

"What are you doing here?" Cruz asked.

"Visiting with your friend," Harry said, turning his surprise into something else.

"What makes you think he's my friend?" Cruz demanded, glaring at Harry.

"Because, Miguel," Harry said, getting slowly to his feet, "it seems obvious to me. Why does my saying it offend you? I think Tyce is a good man. I like him, and I'm deeply troubled by what has been done to him. I would like nothing better than to find the person responsible."

Harry had deliberately made it a long speech, giving Cruz time to calm down and also to say something that Harry felt needed saying. He regarded Cruz as an important piece in this bloody puzzle and wanted to know where to place him. To do that, he had to find a way to persuade the fiery young man to talk with him.

"You still work for Mrs. Brandon?" Cruz asked in a marginally less hostile voice.

"Yes, I do, and I think that whoever killed her husband did this to Tyce."

Wherever Cruz was going, Harry's statement had apparently caused him to shift direction because he asked how Harry could know that.

It was a good question, and Harry took a few moments to think about his answer. The room slipped back into its sunny quiet, broken only by the muted ticking and bubbling of the machinery keeping Yellen alive.

"If I could answer you the way you want me to," Harry said,

"I think I would know who killed Brandon Pike and who beat Tyce Yellen almost to death."

"I suppose I already know the obvious answer," Miguel said, moving to the bed and resting a hand on Yellen's arm as if in greeting and then turning back to Harry, "but is it the right one?"

"Do you have any reason for thinking it isn't?" Harry asked.

They were interrupted by three nurses who told them to leave because they were going to change some of Yellen's bandages and dress his wounds.

Harry left without protest, but Cruz tried to persuade them to give him an update on Yellen's condition and failed, two of them taking him unceremoniously by his elbows and trotting him into the corridor and closing the door firmly behind him.

"I get thrown out of there a lot," Cruz said, managing a grin. "They've given up even pretending to be polite."

"This place has a cafeteria," Harry said. "How about a cup of coffee? I'm buying."

To Harry's surprise, Cruz agreed.

"For Tyce's sake, I hope the care in here is better than the coffee," Cruz said, setting down his mug in disgust in the cafeteria a few minutes later.

"Institutions are forbidden by hallowed custom from preparing edible food or making drinkable coffee."

"Have you been in here as a patient?"

"Many times. Each time they've healed me and shrunk my waistline," Harry said.

Cruz laughed and Harry, having had a chance to observe him when he wasn't scowling, realized that he was a remarkably handsome man.

"Can I ask you some questions?" Harry said, adding quickly, "I understand I'm taking advantage of the situation, so feel free to say no."

"What do you want to know?" Cruz said.

"I don't want to push you where you don't want to go," Harry responded, surprised by Cruz's sudden capitulation.

"Don't worry. I'm at least as tough as Tyce to nail down."

Harry nodded, gathering that the two had discussed his sessions with Yellen.

"Have you talked with the police?"

"Oh, yes, but they seemed a lot more interested in Tyce than they were in me."

"The Yellen and Holly Price thing," Harry said in a way suggesting that was a cold trail.

Cruz gave a short laugh and nodded. "When they found out my mother ran Oleander on a lease, they seemed to lose interest in us."

"Yellen refused to admit that you and he had ever discussed either Brandon Pike or the lease," Harry said, going for broke. "I told him I didn't believe it, but he stuck to his story."

"What makes you think it's a story?"

"Because that lease is running out. You've given most of your adult life to that farm and made a success of it."

Harry paused to give Cruz a chance to speak. When he didn't, Harry continued.

"You must have thought about what was going to happen if Brandon died. His health had been poor for several years, and now he's dead. Where does that leave you and your mother?"

"Doesn't Holly Pike know?" Miguel asked in apparent surprise.

The question stymied Harry. He had expected an entirely different response, and it had not occurred to him that Holly might have been lying to him about the lease.

"You have asked her, haven't you?" Miguel said with a taunting grin.

"And had an answer," Harry replied. "Now I'm asking you.

Of course, you're not obliged to answer, but I can't think why you wouldn't."

"What did my sister tell you when you asked her the question?" Miguel said, serious again.

"Nothing," Harry said, wondering how much her brothers knew about her relationship with Brandon. "Maybe there was nothing to tell."

"As long as I have known her, my sister has been an extremely private person," Miguel said. "When I was in my early twenties, she went through a very bad marriage. She came out of it more silent and withdrawn than when she went into it. I'm surprised she agreed to talk with you at all."

"She wanted to know whether or not I thought any of you were involved in Brandon's death."

"Do you?"

"Based on what I know now," Harry said, having given up playing cat and mouse as to what Miguel knew and didn't know about the lease. "I don't think so."

"You're right," Miguel said. "My sister loved Brandon very deeply. He was both brother and father to her. As for Felipe and me, what possible motive could we have?"

"I've never met your brother," Harry said.

To that, Miguel made no response and got to his feet.

"Do you visit Tyce often?" Harry asked, getting up with him.

"Every day," Miguel said, leaving Harry asking himself why.

Harry watched Miguel drive out of the parking lot, giving him a final wave that went unanswered.

Harry arrived home to find Katherine sitting on the lanai, asleep, with an open book on her lap. She did not awaken until he opened the screen door.

"Sleeping Beauty," Harry said, but thinking that she looked very pale.

"Hi," she said without moving. "What time is it?"

"A little after twelve. How are you feeling?"

"That wretched headache came back after you left," she said, swinging her feet to the floor. "It seems to be better now."

"That's good. You're a little pale. Are you sure you're okay?"

She had thrown up again that morning as soon as she had gotten out of bed.

"I'm fine," Katherine insisted, but when she stood and started to walk toward the kitchen, she was unable to progress in a straight line, and Harry had to put his arm around her to keep her from falling.

"I'm dizzy," she said, pressing a hand against her forehead.

"Don't try to walk," Harry said. "Lean on me."

She did lean on him for a moment, her eyes closed; then she pulled away.

"I'm all right," she said. "I must have gotten up too quickly. What would you like for lunch?"

Harry followed her into the kitchen, thinking hard about how he was going to handle this, and decided that the key lay in not showing that he was worried.

"You choose," he said, "but first I want to talk with you."

"Harry, I'm not sick," she said emphatically, turning by the table to face him, and in turning, she started to pitch over again but saved herself by grasping the table and steadying herself.

Harry pulled out a chair.

"Here," he said, "sit down."

To his relief, she did. She rubbed her face in what Harry saw was a recurring action, done almost automatically.

"Is there something on your face?" he asked, knowing there wasn't.

"I just feel as if I need to rub it."

Harry leaned over her and gently pulled her head against him.

"I want you to see Esther Benson," he said. "I expect you're right. It's probably nothing, but would you do it for me?"

"I suppose I won't get any peace until I do," she said, showing no enthusiasm.

"Thank you," he said, feeling relief that did nothing to lessen his concern.

"If I had to live with him," Dr. Benson said to Katherine as she was peering into her left eye through an ophthalmoscope, "I'd have headaches. Hold still."

Katherine had begun to laugh at Benson's comment because Harry was sitting behind Benson. She had allowed him into the examination room but only if he kept quiet and didn't fidget.

Esther Benson was a slender, prematurely gray-haired gynecologist with the bedside manner of a pit bull and a seriously warped sense of humor. She had treated Katherine for years and had played a major role several years ago in restoring Minna to mental and physical health following a physical assault that had left her ill, withdrawn, and suicidal.

Harry thought she walked on water.

"Well, I can't find anything wrong," Benson told Katherine when the examination was over. "The skipped periods are probably connected with the onset of menopause, but the vomiting, headaches, and other physical manifestations are less easy to account for."

She hung her stethoscope around her neck and glowered at Harry.

"Try not to upset her—if you have any idea what I'm talking about, which you probably don't," she told him.

Harry did not extend their long-standing game because he heard the message. She had either found or suspected the existence of something she did not want to discuss with Katherine in any detail. He felt a cold trickle of fear trace a path around his stomach.

"Then I'm all right," Katherine said, straightening her skirt and picking up her purse.

Benson dropped a hand on her shoulder.

"Probably, sweetheart," she said, "but I want to think a little."

"What does that mean?" Katherine demanded, obviously disappointed.

Harry's suspicions were confirmed. She was on the trail of something.

"It's nothing to worry your pretty head about," Benson told her. "I just want to chase your symptoms a little. When I've done that, I'll tell you. Okay?"

"If you say so," Katherine replied, still wearing a skeptical expression.

"And as for you," she said, patting the bald spot on Harry's head, "try not to be a constant pain in the ass. The woman could use some rest."

Another message, buried in an insult. Harry opened the door for Katherine. As he was following her into the corridor, he paused and said over his shoulder to Benson, "You could have been a code talker in the Second World War," he said. "You're old enough."

"Try not to get run over," Benson replied, making Harry feel even more anxious.

13

Katherine did not speak until they were getting into the Rover. Then she said, "I don't want to talk about this until I've heard from Esther. Is that a problem for you?"

"No," Harry said, trying to sound as though he had already forgotten about her having seen Benson.

"Good," Katherine responded, making putting on her seat belt look like the beginning of a long, unpleasant trip.

Harry groaned inwardly.

"I want to talk about us, Harry," she said. "I made up my mind about it while I was throwing up this morning. It can't be ignored any longer."

Harry thought that placing the "us" in close proximity to vomiting was not an auspicious sign, but he ruled out saying so and waited for whatever had broken loose to land on his head.

"You and I have been trying to wear out our personal equipment ever since I got here," Katherine began, then paused as if reflecting unfavorably on those activities.

"Speaking for myself," Harry said bravely, "I don't really feel any the worse for wear, and, to be frank, I've enjoyed our workouts. How about you?"

Katherine gave a snort of laughter, looked at him, pink-cheeked, and said, "You're hopeless, so I've got to be the one to say this."

"Well," Harry said with increasing desperation, "if you're going to tell me you haven't enjoyed it, don't. Let me stay blissfully ignorant."

"Of course I enjoyed it, you fool," she said, "and don't think I don't know you're trying to change the subject."

"What subject?"

"Okay. I'm sharing you with Soñadora, and don't pretend I'm not," she said.

"Not since you arrived," Harry said.

It was a mistake.

"What did you say to her?" Katherine demanded, her voice rising. " 'Look, Katherine's coming for a couple of weeks. I'll be shagging her, so pack it in ice 'til she's gone'?"

The question made Harry angry, not because it was so far from the truth but because it robbed what they had been doing of all its love and passion and because it forced him to put both Soñadora and Katherine in one mental compartment instead of two, something that up until now he had been resolutely and successfully refusing to do while, at the same time, denying he was doing any such thing. Soñadora had been right about that, but he refused to give it breathing room.

Hence the anger.

"Well, don't sit there trying to yank that steering wheel off its post. Answer me," Katherine said, her face pale with whatever emotion was gripping her.

Harry was so angry, his voice, when he began speaking, was shaking, and his knuckles were white from gripping the wheel so hard.

"Do you think it's remotely possible for me to be with you and not want to make love to you? Do you? Do you think there's anyone on the face of this Earth I love the way I love and want you?"

She started crying and shouted, "Oh, shit!"

She hated crying. Harry knew that when she started crying, she became furious with herself and everyone around her and that what followed was usually a preview of World War Three.

"That's not fighting fair," she said, struggling to find a tissue. "That's a dirty thing to do."

"In the cubbyhole," he said, reaching to open it.

She slapped his hand away and found them herself. A terrible lull followed during which Harry steered the Rover over the bridge without driving them into Puc Puggy Creek, Katherine blew her nose, gasped and wept, and gradually regained control of her tears.

"You did that on purpose," she told him, red-eyed and steaming.

"I told you the truth," he said. "If you can't deal with it, tough."

He parked under the oak, and they walked together in armed silence toward the house.

Once on the lanai, she said, "What do you want for lunch?"

"You," he said.

"Okay," she answered calmly, all traces of her anger gone, and walked through the kitchen and up the stairs with him following.

Astonished by what was happening, he found himself wanting to quote Hamlet's comment to Horatio on the limits of human knowledge but wisely kept his mouth shut, being sufficiently in command of himself to know you don't talk during miracles.

Much later while Harry and Katherine were eating a late lunch in a companionable silence, Katherine asked Harry the name of the Episcopalian priest he mentioned from time to time.

"Rowena Farnham," Harry answered, leaning back from his plate with a sigh of satisfaction. "What made you think of her?"

"Her church sponsors a safehouse for battered women, doesn't it?"

"Haven House," he said. "You thinking of taking refuge there?"

"Maybe," she said. "Do you suppose I could talk with her?"

"Of course," Harry said. "Shall I call her?"

Curious as he was, he decided to let her tell him why when she was ready.

"Yes," she said, getting up to clear the table.

Harry dialed Farnham's office and, as usual, found her at work. They talked for a few minutes, and then Harry asked Katherine if she wanted to see Rowena in an hour. Katherine nodded, and Harry confirmed the appointment.

When he had hung up the phone, Katherine said with a slight flush, "Would you be willing to drive? I feel foolish asking, but I'd like you to introduce me to Farnham."

He was surprised by her request. When they were married, she had a deep dread of meeting new people, but over time she had gotten beyond that; Harry wondered if this resurging shyness—if that's what it was—had been a factor in her turning down the recent job offers.

"Glad to," Harry said, careful to keep his puzzlement out of sight.

St. Jude's Episcopal Church, located on a square of well-tended grass a block from the Gulf in one of the most affluent sections of town, was a white clapboard building with a graceful spire and beautiful stained glass windows. Rowena's office was in a long, low administration building across the street from the church, which, like the church, was dwarfed by the fichus trees towering over it.

"Come in, come in," Rowena said, beaming and throwing open her office door to greet them and giving Harry a hug that all but engulfed him.

She was a large woman with a short cap of snow white hair,

shrewd blue eyes, and a round, rosy face almost devoid of wrinkles, despite the fact she was in her sixties. Dressed in easy-waist blue slacks, a green Celtics sweatshirt and white topsiders, she looked like a fairly prosperous street person. While she and Harry rattled on, catching up with things, Katherine stared at her, not quite open-mouthed.

"You have no idea how glad I am to meet you, Katherine," Rowena said, turning to her suddenly and grasping her hands. "Harry has talked about you so much, I feel as though I already know you. You're even lovelier than he led me to think. Let's sit down over here and get to know one another."

"There isn't room to sit anywhere else," Harry observed, trailing after them. "This place is more of a wreck than it was the last time I was here."

"Harry!" Katherine protested, her face flaming.

"Just look at the place," Harry said.

He had a point. Every wall space was covered with books, floor to ceiling. Rowena's desk was buried under more books, files, notebooks, and fliers that had spilled out into the seats of the nearby chairs.

"Don't pay any attention to him," Rowena told Katherine. "I don't unless I need him. Then I make him work his tail off for nothing. Sit down, sit down."

She all but lifted Katherine into a chair and, taking a linen napkin off the small, round table at which she had seated them, dropped it on Katherine's lap.

"Tea and hot buttered scones coming up," she said in her rich and powerful voice, then picked up a large silver tray burdened with a silver tea service, cups and saucers, jars of marmalade and jam, and a stack of scones with a white napkin draped over them, and set it without apparent effort on the table and whisked the napkin off the scones like a magician conjuring a rabbit.

"I didn't have time to ask Harry what brought you to the Hammock," she continued as she poured the tea and passed around the plates, loaded with the hot scones, which instantly filled the area where they were sitting with a glorious aroma.

"Eat and talk at the same time," she ordered, settling into her chair more comfortably as she spread marmalade on her scone.

Katherine's answer was vague, but Rowena was not put off.

"By the way," she told Katherine, "call me Rowena. The problem doesn't arise with God, but for the rest of us, which name to use can become a nuisance."

She had the kind of full-bodied laugh that made it almost impossible not to join in. Harry was delighted to see Katherine break through her reserve to laugh with Rowena, who continued asking Katherine questions that had no apparent destination, but Katherine began answering them more and more fully, and the moment came when Rowena turned to Harry and said, "This would be a good time for you to run those errands, and don't feel rushed. We're going to be just fine."

Harry expected Katherine to protest. When she didn't, he polished off the last of his second scone and left.

Katherine was quiet when she got into the Rover, but before they were out of Avola, she said, "I'm going to be working at Haven House for a while. Their bookkeeper is in over her head, and I've agreed to help out."

Here was another disturbing surprise for Harry.

"I thought the idea of your coming here was to get some rest," Harry said, not wanting to say anything about it's being out of character. "Benson told me you needed to rest."

"Benson doesn't know everything," she replied.

Harry did not want this to turn into a quarrel and tried changing the subject slightly.

"Was your going to Haven House Rowena's idea?"

"No. It was mine. I asked her if she needed any volunteer help. Are you surprised?"

"No, but I thought you wanted to talk over something with her."

"Like what?"

"I didn't get that far," he lied, not wanting to say he thought it had to do with the way she was feeling.

"Thanks for being concerned," she said, leaning over and kissing his cheek.

"Don't worry about me, Harry," she said. "I need to do this. I need to begin to pull myself out of whatever this hole is I'm in. You're busy. It's not good for me to sit around doing nothing but read or visit with Tucker."

Harry made supportive comments and tried to persuade himself that he should be glad that she was interested in working again, but it was heavy lifting.

"Esther Benson may be able to help," he said.

She looked at him as if she didn't know what he was talking about.

"She should call you soon about the throwing up and the headaches."

"Oh! Of course," Katherine said with what Harry thought was a forced laugh.

They finished the ride to the Hammock in silence with Harry wondering if it was possible that Katherine had forgotten seeing Esther.

The following morning, to Harry's relief, Katherine got up cheerful and displaying none of the symptoms of illness. While they were getting breakfast, she said, "I'm going to Haven House a little later. What are you doing?"

"I'm chasing a will o' the wisp," he said. "So you're really going to follow through on this Haven House thing?"

"Yes, and what do you mean?"

"As you've heard me say so many times since Brandon Pike's murder that you must be sick of hearing it, I don't see any light in the darkness surrounding his death and the attack on Tyce Yellen. From what Jim and Frank Hodges have told me, they're chasing their tails as well."

"Frustrating," Katherine said, putting plates on the table. "Are you still sure the same person committed both crimes?"

"There's no solid evidence to prove it, but the likelihood of there being no connection between them is so remote that I'm left having to believe the connection is there even if I can't find it."

He heard the tension in his voice and realized that the case was disturbing him more than he had admitted.

"And there's no one working for Pike who would have any reason to harm him or Yellen?"

"Not as far as I know, but, pretty much out of desperation, this morning I'm going to dig a little into that episode a few years back in which Brandon killed Henry Jackson."

She was about to crack eggs into a frying pan and paused, asking with an expression of surprise, "Brandon Pike killed someone?"

"Yes," Harry said, "I told you about it a few days ago. Jackson was drunk and stepped in front of Brandon's car. You don't remember my mentioning it?"

"Nope," she said in an unconcerned voice, and turned back to her task.

Harry paused a moment, then set aside his uneasiness about the forgetfulness but determined to tell Benson about it.

"Well, he was arrested and tried for vehicular homicide and found innocent. Then, although there was no record of their having been married, Rosalee Franklin, the woman who claimed to be Jackson's wife, brought a wrongful death suit against

Brandon, which the judge dismissed. There might have been some lingering resentment there somewhere."

"It certainly sounds weird enough," Katherine said. "Put the toast down and turn the bacon. These eggs are almost done."

She hasn't listened to half what I've been saying, Harry thought, dealing with the toast and the bacon. *I wonder if she's worrying about what Esther Benson is going to tell her?*

"I'm really looking forward to seeing Haven House," Katherine said with a smile just before they began eating. "It feels good to be starting something new."

The Scrub-a-Dub office was located on Locust Avenue in a depressing, dingy section of East Avola with peeling paint, cracked stucco, and blinds hanging by one bracket and creaking in the fitful wind, spinning dust devils on the potholed street. Walking up the cracked cement walk to the door, Harry, feeling the sweat begin to prickle under his collar, thought it must be at least fifteen degrees hotter here than it was on the Hammock.

A young woman with spiky black hair and a pasty complexion was seated at a gray metal desk in the cramped and cluttered reception room, typing on a computer keyboard. Behind her was a large poster board covered with rows of postcard-sized rectangles of curling paper with names written on them in longhand. Pinned under most of the names were typed addresses and a surname.

"You need a cleaner?" the girl asked without looking up.

"Does Rosalee Franklin still work here?" Harry asked.

The girl stopped typing and looked at him with a blank expression.

"Who wants to know?" she asked.

"Harry Brock. I'm not a bill collector. I'm not from the police. All I want is to speak with her."

"About what?"

"It has nothing to do with your company. Is she still working for you?"

"I'm not supposed to give out information about an employee."

"Okay, I really do need a cleaner. I've been told she does good work, and I want her to clean my office. Does she do windows?"

Harry was beginning to enjoy this.

"Yeah, she can do that."

"Is she free today?"

The girl got up and studied the board. Then she turned back to Harry and said, "She's off the roster today. You want me to call her?"

"Yes, and if she's willing to do the job, tell her I'll pick her up."

The girl made the call.

"She'll do it. What's the address?"

Harry gave her the address of an office building on Oyster Street where the State Attorney's offices were located, adding a floor to the building.

"Upscale address," the girl said.

"Good security," Harry said with a straight face.

"We could use some. We been burgled twice this year already."

When the paperwork was done, Harry paid the deposit, and the girl gave him Franklin's address.

"You take care," he said. "We live in perilous times."

"Don't I know it," she said and went back to typing.

Rosalee Franklin was standing at the end of her walk in front of a small, pale yellow stucco bungalow with a red tile roof on Frye Street, a modest street lined with Canary Island palms shading a dozen other houses identical to Franklin's except for being painted in a variety of pastel colors. Dogs barked at the

Rover. Half a dozen boys, who should have been in school, were riding bicycles in the street, shouting either at one another or at him. Harry couldn't tell which and decided they were too old to need watching.

Holly had been right. Rosalee Franklin could not have been over thirty-three or thirty-four, but the years since her court case against Brandon had not been kind to her. She was overweight. Her face was lined, and her short, carelessly brushed hair was already sprinkled with white. She stood watching Harry get out of the Rover and come toward her with a look of weary indifference.

"My name's Harry Brock," he said, extending his hand, which she held briefly and then dropped as if glad to be rid of it.

"You already know mine," she said, avoiding his eyes. "You got an office needs cleaning."

"No," Harry said. "I don't, but if you'll stand here and let me ask you a few questions—it won't take much time—I'll pay you for three hours' work, and you can tell Scrub-a-Dub anything you want to."

"You from the po-lice?" she demanded, stiffening. "Because if he's in jail, he can stay there. I've bailed him out for the last time."

"No, and I'm not a bail bondsman," Harry said quickly. "I don't want anything from you but the answers to some questions, which you can answer or not. I won't press you."

He suddenly did not like his job. Seeing the look of mingled fear and defiance on Rosalee Franklin's face told him all he needed to know about her life and what he represented in her eyes.

"What you want to ask me about?" she demanded, eyes narrowed in suspicion.

"Do you know that Brandon Pike is dead? That he was murdered?"

146

"I didn't have nothing to do with that."

"Of course you didn't. I want to ask you about Henry Jackson."

"Brandon Pike killed Henry Jackson," she said.

Harry could see the old anger boiling up.

"Henry was the father of two of my kids," she continued, "and that Pike didn't pay me nothing toward their upkeep. Henry didn't neither, but that don't make no matter." She paused to catch her breath, then went on with increased vehemence. "He should have, and had he lived, he might have. Dead, he ain't never going to make no payments. That's why I went to Pike, but that judge said I lacked grounds. *Grounds!* I could tell him sumpin' about *grounds*. I got six *grounds* needing care, and two of them belonged to Henry Jackson."

"Aside from you and the children," Harry asked when she paused a second time for breath, "did Henry Jackson have any other family?"

Franklin startled Harry by bursting into genuine laughter.

"Family!" she said, her eyes wide. "Lord above! You can't shoot off a gun in this part of town without laying out a Jackson, and there ain't one not related to all the rest."

Harry was unable to keep from laughing with her.

"Was there any of them he was especially close to?"

"He thought a lot of his mother, I know that," she said reflectively.

"Is she still alive?"

"Far as I know."

"Do you remember her name?"

"Gladys, I think."

Harry thanked Franklin for talking with him and gave her a fifty-dollar bill.

"It's too much, Mr. Brock," she said, her suspicion returning.

"No," Harry said. "It's probably not enough. Thank you again."

"Doesn't seem to me I told you anything worth fifty dollars."

"Hearing you laugh, Mrs. Franklin," he said, getting into the Rover, "was worth more than fifty dollars. Take my word for that."

14

Harry felt better after giving Rosalee Franklin the fifty dollars but not a lot better. Driving away from Frye Street, he reviewed the experience and decided that the only wholly satisfying thing about it *was* hearing her laugh. Whatever life had done to her, it had not destroyed her sense of humor. As for his efforts, he thought they had probably been a waste of time; he doubted if talking to Gladys Jackson would be worth the time it would take to find her, but he made a note of her name and turned his mind to a more pressing matter.

Over the past few days, at unguarded moments, he found himself revisiting his most recent conversation with Soñadora. Recalling it left him feeling guilty and ashamed, and the more he thought about it the more obvious it became that from the time he'd known Katherine was coming to visit him until the present, his treatment of her had been absolutely shabby. At the same time, her message and its tone had left him feeling badly done to. In a flurry of shame and self-pity, Harry decided to stop by *Salvamento* on his way home and talk to her.

When he arrived at *Salvamento*, she was in a meeting. He sat muttering and fidgeting in her office for nearly half an hour before she finally appeared.

"I'd like to talk with you," he said, trying to pretend that she wasn't looking at him with all the bonhomie of a female panther stalking her dinner.

"You might have called me," she said.

149

It was not what he wanted to hear.

"Are we making appointments now?" he asked.

"*We*," she told him, "are not doing anything, and until Katherine leaves your house, we will not be doing anything. I'm very busy. Please leave."

Furious, humiliated, and hurt, Harry turned and stalked out of her office and through the large room where the fifteen women who ran *Salvamento* sat at their computers, typing and speaking through their headsets, mostly in Spanish, to the dozens of people who every hour of the day called in search of help or who were being called in to give them support.

As he strode toward the door, the room gradually grew quiet, then exploded in laughter as he slammed the door behind him. His face burning, Harry fled to the Rover, fleeing that mocking sound, and kicked gravel driving out of the yard. It was a significantly bad moment, made worse by knowing that the women knew what Soñadora had done to him and probably why.

Guilt is said to be the gift that goes on giving. Under all of Harry's outrage and pain of rejection lay, coiled and venomous, the snake of his guilt. It struck and pierced his self-righteous anger as he turned north onto Interstate 75. He groaned out loud as the shock of it brought him face to face with just what he had been doing and that he wasn't going to get away with it.

The worst of it was that there was no one to blame but himself. No, perhaps that wasn't quite the worst of it because this newfound clarity did not diminish the hurt that Soñadora's ordering him out of her office had caused him nor the sting of the women's well-deserved laughter.

Gradually, he eased his foot back from the accelerator. The adrenaline drained away. His face stopped burning. Gradually, he stopped rehashing the encounter and splashing around in his lurid grievances. In the ensuing silence, Harry saw that, for only

God knew how long, he and that miserable snake were going to be constant companions.

Feeling guilty or not, Harry had an appointment with Holly Pike and called her to say he was coming.

"I'm glad you are," she told him. "Tuck is sick and Heather Parkinson is with him."

"Is it serious?" Harry asked.

"I don't know. We're in Stable Two."

Nip was waiting for Harry in the parking area and led him through the light shower that was sweeping over The Oaks, riding a brisk wind, and briefly giving relief from the sun. Harry took off his hat and lifted his face into the cool sprinkles. By the time he and the dog reached the stable, they were bone dry and the sun was blazing again.

"I don't like the looks of this, Harry," Heather said with her usual disregard for formalities.

She was bent, hands on knees, over Tuck, who lay on the floor, panting heavily. Beside the dog were a rubber hose, a small funnel, and a pail, the contents of which Heather had used to induce him to vomit. What she had not bottled for lab work was still on the stable floor, giving off a vile stench.

"What's wrong with him?" Harry asked.

"I won't know for sure until I've run some tests," Heather said, peeling off her plastic gloves, "but I think he's been poisoned."

"Where's Holly?" Harry asked.

Without taking her eyes off Tuck, she tilted her head toward the other end of the stable.

"She's down there with Elijah. Watching me make the dog puke was too much for her."

Harry heard footsteps and, glancing down the corridor, saw Holly hurrying toward them.

"Now Sueño's limping badly," she told them, looking very stressed. "Elijah pastured her after she was bred. I don't see how she could have hurt herself in that pasture."

While she was talking, she had knelt down and was stroking the dog's shoulder.

"I can't look at the horse now," Heather said, none too gently.

"I know that, Heather," Holly said in a stricken voice. "What are you going to do with him?"

"I've given him an injection for the pain and to sedate him. I've also given him a healthy dose of Milk of Magnesia to soothe his digestive track and hurry whatever's in there out of him," Heather told her. "To do the rest, I've got to move him to my place. While I'm backing my truck up to the door, get someone to help Harry load Tuck."

"I'll get Elijah," Holly said, straightening up and running back along the corridor.

"Harry," Heather said, stuffing things into the pail, "don't tell her, but if this is what I think it is, the dog is probably not going to make it. How bad a hit will that outcome be for her?"

"Very bad," Harry said. "Give me a call before you tell her. If I can, I'll drive out here."

Elijah and Holly arrived, and the two men lifted the dog into the covered bed of the truck, laying him on a thick layer of pads. Heather, having clambered into the space ahead of them, adjusted the dog's position and then strapped him down.

"I'm out of here," she said, scrambling out and closing and locking the doors.

"Take good care of him," Elijah said.

"I don't need to be told that," Heather said, looking at him through slightly narrowed eyes.

"Sparky, ain't she?" he asked as the truck sped out of the yard.

"I want to look at Sueño," Holly said, making no response to the comment. "Harry, do you want to come?"

"I've arranged to see Jim this morning," he replied.

"Go," she responded, striding away. "Call me later. I want to discuss some things with you."

"Frank's with the C.I.D. people, looking into a hit and run on Seventy-Five near the Marco Island turn-off," Jim said, leaning his elbows on his desk and rubbing his head.

"What's got you worried?" Harry asked.

"Too much work, too few people, too little funding. Aside from that, I'm fine."

Jim pushed his chair back and planted his feet on the corner of the desk.

"What about you?"

"I'm stymied," Harry said, letting his frustration show in his voice. "Unless you're holding back, I don't see that we're making any progress with either Brandon's death or the attack on Yellen."

"I'm surely not," Jim broke out.

"And there's something else," Harry said, hurrying on, "one of Holly's Rottweilers has eaten something that Heather says is likely to kill him. If he dies, Holly is going to be seriously upset."

"You must have heard the dogs' universal philosophy," Jim said with a straight face.

"If I ever did, I've forgotten it. You'd better tell me."

"If you can't eat it or fuck it, piss on it."

Harry couldn't believe his ears. He had never heard Jim tell a joke, and he had certainly never heard him use language like that. For a moment he just stared in astonishment, his jaw actually dropping.

"Well, I know it's crude," Jim said, his ears coloring. "Frank told me it sometime or other, and I remember having to laugh even though I didn't want to. I don't like to encourage him in things like that. Of course, he doesn't need any encouragement. But you don't think it's funny?"

Harry finally laughed but not at the joke.

"I heard it when I was about twelve years old, but I never expected to hear it from you."

"I'm regressing," Jim said with a sad shake of his head. "I know it's no excuse, but between Frank and this job, it's all downhill."

"Try to hold on," Harry said, grinning. "Help is coming."

"It's too late," Jim said with a sadder shake of his head. Then, appearing to make an effort, he dropped his feet to the floor and said, "I'm sorry about the dog. What did he eat?"

"Heather's trying to determine that. I'm wondering, without any evidence to justify it, whether or not the animal was deliberately poisoned."

"Do you really think he might have been?"

"I don't know. Those dogs are seldom out of Holly's sight. They certainly don't run the woods."

"Nowadays, there's a lot of stuff around farm buildings in the way of sprays and whatnot that can be lethal if they're swallowed. I've known dogs to cash in from drinking antifreeze. It tastes sweet to them, and it's usually their last enjoyable moment."

"I would think so," Harry said, guessing Jim was in a worse mood than he was. "Are the background checks of everyone working at The Oaks finished?"

"Yes, whose do you want to see?"

"I'd like to take a look at Elijah Blue's file if you're willing to show it to me."

Jim leaned forward and called up the file on his computer.

"There it is," he said with no show of interest, pushing the monitor around so that Harry could see it from his side of the desk. "Read away."

Pulling his chair forward, Harry read and, reaching across the desk to the mouse, scrolled down the pages until he had read the entire file. As he did that he memorized Elijah's home address.

"He's done about everything, including spending three years in jail for boosting cars," Harry said, moving his chair back.

"Frank looked into that," Jim said. "Elijah never actually stole any of the cars. He just drove them from Avola to chop shops in Miami after they'd been stolen."

"That was after he stopped boxing," Harry said.

Jim nodded.

"He was good. I don't think he ever lost a fight."

"Why did he get out of it?"

"Almost killed a man in a bar brawl in Fort Myers, and the Florida Boxing Commission barred him. He had been charged several times with assault, but up to that one, none had ever stuck."

"An angry man, but that appears to be the last time he got into trouble with the law," Harry said, taking another look at the file. "A fine but no jail time."

"That's right. Later on, he went to work for Brandon Pike and apparently settled down."

"Did you look into his family connections at all?"

"Didn't seem any point in it," Jim said.

"Probably not," Harry said, deciding to look anyway.

If he was going to look into Elijah's family, he might as well talk with Gladys Jackson.

"Is it okay for me to ask O'Reilly for a phone book?" he asked.

"Is your health insurance up to date?"

Harry left on a weak laugh.

Sergeant Maureen O'Reilly of the flaming red hair was Jim's administrative assistant.

"Don't try to tear that in half or do anything else stupid with it," she told him, looking down on him without a smile to soften the square-jawed menace of her handsome face. "That's the property of the County, and I'm responsible for it."

It was a very thick book with a lot of weight, but she was holding it out to him as if it was a sheet of paper. Harry took it with both hands and pretended to drop it.

"Very funny, Brock," she said evenly, "but you won't think it's funny if I have to put my hands on you."

Harry met the gaze of her icy blue eyes and, clutching the book against his chest, took a step closer to her. She was half a head taller than Harry and lived in a heroic body that might have modeled the figurehead on the good ship *Venus*.

"Sergeant O'Reilly," he said bravely, "is that a threat or a proposition?"

"You'll need to grow about a foot for starters," she began, then collapsed in a gale of laughter.

"But I love you, O'Reilly," Harry protested, slipping an arm around her waist.

"Get away, you randy devil," she gasped, pulling a handkerchief out of the front of her bursting tunic and dabbing her eyes. "You're a wicked tempter, Harry Brock, and mind you give me back my directory."

With that she grasped his arm with one hand and marched him out of her office, leaned down, planted a kiss on his cheek, and, still blushing, slammed the door shut. Hodges was hurrying along the corridor toward him just as the door banged, shaking the wall.

"My God, Harry," he said, his round face red with the exertion, "I heard O'Reilly laughing and thought she was killing someone. Then I saw you come flying out of her office. Are you all right?"

"Never better," Harry said with a ridiculously wide grin, still clutching the directory. "O'Reilly just kissed me on the cheek. I'm not going to wash my face for a week."

"You're lying," Hodges said in a derisive voice, "she's never kissed anyone since she nursed at her mother's breasts and left them permanently scarred."

"I am incapable of lying," Harry said and went off to consult the directory.

Elijah's address was in the same part of town as Rosalee Franklin's. Gladys Jackson's was only a couple of streets away. After leaving the Sheriff's compound, Harry decided after a little reflection that showing up on Elijah's street and asking questions about him of the neighbors was probably going to do nothing but make Elijah angry if he learned about it, as he surely would. He would have to do his work on Elijah another way.

Gladys Jackson's house was in much worse repair than Rosalee Franklin's and located on a more rundown and neglected street. Grass was growing through the cracks in the pavement, and to a lizard the sidewalk must have looked like a climbing wall. Harry wasn't sure he should trust himself to the tilted steps and creaking and unpainted lanai, but the boards held.

"Mrs. Jackson," Harry said to the tiny, neatly dressed, white-haired woman who opened the door, "my name is Harry Brock, and I'm not selling anything."

"Should I know you?" she asked with a small, cheerful laugh. "I find I have to ask that because I appear to have forgotten more than I ever knew—not that I ever knew all that much."

She backed up and opened the door wide.

"Come in, Mr. Brock," she said with a smile. "Sit down. I

was about to make myself a cup of tea. Will you have one?"

The door opened directly into a small living room that looked to Harry as if not even a speck of dust had ever found a home on the furniture and the collection of framed pictures on the walls of people he assumed were her family.

"I'd like that very much, Mrs. Jackson," Harry said, stepping into the room, "but perhaps you'd like to have me tell you why I am here before you make me welcome."

"Mr. Brock," she said, turning to him, "I've learned that if you want a cup of tea, you'd better have it because if you wait for the perfect time, you might never get it."

With that she hurried off toward the kitchen, calling over her shoulder, "Sit anywhere, Mr. Brock. The choices won't tax you, but try to be comfortable.

"I take mine in a mug," she said when she returned. "I find it stays hot longer and there's less getting up and down. I hope it suits you. Milk and sugar?"

"I'll have it as it is, and I drink my tea in a mug."

"Good. It's nice to see a man sitting in this room, Mr. Brock," she said, taking the chair facing him.

She waved a hand at the pictures.

"I've got a lot of family, as you can see, but those still walking the Earth are scattered to its far corners," she said in a darker voice.

"It's one of your family that brought me here."

"Oh, Lord! Is it bad news?"

"No," Harry said quickly, "it's about your son Henry, and if you'll let me, I'll explain why I'm here."

"You know, don't you, that Henry's passed on?" she said gently.

"Yes, Mrs. Jackson, I do. It was a terrible thing that happened. I don't suppose it's a thing a mother can get over."

"Do you have children, Mr. Brock?"

"Five in all."

"Do you see a great deal of them?"

"No. Their mothers live in other states, and two are adults now."

"It's the modern world. What is your interest in Henry?"

Harry quickly told her about Brandon Pike's death and the fact that he was working for Holly Pike. When he was finished, she sat staring into middle space for so long that Harry thought, perhaps, he should leave. But when she spoke, he could hear no hostility in her voice. In fact, she sounded, he thought, sympathetic.

"I feel sorry for Mrs. Pike," she said, pausing again. "To lose a husband in that way must be a terrible thing. It was hard to reconcile myself when Henry was killed to the fact that Mr. Pike had not killed him through carelessness or indifference, but in time I came to see that it had not been his fault. Henry had sunk pretty far down by the time he died. There was nothing I could do to stop it."

"No. There never is. Do you think there is any way in which Henry's death and Brandon Pike's death could be connected?"

"I don't see how, Mr. Brock. I surely don't. The years seem to have wiped away all traces of bitterness and trouble brought on by Henry's dying."

"Did you know Rosalee Franklin?" Harry asked.

"Oh my, yes. I don't see her and my grandchildren very often nowadays, but she brings them over now and then. She's a good, hard-working woman. I'm sorry to say that Henry did not do well by her, and, of course, she was taken advantage of by the lawyers who persuaded her to bring that suit against Mr. Pike."

She brightened slightly and asked, "Is Elijah Blue still working at The Oaks? He went there, you know, shortly after Henry's death."

159

"Do you know him?"

"Yes. He is Rosalee's half brother. He was living with Rosalee when Henry was killed. He and Henry got on well. He visited me with Henry two or three times."

She paused to laugh quietly.

"He was a hard-looking man, but he was always gentle and polite in this house. As I recall, he and Rosalee shared the same father."

"Isn't Rosalee's maiden name Franklin?" Harry asked in surprise.

"Yes, Franklin was her mother's name. Elijah must have kept his father's. Elijah took a great interest in Henry until there was too little left to be interested in."

"Aren't three of Rosalee's children your grandchildren?"

"There were three boys," she said quietly. "Duane, the middle one, died some time past. He had been sick for a long time."

"I'm sorry," Harry said.

She sighed and shook her head.

"Down here," she said in a sad voice, glancing out the window, "so many just give up on living,"

"Perhaps someday . . ." he began and then realized there was nothing he could say that wouldn't add to the pain.

Mrs. Jackson, however, went on with what she had been saying. Going on, Harry thought, was what she had been doing all of her life.

"Of course, Elijah was older than Henry," she said, "and his life had its own turns. I'm told he took Henry's death to heart and what happened to Rosalee in the court case and then losing Duane only deepened the pain."

"Does he have any other family?" Harry asked, setting down his mug, thinking about what he had just been told.

"Not that I know of."

"I want to thank you for talking to me and for the tea, Mrs.

Jackson," Harry said, standing up. "You've been most gracious. I've enjoyed our conversation, and I understand some things much better than I did before talking with you."

"It's very kind of you to say so, Mr. Brock," she said, getting to her feet with some effort. "I hope you'll come back. My late husband used to say I could talk the hind leg off a donkey. I hope I haven't afflicted any of your limbs."

Harry laughed and glanced down at his legs, lifting his hands from his sides as he did so.

"All present and accounted for," he told her.

Having said his goodbyes, he crossed the porch, stepping carefully. Mrs. Jackson, standing in the door, called his name. He stopped and turned to her.

"The world has become a dangerous and unforgiving place, Mr. Brock," she said in a strong and somber voice. "Go carefully."

15

Gladys Jackson's warning troubled Harry more than he thought reasonable, especially given the fact that she was an elderly woman, living alone and likely to find the world outside her house alarming. He tried to turn off the cold trickle of anxiety her words had set running through his insides and focus on the news that Elijah was Rosalee Franklin's half brother. Turning onto the Hammock, he began as he often did to feel the uneasiness subsiding.

He had intended to go home but, seeing that Katherine's car was not in the yard, he parked the Rover and walked up the road to look in on Tucker and see how the old farmer was getting along. Harry loved the walk even in the heat of the day because the white sandy road was shaded by tall oaks and gums and rattling palms that in the steady breeze threw a shifting latticework of sun and shadows across the narrow track, and the air was bright with the strident fiddling of the locusts and the cicadas and a dozen other orchestras of insect musicians in the trees.

"Did you hear Benjamin?" Harry asked Sanchez and Oh, Brother!, who had met him at the end of Tucker's driveway, when the ritual greetings of pats and nose bumps and attempted boosts in the crotch by Sanchez, indicating dog fellowship, had been dealt with.

Benjamin was a very large alligator that emerged from the Stickpen Preserve in the spring to breed with the mature females scattered along Puc Puggy Creek and announced his candidacy for their affection by a booming rumble, sounding like a giant cat purring. The rumbling set the water around the alligator rippling in agitation whenever he sent out his call.

"He's starting a little early," Harry said, walking with his hand on Oh, Brother!'s shoulder while Sanchez led them up the drive.

It had been a long struggle, but Harry had finally capitulated and begun talking to the two animals as if they could understand him. He wasn't as far along that path as Tucker, however, who took it for granted that they talked to him as well. Sanchez led the little procession to the garden where Tucker was shoveling compost out of an ancient red wheelbarrow and spreading it around under the pole beans.

"Are you sure you ought to be doing that?" Harry asked, a mixture of concern and anger raising his voice.

Tucker leaned his shovel against the wheelbarrow and paused to wipe his face with a blue-and-white bandanna before answering.

"Certainty," he observed, beaming at Harry and shoving his bandanna back into an overall pocket, "is said to be a category limited to death and taxes."

"Smart-alecky answers don't change facts," Harry said, unable to resist grinning back at his old friend. "You are recovering from a fairly serious accident."

"We're all recovering from a worse one," Tucker answered, taking up his shovel again.

"What do you mean?" Harry demanded.

"Birth," Tucker said with a grunt as he drove the shovel into the black mound of compost, "and we're not going to recover from it either."

"You're changing the subject on me," Harry protested, "and I'm not going to ask you why not."

Tucker spread the compost carefully and then turned back to Harry, full of smiles as ever.

"Then I'll tell you anyway. We're going to die before we're healed."

"There are times," Harry said, mixing humor and a kind of heaviness in his response, thinking for some reason of Rosalee Franklin and Gladys Jackson, "when I wonder if even death cures that catastrophe."

"My, you certainly are glum today," Tucker said, leaning his shovel against the wheelbarrow. "Let's get out of this sun and have a glass of cider. I'm dry as a split stick."

"That's the best cider I've ever tasted," Harry said when he had settled into one of the rockers on Tucker's back stoop while Tucker filled his own glass from the stone jug.

"I tapped the barrel yesterday," he said, setting the jug on the floor and easing himself into the other rocker with a grimace of pain.

"That hip bothering you?" Harry asked.

"Getting into a chair this time of day reminds me that it's there. Otherwise, I seldom notice it."

"And the arm?"

"It aches and won't do a lot I ask of it, but it's getting better. By the way, how's that Rottweiler belonging to Holly Pike doing?"

"Hanging on by a thread. Heather Parkinson said he must have drunk some antifreeze. Add that to the nail in Sueño's hoof and she's pretty low."

"Sounds nasty," Tucker said. "I hope you and Jim crack that pretty soon. Now, tell me what's going on with you and Katherine."

"You know she's taken a job at Haven House," Harry said, his mind pulled to the fact she had heard nothing from Esther

Benson as to whether or not further tests were needed.

"What do you think about that?" Tucker asked.

"I suppose she needs something to occupy her mind," Harry said noncommittally.

"You have no idea what's wrong with her?" Tucker asked.

"You and she have spent quite a bit of time together," Harry said. "Do you think she's seriously ill?"

"I'm going to risk stepping over a line and say that I do," Tucker replied.

"Well," Harry responded, noting that his heart rate had increased, "you wouldn't know it living with her. Aside from occasional episodes of morning sickness—and she isn't pregnant—she's fine. Her appetite is good. She sleeps well, isn't brooding about anything . . ."

He stopped short of describing their sex life, which was more active and satisfying than it had ever been.

"You haven't noticed anything unusual in her behavior?" Tucker asked quietly.

Harry suddenly felt angry, not exactly with Tucker or not only with Tucker but also with the confusion that was a part of the anger. And, yes, he was angry with Benson for not having noticed those things about Katherine's behavior he had noticed and for having left them dangling as she had done.

"It may be change of life," Harry said, avoiding what he knew Tucker had asked him.

"Or it may be the pip," Tucker replied, sharply enough to make Harry stop staring at his cider.

"You'd better tell me what you're thinking," Harry said.

"Something's awry," Tucker said. "She's having headaches for no apparent reason. She's throwing up after getting out of bed for no obvious reason. She's forgetting things she would normally remember. She drifts off in conversations and says things in a way that I never heard her speak before."

Tucker paused.

"This must be very upsetting to you, and I'm not at all sure I should be telling you these things, but I can't believe you haven't noticed them yourself. If I'm wrong, please say so."

Harry set his empty glass on the floor, then leaned back in the rocker and closed his eyes. His head was swimming, and it wasn't from the cider. What he was experiencing had come surging up with the realization that not only was everything Tucker had said true, but also Katherine's uninhibited sexual responses to him, which he had refused to question, were totally out of character, given his relationship with Soñadora.

"No," Harry said grimly, "you're not wrong. I've been in a state of denial about their seriousness. I suspect that Benson guessed some of it and may even have found some physical evidence of the problem—if it is a problem."

"She hasn't gotten back to you yet," Tucker said.

"No," Harry said, his mind still fixed on the implications of his own eager complicity in their lovemaking.

Then for a moment he began to grasp that he must explain to himself why he was sleeping with Katherine when it was clear something was wrong with her and why he was so recklessly destroying his relationship with Soñadora.

Oh, Brother!, who had been leaning comfortably against one of the uprights, and Sanchez, who had been lying between the mule's front feet, broke his concentration by suddenly becoming alert and hastily backing away from the stoop. Jane Bunting appeared out of the bushes and jumped onto the stoop, followed by her two large children. She began her usual circuitous advance toward Tucker's lap by walking around Harry's chair. Experience had taught him not to try to stroke her as she passed him. Then she circled the butter churn standing in the corner behind Harry's chair.

Aurelius, the young tom, showing marked indiscretion, trotted straight to Tucker's rocker and jumped into his lap. Harry, who had been watching this drama unfold, turned to see how Jane Bunting responded to the usurpation. To his surprise, she continued her regal approach with apparent insouciance.

"I don't think Jane Bunting saw that," Harry said.

"She sees everything," Tucker said in an oracular fashion. "Just watch."

A moment later, her circumambulation of the stoop complete, Jane Bunting jumped onto Tucker. His lap being already occupied by fourteen pounds of juvenile cat, she landed on Tucker's stomach, eliciting a grunt from him.

"That's a lot of cat . . ." Harry began when suddenly Jane Bunting rose onto her hind feet with a hair-raising growl and tore into her son with both front feet, claws unsheathed.

For a long moment in Tucker's lap there was a blurred ball of whirling fur made up of two yowling cats. Tucker sat rigidly, gripping the arms of the rocker, his eyes closed and his head pressed back as far as he could get it. Harry pushed forward, looking around desperately for the broom, but before he even began to get out of the rocker, Aurelius, screaming pitifully, exploded out of the ball, his lost hair drifting in his wake like a comet's tail, and fled into the woods.

Sanchez barked gleefully, and Oh, Brother! gave a snort that Harry thought was as close to a laugh as makes no matter.

"I guess she saw him," he said.

"She runs a tight ship," Tucker responded.

Meanwhile, Jane Bunting, purring sweetly, licked her claws free of hair and blood, then settled herself in Tucker's lap, rubbed her chin briefly against his shirt front, drew her tail around herself, and went to sleep. Frederica, who had throughout the event sat demurely between the two rockers, watching with apparent interest, leaped into Harry's lap, batted her emerald eyes at him seductively, stretched, pressed against him, then wriggled herself into a comfortable position and slept.

Sanchez and Oh, Brother! drifted back to their original positions, keeping their eyes on Jane Bunting as they did.

"You really ought to sell tickets," Harry said, then shifted ground. "I've got a question for you. Can you tell me anything about Elijah Blue?"

"I'm not really sure," Tucker said, showing interest. "What kind of information do you need?"

"Anything that's not likely to show up on a police dossier."

"I gather you've read his."

"Jim stretched things a little and showed it to me," Harry said, feeling frustrated just thinking about Elijah. "There's a lot of information there, but nothing that gives me any insight into the man. When I first talked with him, he tried to intimidate me. I think he was amusing himself, and I didn't get the idea he was trying very hard. Nonetheless, he convinced me he was capable of a lot of mayhem."

"His record bears that out," Tucker said with a nod. "As I remember, Brandon hired him just after the Henry Jackson affair."

"That's what Gladys Jackson told me," Harry said. "Also, according to Mrs. Jackson, who is an impressive woman with courage and integrity, Elijah is Rosalee Franklin's half brother and was her son's friend."

"Now I remember," Tucker said. "Rosalee Franklin claimed Henry was her husband and the father of two of her children. Brandon felt very bad about that suit she brought against him. He thought she had been given a lot of very bad advice by her lawyers."

"Holly Pike said he wanted to give her money but was warned that doing so would almost certainly come back to bite him."

"That's what he told me," Tucker said, "and I think it had something to do with his hiring Elijah. I didn't see the connection then because I didn't know Elijah was Mrs. Franklin's half brother. Now it makes more sense. I remember that, at the time, I argued pretty strenuously against his hiring Elijah. I didn't know the man, but I knew his reputation for violence."

"Did Elijah know anything about horses?" Harry asked, expecting the answer to be no.

"Surprisingly, he did," Tucker said, getting into the story. "His father, Homer Blue, had worked for Tillman Hanks at Filigree Stock Farm in Bonita Springs. Among other things, Tillman raised and trained standard-bred trotters and pacers. Thirty years ago, Hanks was a big name in harness racing circles. Homer Blue had the reputation of being a first-class trainer, and when he wasn't fighting or in jail, Elijah worked for Tillman as well."

"Do you think Brandon hired Elijah as a way of helping Rosalee Franklin?"

"It's hard to say," Tucker replied. "Brandon had a wild streak in him. He liked taking chances. Look at that stallion he bred from and rode."

"You mean Elijah's history might have appealed to him?"

"Yes, that and the fact that Elijah had been around horses since he was a toddler. His mother died soon after he was born, and his father brought him up."

Harry lifted Frederica off his lap, causing her to give a plaintive cry of protest. At the sound, Jane Bunting raised her head and stared balefully at Harry. Harry got up quickly and stepped away from Frederica, keeping his eye on Jane Bunting while he did so. Oh, Brother! snorted and Sanchez got to his feet, eyeing the cat and giving a soft, warning growl.

"That cat has these two animals crowded into a corner," Harry said, half amused and half irritated.

"Well, the thing was with Oh, Brother!," Tucker said, "when she first came in with the kittens, in his first efforts to look them over, he stepped too close to Frederica and Jane Bunting, and before he could respond to her growl, she went up his left front leg as if it was a tree and over his back and down the other side, leaving scuff marks in his hide as she went. Sanchez laughed at him. Jane Bunting took exception to his barking near the kittens and danced up and down his back for a few seconds, sending the fur flying. Later, Jane Bunting made some friendly overtures to them, but they were rejected."

"I'm going home," Harry said.

Oh, Brother! and Sanchez walked Harry to the road. Walking home, Harry wondered if he was losing his mind. Before he left them, he had encouraged the two to make peace with Jane Bunting and said he thought Tucker would be pleased.

16

Harry found Katherine sitting on the lanai.

"Hi," she called cheerfully as he crossed the sandy lawn toward her. "Guess what! Benson called and wants me to come in and bring you with me. She's got an appointment for tomorrow morning. Can you make it?"

"I can make it," Harry said, trying to sound unconcerned as he leaned over to kiss her.

"Mmm, good," she said, finally letting go of him. "How's Tucker?"

"He was shoveling compost when I got there about an hour ago. Are you worried about this?"

"About his shoveling compost?" she asked with a laugh, holding his hand as he sat down beside her. "No, I'm glad he's feeling up to it."

"I meant about Benson's call," Harry asked, trying to keep his tone light.

"No, but I'm glad to see you. I missed you while I was working."

"I missed you, too," he said, giving her hand a squeeze. "What else did Benson say?"

"The usual stuff. She asked me how I was feeling, was I still having headaches, was I still throwing up in the morning, and I told her, 'Great, sometimes,' and, 'now and then.' "

She told Harry this with an apparently happy smile.

"Okay," Harry said, uncertain about what he was hearing

and seeing. "Have you been waiting for me long?"

He had noticed that she was stretched out in a lounge chair on the lanai without anything to read.

"About forty-five minutes. Except for getting up to answer the phone, I've been lying here ever since. Oh, when I answered, Benson asked if you were here. Have you got something going with her too?"

"She's really hot, you know," Harry said, hoping to deflect the question. "You must be tired. Did you fall asleep?"

"No! What is this?" Katherine cried. "Why are you asking me all these questions? And if I'm not hotter than Esther Benson, I'd better be measured for a box!"

"Believe it," he said, "you're much hotter than she is. So, you were just lying out here, staring at the lanai ceiling?"

He tried to make it sound like a joke, but he knew that for Katherine to spend five minutes not doing anything was a major change in behavior.

"That's right. I was thinking about us and how much I liked being back on the Hammock with you. It's really great, Harry."

She started to get up, but halfway out of the lounge, she paused. Harry saw that she had gone white.

"Oh, oh," she said. "I think I'm going to be . . ."

With that, she struggled to her feet, and in three quick but unsteady strides, she was out the door and throwing up. Harry caught her around the waist as she bent forward, retching, and kept her from falling. Gasping, she tried to straighten up, but her knees buckled. Harry threw his other arm around her and eased her to the ground, resting her head and shoulders against his legs.

"On a good day I'm hotter," she murmured, still breathing in short, shallow gasps, her eyes closed. "Today, I smell of puke."

"Do you have a headache?"

"Oh, that makes me dizzy," she groaned after rolling her

head in a no movement.

"In a couple of minutes the ants will find us," he told her. " 'Til then, just lie still and rest."

"I remember when you could just pick me up in your arms and carry me into the bedroom," she said in a slurry voice.

"I still can," he said.

"You can't," she said weakly, "my ass alone must weigh fifty pounds."

Harry laughed in spite of himself, but it was a laugh filled with pain. In the past, Katherine would never have referred to her bottom as her *ass* and never have mentioned it to him at all without blushing. She was not a prude, but she had never shaken off her childhood prohibition against mentioning what she sat on.

Harry was right. The ants found them, the big, red, biting kind. With Harry's help, Katherine struggled to her feet. With one of her arms around his neck and one of his around her waist, they made good time getting back onto the lanai. Once in the kitchen, she called a halt.

"I think I'm okay," she said. "Let's see."

She was.

"You see?" she said, taking a glass out of the cupboard and rinsing her mouth with water.

Then she drank some diet Coke.

"That's better," she said, "I'm not dizzy, and my mouth doesn't taste like a sewer."

She had lost that gray pallor, Harry thought, but it was clear to him that something was very wrong.

"I want to run you through some tests," Esther Benson told Katherine.

She had begun by telling Harry to sit still, listen, and keep quiet.

"Why?" Katherine demanded. "I worked all day yesterday and felt fine until I got up too quickly from that lounge chair, made myself dizzy, and threw up. How complicated can that be? It's probably just some inner ear thing."

Benson, wearing her white coat, was leaning against the examination table with her arms folded.

"You're probably right," she said with what Harry thought was uncharacteristic patience. "But I can't make out what's going on there. So we'll take some pictures and see. How's that?"

"Harry?" Katherine asked, smiling at him. "Want me to tell Esther what you said about her yesterday?"

"I'd rather hear more about what Dr. Benson has in mind for tests and what she'll be looking for," Harry said, fearing for his life.

"He said you were hot," Katherine said with a wide grin.

"Well, we both know he's an idiot, don't we?" she said, turning tomato red and avoiding looking at Harry.

"I don't know about that. He's been getting it on with that Soñadora, who runs *Salvamento*," Katherine said, fanning her face with a hand. "You talk about hot!"

Katherine laughed as if she had made a very good joke.

Harry sat tongue-tied, but Dr. Benson pushed herself quickly away from the table and took Katherine by the hand.

"Come on, sweetheart," she said in an affectionate tone. "Let's not keep the lab people waiting. They're grumpy enough as it is. Harry, follow along and keep your hands off the nurses."

Katherine thought that was very funny.

"This is Katherine Brock," Benson said to the small group of green-suited doctors and nurses gathered around the large, gleaming resonance imaging device, filling a third of the otherwise bare, white-walled room, "and somebody get her a blanket. It's cold as a meat locker in here."

The youngest woman present said, "I'll do it," and set off at a run.

The tall technician in charge introduced himself to Katherine, shook hands with her, and gave her the first names of the other three people. By the time that was over, the young woman was back with an armful of blankets.

"I'm Becky," she said to Katherine with a beaming smile as she draped one of the blankets over her shoulders, "better known as *You*. Being frequently insulted and assigned the most degrading tasks is part of the training. Okay, come over here to where the important people are pretending to be doing serious things with this Star Wars machine. Ignore them."

Harry saw with relief that Katherine was following Becky and occasionally laughing.

"Let's go," Benson said, taking Harry's arm. "She's in good hands. They'll work on her for a while, and when they're done, I'm hoping we'll have some answers."

When the heavy door sighed shut, and they were in the corridor, Benson said, "I'll call you when the results are in. It may take a while."

"Okay," Harry said, threading his belt with its metal buckle back into his shorts and noticing with alarm that Benson's neck was turning red again.

"I want you to know," Benson said in a steely voice, "that I don't appreciate being made a joke of."

"I don't blame you," Harry said, assembling swiftly all the fragments of sincerity he could lay hold of in a hurry, "and while Katherine chose to think I was joking when I said you were hot, I wasn't. I meant it."

"You are such a liar, and you are so busted," Benson said, planting her fists on her hips and glaring at him.

"Hold on," Harry said. "Let's look at this calmly. First, you're the most intelligent woman I know. You've got a marvelous sense of humor." He paused and held up his hands. "Now don't hit me," he said. "You've got a knock-out body."

"How the hell would you know that?" Benson demanded.

"Unbutton your coat," Harry said.

"I will not!"

"You don't dare to, do you?"

"No," she said, her face aflame, "because God knows what you'd do."

"I've got to run some errands. Want to come?"

"Get out of here," she said and banged him on an arm with her clipboard hard enough to hurt.

"Looking good," Harry said, rubbing his arm as she hurried away from him.

She didn't look back, but she put more action into her walk.

Harry and Katherine had to wait two days before Benson called them into her office where a nurse took Katherine away.

"This won't take long," she said, "Dr. Benson wants me to take your blood pressure and ask you some questions. Mr. Brock, you can go in and wait for Mrs. Brock there."

"Come in, Harry," Benson said, "I want to talk with you alone for a minute."

"Bad news?" Harry asked.

"Not entirely," she answered after they were seated. "As I suspected, she has a small tumor on her brain, and the blood vessels around it have been leaking blood and increasing the pressure around it."

She paused and asked, "Shall I go on, or do you have to ask something?"

"Finish what you were saying."

"All right, that's the bad news. The good news is that it's operable, and I don't think it's malignant."

"How can you tell without a biopsy?"

"I can't for sure, but from its shape, its size, and where it's located, I will be very surprised if it's not benign."

"Well, I want to believe you, but I can't let myself yet."

"Right. Now, about Katherine . . ."

"She's got to be told," Harry said.

"Agreed. The question is how," Benson said, putting a hand on Harry's arm as if she was steadying him.

"You tell her with me there," Harry said without hesitation.

"Okay," Benson said. "Next issue, beginning tomorrow, she's going into the care of Ray Carver. He's one of the best neurosurgeons in the Southeast."

"Is he the best?" Harry demanded.

"Probably in the top fifteen in the country," she said, showing no surprise at the question. "If you want, you can go online and look at what's on offer, do it with my blessing. But Carver is very good. He's looked at the scans. He'll make himself available."

"Does he do a lot of these operations?"

"It's almost all he does. People are being flown in from all over the state and out of it," Benson told him. "Harry, don't let her drag out the decision. She's leaking a lot of blood up there, and the pressure on her brain could trigger a stroke or something else just as nasty."

"Okay," Harry said. "When?"

"The day after tomorrow at 9 A.M."

Harry slumped back in his chair.

"God," he said.

"Come on, soldier," Benson said, giving his arm a squeeze. "Let's bring her in."

"It went well," Raymond Carver, a thin, wiry man with slate-gray hair and a scratchy voice, told Harry, dropping into a chair beside him, resting his elbows on his knees.

He was still in his green scrubs, his face mask pushed up onto his head.

"How is she?" Harry asked.

"All her vital signs are normal," Carver answered, rubbing his face with his hand. "She's in recovery and being monitored. She'll be awake in half an hour or so, but she won't make much sense for a while."

"Is she going to be all right?"

Since sitting down, Carver had been staring at the floor while he talked, making Harry want to grab him by the ears and turn his head around, but now he sat up and looked at Harry.

"I don't see why not," he said, sounding to Harry a little ruffled. "Now that thing's out of there and that puddle of blood siphoned away, further reducing the pressure in her brain, I'm looking for a full recovery. Any more questions?"

"Does that mean the oddities in her behavior are cleared up?"

"Probably," Carver said, looking at his watch and getting to his feet. "We'll keep her here for a couple of days. Then you can have her back. Before she's discharged, she'll have everything she needs to know in writing, with a copy for you, including things to do and not do, appointments for check-ups, the whole ball of wax. Read it, and make sure she's following the instructions."

With that, he shook hands with Harry and walked away, leaving Harry relieved but wondering if he were to meet Carver on the street would the man recognize him. He was still standing in the same spot, trying to sort out his emotions, which were seriously jumbled, when Benson came flying into the room, her hair and her coattails streaming out behind her.

"Shit!" she said, seeing Harry standing alone.

Harry and the other people in the room looked up with varying degrees of alarm on their faces.

"Has he seen you yet?" she demanded, slowing to a walk as she advanced on Harry.

"Yes," he said, uncertain as to whether to say more.

"Katherine's all right," Benson said, panting a little and stopping in front of Harry. "I was supposed to be here when Ray talked to you, but a damned fool ten-year-old kid ran a knife into his hand and I had to sew him up and give his idiot mother a tranquilizer. How are you?"

"I'm fine. Your coat's unbuttoned."

"To hell with my coat," she told him in a loud voice, snatching it around her, closing it at the waist with a single button. "Come with me, and keep your hands to yourself."

"I'm surprised someone in there didn't dial 911," Harry said, trying to sound offended and struggling to keep up with her as they sailed along the corridor, a threat to pedestrian traffic.

"Christ," she said over her shoulder, "Katherine's just out of brain surgery, and you can't keep your eyes off my boobs. What are you, some kind of pervert?"

They reached her office. Harry hesitated, and she pushed him through the door.

"Probably," he said.

"Probably what?" she demanded, pointing Harry toward a chair.

"Some kind of pervert."

"Joke's over," she snapped. "Tell me what the asshole said."

17

Harry had just returned from the hospital and was talking with Minna and Thornton. The conversation was not going any better than it had gone with Jesse, who had just hung up on him.

"Now listen to me, you two," Harry said, running out of patience. "Your mother threatened me with several options for dying slowly and painfully, which she laid out in hair-raising detail, if I told you she was being operated on. The tumor may have brought on some character changes in her that were alarming, and it's true that her physical symptoms were intensifying, but she knew what the keys to her car were for, and she could tell you what she had for breakfast yesterday. As bad as it may make you feel, she didn't want you here."

Thornton started to say something, but Minna cut him off.

"Not good enough, Harry," she exploded. "You should have told us. We should have been there. We all know you're thin in this area, but that's what families are for."

Harry winced. His record as *pater familias* was as erratic as the markings on a spotted horse, and he knew it.

"I always learn something talking to you, Minna," he said instead of letting it go, which was, he knew, what he should have done and tried to compensate by asking, "when are you and Thornton getting here?"

"When's Jesse coming?" Minna snapped back.

"He's not. After all his righteous indignation at not having been told about the operation, he is committed to a department review of his latest project, and he isn't sure when he can get away."

Minna sighed heavily.

"The truth is, I'm looking at a week of finals. That leaves Thornton to carry the flag."

"Okay. What about you, Thornton?" Harry asked

Thornton said he was going on a class picnic, but he would give that up to come.

"Your mother wouldn't know you from the man in the moon," Harry said. "Go on your picnic, and when Minna has flunked all her finals, come up with her. You might even work out a time with Jesse. Your mother would like that. She ought to know who you are by then."

"I'll call when I've sorted this out with Jesse," Minna said with a certain amount of grumbling about burdens, then added just before signing off, "try to stay out of jail."

After hanging up the phone, Harry told the mockingbird, sitting outside the kitchen window in the wisteria vine at the end of the lanai, running through his repertoire of other people's songs, "Well, today, we've learned what families are for. They exist to enable the children to do what they want to do and feel good about doing it. It builds their confidence and over time totally marginalizes the parents, which is the whole point of the exercise."

After saying that, he felt better and drove to The Oaks.

"How is Katherine?" Holly asked him.

Harry wasn't sure whether she or Nip looked farther down in the mouth. Her face was pale and drawn, and she looked somehow diminished. The visual proof of her suffering made Harry feel frustrated and angry.

"The doctors say she's doing fine," he said, hiding his feelings. "They're pretty sure the tumor is completely removed and expect a full recovery, although her hormone balance may remain askew."

"Then it wasn't menopause."

"No. What about Tuck?"

"Heather isn't optimistic. I guess the renal damage is fairly extensive."

"I'm sorry to hear that. What about Sueño?"

"That nail was driven two inches into the frog of her foot," Holly said, her anger erupting. "I don't see how she could have done it on turf. The men have combed that paddock, and except for the fence, there's not a piece of wood in it."

"Then someone did it. Is that what you're saying?" Harry asked, not surprised by her response.

"That's exactly what I think."

Just then Thahn came silently into the study and said, "Forgive me for disturbing you, Mrs. Pike, but the hospital has called with very welcome news. Mr. Yellen has recovered consciousness. Visitors, however, are not allowed at the moment."

"Why not?" Holly demanded, having jumped to her feet at the news.

"I was told that at this juncture he would be fully occupied adjusting to his new situation, sleeping, and undergoing tests."

"Thank you, Thahn," Holly said. "You may notify the rest of the house staff and please get word to Mr. Blue."

"Certainly," Thahn said with a slight bow and left as silently as he had arrived.

"This is good news," Harry said as Holly dropped back into her chair.

"Yes, and we will soon know who attacked him," she replied, suddenly looking very serious as though the pleasure the news of his recovery had brought her was already supplanted by concern.

"We may," Harry said, his mind turning to Katherine.

Benson had warned him that her emergence into full consciousness might bring with it some surprises. Given Benson's crepuscular view of things, he expected those surprises not to be wholly pleasant.

"Why do you say *may?*" Holly demanded, her voice hardening.

There's a lot of anger around today, he thought, studying the expression on her face.

"Severe head injuries often leave their victims with all sorts of problems," he told her, "loss of memory among them."

"Are you concerned that Katherine may come out of her operation mentally impaired?" Holly asked.

"I suppose I am," Harry said, "but Yellen's situation is much more fraught than hers."

"You mean because of the attack?" she asked.

"He was very badly hurt," Harry said, regretting he had mentioned the severity of Yellen's injuries.

"Yes," Holly said with a shudder, pushing herself to her feet as if by sheer will power. "I want you to see Sueño. She is fond of you. Have you time to do that? If you have to get back to the hospital, please say so."

Harry knew the formality of her speech meant she was retreating, closing emotional doors as she went.

"I have the time, and I would like to see her," Harry said, determined to lift her spirits if he could. "Do you think your kitchen has a spare apple I could give her?"

"Great idea," Holly said, brightening, and pressed a button on her desk. "I'll give her one, too. Thahn will provide."

But they had to wait for their apples because Thahn met them in the hallway to explain to Holly that Elijah was waiting to see her and would not be put off.

"It's all right, Thahn," she told him. "Is it about Mr. Yellen?"

183

"I don't know," Thahn said apologetically. "Mr. Blue did not wish to give his reason for wanting to speak with you."

"Did he threaten you, Thahn?" she asked.

"No, Mrs. Pike," he answered, "but he is in one of those moods in which, when you look into his eyes, you hope they are not the windows of his soul."

Holly responded with a tight smile.

"Go about your business, Thahn, and thank you," she told him. "No, wait. Give Harry the bag of apples. I will attend to Mr. Blue."

Thahn had not exaggerated Elijah's state of mind. He filled the door, his huge frame tense and his heavy face a frowning mass of lines and bulging jaw muscles.

"I need to know more 'bout Mr. Yellen than I been told," he said to Holly in his rasping bass, ignoring Harry.

"I'll tell you what I know, Elijah," she said in a calm voice. "I know you must be concerned. We all are, but I'm afraid there's not much to tell."

"Thahn, he only said that Mr. Yellen had come to. You got to know more than that."

"That was the message from the hospital, that and he couldn't have any visitors."

"Why is that?" Elijah demanded. "Why can't none of us see him?"

Elijah's questions had become more hard-edged, and Harry saw Holly's hesitation in answering the big man.

"When people come out of a long coma," Harry said, coming forward, "they are in a very frail condition, and right away, the doctors have got to run a bunch of tests to find out what needs to be done to keep them conscious and to improve their chances to recover."

"You just guessing," Elijah growled, dismissing Harry with a slashing glance.

"No, Mr. Blue, I'm not," Harry said, recovering Elijah's hostile attention. "I've had to deal with a lot of seriously injured people, enough to know how hospitals handle them. If the doctors don't get it right, and Mr. Yellen slips back into a coma, the chances are they'll lose him."

"You mean he'll die?" Holly asked, her eyes widening.

"It's their business not to let that happen," Harry said quickly, keeping his eyes on Elijah. "That's why they don't want people tiring him and distracting them."

"That may be," Elijah said, clearly not satisfied. "Mrs. Pike," he continued, "I got some bidness to see to. The others been told what needs doing. I'll be back in the morning."

Before Holly could answer, Elijah swung around and set off at a lurching trot for the stables.

"At least," Harry said, "he didn't wring our necks."

"Be grateful for small favors," Holly said sourly, staring after Elijah. "Let's go see Sueño."

The gray mare whinnied when she saw them and limped toward the paddock gate. She had a brown leather boot on her left front foot, but Harry supposed it was pain rather than the boot that was making her limp. She went directly to Harry and pressed her head against his chest. Harry held her head with one hand and stroked her neck with the other. She snorted contentedly.

"I just own her, feed her, pay her veterinarian fees, see that she gets bred," Holly said in an exaggeratedly offended voice, smiling as she spoke and stroking the horse's shoulder.

Sueño caught a whiff of the apples in the bag Harry had set down, lowered her head, and sniffed loudly.

"Treats," Harry said and passed the bag to Holly.

While the horse ate the apples and nodded her head in pleasure, Holly unburdened herself.

"Even thinking that Tyce won't be able to tell us who attacked him," she said in a breaking voice, her face drained of color, "is almost more than I can bear. Lying in my bed night after night, knowing as surely as if it was written on the wall that whoever killed Brandon tried to kill Tyce, has probably killed Tuck, maimed Sueño, and is on his way to me, has driven me to the place that I wish he would do it and get it over."

She turned away from Harry, dropping her forearms on the top plank of the fence, pressed her forehead against her arms, and wept. Nip clambered to his feet and pushed a shoulder against her thigh and whined. With Nip already disturbed, Harry did not dare touch her. The dog even growled at Sueño when she pushed her nose into Holly's back, inquiring about the possibility of another apple.

The dog's growl reached through Holly's misery, bringing her head up.

"Stop it," she snapped at the dog and reached out and rubbed the horse's nose. "Do you suppose I could get a hug out of you?" she demanded harshly of Harry as soon as she had blown her nose. "I know comforting widows isn't in your contract . . ."

She tried to say more but couldn't, and Harry, thinking it might cost him a leg, reached out and pulled her into his arms, pressing her against him. She clung to him and cried like a child. After a few moments, Nip began the most mournful howling and Sueño, because Holly's back was turned toward her and Harry's arms were around her back, began bumping Holly's bottom with her nose.

Holly's head snapped up.

Staring at Harry through her tears, she demanded in a choked voice, "What are you doing?"

"It's not me, it's Sueño. Could you tell Nip to stop howling? I can't hug him and you at the same time, and the sound is wrecking me."

"I thought you were . . ." she said between sobs.

"I know what you were thinking," Harry said. "Don't tell me. Get Nip to stop what he's doing."

Holly buried her face again in his shoulder. A moment later, to his consternation, her body began to shake. The horse was still bumping her bottom and the dog was howling.

Oh, God, he thought and at the same time began urgently repeating, "It's all right, Holly. It's all right."

The shaking increased and finally, having to breathe, she lifted her head and, to Harry's disgust, burst out in helpless laughter. Harry let go of her; still in the grip of her laughter, she sank onto the grass and hugged her knees against her chest for support while Nip began to jump around barking and Sueño, finding Harry free, pushed her nose into his chest.

Giving up, Harry threw his arms around the horse's neck and leaned against her, laughing himself.

"Is there anyone you could stay with for a while?" Harry asked when they had recovered and were walking back toward the house.

"You mean in another city?" she asked.

"Preferably in another state," he answered.

"But I'm not supposed to leave Avola," she protested.

"I'll take care of that," he said. "You should leave without telling anyone, and I mean anyone, including me. Then, when you get to where you're going, you can make one call to Jeff Smolkin. If the police or I need to reach you, we can do it through him."

"Then my night fears aren't entirely foolish?" she asked solemnly.

"They may be, and I hope they are, but until we see where this is going, let's pretend they're not."

"Thanks for the suggestion, Harry," she said, putting her arm through his, "but I'm not going to allow myself to be driven out of my home."

Harry was quiet for a few steps and then asked, "Do you know how to use a gun?"

"Yes," she said.

"Do you have a shotgun in the house?"

"Brandon's got a locked case of them in the gun room. One is a Parker, side by side twelve gauge. I've used it a few times."

"How did it handle?" Harry asked.

"Brandon said it was as close to perfection as you could get."

"I envy you. Is there a twelve-gauge pump in the collection?"

"Yes, an Ithaca."

"Have you fired it?"

"It's a brute, but it does what it's supposed to do."

"From now on, keep it in your bedroom," he said. "I'll buy you a box of double 00 buckshot shells. I want you to put the gun beside your bed, fully loaded, a shell in the chamber, safety on. Are you comfortable with that?"

"Yes, and don't worry about the shells. I could support a small army with Brandon's supply."

"Take it to the Rod & Gun Club. Let them suggest a practice that lets you empty the gun into something, a moving target would be best. Can you do it?"

"It's not much fun, but I will."

"Good, give me a call when it's over. I have to go."

She and Nip walked him to the Rover.

"Thanks for holding me together, Harry," she told him as he was getting into the Rover. "I hope Katherine is awake and feeling as good as one can in her situation." Then she added with unconvincing seriousness, "I found having my bottom bumped comforting. You might remember that if I collapse on you again and Sueño isn't available."

"I will," Harry said, managing to keep his face straight, "and you remember the Ithaca."

He drove away wondering whether or not she was in danger

and hoped putting her to work on the pump gun would ease some of her anxiety.

When Harry reached the hospital, he found that Katherine had been moved from Recovery to Critical Care and was still asleep and heavily sedated.

"She's doing fine," Colin Baker, a stocky, red-haired young male nurse, told Harry and gave him a rundown of her condition. "You're free to stay with her if you wish, but she's out for a while, and I'd be surprised if she was going to be very responsive before tomorrow. Dr. Carver likes to ease his patients back into the world very gradually, testing as he goes."

Harry said he would come back later.

"Good thinking," Baker told him. "Sitting around in these places, watching someone sleep, would depress a bullfrog."

Harry stood for a few minutes beside Katherine, watching her breathe quietly and listening to the soft, purring background sounds of the monitoring systems. The parts of her face not covered by bandages were so free from stress, so angelically calm, that he thought for a moment they actually belonged to the young woman he had married and so often awakened beside to stare at in wonder in their moonlit bedroom all those years ago.

With an effort he pulled his mind back from that thought and struggled to free himself from the scarifying emotions that memory had sent surging through him. As he left the hospital, he wondered what, if anything, she would remember about their days together before the operation and what changes, if any, he would find in her.

These were sobering ruminations, which set him thinking about Soñadora and whether or not he should ignore her demand that he stay away from her. Increasingly he missed seeing her, perhaps because he was ashamed of the way he'd acted,

189

but most of all he felt responsible for the troubles that were separating them. These painful reflections gave rise to another, much more serious one. Was it possible that in turning to Katherine with such passionate intensity he was trying to withdraw from Soñadora?

Was it possible that he was afraid of the increasing seriousness of their affair? He made no progress in trying to answer the question and veered away from it as quickly as he could. For the moment, he escaped thinking about the possibility by deciding it was cowardice and poor judgment that were to blame for what had happened between them. He eased his conscience further by assuring himself that he would do his best to make amends for his mistakes. Besides, he wanted to tell her about Katherine. Not asking himself why he wanted to do it, he pulled out his cell and punched in the numbers.

"Before you hang up," he said when she answered, "I want to tell you that Katherine is in the hospital. She had a benign brain tumor removed this morning."

There was a fairly long wait, during which the line crackled faintly, a pause that gave Harry adequate time to wonder just how big a mistake he had made in calling her.

"By whose authority do you say I am going to hang up?" Soñadora said at last.

Overwhelmed again by his smartass virus, reason failed him, and Harry said, "In our last chat, I think the Pope said something . . ."

"Enough!" Soñadora said. "How is Katherine?"

"She's not sufficiently awake to tell for certain," Harry answered, "but the doctors are saying the operation was successful."

"When was this done?"

"This morning."

"Are you calling from the hospital?" And then when he said

he wasn't, she demanded, "Why not?"

"She's asleep, sedated, resting comfortably," he replied. "I'm going back later."

There was a trace of panic in his voice.

"You are upset," she said, "and should not be driving in your condition and certainly not talking on the phone while you are driving."

"Soñadora," Harry said, lowering his voice an octave, "I'm not upset. I'm starved. I haven't eaten since breakfast. Otherwise, I'm fine."

"The staff is just leaving," she said. "Come over here right now. Buy a bottle of wine on the way. I'll make you something to eat, and remember that you must drive later."

Okay, Harry thought, *I won't be staying over.*

"Is it cold where you are?" Harry asked, having missed the idiocy of his "not staying over" thought.

"It has become much colder lately," she said and severed the connection.

Well, you asked, Harry said with a sigh.

"Beer was a good choice," she said when he set a six pack on her kitchen table.

"It wasn't a choice," he said. "The 7-11 was out of my Silverado Merlot."

Soñadora smiled bleakly.

The kitchen was filled with the delightful smells of cooking, but they did nothing to cut the chill Harry felt emanating from the cook.

"Sit down," she said, pulling a chair out from the table and pointing him into it. "Did Katherine know about the tumor before she came to visit you?" Soñadora asked in the arboreal voice she had been using ever since his arrival.

"No," Harry said. "Minna was worried about her, but Katherine was sure nothing was wrong, and she came to stay with me to get away from Minna, who was demanding she see a doctor."

"Why you?"

She was working at the stove and assiduously keeping her back turned toward him.

"Minna and Jesse loved the Hammock," Harry said, determined not to criticize anything Soñadora did or said. "For Minna, it continues to be a magical place. She thinks miracles happen there. It's where she came to recover from the attempted rape when she was thirteen."

"I remember," Soñadora answered in a slightly warmer voice, lowering the heat under the pan she had been stirring and turning to face him.

It had been his first opportunity to study her face, and he was disturbed to see how tired and troubled she looked.

"I made a very serious mistake in not telling you she was coming," Harry said. "I'm sorry."

"Are you sure it was a mistake?" she asked.

That was much too close to the question he had asked himself earlier and refused again to confront.

"What else could it be but a stupid mistake?" he responded.

She was dressed in a yellow blouse and long, purple skirt, an outfit he particularly liked. He wondered for a moment if she had put it on remembering that, but his thought was quickly interrupted.

"You are still in love with her, aren't you, Harry?" she asked in a voice that Harry might easily have thought freighted with sorrow, had he not instantly suppressed it, determined not to indulge himself.

"I suppose that at some level I am," he told her, taking a small step toward clarity. "It's not something I can do anything about any more than I can do anything about the fact that she and I can't live together."

"So you must have an alternative life," Soñadora said. "Is that so?"

"That's what I'm hoping for," he said.

"With me?"

"If you want me, yes."

Suddenly she smiled at him, the first smile with any warmth in it that she had given him for a long time.

When they began eating, Soñadora said, "There has been a very important development in Guatemala."

Harry groaned silently, expecting to hear more of Father Pierre Robichaud's exploits, but she did not mention him. Instead, she began by speaking about the widespread slaughter of the Mayans in the seventies and later under the leadership of General Rios Mont.

"My mother was killed, my uncle, and nearly half the people in my village were murdered in a single attack," she said, pausing to stare at the wall behind Harry. "I was eight. After that, Father Paulus Jogues became my only family."

"Your father," Harry said, laying down his fork to give her his full attention.

She did not talk about herself very much, but when she did, Harry listened.

"Yes, my father," she agreed with a short, grim laugh, "a white man and a priest. Of course, as you remember, I did not know he was my father then and not for a very long time. My mind is my father's, but my heart is my Mayan mother's," she said somewhat somberly. "You have no idea what a struggle it has been to find a way to live with those two always at war with one another."

"No, I suppose I don't," Harry said, "but I'm sure of this— your parents loved you, and I'd wager they loved one another."

"I try to believe it. But enough of that, I have good news.

President Alvaro Colon has begun making public records left by the Guatemalan government, the police force, the army, and many of the so-called death squads that in the seventies and eighties killed upwards of two hundred thousand people, a very large portion of them Mayans."

"Colon is the president of Guatemala now, right?"

"Yes," she said, beaming at him across the table, "and if he is not killed or ousted from office by the army, he will see to it that those who are revealed by the records to be guilty of atrocities will be tried and punished. It is possible that my mother's killers will finally be brought to justice. Is that not good news?"

He had no intention of diminishing her hope for justice, but it seemed probable to him that once the law began to implicate powerful men like General Rios Mont in those crimes, Colon and his government would find themselves under enormous pressure to stop what they were doing.

"It's long overdue," Harry said.

"I wish I were there, taking an active part in the work," she said, somewhat deflated.

"I can understand that," Harry said, "but what a loss it would be to the Latinos in this corner of the world if you were to leave. There, people are no doubt flocking to help the government. Here, there isn't another person in the county who could or would take your place."

"No one is indispensible," Soñadora told him, shaking her head at him.

"I'm not sure that's true," Harry said, forgetting that he had told himself to support her newfound joy and not argue. "Just think how different human history would be if certain people had not been born when they were."

She leaned back from the table and laughed brightly.

"If you are comparing me with Napoleon Bonaparte," she said, "I'm flattered but decline the honor."

"You are incomparably more admirable and more beautiful than Emperor Bonaparte," he told her.

She threw up her hands.

"You are hopeless," she cried. "I do not know why I bother trying to talk seriously with you."

"Well, the truth is sometimes hard to accept," he said with a smile and pushed his chair back. "I must go to the hospital. Thank you very much for dinner, and I really am pleased by what's happening in Guatemala, especially for you."

They had reached the door, and Soñadora, somber again, said, "I hope you find Katherine as safe as the doctors say."

"Thank you," he said. "Shall I call and tell you?"

"Yes, Harry," she said and gave him a quick, chaste kiss on the cheek. Then, suddenly stepping back from him, she said in an unsteady voice, "No, don't call. I miss you terribly. I want you and I can't have you. Your calling only makes everything worse. When Katherine leaves, perhaps we will talk again—if you still want to."

Harry stepped into the suffocating darkness, feeling as if he had been run over by a twelve-wheeler without the compensation of unconsciousness. Her words had blindsided him, leaving him with no clear idea of how he had responded or even if he had said goodbye. But what was there to say? That he loved her? That he was sorry? For what? Loving Katherine? For sleeping with her?

He drove away, seething with hurt, self-pity, and anger, the adrenaline slowly draining from his system, bringing him to the moment when he saw very clearly that in not telling her that Katherine was coming, in making love to Katherine even after he knew that her passion was fabricated by her illness, he had selfishly and without hesitation, without asking what pain he was inflicting on Soñadora, he had done exactly what he wanted to do—or so it seemed. The qualification frightened him much more than pretending he had been the victim of love and desire.

18

The phone jumped Harry awake at four in the morning.

"We've had a fire," Holly said in a choked voice. "Barn One is burned to cinders and ashes. I'm sure it was set, and I'd really like you to be here."

"The horses?" he asked, turning on the light and starting to dress.

"All in the paddocks, thank God," she told him, "except for Jack and Shadow, a mare we brought into the barn to foal." Her voice nearly failed, and Harry could hear her fighting her tears. "Shadow died," she continued, "but Jack escaped. He must have kicked down the back wall of his stall. It was a close thing because his tail is singed and he's got a torn left hip, probably ripped open by one of the splintered boards when he plunged through the wall."

Twenty minutes later, Harry was standing under the yard lights with Holly, staring at the smoking and charred remains of the stable. The charred body of the mare, smelling of burned hair and flesh, lay in the blackened ruins of her stall, a still-smoldering rafter lying across her neck. The firemen and their trucks had already left.

"It's a miracle all the stables didn't go," Holly added.

"With that wind, how was it prevented?" Harry asked, trying not to look at the dead horse and wanting to lift that smoking four by four off her neck even though he knew she was beyond pain.

He could watch an autopsy with a steady pulse and a calm stomach, but the sight and smell of dead animals distressed him, especially if people had killed them.

"I've got Thahn and Nip to thank for that," she said. "Thahn has always had charge of the dogs at night, and at three Nip began barking and refused to stop. I didn't hear him. My bedroom is at the other end of the house, but the thunder had wakened me. I remember pulling a pillow over my head, then I must have gone back to sleep. Thahn, however, finding he couldn't quiet Nip, dressed and took the dog outside in spite of the weather and immediately smelled smoke. He quickly found the fire and called it in. By then, he said, it had begun burning through the roof, and sparks were shooting into the air."

"What time was that?"

"Just a little after three. I remember glancing at the clock when Thahn knocked on the door."

"Did the firemen say anything about what started it?"

"No, but the man who appeared to be in charge said there would be a forensic team coming out later this morning and not to let anyone poke around in the remains of the stable until they were finished with their investigation."

"You're going to have a visit from your insurance company as well," Harry said.

"I'd forgotten about that," she said. "It won't amount to much."

"How much was Shadow valued at?" Harry asked.

"Possibly ten thousand. Oh, wait! She was with foal," Holly said. "That will add something."

"You're leaving out a little," Harry said. "There's the veterinarian fees for Jack and all the equipment in the stable, plus the cost of reproducing the records in Yellen's office that went up in smoke, plus the cleanup and construction costs of rebuilding the stable. I don't think you're going to be far away from a hundred thousand dollars when all the bills come in."

"God, I feel wretched about Shadow," Holly said, turning away from the burned stable. "She was so beautiful and full of promise. I had great hopes for her. She was only four, and this was her first pregnancy."

"It's bad," Harry agreed, wondering if she had realized that the fire had probably been set.

He did not have to wait long.

"It wasn't started by oily rags or a bad electrical connection, was it, Harry?" she asked in a way requiring no answer, but Harry did not want the question left to drift with the tendrils of smoke still rising from the stable.

"Probably not," he said, "but you won't know for sure until the forensic team completes their work."

"I hope my coming up to say I'm really sorry about this isn't an intrusion."

They turned and saw Miguel Cruz coming toward them.

"I heard the fire engines earlier and dithered around for a while before deciding to come up to see what had happened. I hope I'm not being a nuisance," Miguel said, giving Holly a brief hug.

Harry noticed that Cruz's boots were muddy and the bottoms of his dungarees stained with mud and water.

"I walked," he said, turning to Harry and shaking hands. "The ride between our places is flooded in spots, and I had to wade."

He paused a moment to scan the burned remains of the stable and said, "Holly, I'm very sorry. I can see that one horse was lost. Did you lose any others?"

Then, as if remembering something, he asked, "Where's Jack?"

"In Stable Two. I found him and put him in there for now.

He was in One but, apparently, kicked his way out," she said. "Thanks for coming, and you're not being a nuisance."

"Good. Do you know how it started?"

"Not yet, but I'm sure it wasn't lightning. I would have heard the crash."

Cruz nodded, then said quietly, "I'm glad Tyce was spared seeing this."

"Yes, he would have been devastated, *and* he would have blamed himself."

"I meant to call you about Tyce," Cruz responded, "but that's something else I've been dithering about. Look, I know you've got a small army working for you, but if there's anything I can do to help, you know where to find me."

"Thanks, Miguel, I may call just to talk. Harry here has to listen to me too much. How's Clarissa?"

"Not good. Brandon's death . . . well, no need to tell you. Don't forget. Call me."

With that, he left as quickly as he had come.

"Have you two been talking with one another?" Harry asked.

"He called after Tyce was attacked and asked if I thought Tyce was going to need help with the hospital costs. I told him the stud's insurance would cover them and I would see to the rest."

Not exactly an answer to his question, but he decided not to press her. It had been clear they had some sort of regular contact. He wondered why but moved on.

"Did you know he's been visiting Yellen every day?"

"I'm not surprised. Who told you?"

"He did. I met him there right after Yellen had been put in the IC unit."

"Was he as disagreeable as he was when you were talking with Clarissa?"

"No. He was very decent and left me liking him."

"He's a very sweet man, and I feel sorry for him."

"Why?"

"Clarissa Cruz is as dark inside as out. I can't begin to imagine how Brandon . . ."

She caught herself and turned away from the burned stable.

"I'm exhausted," she said, looking up at the wash of pale gray in the east, outlining the black shapes of the trees. "Can you stay a little longer? We could have coffee and, if anyone's up, some breakfast."

"Of course," Harry said, thinking it unlikely that she was hungry and supposed the food and drink were inducements.

She was an odd mixture of hard realist and vulnerable innocent, he thought as they walked in silence back to the house.

It turned out, however, that people were up, and she was hungry.

"So we're adding arson to murder and attempted murder," Hodges said later that morning in Jim's office where Harry was listening to Jim's summary of the Fire Department's report on the fire.

"The accelerant had been thrown around pretty freely," Jim said, tossing the report onto his desk.

"And especially around the stalls where the two horses were located," Harry added. "Very nasty."

"Is there any possibility that maiming the horse, poisoning the dog, and setting fire to that stable were not done by whoever murdered Brandon Pike?" Jim asked in a harsh voice.

"Hell, no," Hodges put in.

"I believe that's called a rhetorical question," Harry said, "but the answer to your grim query is that, at the moment, there's no way of knowing."

Jim kicked back from his desk and unfolded his long length to begin pacing around the office as if he was preparing to jump out a window. Harry watched with interest. It wasn't often that Jim lost his composure, but this, Harry thought, might be such a moment.

"There's the possibility that Tyce Yellen will remember who attacked him," he said with almost total lack of conviction but trying to give Jim some hope.

"Good try, Harry," Hodges said with a loud laugh that set his folding chair creaking.

Harry's contribution to the conversation did stop Jim from pacing and perched him on the corner of his desk, to glower first at Hodges then at Harry.

"Since I've caught you in a good mood," Harry said, "what about putting a guard on Yellen's hospital room?"

"Do you know something I don't?" Jim demanded.

"Possibly," Harry said. "When Elijah Blue heard that Yellen had regained consciousness but couldn't have visitors, he became agitated and demanded that Holly and I tell him why he couldn't see him."

"You know, Harry," Hodges, said, suddenly serious, "Blue and Yellen have been working together for a long time. He might have been looking forward to Yellen's waking up."

"He doesn't strike me as the sentimental type," Harry said.

"How did Mrs. Pike respond to him?" Jim asked, showing interest.

"The way she does to Jack," Harry answered, his admiration showing, "with respect but no obvious fear. She's also ac-customed to him and his rough edges."

"He's got a history," Hodges put in, "but we don't have any reason to think he beat on Yellen. Nobody we talked to ever heard him and Yellen so much as argue."

"That's true," Jim said with a sigh, "and aside from the fact he had access, there's not a scrap of evidence to indicate he's involved in Pike's death or any of the other crimes at The Oaks."

"One thing," Harry said. "Mrs. Jackson said he was very upset over Henry Jackson's death and Rosalee Franklin's losing out in that suit against Brandon. She also said that when one of Rosalee and Henry's sons died, Elijah took it hard."

"Did she say he'd ever threatened Pike?" Jim asked.

"Not to me," Harry admitted. "This may not be anything more than what it appears to be," Harry continued, "but while Holly and I were talking and looking at what was left of the stable, Miguel appeared. He was soaked to the knees and said he had walked over and had to wade part of the way."

"What time was that?" Hodges asked.

"A little before five."

Jim glanced at the fire report.

"The 911 was called in at 3:05," he said. "Cruz wasn't making a social call."

"In a way, yes," Harry said. "He said the sirens woke him, but he dithered around for a while, making up his mind whether or not to come over and offer his help if it was needed. It would have taken him about half an hour to walk over from Oleander, giving him an hour and a half to 'dither.' "

"Unless he spent the time out there in the dark somewhere, watching the barn burn," Hodges said.

Jim shook his head.

"I can't see it happening that way," he said.

"No," Harry said, getting to his feet. "I think he and Yellen are friends. He and Holly are on good terms—how good I couldn't say, but they talk to one another from time to time."

"Any chance that she got knocked up talking on the phone?" Hodges asked with another guffaw.

Harry wanted to say there wasn't, but he found he couldn't. Why, he wondered as he left the office, did he find it so unpleasant to think of Holly and Miguel as lovers?

★ ★ ★ ★ ★

Harry counted two nurses and three doctors clustered around Katherine's bed, blocking any hope of his catching more than a glimpse of her face, but he could see enough to realize that she was sitting up with only a drip attached to her, all the other devices that hummed and whirred, registering digital messages, were gone. His disappointment at finding her so surrounded was more than balanced by the fact that, except for the serious bandage covering her left eye and the incision area above her eye, she was free of encumbrances.

Colin Baker looked up from the scrum around the bed and saw Harry standing in the door. Stopping whatever he was doing, he joined him.

"She's fully conscious and in good spirits," Baker said, his red hair flaring. "It's going to be at least another half hour before we're done with her. Everyone, including Horace Peters from the psychiatric wing and William Morrissey from the rehab unit, is in there. She's going to be seriously pooped when they're finished putting her through her paces."

"And I should go away," Harry said, struggling to stifle his frustration. "You're beginning to sound like a stuck record."

"Be brave," Baker said with a broad grin as he grasped Harry by the shoulder and shook him vigorously.

"Okay," Harry said, judging from the feel of his shoulder that Baker should have been a lumberjack instead of a nurse. "I'll see if I can visit Tyce Yellen."

"Give it a try," Baker said, running a large hand over his spiky hair, "but he's not in great shape. Talk to someone down there before you try to go into Yellen's room. The team's a little edgy. They had some trouble yesterday with a very big, very fractious black man who wanted to see him and didn't take kindly to being told he couldn't."

"Elijah Blue," Harry said, half amused and half worried.

"That's the man," Baker said with a laugh. "He scared the bejesus out of them."

"I don't think they'll mistake me for Elijah," Harry said.

"I hope not," he said, going back to what he'd been doing. "They have orders to sedate on sight."

Harry went down two floors and stopped by the nurse's station. Recognizing Michelle, who had been on duty during his last visit, he asked if he could see Yellen.

"If the deputy clears you, you can go in for a few minutes," she said.

"Got it," he said, responding to her probing gaze.

"Especially don't ask questions about what happened to him or tell him anything about what happened to him," she added. "You can give him your name if you want, but skip the rest. This man is still seriously ill. He's easily upset and easily frightened. Are you with me?"

"Yes," Harry said. "I hear you had a little excitement yesterday."

"You could say that," Michelle replied, softening her tone slightly. "There was a minute when our deputy had his gun out of its holster. That was right after Mr. Blue told us he might have to throw someone through one of our sealed windows, to persuade us he was serious about seeing Mr. Yellen."

"Did he say why he wanted to talk with Yellen?"

"He said he was a friend and wanted to know if Mr. Yellen knew another part of his anatomy from his elbow."

A smile begin to tug at the corners of the nurse's mouth before it was suppressed.

Harry laughed for her.

"It sounds right," he said. "He's an impressive man."

"*Dangerous* comes to my mind. I would say his bite's worse than his bark," Michelle said. "You can go along in if you want, but don't expect much interaction."

The deputy guarding Yellen was Fred Robbins.

"Congratulations on your promotion, Corporal," Harry said, shaking hands.

A year ago they had worked together for a few days on a burglary case.

"Thank you, Harry," the young man said, coloring a little under the compliment. "I guess you've heard about the excitement here yesterday."

"Michelle and I were just talking about it."

"How's Mrs. Brock? When I was assigned to this job, Sergeant Hodges told me your wife was in the hospital."

"They won't let me see her yet," Harry said, "but the doctor and the others working with her say she's doing well. I hear you had to put your gun on Elijah."

"I don't know whether I needed to or not," Robbins said, "but I decided not to risk letting him get his hands on somebody, especially me."

"He's impressive, coming straight at you," Harry said with a grin. "Did you find out why he wanted to see Yellen?"

"I gather he wanted to talk to him."

"What about?"

Robbins shrugged.

"His language was a little colorful, but I think he was worried that Yellen wouldn't recognize him."

"They've worked together for a while," Harry said, thinking the opposite might be what Elijah was really concerned about. "Is Yellen conscious?"

"More or less," he said with a wry grin.

Robbins turned and opened the door.

"Don't expect much," he said quietly as Harry stepped past him.

Although his head was heavily bandaged, Yellen looked less like a mummy, Harry thought, but that was about all he could say that was hopeful. The pallor of his face accentuated the bruises, staining the flesh around his eyes in ugly streaks of yellow, purple, and green. Harry placed himself beside the bed so that Yellen could see him without turning his head.

"Hello, Tyce," he said. "How are you feeling?"

At the sound of Harry's voice, Yellen's eyes flickered open, but Harry still found himself looking at someone who appeared to be a full ten years older than the Yellen Harry had last seen.

"Do I know you?" Yellen asked in a dull voice.

"Maybe not, but I used to see you at The Oaks now and then."

"The Oaks?" Yellen asked.

"Holly lives there," Harry said, beginning to worry that what he was saying might be upsetting Yellen.

"Stop talking like a horse's ass," Yellen said.

Michelle walked in just as Yellen was issuing his command.

"I'm coming back in a minute," she told her patient, putting her hand on his forehead, then removing it and turning her attention to Harry. "Mr. Brock is leaving now," she said, taking Harry by the arm, just in case, he thought, he was deaf or feeble.

Once out of the room, Michelle turned to Harry and said in an everyday voice, "Don't pay any attention to that. Saying inappropriate things is just part of his healing process. If things go okay, after a while he'll stop doing it. Now, he doesn't know the difference between *fart* and *hello.*"

Her illustration startled Harry a little, but he rallied.

"Does he have any memory left?"

"Not much. By now he will have forgotten we were in the room with him," she said, "but it will take a while before we'll know how much of his long-term memory is intact. Right now he can't access any of it, but that's not at all unusual."

"Thanks for the tour," Harry said.

She had a lovely smile, and Harry gave himself two points for having prompted it.

"It comes with the package," she told him and went about her business.

"She's got more corners than a good-sized town," Robbins said as he and Harry watched her hurry away, "but she improves over time. I'm getting to like her."

"Be careful," Harry told him. "My experience is that getting to like a woman is like hitting black ice going sixty. By then it's way too late to brake."

19

Having been cleared by Colin Baker, Harry walked into Katherine's room with his heart trying to pound its way out his shirt pocket. His throat was dry, and his hands were cold, but he wasn't sure where the terror was coming from.

"Hello, Harry," she said, having turned her head on the pillow, bringing her unbandaged eye into play.

"God!" Harry said, finding his fear, "I was afraid you wouldn't know me."

She gave him a wan smile and reached a hand toward him.

"Your hand is cold," she said. "Are you all right?"

"I am now," he answered, pulling a chair to the side of the bed, then taking her hand in both of his. "How are you feeling?"

He wondered briefly if he was still under Michelle's spell.

"Did you really think I wouldn't know you?" she asked, expressing concern.

"I wasn't sure. How *are* you feeling?"

"Weak," she complained. "I want to frown, and I can't."

"After all you've been through, I'm surprised you can talk."

His terror had submerged like an alligator, leaving only a ripple on the surface, but his mind was still uneasy and kept glancing around, trying to anticipate where it would rise next.

"Have you been talking to the kids?" she asked.

"I have, and now you're back with us, they'll be coming to see you. They wanted to be here when you went into the hospital and were not pleased with me. I'm seriously worried that when she gets here, Minna will beat me up."

Harry's effort failed even to produce a smile.

"I wish they weren't coming," Katherine said. "I'm tired enough as it is."

"They won't be here long," Harry said to comfort her, "they've all got lives to live."

"Good," she said, hitching a little onto her left hip to bring her eye to bear more directly on him. "I want to ask you some questions, and I want honest answers."

"Sure," Harry said, uneasiness slipping in like the fog, obscuring landmarks.

"I'm having trouble sorting out some things that happened before the operation. Were you and I sleeping together?"

"Yes," Harry said, guessing where this was going and wishing it wasn't.

"Am I right in thinking that I took an active part in causing that to happen?"

"I'd say your memory is fairly accurate," he hedged.

This was going to be even more difficult than he could have imagined, probably because now that he thought back, his behavior seemed more inexcusable than ever.

"And when I arrived, you made a smooth transition from Soñadora to me?"

"I wouldn't describe it that way," he said, hoping he wouldn't be called on to explain himself.

"I don't remember your saying that there was anything problematical in our sleeping together."

"I didn't."

"Why the hell not, Harry?"

He started to say something about gift horses but veered away from that option. Telling her that it didn't seem relevant was equally unattractive.

"I thought of it," he said, "but at first I couldn't find the right time. Then it got to be too late."

"That is so lame," she told him.

"I could have taken the fifth," he said.

"Never mind," she said, averting her eye and ignoring his feeble attempt at humor. "I know the answer. My memory isn't totally shot. You told me you loved me and would never turn down the chance to make love to me."

"The truth at last," Harry said.

"Aren't you ashamed of yourself?"

"No. Are you?" he demanded, beginning to feel threatened.

"I have an excuse."

"Lucky you."

She was looking at him again. Being stared at by that one eye made Harry feel as nervous as the narrator in *The Tell-Tale Heart*.

"You're twisted," Katherine said.

"That too."

"Harry, do you know how bad we've been?"

"I love you too. What if I was to lock the door and . . . ?"

She gave a shout of protest, laced with laughter, which brought a nurse running into the room.

"You're supposed to be resting," she said sternly. Scowling at Harry, she pointed at the door and said loudly, "Out! Now!"

Harry was scarcely out of the hospital when Rowena Farnham called him.

"Harry," she said, "we need to talk."

Rowena's oval face was not made for frowning, but she wore one as Harry sat down with his cup of Earl Grey tea and buttered scone, prepared for bad news.

"What's going on between you and Soñadora?" Rowena asked in her rector's voice.

"Nothing," Harry said. "I have been banished from her presence as long as Katherine is in town."

"Is that all?"

The answer had clearly not satisfied Rowena, but she did allow herself a nibble at the scone and a sip of tea.

"I didn't tell her Katherine was coming to stay with me, and she called me and got Katherine."

Rowena set down her cup with a clatter.

"You idiot!" she said, straightening her back.

"Fair assessment," Harry agreed.

"But that's not all of it, is it?"

"What do you mean?" Harry asked, now seriously worried.

"You know damned well what I mean. You and Soñadora were engaged to be married or next thing to it. You were intimate. Do I have to tell you what Soñadora concluded from your not telling her about Katherine's arrival?"

She took a deep breath that expanded her voluminous bosom and made Harry feel as if he was inside the First Little Pig's house.

"And *no* is not an optional answer."

"Okay," Harry said in full flight, "where is this leading?"

"Guess, Harry."

"She's been talking with you about breaking off our relationship."

"Something's breaking," Rowena snapped, "and I'm afraid it's her heart. Don't you know by now how fragile she is?"

Harry knew that she didn't expect an answer because it was an accusation, not a question.

"What do you think I should do?" he asked, resentment beginning to build. "She doesn't want to talk to me. She won't take my calls and has told me to stay away from *Salvamento*, but preventing Katherine from coming was never an option and neither is sending her away."

"Self-pity and self-righteousness belong under a bridge with the rest of the trolls," Rowena told him. "Confront the truth, Harry. You have been sleeping with Katherine. Shame on you."

"How could you possibly know that?" Harry demanded, reduced to bluster.

"Because she told me."

"Before the operation or after?"

"Most recently this morning. I saw her just before her medical team arrived. Of course, being Katherine, she blames herself for what happened."

"We talked about it," Harry admitted, losing all inclination to avoid the issue. "Of course it wasn't her fault. I knew that under the circumstances her sharing my bed was way out of character, but I didn't link it to her tumor. When we started, neither of us even guessed what was wrong."

The possibility that he had acted as he did for reasons that stemmed from his relationship with Soñadora surfaced again, but he shrank from sharing them with Rowena.

"A fine mess!" Rowena burst out.

"Yes," Harry agreed. "Katherine and I did have a fight about my not telling Soñadora, but she seemed to dismiss it as a problem for us."

"And you found it convenient to let her."

"That would about sum it up."

"What do you want to see happen?"

"I asked you first."

"Don't be a child. Answer me."

"I want Katherine to recover fully. I want to find some way to undo the harm I've done to Soñadora. Beyond that, I don't know."

The tea was cold. The butter had congealed on the scones. Rowena stood up.

"Harry," she said, "you'd better find out what you want, or you may end up with nothing."

Buoyed by that cheerful thought, Harry drove away from St. Jude's reluctant to have any further contact with his fellow men; but when the phone whistled its happy tune, he answered it. It was Heather Parkinson.

"Iffy news, Brock," she said on hearing his voice. "I'm taking Tuck home to Holly. He's on his feet, and I've done all I can for him. You anywhere near her?"

"Give me half an hour, but why do you need me?"

"I've got to tell her that the dog could go into renal collapse any time. If that happens, it will be, 'Goodbye, Tuck.'"

"Okay. What's the problem?"

"Here's the thing, Dummy. We're dealing with a woman three months pregnant who's just lost her husband, had one of her horse barns burned down, incinerating one of her pregnant mares, and now she's going to hear that half of her favorite dog team may fall down and die. She's going to need support. Support takes time I haven't got. I'm on call for a collapsed horse and a bull that, according to his owner, has eaten half a coffee can of roofing nails."

"That's not it, Parkinson," Harry told her.

"What do you mean?" she demanded.

"You're afraid she's going to start crying and that you'll have to comfort her, maybe put your arms around her. Then she'll put her arms around you . . ."

"All right! Cut it out! It's not funny."

"Sorry. I'll be there. She can cry on me. I kind of like it."

"You know what, Brock?" she shouted. "You'd make a corkscrew look straight."

She slammed her cell phone shut so hard Harry winced and smiled at the same time. Having Heather insult him always made him feel better, but he lost his smile when he remembered that she was the second woman since breakfast to call him twisted.

"Have you and she got something going?" Holly asked as Heather was ripping her pickup out of the yard.

"Why would you think that?" Harry asked in surprise.

"Every time she looked at you, her face turned red."

"It was probably rage," Harry said and laughed. "I tease her more than I should."

The two dogs that had been bumping and chewing each other in their excitement at being united came running back and plowed into Harry and Holly, nearly taking them down.

"You wouldn't know, looking at Tuck now, that he'd been drinking antifreeze," Holly said when she had straightened out the tangle and sent the dogs off toward the barns.

"So that's what nearly killed him," Harry said.

"That's what Heather told me," Holly answered.

"Do you keep antifreeze here for any reason?" Harry asked.

"I don't think so. At least I can't recall ever seeing any here," she said, frowning. "When did we last have a frost?"

"It's been at least two years," Harry said. "When I first moved down here, we had one or two frosts every winter."

"Still no reason to keep antifreeze on the place," she said in disgust.

They had been following the dogs, and Harry was surprised to see a man on a large yellow front loader clearing away the remains of the burned barn. Having regained their composure, the dogs trotted back to stand beside them and watch the loader scoop up the charred beams, planks, and ash and tip them into an enormous red ten-wheel dump truck with the logo Southwest Construction painted on the doors. Stirring up the ash had put the dank smell of burning back into the air.

"I don't want to watch," Holly said, turning away from the

scene. "All I can think of is Shadow being burned to death."

"There's no doubt she would have been terrified by what was happening," Harry said quietly, bending toward her as they walked, "but she was probably asphyxiated before the flames reached her."

"Are you just trying to make me feel better?"

"I hope it does," Harry said, "but it's also true."

"I would like very much to believe you," Holly said.

"Believe it," Harry said, then, wanting to take her mind off Shadow's death, he added, "I'd like to talk a little more about Tuck's being poisoned."

"What more is there to say?" Holly asked, staring at the ground with a glum expression.

"I think it's safe to say there isn't any antifreeze here."

"But it had to have been there," Holly protested. "Heather detected it in his system when she ran the tests."

"Not necessarily."

"You mean someone had to have gotten rid of it before we found Tuck?"

"Yes," Harry said, "I've been giving it a lot of thought, and while I can, just barely, make myself believe that someone from outside The Oaks might have come in and put it where the dogs could have found it, I can't believe that person could have come back and taken away whatever had contained the antifreeze."

"Then it must have been someone who lives or works here," Holly said in a hollow voice.

"I think so."

Holly's cell rang and, obviously still thinking about the implications of what Harry had said, she answered the call.

"Oh, my God! Where are you?" she cried, paused, and said, "I'll be there as soon as I can."

"What is it?" Harry asked, alarmed by her loss of color.

"It was Miguel," she told him, her eyes wide with shock. "Clarissa's dead. She's been shot."

20

"So it's settled," Tucker said. "She committed suicide. Anyone know why?"

He and Harry were in the shed where later in the season Tucker would bottle his honey. They were stacking newly painted hive sections against one of the walls. Clean and scrubbed as the place was, the room still smelled of honey, and bees and hornets hummed at the screen door and the open, screened windows. Surrounded by tall fescue grass, scattered through with a rainbow of day lilies, lupine, and larkspur, it was one of Harry's favorite places on Tucker's farm. Even the darkened pine board walls of the inside of the shed, dappled with sunlight, seemed to have taken on the color of warm honey.

"I drove Holly to Oleander," Harry said, making sure not to make his stack taller than Tucker could manage alone without a ladder, "but, of course, Jim's people were there and the medical examiner and her crew. I got to talk with her for a moment."

"We're done," Tucker said, stepping back to view their work and nodding in satisfaction. "Kathleen Towers is still Tequesta County M.E., isn't she?"

"That's right. She said that prior to an autopsy and a full report from the crime scene crew, Clarissa appears to have been lying on her back on her bedroom floor when she put the barrel of a Sig Sauer .380 in her mouth and pulled the trigger. A photo of Brandon Pike was lying beside her."

"Powerful gun," Tucker observed, wiping his face with the

blue bandanna he had been wearing around his neck. "It must have made a mess."

"That's right," Harry said, trying not to picture it.

"What would you say if I was to tell you that I suspect she and Brandon had been lovers for years before he married Holly?" Tucker asked suddenly.

"If anyone but you had said it, I'd say the person was crazy," Harry replied, taken by surprise, "but because it's you—and I can't say more—you've made a shrewd guess if it was a guess."

"Not entirely. You have confirmation then."

"I never said this to you, okay?"

"Of course," Tucker said. "If we can manage it, let's walk and talk at the same time. There's a pitcher of fresh lemonade calling to us from the refrigerator."

"Now that you mention it . . ." Harry replied, pulling open the door.

Oh, Brother! and Sanchez appeared and walked with them from the honey shed to the house but stopped somewhat short of the stoop and looked around carefully. Sanchez whined pitifully and backed away.

"What's wrong?" Harry asked.

"We've got a delicate situation," Tucker said as they stepped onto the stoop. "A female skunk has dug a den under our feet, and we're all expecting her to bring out a family one of these days. Meanwhile, everyone, including Jane Bunting and her group, are treading carefully until the happy event occurs, and our odiferous guest can go back into the woods."

"What if she doesn't?" Harry asked.

"Have her family?" Tucker asked, taking the pitcher out of the refrigerator and filling two glasses set out on the counter.

"No," Harry said, picking up one of the glasses, already rewardingly cold, and following Tucker back onto the stoop. "I meant decides to stay, family and all."

"We'll just adjust," Tucker said with a comfortable smile, settling into his rocker. "Sanchez will find it hardest. He's terrified of skunks. I expect he was sprayed as a pup and has never recovered from the shock. You heard him whining. Go on with what you were saying about confirmation."

"I think you have to be right, and that's all I can say now," Harry answered. "One day I hope we can discuss this properly."

"So do I," Tucker answered. "Meanwhile, I take it Clarissa left no letter explaining herself."

"Nothing so far," Harry said, "but these are early days. Jim is going to be all over this. We haven't talked, but I'm guessing he is going to take the possibility that she was murdered very seriously."

"As he should," Tucker said, refilling their glasses. "What's your thinking on the matter?"

"At least for the moment, I can't see any reason for whoever killed Brandon wanting to kill her."

"Nor I," Tucker agreed.

They talked about Holly for a while, and before Harry got up to leave, Tucker thanked him for his help with the hive sections and accompanied him to the Rover. On the way, Harry asked him if he had seen anything of the coyotes.

"No," he said, "but Bonnie and Clyde are acting as if they expected to be jumped any minute."

"Have those gray foxes been bothering the hens?" Harry asked with a grin.

"Not so far, but I expect their cubs are still in the den. Wait 'til they get a little older and a lot hungrier. Then we'll see."

He paused while Harry got into the Rover. Then before Harry closed the door, he said, "You're the expert here, but shouldn't you be more worried than you seem to be about Holly?"

"You think the noose is tightening."

"I do."

"Well, so do I, but she's determined to stay at The Oaks, and short of moving in with her, I don't see what more I can do to protect her."

"For the time being," Tucker said, shutting the door, "I think you're living with enough women."

Jesse arrived, tall, intense, and rangy with his father's saturnine good looks. Pleased as he was to have his stepson back in the house, Harry had trouble now and then remembering that he wasn't looking at a young Willard Trachey, but Jesse had his mother's green eyes, and that was enough to settle the hair on the back of Harry's neck.

His greeting had been, "How's Mom?" followed by, "Are you holding up?"

Having been reassured by Harry's responses, he immediately began messaging his team.

"I've got to stay with this project," he said by way of apology. "It's not that I don't trust my crew, I can't afford to fall behind. I've brought a bunch of work with me."

Well, Harry thought, so much for walks and long conversations.

Then Minna and Thornton came, and the remaining vestiges of quiet and decorum vanished, a development that alternately delighted and appalled Harry. Minna and Jesse fell on one another like long parted lovers, and Harry was struck hard by the reminder of the way in which the two had protected one another as children when they and their mother were living without anything but a car roof over their heads at night and seemingly nothing but the road in front of them. They flowed around the smiling and imperturbable Thornton like a tumbling brook around a rock.

"I've decided not to throttle you, Harry," Minna said, emerging through the Arrival Gate and smothering him in a hug while

Thornton watched with a tolerant smile. "K wouldn't approve, although by now she would probably like to do it herself."

She was almost as tall as Jesse with the same arresting looks except that she was as fair as her mother.

"Hug your father," she told Thornton when she let go of Harry, which didn't happen right away. "Don't stand there gawking like an idiot."

There were two days of this sort of thing, and then they were gone.

"I need another operation," Katherine said when Harry returned to the hospital after driving them to the airport.

"Why?" Harry asked in alarm.

"I'm so exhausted and muddled, I think the tumor must have grown back."

Harry was glad to be able to laugh.

"You're coming home," he told her. "You can rest there."

She was sitting up now in a chair, dressed and with most of the bandages off her head except for a small patch above her eye.

"No, Harry," she said calmly, "the Hammock's no longer my home."

"It could be," he said.

"You know better than that," she told him with a small frown of either rebuke or regret.

Harry couldn't tell which.

Harry had just gotten Katherine back to the Hammock and settled in a chaise lounge on the lanai when Jim called, asking him to come to the Oleander.

"Go," Katherine said, waving him away, when he told her. "I've got iced tea, books, morning sun in the oaks, cicadas for company, and no one jabbing me with anything. Don't hurry back."

"Four days!" Jim said with groan. "And I still don't have closure on this investigation."

They were standing in the garden in front of the house, surrounded by the humming of bees, waiting for Kathleen Towers and Lieutenant Millard Jones, the ranking officer of the Crime Scene team that had made the initial examination of the death.

"Where's Miguel?" Harry asked.

"He's inside with his brother and the brother's wife. They seem pretty sensible people, but Miguel is another thing altogether. He refuses to accept that his sister killed herself."

"Is that why I'm here?" Harry asked.

"I suppose so. What I'm doing here or hoping to do is not conventional procedure, but it's all I could come up with. I've decided to bring Millard Jones, a senior officer on the Criminal Investigation team, and Kathleen and you together with Felipe, his wife, and Miguel to try to persuade Miguel that his sister was not murdered. He's raised such a stink at the State Attorney's Office, insisting she was, that unless we can get him to back off, we'll never be free of this thing."

"It doesn't sound like our fearless Harley Dillard," Harry said, "to let himself be influenced by someone like Miguel. What's got him spooked?"

"Clarissa Cruz was an important Hispanic woman in some very influential circles in the county. Those two chips have big numbers on them," Jim said grimly. "Don't forget, we're talking about election cycles here."

"When are we not?" Harry asked.

Just then one of the department's unmarked cars came up the drive.

"Let's get this over with," Jim said, striding toward the car.

Millard Jones was short and slim, wearing perfectly creased gray trousers, polished black shoes, and a short-sleeved black silk shirt. He was tanned, his mustache was perfectly trimmed, and not a hair on his head was out of place. Kathleen waited for Jones to walk around the car to open her door. Half a head taller than Jones, she stepped out of the car, taking his hand and blushing prettily as he handed her down.

"Jesus," Jim muttered savagely as he watched.

"You've got to admit it, Jim," Harry said, knowing that his friend swore about as often as hens have teeth, and gleefully twisted the knife, "the man's got style."

Jim muttered something about balls and brass monkeys as Harry followed him to the car, choking back his laughter.

"Captain," Jones said smoothly in a surprisingly deep voice. "I've had a very pleasant ride out here with your charming fiancée. It ended much too soon. I hope it's not going to be spoiled by anything sordid."

When Jones finished speaking, Jim was the only one of the little group not smiling.

"Our job here is fairly straightforward," Jim said as though he hadn't heard Jones. "We're here to persuade Miguel Cruz that his sister committed suicide. His brother Felipe wants the body released from custody and the memorial and burial services to go forward. Everyone wants that to happen except for Miguel."

"I think we can manage that, Captain," Kathleen said in her most pragmatic voice, slipping Harry a wink and stepping forward to link arms with Jim and start him toward the house.

"Hello, Brock," Jones said, falling in beside his taller companion as they got under way. "I hear that your ex is with you and that she's been under the knife. I hope she's recovering well."

"She's much better," Harry replied. "Thanks for asking."

"I'm glad to hear it," Jones said. "I knew her only casually, but she is a lovely woman."

"Yes," Harry said, relieved that he hadn't known her better.

Harry was sure that, except for his burglar friend Ernesto Piedra, he had never met another man who loved and admired women as much and had that liking reciprocated as often as Millard Jones.

"Of course she is," Jones said. "With bone structure, skin, and coloring like that, she'll be a beautiful woman all her life, and when I think of the way she carries herself . . ." He sighed. "A striking woman."

"Are you married, Jones?" Harry asked, knowing he wasn't but anxious to get his mind off Katherine.

"Unfortunately, no," he said, sounding more than ever like a man with his collar on backwards. "It has been my fate to go through life in the bachelor state."

"How do you account for it?" Harry persisted.

"Bad luck, Brock, extremely bad luck. I've been called many times but never chosen," he responded in a deep voice rich in conviction and tinged with melancholy.

"I'm sorry to hear it," Harry said, holding up his end, "but I wouldn't have said that you were a lonely man."

"No," his companion replied, an irrepressible smile flickering at the corners of his mouth, "there have been compensations."

"Have you ever counted them?" Harry inquired.

"Heavens, no!" Jones protested as if he'd been asked to vandalize a priceless painting.

"I expect it's approaching three digits," Harry observed, unable to stop himself.

Jim was holding the door to the house open, and Harry did not get to hear Jones's response.

Jim made the introductions, and Jones lingered over Constanta Cruz's hand. Harry watched with admiration tinged with envy as color brightened Constanta's face and her body swayed gracefully as a willow in the wind in response to Jones's touch.

"Let's get to it, Captain," Felipe said more loudly than necessary to be heard, shooting a dark look at his wife.

Harry thought that Felipe and Constanta looked exactly like what they were, a handsome, prosperous, self-confident couple, appropriately subdued by Clarissa's death, but moving up the economic ladder and enjoying the climb. Miguel was another case altogether. He was hunched on the couch, elbows on his knees, where Harry recalled sitting when he talked to Clarissa. Miguel looked like a storm cloud, filled with misery instead of rain. He had not looked up when Jim was giving everyone names, and he made no response to Felipe's call for action.

"I suppose we all know why we're here," Jim said when everyone was seated in a rough circle facing the fireplace.

That was as far as he got because Miguel suddenly leaped to his feet, fists clenched, and shouted, "Fuck this! No one is convincing me my sister committed suicide. She didn't. She was murdered."

He stood trembling but unyielding, facing the silence that met his outburst as if he was leaning into a strong wind. Constanta was the first to respond, crossing the space between them quickly and embracing him. For a long moment she said nothing, just held him. Although Miguel gradually stopped shaking, Harry thought he still looked as if he was being crucified.

"Miguel, darling," she said after kissing his cheek, "no one wants to make you do anything that you do not want to do, but we should hear what these people have to tell us. I want to listen to them. It may help me to understand this awful thing. Will you be very kind to me and listen with us?"

Harry was sure Miguel would bolt, but Constanta was still holding his arms, and that may have been enough to constrain him. In any event, he looked at her and, with tears flooding his eyes, sank back onto the sofa. Constanta sat down beside him. Scowling, Felipe went to sit with her. Harry shared in the general relief.

"I think we should hear from Lieutenant Jones first," Jim said. "The Lieutenant and the other members of the crime scene team were the first Sheriff Department's responders. I would like to hear what the team was looking for and what they found. Lieutenant Jones."

Whatever else Jones was, he was a competent police officer, and Harry had great respect for his work. Unceremoniously and with an obvious awareness of how sensitive the issue was for the Cruzes, Jones described briefly police procedure in such situations and then said what he and the team had found.

"Your conclusions, Lieutenant?" Jim asked.

Harry, already bored, glanced around the room and the circle of listeners and thought all that was lacking was Miss Marple, but finding his mind beginning to expand on that amusing idea, he forced himself to listen to what Jones was saying.

"There was no trace of a second person having been in the room with her. Our medical examiner can expand on the corroborating evidence, but our unanimous conclusion was that Clarissa Cruz had taken her own life."

Miguel was holding his head and offered no response to Jones's presentation, which was followed by Kathleen Towers's more technical explanation of why from her examination she concluded that Clarissa had put the gun in her mouth herself and pulled the trigger. Miguel went on sitting, apparently oblivious to what was going on around him, but the moment Jim started to speak, Miguel interrupted him.

"Harry," he said, "you talked with my sister a short time ago."

"That's right," Harry said.

"Did you see or hear anything in that conversation that led

you to think that she was a suicide risk?"

The question surprised Harry, and he took a moment to reflect before answering.

"She was in mourning for Brandon Pike, her half brother," Harry said for Jones and Kathleen's benefit, "and, possibly, somewhat subdued, but she talked freely and graciously with me. I was impressed with her dignity and her intelligence. There was nothing in either her manner or her words that suggested to me that she might take her own life."

"Then what could have changed?" Miguel demanded.

"She was threatened," Constanta said quietly.

"Constanta!" Felipe burst out angrily and pushed himself halfway to his feet.

"Mr. Cruz," Jim said, "please sit down and let your wife finish what she was saying."

Still glaring at his wife, Felipe subsided.

"Mrs. Cruz," Jim said.

"I was going through some of my sister-in-law's things and came upon her diary . . ."

"You had no right looking at it!" Miguel protested.

The anger darkening the young man's face led Harry to wonder whether it was offended propriety or jealousy that was making Miguel so wrathful.

"I wasn't reading her diary, dear," Constanta said quietly. "I had something else in my hands when I picked it up and dropped it. This fell out."

She pulled a folded square of paper from the front of her dress and extended it toward Jim, who rose quickly and took it. In the silence following Constanta's remarks, Harry had a flash of vivid memory. He saw a favorite aunt rummage in her bra for an embroidered handkerchief, to wipe her eyes after a fit of laughter brought on by something he had said or done. It was gone as swiftly as it had come, but it left a twinge of longing for the woman, the sunny room, the smell of lilacs in the open window, and the warm breeze unfurling white curtains.

"Why have you waited until now to show this to me?" Jim demanded.

"Because nothing useful will be served by showing it to you," Felipe exploded, flinging a steely glance at Constanta. "Clarissa is dead, making everything in that note moot."

"This is essential evidence," Jim shot back. "Weren't you aware of that? Withholding evidence from the police is a serious offense."

"What does the note say?" Miguel demanded, on his feet again.

"For now," Jim replied, "you will have to ask your brother and your sister-in-law to answer that question."

"And you will not tell him," Felipe said to Constanta in a savage voice.

Constanta's back stiffened, but she made no response beyond avoiding her husband's angry stare. Jim, having remained standing to read the note, broke in.

"Mrs. Cruz, why have you decided to give the note to me now?"

"Because it may lessen Miguel's pain. We have in the note the reasons for Clarissa's suicide."

"And I say the contents of that note must not be made public," Felipe shouted.

"And I will tell him if you won't," Constanta insisted. "He's suffered enough."

"Learning the contents of that note can only increase his pain," Felipe insisted.

"Lies and secrets increase suffering for everyone made victims of them," Constanta replied, her voice growing stronger.

"We're finished," Jim said to Felipe, then turned to Constanta. "Mrs. Cruz, please give the diary to Lieutenant Jones. It and the note will be entered in evidence. You and Mr. Cruz will hear from me soon."

Harry trailed out of the room in Jones's wake, leaving Miguel and Felipe staring at one another like gladiators and Constanta, head high, moving purposefully toward her husband.

"I'd like to be a mouse in the wall," Harry said to Kathleen, who had waited for him on the garden path, having sent Jones after Jim who was striding away in ten-league boots.

"Yes," she said, staring after Jim. "I don't know when I last saw him this angry." Then she returned her attention to Harry as they moved away from the house. "Okay, what's in the note?"

"I'm giving odds that it's a blackmail note," Harry said, avoiding the point.

"I got that far," Kathleen said in disgust. "Come on, Harry, what's the skinny on Clarissa Cruz?"

Harry shook his head.

"I've got Holly Pike on one side of me and Jim on the other," he answered ruefully, "shaking their heads at me."

"I might have known you'd weasel out on me. Damn! Now I'll have to wring it out of Jim."

"Give him time to cool down," Harry advised with a grin.

"Who do you think wrote the note?" Kathleen asked.

Harry paused for a last look at the garden, brimming with color in the blazing light.

"I don't know," he said, "but if I was a better investigator, I would."

21

Despite his advice to Kathleen, Harry followed Jim to the office.

"People think they can do what they want without consequences," Jim said, visibly still stewing.

Hodges, just back from another pile-up on I-75, winked at Harry, having instantly run into the gale-force wind of Jim's discontent over a misspelling in his report.

"Read this," Jim said and passed Harry the note Constanta had given him. "It sounds crazy to me. It can't be why she killed herself."

Harry had a severe sinking feeling in his stomach as he took the note.

Pasted on a piece of cheap yellow note paper, the message was crudely constructed of letters cut from a newspaper. The message itself was as crude as the construction:

YOU BIN FUCKING YOUR BROTHER. You kid brother's bln butt fucking tyce yellen. You give me $10,000 or everybody's goln to know it.

"Hasn't Holly talked with you about this?" he asked, passing the note back.

"About what?" Jim demanded.

"About Brandon and Clarissa."

"You mean it's true?" he asked, his eyes widening in astonishment.

"Yes," Harry said.

"What's this nonsense about her being Pike's sister?"

"Half sister," Harry said and gave his listeners a quick summary of Zebulon Pike's marriage to Elspeth Mortimer, the birth of Brandon, and his affair with Alejandra and the building of Oleander as her home, followed by the birth of her three children—Felipe, Clarissa, and Miguel.

"Why in the name of the Divinity am I just learning this?" Jim asked, his astonishment turning instantly and obviously into anger as he loomed over his desk at Harry.

"Holly found letters from Clarissa to Brandon. I've read them," Harry began. "There's no doubt about the nature of their relationship. It had been going on for years."

"You've read the letters," Jim repeated.

"Yes. I think they're genuine."

"When did you read them?"

Harry took a deep breath. "Shortly after Brandon was murdered," he admitted.

"Ha!" Hodges shouted, his round face shining with delight. "Now your dick's in the wringer."

"That's enough, Sergeant," Jim barked. "This isn't funny, and neither are you."

"Holly wasn't trying to keep information from you," Harry said, jumping what he guessed were two questions ahead. "Neither was I."

"Let's hear it," Jim said, slumping back into his chair and rubbing his head furiously as he barreled into the wall. "Lord in Heaven!" he groaned, hitching the chair back to the desk. "Go on. I'm listening."

Harry quickly described reading the letters and, a few days later when he learned she had not told him about the letters, telling Holly to make the call.

"Things were piling up on her, Jim," Harry said. "She was

none too stable. It's more my fault than hers. I should have checked with you. Instead, I got busy, let it ride."

"Don't be too hard on yourself," Hodges said in a sympathetic voice. "It must have been right after that you learned about Katherine."

"How long had she known about the letters?" Jim asked curtly.

"They were in Brandon's office safe. She told me she came upon them the day he was killed. Tyce had brought her Brandon's wallet and his keys. She used one of the keys to open the desk where she found the combination to the safe."

"Captain," Hodges said, "I remember Millard Jones telling us he had to get them back from Mrs. Pike. Yellen told him he had given them to her."

"Doesn't matter," Jim said angrily. "She was withholding information. She may have learned earlier in some other way about her husband's infidelity—God spare us—with his half sister, most likely."

He gave his head another scrub.

"Don't you all see? It gives her and Yellen a motive for killing Pike."

"Can we go off the record here for minute?" Harry asked, taking no pleasure in having warned Holly about the risks of not telling Jim about the letters.

Jim hesitated, then nodded.

"What I'm going to tell you stays right here," Harry said, looking from Jim to Hodges. "Agreed?"

"I'll be still as a grave," Hodges said with intense gravity, leaning forward in his chair.

"Let's not turn this into a soap opera, Frank," Jim said, displaying his usual irritation at Hodges's love of gossip.

"I can't prove she wasn't lying," Harry said, interrupting before Jim and Hodges began wrangling over the difference between gossip and a human interest story, "but I'd stake quite a lot on her honesty. As for why she didn't make that call, several things must have factored into the failure."

"Deliberate failure?" Jim persisted.

"Always a possibility," Harry admitted, "but I don't think so. Back to my points—the first is that she'd just lost her husband. Next, she had just had the additional shock of finding out he'd been sleeping with Clarissa for years and years. Finally, she's pregnant and not, she assures me, by either Brandon or Yellen. My guess is she went to a fertility clinic and chose an anonymous donor."

"Why?" Hodges demanded in an offended voice. "A woman as good-looking as she is could have picked any man she wanted and had some fun in the process."

"I gather the pregnancy itself is going all right," Harry said, moving on, "but she hadn't counted on finding herself a single mother so soon."

Jim shook his head.

"Given Pike's medical condition and the way he was behaving—riding Jack and so on—she had to know he was likely to go anytime."

"Yes, but knowing a thing might happen and having it happen are different things," Hodges put in. "Another thing. If she knew he was at death's door, why kill him?"

Jim glowered but stayed silent.

"I only want to add one thing," Harry said. "Holly has insisted all along that she and Yellen are not lovers and never have been. The blackmail note may lend credence to her claim."

Jim sighed.

"I'd like to believe Mrs. Pike is an innocent party," he said, his voice making an abrupt shift into a more sympathetic tone. "Unless she's unbalanced, I can't really believe she poisoned her dog, maimed one of her favorite horses, and burned down a barn, killing another animal and almost killing a third."

Jim hung fire, frowning at the sunlit window.

"You're not thinking Holly sent that note!" Harry said, his incredulity declining even as he spoke.

"What would she need with ten thousand dollars?" Hodges asked in a huffy dismissal of the idea. "If you ask me, I think Elijah Blue is a better prospect."

"Just what she might want us to think," Jim shot back. "Who else would know her husband had a sexual relationship with Clarissa Cruz?" Jim asked.

"Me and possibly Clarissa's ex-husband and Thahn," Harry said, "and that leaves out Clarissa's two brothers."

"Well, I suppose the language and the ten-thousand-dollar demand could be cover," Hodges admitted with obvious reluctance.

"Maybe that's what Clarissa Cruz thought," Jim said gloomily. "I hadn't thought of Thahn or Miguel and Felipe," Jim added, "but it's possible they knew."

"Felipe anyway," Harry said, turning over options. "It would account for his anger with his wife for giving you the note."

"Maybe he knows and Miguel doesn't," Hodge added.

"Remember," Harry said to Jim, "Constanta said she would tell Miguel if her husband didn't. So, I think it's safe to assume Miguel did not know about the relationship."

"Too many *maybes*," Jim said, "Well, I'll send the note and the diary to the evidence section and have Jones and his people comb through the diary. The local labs and the FBI will make the usual tests," Jim said. "Then, when we get the reports back, we'll take another look."

Harry nodded, although he had no intention of waiting.

He left Jim's office in a very troubled frame of mind. The possibility that Holly had sent that note was deeply disturbing to him. At first he had thought it an outrageous suggestion and felt guilty for even suspecting it might be true; but once it was in his mind it stuck there, and the longer it stuck there, the less ridiculous it became.

"No," he said aloud as he clambered into the Rover, "it can't be true."

"Have you been sitting out here all the time I've been gone?" Harry asked in dismay when he found Katherine on the lanai.

"Except for taking short walks," she said easily, closing her book. "I find reading tires me. Sentences can suddenly get all mixed up in my head. By the way, I saw a pair of medium-sized dogs between here and Tucker's place. They jumped into the road in front of me, paused for a look, then ran on."

"What color were they?"

"A pale, streaked brown, I guess. They didn't seem interested in me."

"Coyotes," Harry said in disgust. "I expect they were on their way to scout out Tucker's hen house."

"Coyotes!" she said, getting up. "How long have there been coyotes on the Hammock?"

"A young pair, the two you just saw, moved in awhile back," Harry told her. "They're thinning out the rabbits and the young raccoons when they catch one without its mother."

"I love this place," she said with a sigh, getting up, "but it's got its savage side."

"Mother Nature is not sentimental," Harry agreed, "but she maintains the balance."

"You don't look well," she said, putting glasses back on to look at Harry more closely. "Are you feeling all right?"

"I don't think I'm coming down with anything more serious than middle age," he said with a show of liveliness, which clearly failed to impress Katherine.

"I'll make us some coffee," she said, pushing him toward the kitchen, "and you'll tell me what's wrong."

"Do you think Holly is angry enough with her husband and the Cruz woman to do such a thing?" Katherine asked skeptically, sitting down across the table from him when he finished talking. "It doesn't sound like the woman you've been telling me about."

"I don't want to think so," he said. "I'd rather it was Elijah Blue."

"Is there any way of telling?"

"Jim is sending the note to the labs to see what information can be lifted from it. I'm not very optimistic, and so far at least, no envelope has been found."

"So you don't know how long ago she got the note."

"Right. It was inserted in the entry that Clarissa had written three days before her death."

"Does she mention it in the entry?" Katherine asked, refilling their cups.

"I didn't see the diary, but Constanta said there was no mention of the note in the entry for that day or any of the final three."

"Who has the diary now?"

"Millard Jones and his team."

"Millard Jones," Katherine said with a pensive smile that did not include Harry. "I haven't thought of him for years. Is he still . . ."

"Whatever you were going to ask," Harry said a little sourly, "the answer is yes."

"Yes," Katherine said, going a little pink, "I remember now." She paused to laugh. "There was something . . ."

"Don't tell me," Harry said, holding up both hands. "I've just had to watch two women light up like Christmas trees in his presence. One of them was Kathleen Towers. He had Jim swearing just watching him hand Kathleen out of a squad car."

"By the way, speaking of swearing, Soñadora called while I was out and left you a message."

"What is it?" Harry asked, instantly worried.

"I don't know. As soon as I heard her voice, I shut it off."

"You didn't need . . ."

He stopped, and they sat for a while in an uncomfortable silence.

"You know, don't you, Harry, that I should never have come here?" Katherine said at last.

Harry wasn't sure whether it was sadness or humiliation that was darkening her voice, but whichever it was, it was a knife in his side.

"I'm sorry you feel that way," he replied. "I'm particularly sorry it's now giving you pain. For my part, I'm glad you came, that you're here, and that the operation is a success."

"I'm very grateful to you for caring and caring *for* me," she told him, reaching across the table to take his hand, "but I'm not sure I'm going to forgive either one of us for behaving the way we did up to the time I went into the hospital."

" 'Somewhere, out beyond our ideas of right doing and wrongdoing, there is a field,' " Harry said, struggling for a way out of the trap she had sprung. " 'I'll meet you there.' "

Katherine gave a small, wry laugh.

"I don't think Rumi had us in mind, Harry," she said, patting his hand, then leaning back in her chair.

Harry saw her leaning away from him as something more than easing her back. He experienced a profound sense of her withdrawing from him, and it hurt. It hurt even more when he considered what she had said about not forgiving him or herself.

"How much of what happened between your getting here and going to the hospital do you remember?" he asked, deciding that he should try to get all the way through this ethical briar patch.

"As I said before, it's patchy, but bit by bit it's coming back."

"And the more you remember, the worse it makes you feel."

Katherine looked at him sharply.

"If talking about this is going to make you angry, I don't want to go on with it."

"I'm not going to break the furniture. I'm just trying to separate what you think in hindsight from what you experienced while we were sleeping together."

"It doesn't matter what I felt. I had a growth pressing against my brain that prevented me from thinking straight. What was your excuse?"

She paused, and Harry thought, *I was in that field waiting, and you came.* Too easy, he told himself. I may have been in full flight into your arms, hoping never to leave them, and for that I abandoned Soñadora. Lost in that thought, he forgot Katherine's question.

"All right," she said, apparently tired of waiting or, perhaps, impelled by her own train of thought. "I'll tell you what I felt. It was wonderful. It was the best sex I ever had in my life."

She stopped, a shadow of what Harry thought was sadness passed over her face, making her look suddenly old.

"Don't lose it, Katherine," Harry said quietly.

"What do you mean, *lose* it!" she demanded, her voice rising and hardening. "I never had it. Whoever I was with that tumor had it."

It was the old Katherine in her old place, riddled with guilt and responsibility. It was the woman he had married. He gave up hoping they could recapture it.

"I'm sorry you feel that way," he said quietly, "but it's over, and it can't be undone."

"No," she said, "and we'll just have to live with it."

And I wish you joy in the task, he thought, but, fortunately, did not say it.

22

Katherine had gone up to her room to rest, and Harry, feeling the walls pressing in on him, decided to walk to Tucker's place and call Soñadora on the way. The sun was throwing long shadows over the white sand road, and the Gulf wind was stirring the leaves, making their shadows dance on the sand. On an ordinary day, the sight would have cheered him, but he dialed Soñadora's number with no lift in his spirits.

"I wanted to hear your voice," she said, not sounding very cheerful herself.

"What's wrong?" he asked.

"Why must you always ask me what's wrong when I say something?" she demanded.

"Okay, I'm pressing the rewind button. Now we're back to the beginning. How are you?"

"I'm all right, but I have several things to discuss with you, and I don't want to do it over the phone."

"Lunch tomorrow?"

"I wanted to see you tonight, but that is not realistic, I suppose. How is Katherine?"

"No complications so far, which is good news. She still tires very easily. I'm keeping house and also working. I can leave her during the day. Are you sure nothing's wrong?"

"Well, *yes* somewhat and *no* a little. We will talk tomorrow. Right now, I have work to do. Goodbye."

Harry shook his head and thought that he had had some of

his least satisfactory conversations with her on the phone. "In fact," he complained, "a lot of the time I don't know what she's saying. What, for instance, does '*yes* somewhat' and '*no* a little' mean?"

He got no answer. Soon after that a six-foot indigo snake dropped from a large live oak limb just as he walked under it, misjudged, and landed on Harry's shoulders instead of on the ground. In its eagerness to escape, it managed to wrap itself briefly around his neck and then entangle itself briefly in his legs before slithering away into the tall grass at the edge of the road. Once his breathing was nearly normal, Harry found the experience had bucked him up significantly.

Harry found Tucker turning over one of his compost piles with a garden fork. After the two men had shaken hands, Harry told Tucker about the snake and concluded by saying, "I think it was more apologetic than frightened. It was really too big to be frightened of anything smaller than an alligator."

"The indigo is one of the most beautiful creatures in God's Kingdom," Tucker said when he stopped laughing. "Do you remember the indigo that wintered in the barn a few years ago? She kept the rats down, you'll remember, but as long as she was in there, Sanchez wouldn't go near the barn after dark. Oh, Brother! got a lot of mileage out of that and teased him unmercifully. What's the news? How's Katherine?"

"She's doing well. This morning she tried to walk over to see you but had to give it up. It turned out to be too tiring for her."

"I'm glad to hear she's improving."

"So am I. Do you want some help here?"

"Yes, there's another fork in the barn."

"I've got some bad news," Harry said, retuning with a fork and setting to work beside the old farmer, who appeared to Harry to have just about fully recovered from his accident.

"Is it about Clarissa Cruz?" Tucker asked.

"The jungle drums?" Harry asked.

Tucker stopped digging and leaned on his fork handle.

"Is everybody sure she killed herself?" he asked.

"Does that mean you're not?" Harry asked, pulling off his hat and using it to mop his face.

He noticed with a sting of embarrassment that Tucker showed no sign of sweating from his efforts.

"I don't know enough to have an opinion," Tucker said, "but I notice you haven't answered my question."

"Kathleen Towers says there are no traces of her having been forced. Aside from the extensive damage done by the bullet at the exit point at the back of her head, there were no bruises, scratches, or abrasions anywhere on her body, and the room where she died showed no signs of a struggle."

"As I remember, she was an average-sized woman and in good health."

Tucker began digging again, and Harry replaced his hat and bent to his task of turning over the dark, crumbling pile.

"Even a strong man couldn't have put a gun in her mouth without a struggle," he agreed. "Except for Miguel, everyone is satisfied that she did the job herself."

"Almost her child," Tucker said, "certainly her favorite, who had always lived with her. He'd find it hard to accept. Why did she kill herself?"

"I doubt we'll ever know for sure," Harry said. "She apparently didn't leave any explanation."

"Unless something went haywire in her brain," Tucker said. "And if it did, I'd wager it had to do with Brandon Pike's death."

"I can't tell you much," Harry said, "because the State Attorney has put a lock on all information, but I can say that someone sent her a blackmail note. Her sister-in-law Constanta found it in Clarissa's diary, held onto it for a while, showed it to her husband, and then, against his wishes, gave it to Jim. He nearly had a heart attack when he found out she and Felipe had been withholding it."

"Which leads me to think I'm right. Five will get you ten it is about her relationship with Brandon."

"I'm not betting against that being so," Harry said, deciding not to bring up the question of Miguel and Yellen. "A thornier issue is who sent Clarissa the letter."

"Have Jim's people finished studying it?"

"Not as far as I know," Harry answered.

"Not, I assume, a literary masterpiece."

"No, but Jim thinks that it may be a ruse."

"As well as the demand for money? Well, I suppose you can't confirm that, but it's a possibility that the person who sent it was trying to fix the blame on someone else."

"Jim thinks so."

Tucker nodded, stepped back, and surveyed their progress.

"We're done here," he said. "I'm obliged to you for your help," he added, staring critically at Harry. "You're going to need a fresh shirt. You've soaked that one through."

"Too much desk work," Harry said lamely.

"Get yourself ready for an unpleasant surprise when you find out who sent that letter," Tucker said, dismissing Harry's excuse. "I think the sender might have guessed the outcome of Clarissa's reading that note."

It was a new and chilling thought, and Harry stopped to consider it.

"If you're thinking what I suspect, there's no way to prepare for that kind of surprise," Harry said unhappily, "especially if you've got Holly Pike in mind."

"Who else had all that information?"

Harry ran over the list in his mind before answering.

"At the time of Clarissa's death," Harry said, "I think only Clarissa, Holly, and I and, possibly, Felipe and Constanta had all the information in the note. Those who might have known would have to include Elijah Blue, Thahn, and Tyce Yellen—unless she told others I don't know about."

"You can take Tyce Yellen and Felipe Cruz out of the list," Tucker said, wiping his fork on the grass and starting for the barn. "One's in no condition to write anything, and the other is, so far as I know, without motive. I also doubt Thahn had anything to do with it."

"Too loyal to the Pikes?" Harry asked, following Tucker out of the shade of the trees and into the sun.

"Not only that," Tucker agreed. "In the years he and his wife have been with the Pikes, Brandon has brought most of Thahn and his wife's relations over here and settled them in Colonial Town in Orlando." Tucker paused to chuckle. "Brandon once told me that he feared he was weakening Vietnam through a population drain."

Harry was too preoccupied with the possibility Holly had written that note to be amused by Tucker's story.

"I've had a really nasty thought," Harry said. "Tell me I'm crazy."

"I've been telling you that for a long time," Tucker said as they went into the barn and put away the forks. "Share your thought with me."

"If Holly sent that note, she put the gun in Clarissa's mouth, pulled the trigger, and didn't leave a mark on her."

Harry filled the time driving to meet with Holly trying to think of some way to discuss his concerns about the sender of the note without alerting her to his suspicions that she might have sent it and not deeply offending her if she hadn't. By the time he stepped out of the Rover, to be greeted by Nip and Tuck, he had not solved his problem.

Thahn met him and his honor guard at the door and led him

through the quiet house, smelling faintly of furniture polish and peonies, its cool air stirred by the slowly revolving fans.

"Before I leave, Thahn," Harry said, "I have something to discuss with you if it's convenient."

"Is it a personal matter you wish to discuss, Mr. Brock?"

"No," Harry said, "it concerns Clarissa Cruz's death."

"Then I will require Mrs. Pike's permission," Thahn replied.

"Okay," Harry said. "I'll ask her."

"I will require confirmation from Mrs. Pike," he said, knocking on Brandon's office door, already half open.

"Harry!" Holly said in a startled voice, dropping her pen when she looked up from the desk where she was sitting among a froth of papers and files and saw him waiting with Thahn. "Come in, come in. I apologize for not meeting you. I completely lost track of the time. Thank you, Thahn."

"Wait, Thahn," Harry said, still standing in the door. "Holly, I want to ask him some questions before I leave. They concern Clarissa's death. Does he have your permission to answer them?"

Whatever she said to him in what Harry thought was Vietnamese was, apparently, adequate for the situation because when she was done, Thahn bowed slightly and said, "Very well, Mrs. Pike," and withdrew silently.

"Did you say yes or no?" Harry asked, approaching the desk.

"I said yes, but he could choose for himself which, if any, of the questions to answer."

"I had no idea you spoke his language," Harry said.

"I don't. That was Mandarin Chinese. Most Vietnamese Thahn's age know some Chinese, although they do not like to speak it. I've always wanted to visit China, and after I married Brandon and the money to go became available, I began studying the language in a very desultory way. What I know wouldn't take me far."

"I'm puzzled as to why you thought it necessary to use it

now," Harry said.

"Simple," she said with apparent frankness. "It's a matter of face. Telling him in a language you understand that he is free to refuse to answer any question he chooses not to would also tell you he requires my permission to refuse to answer. That would cause him to lose some face."

"And that would translate . . . ?"

Harry was fairly sure he had been given the good reason rather than the real one, but how could he be sure?

"Harry," she said, sending her chair skidding back from the desk as she jumped to her feet. "What's wrong? Are you angry with me? What is it?"

It was Harry's turn to be alarmed. He thought he had kept his doubts entirely out of sight. The dogs came onto their feet as suddenly as Holly, staring at her with ears pricked.

"No, no," he said. "I'm not angry with you, but there's something I've got to tell you and . . ."

By the time he had finished speaking, Holly had come around the desk and was standing in front of him.

"Is it Katherine?" she asked, reaching out and grasping his arms, her eyes searching his face.

Harry now added guilt to the medley of feelings that was making him into a monkey puzzle tree.

"It's not about me," he said. "I'm sorry I gave you that idea. It's about Clarissa's suicide."

"Oh, God," she said, dropping her hands. "You had me really worried. Come over here. Let's sit down. What's been going on that has you so upset?"

Oh, nothing, he thought, as she led him, closely flanked by Nip and Tuck, who appeared to be holding up fairly well, to a pair of leather chairs angled toward one of the study's long windows, *except that I think you may have killed Clarissa Cruz.*

"Now, tell me," she said when they were seated.

"Jim Snyder called a meeting the other day at Oleander," Harry began with all of the enthusiasm of a man approaching a colonoscopy.

"Why?" she demanded, sitting forward in her chair, hands clasped between her knees, urging him on.

"He was determined to break the deadlock that Miguel has created in the State Attorney's Office over whether Clarissa's death was murder or suicide."

"Oh!" she exclaimed, throwing up her hands, "I know that. I don't care that I wasn't invited. Why should I have been?"

"How did you learn about the meeting?"

"Ho Xuang heard about it from the Cruz cook."

"Who?" Harry asked.

"Ho Xuang, my cook!" she said impatiently. "Thahn's wife. Didn't you talk with her after Brandon's death?"

"No." Harry said. "Jim's people may have. But that's not the important part."

"You know, Harry, it's odd. I don't remember a lot about those first days after his death." She paused and stared out the window for a moment, then turned back to him and said, brightening, "Well, tell me the rest of it."

Harry had used the pause to gather his own resources. Now, as he went on, he watched her closely to see how she was reacting.

"It was a very contentious meeting. Miguel was furious, insisting that his sister had absolutely no reason to kill herself and that she must have been murdered. Jim, increasingly frustrated, called on each of his team, who tried with equal determination to persuade Miguel it could have been nothing but suicide."

So far as Harry could see, Holly's demeanor showed nothing but interest.

"I'm astonished that the Captain has allowed a hysterical young man, who's obviously distraught with grief, to prevent him from closing the investigation and get back to finding Brandon's killer," she said with sudden vehemence.

Harry was surprised by the intensity of Holly's response, although she had reason enough. The investigation of her husband's death had produced little to bring her any comfort.

"I think it's the State Attorney's Office that's responsible," he said, "not Jim. You see, it's a political issue. Clarissa was an important Hispanic woman in Tequesta County and because an election's in the offing, they don't want even a glimmer of doubt to mar the State's position regarding her death. They especially don't want it said that because she was Hispanic, the State closed the case without seriously considering that she might have been murdered."

Holly stared at Harry, frowning and obviously still unsatisfied.

"Do you think she was murdered?" Holly asked.

Harry hesitated, considered saying, *it depends on what you mean by murdered,* then said, "I think Clarissa was alone when she died. I think she shot herself."

"Why do I detect something not said in your answer?"

Harry felt himself being pushed where he didn't want to go but had to go. But at this point, he knew he had no choice.

"It's possible the person who killed her wasn't in the room."

"Make sense, Harry."

So she hadn't taken the bait.

"Why do you think she killed herself?" he asked, spinning the wheel.

"Did she leave a note of any kind?"

"I don't think so."

Holly bit the corner of her lip for a moment.

"Okay, she had to know something that we don't."

If this was a performance, it was a good one, Harry thought with a mixture of relief and disappointment.

"Oh, we know all right," Harry said, stretching things out, testing again.

"I certainly don't know anything that would have made her kill herself," Holly said flatly.

Harry gave up.

"Someone sent her a note threatening to expose her relationship with Brandon and her brother's homosexual relationship with Tyce Yellen," he said.

"Well, well," she said, dropping back in her chair with a flicker of a smile, "and the threat was enough to kill her. What did the writer want?"

"You mean aside from her death?"

"How could he have known the threat would be enough to do it?" Holly asked dismissively.

"What makes you think it was a man who wrote the note?"

She crossed her legs and began to swing her foot while staring out the window, appearing to be thinking about Harry's question, but when she spoke it was to ask one of her own.

"Harry, be honest with me," she said, turning back to face him, "which you haven't been up to now. Do you think I wrote that note?"

He had no intention of answering the question.

"Did you?" he asked.

"What do you think? No, wait. I'm not sorry Clarissa Cruz is dead. I know it's wicked, but I'm not. Now, answer my question."

The question and her cold gaze both angered and pained him. They were not what he had hoped for, and he stood, too disturbed to go on sitting.

"It doesn't matter what I think," he said sharply, "but ask yourself this question: Who besides you, Clarissa, and maybe Felipe and Constanta knew that Clarissa Cruz and Brandon were lovers and that Miguel Cruz was in a homosexual relationship with Tyce Yellen?"

Harry's leave-taking from Holly was strained and unsatisfactory. He had hoped to broach the question in a much more gentle fashion, but her combative refusal to answer his question, even if wholly in character, and his mixed reactions to the possibility that she might have sent Clarissa that note had left him thoroughly discomposed.

His conversation with Thahn was no more satisfactory. He had planned to ask him if he had been asked recently by anyone, including Mrs. Pike, to dispose of any newspapers that had parts of pages cut out.

"Think very carefully about what I'm going to ask you, Thahn," he said as a lead-in after thanking him for agreeing to talk with him, "because the police may be back to ask you the same thing."

"Being careful comes naturally to me, Mr. Brock," he said with a dry smile, "I was raised where answering carelessly could be fatal. What is it you wish to ask me?"

"Have you come upon any newspapers in the house recently that have had sections of pages cut out?"

"I presume your interest in such matters comes from the way in which the note found in Ms. Cruz's diary was constructed."

"You know of this by way of the Oleander cook."

Thahn answered with a small nod.

It occurred to Harry that the dry smile and the equally dry nod was as close to insolence as Thahn would let himself come, and that Thahn either despised him or was using insolence as a way of limiting Harry's ability to extract information from him. Harry decided to test his theory.

"I suppose you know the contents of the note?"

This time the nod was so slight that it was clearly meant as an insult.

Uh-huh, Harry thought.

"How long have you known about Brandon and Clarissa's relationship?"

"I know nothing of Mr. Pike's activities outside the house," he replied.

"You didn't know that for years he visited her several times a week?"

"Mr. Brock," Thahn said, "why are you asking me these questions?"

"Because I want your help, Thahn."

"Help with what?"

It was, Harry supposed, evidence of progress that Thahn was showing *some* interest.

"To protect Mrs. Pike, which I am paid to do as you are."

"Why does she need our help?" Thahn asked, suspicion showing in his voice.

"Are you aware that the person who wrote that note to Clarissa Pike broke the law?"

"Of course. I believe he was attempting to extort money from her."

"Do you know who the man is?"

"What?"

"You said, '*he* was attempting to extort money from her.' "

For the first time since Harry and Thahn had begun talking, Thahn's gaze wavered. "I assumed . . ."

"Not good enough," Harry said.

Thahn made a bow and said, "You have made your point, Mr. Brock."

"If they haven't already," Harry continued, "the police will soon suspect as I have and possibly you that the form of the note is a ruse, that the person who wrote it doesn't want the money, and wrote the letter to extract something else from Ms. Cruz."

"Her death," Thahn said without hesitation.

"Exactly."

"And of those knowing about the two revelations in the note, the one who would, arguably, most want her dead is Mrs. Pike."

"Bingo," Harry said.

"A strange word," Thahn said, "but oddly appropriate. Are you aware that she has only recently become fully aware of Mr. Pike's relationship with his half sister?"

"The police know that," Harry said.

"It seems unlikely that, even if it could be proved that Mrs. Pike wrote the note, she could be proven guilty of murdering or even intending to murder Ms. Cruz."

"Possibly not."

"I have found nothing that would suggest that Mrs. Pike wrote the note," Thahn added.

"That's good news. Were you surprised by the news of Clarissa Cruz's suicide?"

"Until I learned of the note she had received and its contents. Then, no longer. She was profoundly ashamed of her brother's relationship with Mr. Yellen."

"More ashamed of that than her love affair with Brandon Pike?"

"I do not think she was at all ashamed of that. She loved Mr. Pike with all her heart and would have lived openly with him had he wished it, which he did not."

"And his marrying Mrs. Pike?"

"It was a terrible blow to her, but still she clung to him."

"And his death?"

"A terrible blow."

It was Harry's turn to nod.

"Thank you, Thahn," he said. "Now I have to persuade Mrs.

Pike that she must take this business of the note seriously."

They walked out of the room together, talking easily about the rebuilding of Barn One.

As Thahn opened the front door for Harry, he said quietly as though it was a casual observation, "Mrs. Pike goes most quickly in the direction she thinks she has chosen."

"I've noticed," Harry said with a rueful laugh, stepping out into the blazing light of the day. "Don't think I haven't noticed."

23

"You have been talking about Holly Pike and Clarissa Cruz's suicide for ten minutes," Soñadora said, moving her glass of Perrier water a fraction of an inch to the right.

She and Harry were seated at a corner table in The Conch Shell, a crowded, moderately upscale strip mall restaurant in northern Avola, bright with midday conversation and the cheering aroma of island herbs and spices. Soñadora was there under duress, regarding restaurants without chickens under the table as decadent.

"Sorry," Harry said. "Clarissa's suicide has opened a huge can of worms, and Jim has had no success in keeping them in the can."

"Not a picture I want in my mind while waiting to eat," she said coolly, glancing around the room.

"Okay," he said. "Your turn."

Her hip-length black hair was braided and wound around her head, a style that tended to pull up slightly the outer corners of her eyes, adding to her beauty, and she was wearing a dark blue sun dress he particularly liked, together with a gossamer scarlet shawl, drawn loosely across her shoulders. When they entered the restaurant, Harry noticed there was scarcely a pair of eyes that had not followed her to their table. He also noticed that she was, as usual, apparently either indifferent to or unaware of the attention she attracted.

He thought of that now, looking at her and waiting to hear

what she had to say, but he anticipated her by asking, "Soñadora, do you have any idea how beautiful you are?"

"Harry," she said, abandoning her glass and frowning at him, "try not to be so frivolous. I have serious things to discuss with you."

"I'm listening," he said, frustrated by her refusal to take any pleasure from his compliments.

Their food came and they ate—at least Harry did, listening while she talked.

"I have been training Gabriela Rodriguez to take over parts of my job at *Salvamento*," she began, picking at her salad without actually eating any of it.

"Why?" Harry said, made instantly suspicious by the suddenly casual tone of her voice.

"It was my intention to spend more time with you," she said, the chill still in her voice, "but that has not been possible."

He would have said that their separation was temporary had she not interrupted him.

"I have been thinking a lot about my life," she told him as though it were something ordinary.

"What does that mean?" he demanded.

"It doesn't have to mean anything," she fired back. "I've just been doing it."

"And?"

"I've decided I need more time."

Harry put down his fork.

"Tell me," he said.

Instead, she began to eat.

"Eat and talk at the same time," he said.

"It's impolite," she said.

"You won't listen when I say you're beautiful," he told her. "So let's try this, you are one of the most difficult people to talk with I've ever met."

She paused over her salad and widened her eyes at him.

"Untrue," she complained. "I am very direct."

"You are devious and deliberately obtuse."

She smiled warmly and arched her back slightly, lifting her breasts toward him.

"Do you like me better this way?" she asked in a soft, caressing voice.

"Not funny," he said, feeling his face burn.

"Astonishing," she said, returning to her salad. "You turn on and off like a faucet."

Harry reminded himself that what he was going through was the consequence of not telling this woman in advance that Katherine was coming to the Hammock and that his penance was not yet completed. However, it was also, obviously, too late for regrets.

"When you have pulled your knife out of me and wiped the blade," he said, "why not say what you want to say?"

"And watch you bleed?" she said with a thin smile. "It would give me pleasure."

Then she put down her fork, straightened herself in her chair, and seemed to shake something off.

"I'm sorry," she said. "We must be alone when we talk about my anger, which will not be soon. When is Katherine leaving? Is she leaving?"

"Yes, she's leaving, but for the moment she's still seeing the doctors."

"This has become a *telenovela*," Soñadora said, her voice graveled with disgust. "I cannot cope. Please return me to *Salvamento*."

She did not speak to him again until she was getting out of the Rover. Then she paused and twisting toward him said, "How could you have done this?"

Without waiting for an answer, she flung herself the rest of the way out of the cab and slammed the door hard enough to rock the SUV. Running across the yard, she vanished into *Salvamento.*

As Harry sat staring at the door, two lines of bitter poetry sprang out of the moment and ran roughshod through his head: "All this the world well knows, but knows not well / To shun the heaven that leads men to this hell."

On his way to talk with Jim, who was waiting for him on a bridge in East Avola, Harry cooled down enough to recant his quotation from Shakespeare's sonnet on lust and muttered, "If anyone's listening, I didn't mean it."

The quasi confession, however, did nothing to lessen his sense of guilt as far as Soñadora was concerned.

The first person he met on the bridge was Hodges.

"I've been promoted to directing traffic," he announced while leaning against the bridge railing and looking east and west along the deserted road running through tall swamp grass and occasional clumps of cabbage palms, straight as a ruled line from horizon to horizon.

The bridge itself was crowded with four Sheriff Department's cruisers, two ten-wheel tow trucks, and a derrick, whose steel arm dangled over the water like a huge yellow fishing pole. Harry saw that Jim was engaged in apparently heated debate with three other men, dressed in work clothes. The three troopers were listening to whatever was being said and looking bored.

"What's going on here?" Harry said.

"If you can believe it," Hodges said, pointing at two boys, who looked to Harry to be about twelve, sitting on their heels at the far end of the bridge, their bicycles leaning against the railing beside them. "If you can believe it," Hodges continued, "those two were diving in the canal with homemade spear guns when they found the truck, standing upright on the bottom with two people still sitting in it."

"They were spear fishing in the Louis Faubus Canal?" Harry asked, incredulous.

"Don't it beat two biscuits and a side?" Hodges demanded, his red face lighting up in grin. "And they're alive to tell about it."

"Miraculous," Harry agreed.

"It gets better," Hodges said. "They'd been trying to spear a big alligator. The critter got sick of being poked and swam down into the deep water. Those two idiots followed him down and found the truck. Then they got back on shore, and one of them used his cell phone to call 911."

"What's going on now?" Harry asked.

"There was a screw-up and two tow trucks were called instead of one. The Captain's trying to sort out which one gets the job—supposing there really is a truck down there."

"Why are you and Jim out here instead of some people from your C.I.D. squad?" Harry asked.

"Shorthanded," Hodges grumped. "The Department's doing a half-assed job nowadays, if you ask me. Just look how the investigation of Brandon Pike's killing and what's followed it is being neglected! And we're still waiting to hear from the lab about that damned blackmail note."

The discussion among the men by the trucks having apparently broken up, one of the drivers turned his truck around and drove past Harry and Hodges toward Avola without returning Hodges's wave.

"Pissed," he said, watching him put on speed.

"Poor loser," Jim said, joining them. "They flipped a coin. He lost."

Harry thought Jim looked tired and said so.

"The department's heavy-laden, and that's a fact," Jim said in a resigned voice. "Sergeant, call in and tell Maureen we need

259

two divers out here. If she balks, tell her this water's too dangerous for one person to work in."

"She's been on the warpath lately over the budget," Hodges said with a worried expression, "and you know what that means."

"Just do it. Don't let yourself be talked out of it. It's got to be two people."

"You said you wanted to see me," Harry said as soon as Hodges was out of earshot.

"I need some help."

"All right."

"That blackmail note Clarissa Cruz got before she died," Jim said. "What do you make of it?"

"I think it's why she killed herself, if that's what you mean," Harry replied, watching a blue and white bird with a deeply forked tail swooping and hovering along the north side of the bridge.

"Beautiful bird," Jim said. "Looks like a big barn swallow."

"Swallow-tailed kite," Harry said. "It's a small raptor, feeds on lizards and small snakes and small mammals. It plucks lizards and palm rats off palms and palmettos and probably has a nest nearby."

"I don't think I've ever seen one before. Is it common here?"

"In the summer. In the winter it migrates to South America."

"Where did you learn all this stuff?" Jim asked, turning his attention back to Harry.

"It's better than working," Harry said. "What do you think about the note? You were pretty angry about it the last time I saw you."

"I wanted to wring Constanta and Felipe Cruz's necks," he admitted.

"One of these days!" Hodges roared, hurrying toward them. "One of these days, I swear I'm going to take her down to the river and drown her."

The Sergeant's face was red and streaked with sweat.

"Don't give her an excuse," Jim said, gripping Hodges by the shoulder and giving him a shake. "She'd pull your arm off and gnaw on it while you bled to death. Don't even think of it."

Jim spoke with such conviction that even Hodges, wrathful as he was, fell in with Harry and gave a bellow of laughter. Harry laughed but it rang hollow.

"Did you get the divers?" Jim asked, straight-faced.

"I got them," Hodges said, wiping his face with a red-checked bandanna, "but not before there was smoke on the water."

"Good," Jim said, "Now go talk to those two boys, take down what they have to say, thank them for helping, give them Hail Columbia for swimming in the canal, and send them home. Then get all but one of those deputies back on the road."

Hodges lumbered off, cursing Maureen O'Reilly again under his breath and mopping his face as he went.

"Have you had enough of this sun?" Jim asked.

"Want to use the Rover?"

"Yes, I don't want to listen to my radio yammer at me."

"We were talking about the blackmail note," Harry said as the air conditioner began an assault on the cab's fiery furnace.

"We've eliminated you, Constanta, Felipe, Miguel, Yellen, and Clarissa Cruz's ex-husband," Jim said, pulling off his hat and dropping it on his lap.

"Where did you find the husband?" Harry asked, his curiosity aroused.

"Puerto Rico. He's married, three kids, running a string of travel agencies and about as likely to have sent that note as Frank."

"Jim," Harry said, turning down the blast of cold air, "this is a strange world."

Jim was sitting with his eyes closed and his head resting on the back of the seat.

"When I was a kid," he said wearily, "I thought the people in that mountain hollow where I grew up must have been sorted out for weirdness and put in there to multiply, but after I left home I found the inhabitants of the flat world to be even more peculiar."

"Who put that note together?" Harry asked.

"You're not going to like this," Jim said, opening his eyes and turning toward Harry, "but I think Holly Pike may have done it."

"I could pretend to be surprised and shocked," Harry replied, "but I've been wrestling with that possibility for a while now. Have you decided Elijah Blue didn't do it?"

"No, and I'm working on a warrant to search his house. I should have it by the time I get back to the office. Have you said anything to her about the note?"

"I asked her if she wrote it."

"What did she say?"

"She asked me what I thought."

Harry paused for a long moment without speaking. When he did, he put in words the fear that lay behind his wondering whether or not she had composed the note.

"She will not tell me whether she wrote the note or not," he said, continuing. "She's angry and probably hurt because I asked, but here's the thing, she's not going to answer if your people ask her."

"Then she's going to regret it," Jim said grimly.

Harry got to his feet when he saw Katherine walking down the corridor toward him. She was smiling.

"They've cut you loose," Harry said when she reached him, trying to sound happy.

He put out his arms, and she walked into them, relief

brightening her face.

"I'm good to go," she said, kissing him, then hugging him hard.

Harry held her as long as he could, the knowledge of her release making real the fact that he would soon be losing her. She dropped her arms, and he released her.

"Let's get out of here," she said, no longer smiling. "I don't care if I never have to go into a hospital again."

They left, with Harry aware of a new awkwardness between them, due, he assumed, to the shared awareness that her reason for remaining with him was gone.

"You can stay," Harry said, refusing to pretend nothing had changed, "that is, if you want to."

"Of course I want to," Katherine said with a small frown, "but you know I can't, so why ask?"

"Because I don't want you to leave, and I want to be sure you know it."

"I know it, Harry," she said. "Thank you."

"Then why do it?" He regretted the note of anger that had crept into his voice.

"You *know* why Harry," she replied equally sharply. "Why do we have to keep going over it?"

"Well, tell me again. Obviously, I'm not getting it."

They were close to quarreling. Harry knew it, didn't want it, but couldn't seem to let it go.

Of course I can't, he thought, *because if I do, she'll leave. She's going to leave anyway.*

"All right, I'll tell you again. All I do is give both of us pain," she said. "You and I can't live together, Harry, because you won't stop what you're doing and get a sensible job in which you're not at almost constant risk of being killed—and don't quote actuarial tables to me. Your body is covered with scars."

"You make it sound as if I'm a bullet-riddled Queequeg!"

Harry protested.

"Who?" Katherine demanded.

"Never mind. It's true I've had one or two accidents . . ."

"Let's try to be real here. They weren't accidents. People were trying to kill you."

"That's true," he said, partially recovering his sanity, "and you're right. I'm not going to give up what I'm doing."

"It's also true that you're not going to leave the Hammock."

"Feet first," he said. "Maybe not even then."

She laughed and touched his arm.

"I'll make flight arrangements and call the kids to warn them their good times are coming to an end."

That evening, sitting on the lanai with a bottle of wine between them and a huge yellow moon rising over Puc Puggy Creek, Harry had almost resigned himself to her going, *almost* being the operative word.

He was trying to think of something to say that might change her mind when Katherine broke the silence between them. There was seldom any extended silence on the Hammock, especially at night, with the croaking, buzzing, humming, and sighing of colony frogs, locusts, night jars, and the wind in the trees, rising and falling in waves of sound.

"Harry," she began hesitantly, "there's something I want to say, but if it doesn't come out right, I want you to know it will be my best shot."

"I'm listening," he said.

"I remember now very clearly the way we made love before I was operated on."

"So do I," he said. "It was . . ."

"Please let me finish. It won't take long."

"Go," he said.

"It was wonderful. I just want you to know that. If you hadn't been with Soñadora . . ."

"Stop there," Harry said. "Soñadora is my business, not yours."

"I can't, won't share you, Harry."

"You weren't sharing me. You aren't sharing me."

"Harry, you know it was wrong."

"It didn't feel that way."

She was quiet for a while. Then she reached out and caught his hand.

"No, it didn't," she said with a sigh, "and we both know why."

24

While he and Katherine were eating breakfast, Harry's cell rang. He listened a moment and said, "I'll call you back."

"That was Holly Pike," he said, laying the phone on the table. "She wants to see me."

"Go," Katherine said, refilling their cups with coffee. "I don't need looking after. I have calls to make, shopping to do, and I want to visit with Tucker. Will you be home for dinner?"

"Yes," he said, watching her with mingled pain and pleasure. She was wearing a pair of faded jeans cut down to shorts, and one of his old blue shirts, its tails knotted around her waist.

Seeing her dressed that way had rolled back time for him. It was how she had always dressed when Jesse and Minna were young.

"Whose shirts do you wear when you're home?" Harry asked with a grin.

They had parted friends before going to bed the night before, but, too late, he regretted the question. She returned his grin, however, and, turning away, told him it was none of his business, giving her hips a little extra swing as she carried the coffee pot back to the sideboard.

"God will punish you for that," he said and picked up the phone.

"How long has Elijah been gone?" Harry asked.

"Three days," Holly said.

They and the two dogs were standing outside Barn Two, waiting for their horses to be saddled. Behind them at the Barn One site, the demon howl of power saws and the thump of hammers forced them to raise their voices.

"Has he ever done this before?" Harry asked.

"I don't think so. None of the grooms can recall his missing even a day of work."

"Have you tried calling him?"

"Yes, but I only get the answering service, and he hasn't returned my calls," she said as Buster and Carlyle, two of the grooms, led Scotsman and a tall dun mare with a dark mane and tail out of the barn.

"Are you expecting me to ride her?" Harry demanded as the mare tossed her head and danced her hindquarters into Scotsman as soon as they were out of the barn, while Carlyle, the older of the grooms, scolded her without much success and tried to pull her head down.

"She's just flirting," Holly said with a bright laugh, "and maybe showing off a little for her audience. She's a beauty and knows it."

"Are you sure you should still be riding?" Harry asked, seeking a straw.

"No problem."

Meanwhile, Scotsman was not apparently amused and tried to bite her, but she dodged away.

"What's her name, and how long do you think I'll stay on her back?" Harry asked.

"Sarah," Holly said. "She's one of the best mothers we've got on the farm. Her colts always prosper."

"She doesn't look much like a Sarah," Harry said, not mollified but gamely preparing to mount.

"Just wait, you'll see," Holly said, stepping forward to take Scotsman's reins from Buster. "Hurry up, we're wasting time."

Sarah rolled her eyes at Harry's approach, but settled when Harry reached up and grasped the horn of his saddle and after a couple of failures got his left foot into the stirrup. He saw Buster and Carlyle exchange glances but keep their faces straight.

"Idiot!" Holly shouted suddenly just as Harry gained his seat.

Sarah with a snort of alarm sank slightly and, with the grace of a ballet dancer, sprang six feet to Harry's right.

"Whoa!" he yelled, gripping the saddle horn with both hands, straining for all he was worth to stay on her back.

Glancing to his left, Harry saw Scotsman standing on his hind legs, pawing the air with Holly glued to his neck, trying to yank him down, laughing all the while, apparently enjoying herself. Harry saw that instead of being skittish, Sarah had moved herself and her rider out of range of the gelding's flailing hooves. A moment later, Buster stepped under Scotsman, jumped and caught his bridle, and brought him back to earth. The horse looked very pleased with himself, arching his neck and snorting with satisfaction.

By the time that was all over, Harry had managed to settle into his saddle and gather the reins. Sarah looked back at him from first one side and then the other.

"What did I tell you about her?" Holly asked, her face pink and her eyes sparkling. "She's the best mother in the stables. First she took you out from under Scotsman's shenanigans and just now checked to see that you were properly mounted."

"I don't believe it," Harry said, looking uneasily at the distance between himself and the ground.

Sueño had been much shorter.

"Believe it," she said cheerfully. "Buster, give me a sack of that corn. I'm going to look at the cattle."

Buster fetched the sack and handed it up to her.

"Watch yourself out there," he told her. "A stray bull's been hanging around the pasture, trying to find a way in, and Thor's spoiling for a fight."

"Thank you, Buster," she said. "Do you know who it belongs to?"

"I been calling around, but so far no one's missing one," the groom said, his hand on Scotsman's shoulder. "I suspect he's drifted in from some outlying place east of us. I haven't been able to see any brand on him, but he's got a mean look. If you ride up on him, go the other way quick as you can."

"All right," Holly said. "If you don't locate an owner in the next day or two, I'll shoot him. I don't want him shredding a gate to get at the cows. I don't want Thor hurt either."

"You want to wait until Elijah gets back?" he asked, showing some unease.

"No, Buster, I don't want a wild bull on the place. He's too dangerous."

With that, she called the dogs to her and kicked Scotsman into a trot toward the house. Sarah pricked her ears and without urging from Harry trotted after Scotsman.

"Tuck isn't strong enough for a long run," Holly called over her shoulder. "I'll leave both of them at the house."

Thahn opened the door before Holly reached the *porte co-chere*, and at her command, the dogs ran into the house while Harry tried to come to terms with the fact he was going for *"a long run."*

"I want to talk with you about that note Clarissa got before she killed herself," she said when they reached the pastures ride.

"What more can I tell you?" Harry asked.

"Why haven't the police arrested Elijah?"

Harry was surprised by the anger in her voice.

"Do you think Elijah knew about Brandon and Clarissa, and

is it even true about Yellen and Miguel Cruz?"

"Yes to both questions."

"How can you be sure about Yellen and Cruz?"

"Simple. Tyce told Brandon and Brandon told me. He thought Brandon should know in case he disapproved and wanted Tyce off the place."

"He didn't."

"No, but I did," she said.

Harry had been so occupied with their conversation that Harry had forgotten he was riding a horse. The recollection gave him a small jump of alarm. Sarah, who had been ambling along in a sleepy way, lifted her head and pricked her ears.

"Do you know why she did that?" Holly asked.

"Something must have caught her attention."

"She felt you make that startled move and wondered if you were all right."

Harry leaned forward and stroked Sarah's neck.

"I'm okay," he said and felt as if he was talking to Oh, Brother! "Why did you object?" he continued, feeling the horse relax under him.

"Not to their sexual relationship but to an employee of Oaks having an intimate connection to the Cruzes," she said, frowning angrily as she spoke. "Even before I knew the full extent of Brandon's involvement, I considered the connection fraught with a negative potential for competing interests."

"I don't follow you. How could the Oleander find itself at cross purposes with The Oaks?"

She gave a brief, bitter laugh.

"Brandon's lawyers have a copy of the original lease between Zebulon and Alejandra and all the renewals, including those signed by Brandon, but they have no idea what additional arrangements, verbal or written, Clarissa may have been given regarding renewal of the current lease."

"And if there are none, the lease will simply expire unless you and Miguel and Felipe can reach agreement on terms for renewing it."

"Yes, isn't it wonderful?"

"Have you spoken to Jeff Smolkin about this?"

"What can he do?"

"For openers, he can talk with Miguel and Felipe," Harry said and would have said more, but a thrashing in the trees ahead of them silenced him.

They had entered the most heavily wooded section of the ride, and trees and bushes crowded both sides. A loud thrashing and snapping of branches caused both horses to slow to a walk, their heads raised, ears cocked.

"Harry," Holly said quietly. "If this is what I think it is, give Sarah her head, grip her hard with your legs, lean forward, and hold on."

The crashing increased, accompanied by a deep, rumbling bellow, and a very large, black bull, looking to Harry exactly like pictures he had seen of Spanish fighting bulls, heaved himself onto the ride and stood glaring at them. Harry did not find it a cheering sight. Apparently, Sarah didn't think so either because she snorted nervously and backed up.

"Opening move by the bull," Holly said as the animal slashed his horns free of the vines he had shredded in his charge onto the ride.

"They're not supposed to attack us if we're on horseback," Harry said hopefully.

At that moment, the animal pawed the ground, arched his tail, and came at them, roaring like a train.

"I think this one missed that lesson," Holly said.

Scotsman, apparently deciding he had seen all he wanted, stood on his hind legs, spun around, and came down pointed in the opposite direction, springing without a pause into flight like an arrow out of a bow.

"Trust Sarah," Holly shouted over her shoulder, apparently giving up her efforts to stop the big gray whose hooves were flinging clots of dirt that flew around Harry like grapeshot.

Katherine's face flashed through his mind, followed by Soñadora's, which also vanished. They're saying goodbye, Harry thought as he watched three quarters of a ton of black anger behind lyre-shaped horns thunder toward him. Then all thought was erased from his mind when Sarah did the unimaginable.

She charged the bull!

"Sarah!" Harry shouted helplessly, gripping the pommel with both hands and watching between her ears the approaching catastrophe. The animal lowered his head to drive his horns into the horse, but at that moment, Sarah faded to the right and the beast shot past them, hooking empty air, his left horn missing Sarah's flank by a hair, but the hair was enough. Sarah braked with all four feet, skidded to a stop, and wheeled to face the next charge, but the animal was driving down the ride in pursuit of Scotsman.

"Well done, girl!" Harry shouted, astonished to find himself still in the saddle and alive.

Sarah snorted, possibly in agreement. Holly, Scotsman, and their pursuer had vanished around a curve in the ride. Even the sounds of pounding hooves had faded into silence. Harry sat back in the saddle and waited for his heart to stop pounding.

"What do you think?" he asked the horse, taking the slack out of the reins.

Sarah's response was to start in the direction of the barns.

"Makes sense to me," he said.

Sarah, without urging from Harry, moved easily from a walk to a trot and then into a gentle gallop. Harry found himself enjoying the run. He did not have to worry about Holly. With his head start, Scotsman would easily outrun the bull. A quarter of a mile along the track, Holly was racing back toward them.

"Where is the son of a bitch?" she shouted, reining Scotsman into a skidding halt that almost did to Sarah and Harry what the bull had failed to do.

But once again Sarah saved them by dancing to one side, letting the big gray plow past them.

"Sorry," Holly said, pulling Scotsman around to face them.

The animal was quivering and throwing his head, his eyes rolling.

"Quiet down," Holly commanded, leaning forward and patting his neck. "He's good," she said, laughing, "but he's a damned prima donna. Did Sarah take good care of you?"

"She's a miracle worker," Harry said. "Without my doing anything, she turned and began running right at the bull. Scared me half to death. The bull missed goring her by a fraction of an inch, but she waited until he dropped his head and couldn't see her, then leaped away from his horns like a toreador. Once he was past, she swung around to face him, but he kept on going. Didn't you see him?"

"Not for long," Holly said. "Scotsman decided to show me what he could do. It was great. Then, when we slowed down and the bull didn't show up, I remembered you and Sarah, got scared, and came racing back. I thought you'd be all right with Sarah, but accidents happen."

"So I've heard," Harry said. "He's back in those woods. What do you want to do?"

"Well, we're almost at the pasture," she said, looking around. "I'd like to take a look at Thor and the cows, just to be sure they're in good order."

"Okay," Harry said, "but remember, we've still got to ride back, and that black devil can't be far away."

"It would be hard to see him in that mess," Holly said, standing up in her stirrups to look into the tangle of trees and vines, "but I wouldn't be surprised if I end up having to hunt that black devil."

"As soon as he smelled you," Harry said, "he'd be hunting you. Don't even think of going in there after him."

Holly made a noncommittal sound and turned Scotsman toward the pasture.

"Let's go," she said.

Once they reached the pasture, they rode along the fence and found the animal's tracks sunk in the soft ground and places where the grass had been trampled into mud on both sides of the fence. The fence was not damaged and appeared to be untouched.

"Thor and the competition," Harry said.

"Right. There's no hair on the wire. That's a good sign. Let's go in," Holly said, moving back toward the gate.

"Someone's been here on foot," Harry said, looking down at large boot tracks in the mud beside the ride and near the gate. "It's rained since the tracks were made. I can't tell how old they are."

"Probably Buster," she said. "Help me with the gate."

Scotsman was snorting and dancing and keeping her from operating the lock from the saddle. Harry dismounted, punched in the numbers she gave, and swung open the gate. Following Holly, he led Sarah into the pasture. While closing the gate behind him, he shifted his concern from their earlier attacker to Thor, although the herd was at least a hundred yards from them. Nevertheless, Harry was thoroughly sensitized to the fact that a bull could run. However improbable it seemed, he was easier in his mind when he was on Sarah's back again.

The cows were in good order, but Thor was far more alert than he had been the first time Harry saw him; although he did not threaten them, he showed no interest in the corn Holly poured onto the ground for him and spent most of his time staring at the fence.

"He's dropped some weight," Holly said. "He's too vigilant to be eating much. That black bull's got to go."

Suddenly Thor swung away from the corn and, bellowing as he went, began trotting toward the fence, stopping after fifty yards to paw the ground and rip up the turf with his horns, throwing up divots of dirt and grass and flinging them high over his head.

"He's worked up all right," Harry agreed, wondering how a battle between the two would come out—Thor had the weight, Black, the speed.

"I know what you're thinking," she said, "and we are not amused."

When they returned to the barns, Buster came out to meet them.

"That bull may belong to Mr. Ryan, over there at Hilltop," he told Holly.

"Keep talking," she said.

"His Andalusia's gone missing."

"Idiot!" was Holly's response as she jumped to the ground, tossed the reins to the groom, and ran toward the house. Harry surrendered Sarah after stroking her neck and thanking her for saving his.

Thahn and the dogs greeted him and led him into the study. Soon after, Holly came striding into the room and said angrily, "I've been talking with Geoffrey Ryan. The man ought not to be let out outside without supervision. He's an idiot. Do you know what happened?"

Harry thought the question unnecessary but said no anyway.

"That fool bought a Mexican fighting cow and had her impregnated with semen from one of Eduardo Miura's *Toro de*

Lidia bulls. The demon that attacked us this morning is the result."

She flung herself into a chair, feet thrust out, obviously furious.

"Did he jump a fence?"

"No. Someone took a bolt cutter to the chain on the beast's paddock gate, and *el Toro* ran off, undoubtedly following his nose to my Angus cows."

Harry thought for a moment.

"I take it Ryan's farm is close to The Oaks."

"Gar Creek separates our holding on the north side."

"Not fenced?"

Holly, still scowling, shook her head.

"Ryan spent a fortune breeding that bull and for what?" she demanded. "The beast is a killer and a threat to every living thing that comes in contact with him. What was Ryan thinking of?"

"I don't know," Harry said, his mind elsewhere. "The more important question is why did someone cut that bull loose?"

"I don't know, and I don't care," she snapped.

"You should," Harry said, "because I think the same someone hoped it would kill you."

"It looks like a very long shot," Jim said doubtfully.

"If Blue wants her dead, why not just shoot her or break her neck?" Hodges asked.

"I think his aim is to make her suffer," Harry said.

"What does he gain?" Jim demanded. "And why does he want her dead in the first place?"

"Satisfaction and revenge for Henry Jackson and Rosalee Franklin," Harry said.

"We turned his place inside out," Jim said. "He doesn't own a pair of scissors, and he surely doesn't take the newspaper. I think there's some question as to whether or not he can read."

"And according to his neighbors," Hodges said with a grin, "he didn't ask any of them if he could borrow a pair of scissors or an old newspaper. So, unless he put that note together in the public library, he didn't send it."

"I guess that takes care of everything," Harry said, getting to his feet and for once not finding Hodges's analysis amusing, "unless you can tell me why he's missing and why you're dismissing what Gladys Jackson told me about Elijah's anger over Henry's death and his half sister's losing her lawsuit against Brandon Pike."

He paused, but neither Jim nor Hodges said anything, apparently waiting for him to go on.

"As far as I know," Harry said, angry and frustrated, "you can't name a single person outside of Elijah who has the slightest reason for wanting Holly Pike dead."

"Whoa!" Jim said, scrambling out of his chair, "don't get all aerated. We're doing what we can to find Blue, but you know as well as I do that if he's decided to go to earth, it will be by lucky chance if we ever find him."

Harry had already cooled down. He said in a reasonable voice, "I know, and I don't really think he did construct that note. But I do think he killed Brandon, nearly killed Yellen, lamed Sueño, poisoned Tuck, set fire to Barn One, and took a bolt cutter to that bull's paddock. I also think that if we don't find him and stop him, he will kill Holly."

"What's Geoffrey Ryan going to do about that bull of his?" Tucker asked Harry as they moved along a row, picking green beans.

"Jim called the Fish and Game Department, and the commissioner is putting a warden on the problem. The Oaks and Ryan's properties border some hog hunting areas, and the possibility of the bull wandering into one of them and killing a hunter caught the commissioner's attention."

"Is the Sheriff's Department taking any action on its own?"

"Hodges has gone out to talk to Ryan and remind him that he will be responsible for any damage to property or persons done by the animal."

"You don't seem satisfied."

"I'm not. Jim's not taking the threat Elijah poses seriously enough."

"I have some sympathy for his position," Tucker said, frowning slightly. "Setting that bull loose looks more like an effort to damage Ryan than anything else."

"Point taken" Harry replied, straightening up to ease his back, "but you're overlooking Elijah's motives."

"Which are? By the way, these beans aren't going to pick themselves."

Harry grumbled but bent to his task.

"I think Elijah is setting out to cause Holly as much pain as he can. He knew that bull was dangerous and that set loose it would follow its nose straight to her herd of Angus cattle. He also knows she takes that pasture ride three or four times a week."

"If he got as far as that pasture gate," Tucker asked, "why didn't he force it and create some more havoc?"

"Once it was loose," Harry replied quickly, "Elijah wouldn't have risked walking around there in the dark. In the daylight, he was at risk of being seen by Buster or one of the other men, checking the fences. My guess is he tried that key lock, and when he found that, without the code, he couldn't open it, he left."

"How is he getting into The Oaks without being seen?"

"I think he's found a way through Oleander Farm. There's a

ride between there and The Oaks, and the Cruzes don't keep a dog."

"I see you've given it some thought," Tucker said. "You may be right."

He gave his basket a shake and straightened up.

"I think we've got a mess here," he said, looking from his own basket to Harry's. "What have you been doing over there? I've picked twice as many beans as you."

Harry straightened with a groan.

"You've got to cut me some slack here," he said. "I was yanked around on that horse, and you've had more practice."

"Picking beans isn't like welding," Tucker said. "It doesn't take ten years to master the skill."

"I don't even want to become good at it," Harry said, dumping his pathetically few beans into Tucker's basket.

"You know," Tucker said as they walked back along the row toward the house, "you're right. There's some things a man ought never learn how to do. House painting, for example. There's nothing more mind-numbing on earth than painting shutters, unless it's painting a ceiling. I wish I'd never learned. Can you paint?"

"No," Harry said, seeing where this was leading.

"Good," Tucker said with a broad smile. "I'm planning to paint the barn. It will give you a chance to practice."

"You just said . . ."

Harry let it go.

"How are you getting along with the skunk?"

"Good question," Tucker replied. "There's hardly any evidence of her."

"You mean the smell."

"That's right, but we don't speak of it around the house."

"She might hear you and be offended."

"Yes. She spends most of any twenty-four hours in her den. I think she's very close to giving birth and doesn't want to be far from home when the moment arrives."

"And Jane Bunting's adjusting to the situation?"

"Late at night, I sometimes hear her growl a little when she comes out to forage," Tucker said with a chuckle, "but she's smart enough to leave her alone. The other two take an interest, but don't seem to resent her presence under the house. But I am concerned about her and her young ones," Tucker added somberly as they set their baskets on the table by the kitchen door.

"What's got you worried?"

"Take one of those rockers. I'll bring us out some lemonade. I made a new batch this morning. I've forgotten. Do you take yours with ice?"

"Without," Harry said, easing into the chair.

Immediately after his experience with the bull, he had felt nothing but relief, but he had awakened the next morning to find that every muscle from his neck to his heels and whatever he sat on was either bruised, strained, or tender.

"Coyotes," Tucker said, returning with two frosted glasses. "I keep them in the freezer."

"The coyotes?"

"Very funny. The glasses."

Tucker settled himself and took a long drink.

"They've made two passes at the hens, but the wire has stopped them so far," he said when he had caught his breath. "But what worries me more are the cats. Yesterday in broad daylight, our new neighbors put Aurelius up that oak, and came within a few inches from snatching him right off the tree. They're bold."

"What was Sanchez doing?"

"Just what he's doing now," Tucker said, nodding toward the shadiest side of the stoop, where the dog was sleeping.

Oh, Brother! was standing under the oak where Aurelius had taken refuge, grazing on Bermuda grass.

"Oh, Brother! saw it, but it was all over before he got to the tree," Tucker continued thoughtfully, still staring at the tree. "I've got to say, they were impressive. Aside from a single squall out of Aurelius and the pop of their teeth as they jumped and snapped at him, the whole event unfolded in silence, and when they missed their grab, they vanished without a sound. It's a good thing Jane Bunting was out hunting with Frederica because if she'd been here, she would have tackled them, and they would have killed her."

"Too bad you can't sic that skunk onto them," Harry said, wanting to get Tucker's mind off the possibility of Jane Bunting being killed.

Tucker shook his head. "I'm afraid that lady picks her own fights."

"Speaking of being worried," Harry said, expressing a concern of his own, "I think Holly Pike is in some danger—how much I can't say."

"Are you staying in touch with Gladys Jackson?"

"What are you thinking about?" Harry asked, knowing Tucker usually was responding to his concern by asking a question.

"She talks and listens and takes an interest," the old farmer replied.

"And I should talk to her."

"Might be a good idea. She's close to Elijah. Of course, Rosalee Franklin is closer, but she's not going to help you find him. Which reminds me, I haven't asked after Tyce Yellen."

"Jim is getting daily reports on his progress," Harry replied. "Holly has been looking in on him most days. Both she and Jim say he's growing stronger and that his mind is clearer, but he still can't remember what happened to him."

"Does he recognize people now?"

"Yes, and he's recovered his own identity."

"Dangerous time for him," Tucker said.

"Whoever attacked him must be thinking hard about his recovery."

"And that would be Elijah."

"Yes, a sobering thought."

25

Gladys Jackson appeared glad to see Harry. Smiling, she hurried him into a chair in her living room, redolent with the smell of baking.

"I've just taken a batch of peanut butter cookies out of the oven, and the kettle's singing," she said, having gotten him settled, "I'm thinking tea and cookies. Will you join me?"

"With pleasure," Harry said without having to exaggerate his enthusiasm.

He had been up early, and with still another appointment to keep, lunch was looking a long way off.

She hurried away, lively as a woman half her age, but despite the prospect of freshly baked cookies with tea to go with them— tea that, unlike Tucker's, would not take the varnish off the floor if he spilled any—Harry couldn't settle. He found himself worrying about Holly.

"Here we are," Mrs. Jackson said, reappearing with a tea trolley, laden with teapot, cups and saucers, sugar, milk, and a glass plate heaped with cookies. "I thought we'd take a step up from the mugs."

"Very nice," Harry said.

"I used to just load up a tray and carry whatever was on it all over the house when the need arose," she said with a deprecating laugh as she poured the tea, "but I find this wheeled trolley feels more comfortable now. Do you think I'm being wicked?"

"I don't think your soul's in danger," Harry said with a laugh,

283

forgetting his other concerns for the moment.

He was grateful for the lift in spirits this woman gave him.

"I believe it was one of your New England people," she said, "who, asked on his deathbed if he had made his peace with the Lord, his answer was that he was not aware of ever having quarreled with Him."

"Henry David Thoreau," Harry said, "an exceptional man."

"That's what our minister said," she replied. "It's a year or more since he told us that story, but, you know, it's stayed with me. Perhaps you have to live with it awhile before its full meaning reveals itself."

They ate and drank together in a peaceful silence for a few moments before Mrs. Jackson asked what had brought him to see her, adding that he didn't need an excuse, that he would always be welcome.

Having thanked her, he ate the last bite of his cookie, then put his cup back in its saucer, thinking how best to begin talking about Elijah. Before he had fully decided, she spoke.

"I suspect you want to talk about Elijah," she said, the cheerfulness leaving her voice. "Don't be troubled, Mr. Brock. I've been expecting you."

"It's got to be a painful subject for you," he said.

"Yes, but much of what has to be said and done has pain for a companion. Please go on."

"Elijah has disappeared, and the police are looking for him. Do you know where he is?"

"I'm relieved to say that I don't," she said, and Harry did not doubt that she was speaking the truth. "What has he done this time?"

"Well," Harry said, "I don't know for sure that he's done anything wrong, but the police need to talk with him."

"It's all right, you know," she said gently. "You can tell me. I know that in the past Elijah has shown a gift for getting into trouble of one kind or another."

"Some bad things have been happening at The Oaks," Harry said and went on to give his listener a very abbreviated and sanitized version of the events, admitting that there was a possibility that Elijah had been the author of them.

When he was finished, Mrs. Jackson refilled their cups without speaking, taking the time, Harry thought, to frame her response or, possibly, to decide how far she was willing to go toward helping the police find Elijah.

"This is a small community, Mr. Brock," she told him, putting down the teapot and seating herself again. "Word of things goes around as fast as phones can ring or people stop to exchange a few words on the street. Sometimes," she added with a smile, "I think it blows in the windows on the wind."

Harry laughed, relieved that she could still make a joke.

"Has anything concerning Elijah blown in your window?" he asked.

"You have tried to make it easy to hear the terrible things that have been happening at The Oaks," she said, "but, you know, including Elijah, there are six of our people working out there. I'm sorry to say, I know the whole sad story, and I'm afraid it's not over yet."

"No," Harry said, feeling slightly chastised. "I'm afraid it's not, but you have no news of him?"

"The poor man's life has been marked by violence, Mr. Brock. I will not be surprised to learn that his anger has led him down that path again. Beyond that, I'm afraid I can't be of help."

"I understand," Harry said, and he felt something akin to relief that he did understand, but he also felt the need to make a final try.

"My fear is that if we can't stop the violence, someone else is going to die."

"Then I hope you can find a way to end it," she answered gravely. "I really do."

Harry sat, literally cooling his heels, in Jeff Smolkin's waiting room, trying to ward off the cold by recalling the days when Jeff Smolkin had to supplement his law practice income by making debt settlements by telephone for loan companies. That was a long time ago, Harry thought as he tried to listen to a Bocchereni quintet that was dancing in the icy air.

The receptionist, who on his arrival had instantly offered Harry a large mug of steaming coffee, which he now clutched in both hands, wore a thick pink and gray sweater with the collar turned up. While Harry waited, three of Smolkin's wool-suited and harried-looking but remarkably attractive legal assistants rushed past him, giving him distracted smiles of greeting.

"I may own the building, but it's clear I don't own the god-damned air conditioning system," Smolkin complained, half ushering, half pushing Harry into his office where the meat locker effect was mitigated by partially open windows, an amenity not available in newer, less elegant and hermetically sealed buildings.

Ten years younger than Harry, Smolkin was short and rotund, balding and graying, but not, as far as Harry could see, becoming any less headlong in his plunge through life.

"I'm glad to see you, Harry, sit down, sit down. What's brought you here? Christ! Who has time to just visit somebody anymore? Not me, that's for damned sure."

He dropped into the black leather chair beside Harry's, yanking it around while he talked.

"It's good to see you, Jeff. When are you going to take in a couple of partners and begin to live like a real person?" Harry scolded him. "You'll drop one of these days." For years Harry had been trying without success to get him to slow down.

"What would I do with myself? Play golf?"

He spoke with such wide-eyed alarm that Harry gave up and laughed.

"I need help."

"You came to the right place. Fire away."

"Holly Pike and the Oleander," Harry said.

Smolkin wriggled in his chair and grimaced.

"I've been driving myself nuts over it," he said. "It makes no sense that there isn't something somewhere telling us what the arrangement was between Pike and Cruz. I've done everything but try choking it out of Gus Shriver, but, honest to God, Harry, I don't think the man knows any more than I do. And if he wasn't such a tight-ass, he'd tell me he can't find anything in Pike's papers."

"But you haven't managed to find those belonging to Clarissa Cruz."

"Hell, no. When I've mentioned it to him he has a hissy-fit."

"Who takes care of Oleander Farm's legal affairs?" Harry asked.

"No one in Tequesta County, and if it's an outfit on the East Coast, I haven't found them."

"Then the lease will stand?"

"It looks like it. Not that it makes any sense. The Cruzes have lived there as though it was their place and as if they expected to live there forever. It just doesn't add up that Pike would have hung them out to dry in this way."

"Will Holly renew the lease?" Harry asked.

"I don't know, and I don't think she knows either."

It made him feel better to find he agreed with Smolkin. He did not want to believe she was preparing to reclaim Oleander Farm.

"I take it that neither Miguel nor Felipe Cruz asked you about it?" Harry asked, standing.

Smolkin jumped up and said they had not and shook Harry's hand.

"Think about what I said, Jeff," Harry said from the door. "Man doesn't live by paralegals alone."

On a hunch, Harry went from Jeff Smolkin's office to the hospital, where he found Colin Baker, the red-haired male nurse, sitting behind the duty desk looking bored.

"Have they closed I-75?" Harry asked him.

For a moment he looked puzzled, then grinned.

"You've got a bizarre sense of humor, Harry, but as a matter of fact, we've had three 75s so far today. Fortunately for them, they all walked out of here—one needed a crutch, but he walked."

"How is the patient?"

"Great."

Baker flipped open a register, studied it a moment, and said, "I think Miguel Cruz is in there, but there's no reason not to go in. You know him, don't you?"

Harry nodded.

"How is Yellen?"

"Great," Baker said. "He's making good progress, and he's stopped critiquing the nurses' asses while they were in the room. The hospital became hysterical. Even the OR was breaking into gales of laughter. Now, Yellen can't remember he did it."

"Who won?" Harry asked.

"A candy striper from obstetrics and, get ready for this," he said, grasping Harry's arm and glancing around furtively, "Michelle was runner-up. She pretended to be insulted, but I saw her give him a peck on the forehead soon after. Not that he knew why."

Harry was still smiling when he stopped to say hello to Fred Robbins.

"Everything going well, Corporal?" Harry asked, shaking the man's hand.

"Blue hasn't been back, if that's what you mean," Robbins said. "I'm beginning to think I'm wasting the Department's money, sitting out here."

"I hope you are," Harry said and went into Yellen's room.

"Hello, Harry," Yellen said, sliding off the edge of the bed to shake hands. "You've probably been here before, but I don't remember it. If you were, I hope I didn't insult you. I've been told I was pretty obnoxious. The nurses can't come in here without blushing. I must have been very naughty."

"In fact," Miguel put in dryly, "he developed a whole new interest."

Harry caught that as well as Miguel's expression and barely managed not to laugh.

"I'm glad to see you back, Tyce," he said. "How are you feeling?"

Despite traces of bruising and a shaved head still sporting a couple of livid scars, Harry thought he looked remarkably well.

"Good," Yellen replied. "I don't think I'm ready to ride Jack, but I'm sure that will come."

"You've talked with Jim Snyder, I suppose."

"Lord, yes. I've had half the Sheriff's Department in here in the past few days. It's been frustrating for me and disappointing for them. I don't remember a damned thing about what happened to me."

"If you're lucky, you never will," Miguel said.

He had been sitting on one of the folding chairs near the bed and stood up.

"I've got a lot of work waiting," he said, giving Yellen a quick hug.

"So have I," Harry said. "Miguel, can I walk you down?"

"Sure," Miguel said without enthusiasm.

"Come back when you can stay longer, Harry," Yellen said. "I'd like to talk about The Oaks. Holly won't tell me a damned thing."

When Miguel set a quick pace along the corridors to the elevator, Harry assumed there was still some rancor hanging over from the contentious meeting with Jim and Felipe.

Once in the elevator, he said, "I'm sure the Pikes' lawyers have asked you about the lease and whether your sister has any other documents applying to it. Am I right?"

"They've called, and I'll tell you what I told them and what I told you before my sister's death. I don't know what arrangements beyond the lease she had with Brandon."

"I remember," Harry said, "and it just doesn't make sense that Brandon would have left you and your sister so exposed. Have you and Felipe made a thorough search of your sister's papers?"

"Why the hell are you asking me this, Brock? What business is it of yours? Why should you care what happens to us? What is it that Holly is fishing for?"

"I'll deal with the last question first," Harry said, ignoring the smoldering anger in Miguel's voice.

"She does not believe that Brandon would have left things the way they appear to have been." He paused, but Miguel made no response. "I think that you should protect yourself and your sister by doing everything you can to establish that Brandon and your sister had an understanding that made the lease redundant."

"Thanks to you and Jim Snyder and his people," Miguel said in red-faced fury, "I now know my sister and Brandon were incestuous lovers, that Felipe and Constanta have known for years and kept it from me, that in an act of cowardice she did commit suicide, and because of her folly, I am now at risk of losing Oleander."

The elevator door slid open, and Miguel strode out into the crowded foyer. Wrecked dreams and ruined hope, Harry thought sadly, watching the young man hurry away. He followed more slowly, determined to call Felipe to see if he could be brought to make a proper search of Clarissa's papers, and convinced that Miguel, furious as he was with his sister, would not go near them.

Once in the Rover, he discovered that his cell's phone list contained only Felipe's home number and decided to call it on the chance he would find a housekeeper in the house who could give him Felipe's business number.

Constanta answered and Harry reminded her of who he was and was surprised to learn that she remembered him.

"How can I help?" she asked after they were past the pleasantries.

Harry told her about his conversation with Miguel. Feeling freer to be open with her, he said, "I'm afraid he's still open to suspicion regarding Brandon's death if it can't be proved your family's future at Oleander was assured by agreements that superseded the lease. I think the lease added to the idea that Brandon's and Clarissa's arrangements were conventional business arrangements."

"You may be right," Constanta said, "but I doubt that Felipe will touch her papers. Confidentially, he regards his sister's liaison with Brandon to have been a sinful and base relationship and is deeply ashamed of it. I don't know how he found out about it, but once he knew, he left Oleander. It is why he and our sons have had so little contact with her."

"And you?" Harry asked.

"I think he made a mistake. While I do not think Clarissa and Brandon were wise, wisdom has nothing to do with the heart's affections. They loved one another, and perhaps their love was intensified by their being half brother and half sister. I choose not to judge."

"Did Clarissa have a lawyer?" he asked, finding nothing to add to what had been said, after all, a surprisingly succinct summary of the situation.

"I don't think so."

"Would you be willing to go through her papers?"

"In search of what?"

"Something that guarantees Clarissa and her family the right to live at Oleander Farm for as long as they want."

"Miguel will not be happy. You recall how angry he was with me when he thought I had been reading her diary."

"Can you persuade him that it must be done, for your children if for no other reason?"

"Possibly, but there is Felipe."

Harry had seen them together and did not find her comment daunting.

"Are the children out of school?"

"This is their last week."

"Do you agree with me that this needs to be done?"

"Yes, I do. For everyone."

"Good. Can you make it happen?"

"I can try," she replied with a resigned smile.

"Good," Harry said and experienced a flicker of hope.

It was mid-afternoon when Harry returned to the Hammock. Katherine met him at the door.

"Bad news," she told him. "Holly Pike is at risk of miscarrying," she said, "At least that's what I think her butler was trying to tell me."

"Is she in the hospital?"

"No, she's home in bed, and—can you believe it—Esther

Benson's been out there to see her. Tell me money doesn't count."

As she talked, she led Harry into the kitchen, taking off her apron as she went. The smell of roasting chicken filled the kitchen, despite the open door and windows, and briefly distracted Harry, but he forced his mind away from the aroma and the sight of a rhubarb pie on the sideboard, waiting for its turn in the oven.

"My guess," Katherine continued, "is that she started spotting, panicked, and called Benson. Then, after seeing Benson, she told her man to call you."

"How serious does it sound?" Harry asked.

"Not very," Katherine responded. "If it had been, Benson would have called an ambulance. My guess is that she told Holly to stay in bed and rest."

"They'll handle it by phone," Harry said.

"Right, watchful waiting. However, she wants to see you."

"Want to go for a ride?" Harry asked her.

"No, thanks. You handle your women on your own," she told him with a sardonic smile.

"I think I liked you better before the operation," he said, thinking that in her blue halter and white pedal pushers, she was heartbreakingly appealing.

"Go," she said, coloring as if she had read his mind, and gave him a push toward the door.

"I'm really being treated shabbily," he said, falling back in an exaggerated stagger.

"Dinner's going onto the table at six sharp," she said, "and I'm going out to the lanai and read."

As he was leaving, she stopped him and said, "Harry, no heroics. If she's bleeding or starts cramping, call the EMS."

By then she had put on her reading glasses and was carrying her book. Leaning over, she kissed him on the cheek, reminding him that he was sharing his house with the sexiest librarian in town, but the private joke didn't cure his loneliness.

Thahn and Nip and Tuck met Harry and led him upstairs to Holly's bedroom. With its rose-colored walls, the cherry sleigh bed, the arresting watercolors on the wall of gardens, the Maine coast, Rome, as well as still life paintings, all by the same artist. A woman. He groped for the name.

"Annie Gooding Syke," Holly said sourly, propped up in bed wearing a frilly bed jacket and looking ready to bite one of the dogs.

"Spectacular," Harry said, taking the opportunity to get a good look at her while also letting his eyes drift over the stunning paintings. "How are you feeling?" he asked, still taking in the watercolors.

"Pissed off," she said.

Thahn had vanished as usual without fanfare. Harry came to the bed and stared at her.

"Not bad," he said.

"Watch it, Buster," she said. "There's a gun in this bed, and I might just use it."

"A little pale, but not altogether washed out. Are you in any pain?"

"No," she said, dropping her head back against the pillows, "but I'm scared half to death."

"Did you tell Benson about your Paul Revere ride?" he asked.

Her head popped back up and her eyes widened.

"Do I look crazy?" Holly demanded. "She'd have killed me." Harry laughed.

"But you did tell her you'd been riding."

For a moment, sitting in the bed in her pink bed jacket and just before she responded, she looked to Harry like a little girl being asked a question she would rather not answer. And she didn't. Instead, she shook her head.

Harry tried not to laugh, but he found he couldn't help it.

"It's not funny," she said. "She scares me to death."

"She scares everybody. Are you in any discomfort?"

"No."

"How are you supposed to know if you're all right?"

"No bleeding."

"And?"

"I'm not bleeding. No cramps, no nausea, no nothing," she said, her voice climbing along with the list. "Can we leave this? I'm beginning to feel like I'm talking to Benson."

"All right, why am I here?"

"She's grounded me," Holly complained. "No riding, a lot of bed rest, no strenuous exercise, no tiring myself until further notice. I have to see her tomorrow if I have no further counter indicators."

"If you do?"

"Hospital," she said, then hurried on. "Harry, I need some help with things here for a few days. Buster really isn't up to it. He can take care of the horse barns well enough, but he's no use for the rest. Can you help me?"

"What I know about cattle could be written on a postcard," Harry said, alarmed by her request.

"I know, but that doesn't matter. I only need you to be me for a few days. I'll tell you what needs doing. I just don't want the subcontractors working on the barn to get the idea no one's paying attention. Also, with that damned bull still at large, I want the fence around the Anguses' pasture checked every day. I'll call Geoffrey a little later and ask if he has organized a team to corral that black demon."

She stopped and leaned back against her pillows and closed her eyes.

"Are you all right?" Harry asked.

"Yes, but I'm not sure I like having my body requisitioned this way. I have the distinct sense of an alien presence asserting itself."

Harry laughed in spite of himself and said, "I don't think your alien will have to be naturalized when it arrives."

"If it arrives," she said and suddenly collapsed in tears.

Without hesitating, Harry leaned over the bed and, awkward as it was, managed to gather her into his arms. Holly grabbed him like the last stick floating and for a few moments clung to him, crying it all out like a child.

Then as fiercely as she had clung to him, she suddenly began shoving him away, her tears still flowing. Startled, Harry tried to pull his arms free, and the effort was just enough to topple him forward onto the bed and across her.

"What are you doing?" she shouted, her voice muffled by his fall. "Get off me."

Nip and Tuck jumped to their feet and began growling.

"I'm trying to," Harry said, desperation in his voice. "I lost my balance."

There was a moment in the inelegant scramble when he was backing off her that his face passed over hers. Harry glanced down and saw her eyes still flooded with tears and her face streaked and pale. The sight was too much for him. Lowering his face as he crawled backwards, he kissed her on the forehead and said, pulling something up from his remote past, "Don't worry, sweetheart. It's going to be okay. It really is."

"How many daughters do you have, Harry?" Holly asked him when he had made it to his feet.

"Two," he answered, a bit disconcerted by the way she was looking at him.

"How old are they?"

"One's in her twenties, the other's quite a bit older."

"You used to say that to them when they'd skinned a knee,

didn't you?"

"What?" he asked, feeling his face burn.

"Do you know how sweet that is," she asked him, "or how long it's been since anyone's kissed me on the forehead and called me *sweetheart* in that tone of voice?"

"I'm sorry," he said, "I spoke without thinking."

"It was delightful," she said, smiling and waving away his apology. "Are you going to be my manager until I can get out of this bed or not?"

"Of course," he said, "but I can't be here all the time."

"You don't have to be. A couple of hours a day is enough."

"I'll come out in the morning."

"Thank you."

"When do you see Esther Benson?"

"If I don't start bleeding again, tomorrow afternoon." She put up her hand. "Don't say it. Thahn will drive me."

Harry smiled.

"Rest, eat, watch television, sleep."

With that he left with a familiar ache reminding him that when he wasn't looking, his daughters had become women.

26

Harry got home half an hour ahead of his appointed time to find that Katherine had changed into a blue sleeveless silk dress for dinner and was carrying a drinks tray, freighted with glasses, bottles, and crackers and cheese, onto the lanai. The skirt of her dress, Harry noted with pleasure, swirled gracefully around her legs as she moved.

"What did I do to earn this?" he asked, pleased and surprised.

"It's the only way I can say thank you," she replied lightly, setting the tray on the table between their chairs and turning to greet him. "Sit down. Everything's ready. I want to hear about Holly."

"Just a minute," he said, going into his study to shed his CZ pistol and shoulder holster and drop them on his desk.

When he returned, she was already leaned back in her deck chair with her feet up, enjoying the breeze. He dropped onto his chair, glad to be sitting.

"I think Holly's going to be all right," he began, but Katherine interrupted him.

"Make us both a gin and tonic—a lot of ice in mine. Oops," she said, swinging to her feet, "I forgot the ice."

At that moment there was the heavy slam of a rifle and the center slat in the back of the chair in which she had been sitting exploded into splinters.

"Run!" Harry shouted, throwing his weight to the right, overturning his chair as a second bullet smacked into the wall of the house behind the spot where he and the chair had been.

Rolling onto his hands and knees, he scrambled across the floor and flung himself into the kitchen as the shooter fired again. Harry felt something like a red hot iron press the back of his left leg, making him yelp, but he kept on scrambling until he could come onto his feet in his office and snatch the CZ out of its holster.

"Front or back?" Katherine asked as Harry emerged from the study.

She had kicked her shoes off and was running down the stairs, feeding shells into his twelve-gauge pump gun as she came.

"I've called 911," she said.

"Good. Sprawl out on the floor just inside the dining room door," he told her. "If anyone comes through the kitchen door, shoot them. I'll go out the back and try to draw whoever the shooter is away from the house."

"Oh, no," Katherine said, jacking a shell into the chamber and feeding a last shell into the tube, "I'm not letting you go out there alone."

She was angry and her eyes were blazing. One glance told Harry there was no point in arguing, but before he could say anything else, the window over the kitchen sink disintegrated, followed by the crash of the rifle and the clatter of crockery on the dining room table being reduced to shards.

Harry sucked in his breath, figuring the bullet must have zipped by about a foot from them, then grabbed Katherine and pulled her down onto the floor with him.

"That son of a bitch has wrecked our dinner," Katherine grated, rolling herself onto her stomach and yanking the shotgun into firing position. "If he makes me ruin this dress, I'll kill him."

For the next fifteen seconds, neither of them could say or do anything except hug the floor as the shooter riddled the kitchen and the dining room, spraying the rooms with a swarm of bullets and sprinkling them with plaster dust and bits of flying glass.

When it came, the silence was oppressive.

"From the sound and rate of fire, I'd say it's a made-over Browning automatic rifle, firing on semiautomatic," Harry said.

"I'm glad you told me," Katherine said wryly, trying to shake some of the glass off herself without getting cut. "By the way, your leg is bleeding."

"I was grazed getting off the lanai," he said. "It's nothing to worry about."

"Shot in the leg, no arteries cut," she said, "nothing to worry about."

Harry heard the message and decided not to go there.

"We've got to get out of the house," he said.

"Not an attractive thought," she said, "but better than being roasted alive if he decides to burn us out."

"You're barefoot," Harry said. "I'm going to have to carry you over this glass."

"I remember you carrying me in here the day we were married, but there have been changes since then. Do you have health insurance?"

"I'm going to get onto my hands and knees," he said. "You crawl onto my back, wrap your legs around my waist, hold the shotgun in one hand and put your free arm around my neck."

"Dream on," she said.

"We should talk dirty later," he said. "Climb aboard."

With a certain amount of swearing, groaning, and struggle, Harry managed to stagger to his feet and crunch his way through the glass and crockery into the back hallway.

"Bent over that way," Katherine said, sliding off his back, "you looked like a coolie carrying three sacks of rice."

Harry was standing, head sunk, one hand propped against

the wall, trying to get his breath.

"If you giggle, it's all over between us," he gasped. "Pull your dress down."

"Oh yes, I forgot. This dress wasn't meant for riding bareback."

She wriggled the skirt down over her hips.

"Harry."

"What?"

She had leaned the shotgun against the wall to deal with her dress. Now, she caught it up again and cradled it in her left arm.

"If we don't survive this," she said, "I want you to know I love you."

Harry, his hand on the doorknob, turned back and kissed her.

"I love you, too," he said, striving with doubtful effect to sound brisk, "but we are definitely going to survive, and this is how we're going to do it."

When he finished telling her, he pulled open the door.

"Wait," she said, "if you get me killed, I'm coming back to haunt you forever, and I warn you, the punishment will be severe."

"Fair enough," he said. "You first. Go!"

She cleared the landing and turned at a run to her left. Harry followed and raced for the nearest oak to his right and flung himself onto the ground. Gaining a three-point position, he had the rear of the house, the cleared area under the oaks to the right and left of the building, and the Rover, parked under the big live oak at the front corner of the lawn in view.

The sun had slipped down behind a line of purple thunderheads, leaving the Hammock in pale light and dark shadows. Edges had become blurred and the lavender afterglow on the eastern clouds was all the color left. He tried to locate Katherine to his left but could not see her.

Good, he thought, she's hugging the ground. Behind him the barn was nearly buried in the trees, but he could see that the barn door was closed and padlocked. Then, slowly, he counted to thirty. In that time, nothing in his range of vision moved. With the fading of the day, the onshore breeze had all but died, a breathless silence had settled over the Hammock, and even the locusts were quiet.

Very slowly, he rose to his feet. Holding his CZ in both hands, he ran toward the front of the house for a count of eight and dropped to the ground behind another tree without drawing any fire. He counted again. Still nothing.

Now he could see all of the cleared area in front of the house, the white sand road, and brush on the creek side of the road. He will not be there, Harry thought, he has nowhere to run except into the creek. That meant that if the shooter was anywhere, he was between the road and Katherine. Because there was no cover for him in front of the house, he pulled back in short dashes to his starting point and began moving toward Katherine, a tree at a time.

Here, behind the house, the grass under the trees was nearly knee-high. Harry, making another dash, saw Katherine rise up out of the grass.

"Shit!" he said as he pitched face down into the grass and heard the throaty roar of the twelve gauge. The charge of shot had passed over his head and shredded a cluster of low-hanging branches.

"It's me!" Harry shouted, his voice muffled by dirt and grass. "It's me!"

A moment later, Katherine was standing over him, the muzzle of her gun pointed at his back.

"Don't even think of moving," she said. "One little wiggle from you, and I'll blow you in half."

"I'm not moving," Harry said.

"Harry! What the hell . . . !" Katherine shouted. "You weren't supposed to be over here!"

"There was no cover," he said. "I had to come back. Point that cannon somewhere else."

"Shit!" she said, cradling the gun. "I thought I had him."

"You damned near had me," he huffed, scrambling to his feet.

"What if I had shot you?" she demanded, her voice rising angrily.

"You didn't," Harry countered, still rattled. "Where is our visitor?"

Harry looked around, knowing he was not going to see anyone.

"You damned near got yourself killed," Katherine persisted.

"Think about this," Harry said. "If the shooter was still here, we'd both be dead."

"You're changing the subject," she countered. "You have some explaining to do."

Harry grinned.

"I'll explain it over dinner," he said, feeling suddenly very pleased with himself.

After having surveyed the damage in the house, they decided to leave the mess until morning and eat in town, but some tension had developed over the condition of the blue dress while she cleaned and bandaged the wound on Harry's leg. Just as they were leaving the house, two cruisers with sirens blaring raced up the sandy road and swerved into the yard.

Jim jumped out of the first cruiser and Hodges struggled out as fast as he could. Two very tall deputies eased out of the second cruiser, guns drawn, looking back at the road and slowly scanning the woods before walking toward the four people clustered at the Rover.

"You two look all right," Hodges said in a loud voice.

"What happened?" Jim asked Harry as Katherine came around the Rover to greet them.

"Somebody tried to blow us away," Harry said. "Then, by the time we got organized, he had faded."

"The inside of the house looks like the O.K. Corral when the shooting was over," Katherine said, giving first Jim and then Hodges a hug.

Harry thought that was being done for his benefit and said, "We were on the lanai when the shooting started and made it into the house. That's when he began spraying the house with lead."

The two deputies joined them.

"Deputies Dan Springer and Berker Szalay," Hodges said.

Even Jim had to look up at them. Harry was already grinning. Both men had holstered their guns and tucked their caps under their left arms.

"We're pleased to meet you," Springer said.

"That would be Dan speaking," Szalay added seriously. "I'm Szalay. It's spelled S-Z-A-L-A-Y. I believe we've met Mr. Brock. Would that be right, Dan?"

"Yes, I think I remember, Berk," Springer said, turning to his partner. "Several years ago, we were out here investigating a vandalism charge. A Caterpillar tractor and butterflies figured in there somewhere."

"That's right," Szalay said, addressing Katherine. "We interrogated Mr. Brock and then we interrogated a Mr. LaBeau."

"That's right," Springer said, his voice rising in remembrance. "A large hound and a mule, wearing a straw hat, took part."

The two deputies were now standing facing one another, reconstructing the event.

"And after we had been questioning Mr. LaBeau for a few

minutes, the dog began grinning," Szalay replied. "We thought we had done something to offend him," Springer added, "but Mr. LaBeau said he only grinned like that when he was feeling friendly."

Jim broke the spell that seemed to have gripped the four listeners.

"Springer and Szalay," he said loudly. "Get your flashlights. Quarter the area along the creek. See if you can find any spent shells. You know what to do if you find any."

"Yes, Captain," the pair said in unison, turning and striding away toward their cruiser.

"We keep them around to lift things down from high shelves," Hodges said, still grinning.

"I'd forgotten," Harry said, "until I saw them. They should be on television."

"They certainly are tall," Katherine said as if emerging from a coma. "Do they always talk like that?"

"Always," Hodges said.

"Let's go in the house," Jim said, swatting a mosquito on his neck, "before we get eaten alive."

"I'm going to have to tape newspaper over the holes in the screens," Harry said as he pulled open what was left of the lanai door. "That BAR the shooter was using took out most of the glass in the front and the south side of the house."

"He certainly did a job in here," Jim said when he had crunched his way through the kitchen and the dining room, both seriously shot up.

"Did you hear him drive away?" Hodge asked, looking out a kitchen window.

"No," Katherine said. "As Harry said, we were sitting on the lanai before the shooting started, and we would have heard a car come over the bridge. It's got some loose planks that clatter whenever wheels roll over them."

"Parked off 19 and walked in," Jim said. "Probably left the same way."

"I think that's right," Harry said, beginning finally to register the full effects of what he and Katherine had experienced.

If she had been killed . . . he thought, his heart going cold.

"Did you stay in the house?" Hodges asked, breaking into his delayed fear.

"No," Harry said. "We went out the back door. Katherine had my shotgun. We split left and right. I was on the north side and worked my way around to the front of the house until I ran out of cover."

"He was supposed to circle the house and come toward me from the front," Katherine said, her voice still full of anger "but, instead, he came from the other way, and I damned near killed him."

"It wasn't quite that bad," Harry put in, trying to ease her stress over the incident.

"Every two people should have at least one brain," Katherine shot back, "and in this case it's pretty damned clear who had it."

Hodges gave a whoop of laughter and would have said something, but Jim glared him into silence.

"Who's the shooter?" Jim asked.

"Elijah Blue," Harry said without hesitating. "He's tightening the noose—at least, he's trying to."

Jim nodded. "And after you, Holly Pike," he said grimly.

"I think so," Harry said.

"But he's going to kill you first," Katherine said in a voice Harry couldn't read but that twisted his insides.

27

"What about the bull?" Harry asked.

He was sitting in a pink barrel-back chair in Holly's bedroom, having just come in from Barn Two where he had put in an hour working on the barn books and talking with the construction foreman at Barn One where work had suddenly slowed down. Holly was sitting in a lotus position on her bed with cushions piled in back of her, propping her up. Books and magazines were strewn around her television remote and cell phone.

She had, Harry thought, regained some of her old energy, but she was still pale and showing enough strain in her face and her voice to persuade Harry not to tell her about last night's attack on him and Katherine. Also, being told that delivery delays would push completion of Barn One back a month was enough depressing news for the day.

"No one's seen him for a while," Holly said in a lackluster voice. "Buster says he hasn't been around the cattle. I think he's probably drifted away. Let someone else deal with him."

"I'll take a look around anyway, and, by the way, Heather Parkinson's been by and left a note saying Sueño's hoof is healing much better than expected, but that tear in Jack's hip is still infected, mostly because he keeps reaching around and tearing off the bandage. She recommends confining him to a stall with double ropes to keep him from getting at the wound, at least until she can clean up the infection."

Holly gave a dismissive, "Ha! Try it and watch him kick the stall into kindling wood."

"Try it or not?" Harry asked.

"Yes. You know, I like that animal, but sometimes I think he's more trouble than he's worth."

"Changing the subject, I've been meaning to ask if you've seen Miguel recently."

"He was here yesterday," she said, showing a bit more interest.

"Has he seen Constanta?" Harry asked, taking as much emphasis out of the question as he could.

"He said he had talked with her."

"And?"

"Why the sudden interest in Miguel?" she asked, frowning.

"Because she has agreed to go through Clarissa's papers, something that the Pike Associates lawyers have not made any effort to do."

"Looking for what?" Holly asked, becoming very attentive.

"Anything in writing between her and Brandon bearing on the Oleander Farm lease."

"You're not giving up on that, are you?" Holly demanded, abruptly leaning forward and beginning to throw magazines off the bed. "Why not?"

"Because," Harry said, wondering what had made her angry, "it is inconceivable to me that Brandon and she would not have made some arrangement to protect her and her brothers in the event of his death."

Holly stopped flinging magazines around as abruptly as she had begun and dropped back into her pillows, breathing heavily.

"Damn her," she grated. "Damn her to hell!"

Her voice rose. Harry, alarmed, waited, wondering what would follow.

"Well? Say something!" she said, her face red with anger and her eyes snapping.

"You'd be a pretty good-looking woman if you stayed mad."

She threw the rest of the magazines off the bed and even grabbed her cell phone but caught herself in time and dropped it.

"Even dead, she's still biting my ass," Holly groaned, collapsing against the pillows.

Harry decided not to try again for a laugh.

"If Constanta can find something to settle the issue of the lease, it might help you to get beyond things a little," Harry suggested.

"She got away," Holly said.

"Wasn't that what you wanted?"

"Are you implying again that I wrote that note to her?" Holly demanded.

"It crossed my mind," Harry admitted, "but I also meant the lease for that farm must be a burden."

"Having to stay in this bed is a burden," she fired back. "I'd like to wring Esther Benson's neck for keeping me here."

She attacked the pillows for a moment, then said, punching and restacking them, "If I was deciding for myself, I'd be riding Jack right now, but I'm not, am I? I've got to think of whatever is here."

She pointed at her abdomen as she spoke as though she was going to give herself a poke. God! Harry thought, what if she did?

"It has suddenly impressed itself on me," she continued, "that I'm no longer in control of my body, and I don't like it."

Uncharitably, Harry thought she had adroitly moved the conversation away from the blackmail note. Then he reconsidered and abandoned judgment in favor of sympathy.

"It's been my experience that when women become pregnant for the first time," he said, "the realization that they've given hostages to fortune comes pretty quickly after the initial flush of joy."

"Oh, you'd know about that, would you?" Holly demanded in a mocking voice.

"Two marriages, five kids," he said.

"I hate it when you do that," she snapped.

"What?"

"Keep me from fighting with you."

"I'm experienced."

"Two marriages and five kids."

"That's it," Harry said, getting to his feet. "You've given me a week's work. I'd better get at it."

"When will I see you again?"

"Tomorrow, unless something comes up. Where's the gun?"

She turned and snaked a handgun out from under the pillows.

"I can dot an *i* with it anywhere in this room."

"Colt Defender," Harry said, impressed by her display of assurance in handling it. "Forty-five caliber, aluminum and stainless steel frame, rubber grips, Teflon slide. Top of the line. Have you ever fired it?"

"I've put a hundred rounds through it," she said, holding the gun at eye level, barrel pointed toward the ceiling, turning it back and forth as if she was studying it. "It was Brandon's. I didn't like having that shotgun in the bed and went to the Rod and Gun Club for some training with this. It kicks like a mule, but with a two-hand grip, I can shoot and put another hole in the ten ring in three seconds."

"I'm impressed," Harry said. "It's a gun with a history."

"So my instructor told me," she said, giving him her attention but showing no interest.

"When Benson frees you from the bed," Harry said, "I want you to start carrying the Colt both in and out of the house. Go to a gun shop and tell the clerk you want a small back holster for it and don't stop carrying until this mess is cleaned up."

"Isn't that a little drastic?" she asked.

"No. It's realistic. And one more thing, as soon as it's dark enough for you to put lights on in the house, have all the shades drawn."

"You really think Elijah's coming after me, don't you?"

"I don't know, but it's a distinct possibility."

"I hope I don't have to use this thing on anything but a paper target," she said, staring at the gun.

"I seriously hope you don't," Harry said, thinking of what had happened to him and Katherine.

Harry left Holly with Nip and Tuck for escorts. The dogs had come to like him and pressed against his legs as they walked, hoping to have their ears scratched. Before he left the house, he knelt down and put his arms around their necks and engaged in a very one-sided wrestle with them. Close up, paying attention, Harry saw that Tuck, putting on a show of enthusiasm, really didn't have his heart in it and meekly let Nip shoulder him aside without resisting.

"I'm sorry I missed you leaving Mrs. Pike," Thahn said, hurrying along the corridor to open the door.

"How is Tuck?" Harry asked, having regained his feet while Thahn scolded the dogs off him.

Thanh lost his smile and shook his head.

"Between us, Mr. Brock, I think he is slowly fading. So does Dr. Parkinson."

"Does Mrs. Pike know?" Harry asked.

"I'm not sure," Thahn said, then paused to ask, "I think you have an idiom in English that is applied to a person who does not reveal her feelings easily. Strangely, it is something on a sleeve."

311

Harry laughed when he guessed what Thahn was thinking of.

"I think you mean Mrs. Pike doesn't wear her heart on her sleeve."

"Exactly," Thahn said, looking pleased.

"It also means that a person does not easily show that she or he is attracted to another person," Harry said.

"For her age, she is a woman of great dignity," Thahn said more seriously.

"With so much on her mind," Harry said, "I don't think I will say anything about the dog's condition."

"I have thought it best not to," Thahn said, then added, "I have noticed you are limping. I hope you will not find my observation unwelcome."

Harry's first response was to think that there was very little Thahn didn't see. Until that moment, it had not occurred to Harry to say anything to Thahn about Holly being in danger. Now that he had thought of it, he was angry with himself. What a damned fool he had been. This man and his wife lived here with her. Of course he should be told.

"It's nothing serious," Harry said, "but I want to tell you something, Thahn, that should stop with you. Two nights ago, someone tried to kill me and the person who was with me. I was clipped in the leg. Otherwise we were unharmed. I'm quite certain we were attacked by Elijah Blue. Unfortunately, he got away. The police have beefed up their search, but I don't expect good results anytime soon."

"I am glad you escaped with a minor injury," Thahn said, "but I am not surprised by what you have told me. I fear that Mrs. Pike is also in danger."

"Yes, and I'm sorry I haven't talked about this sooner," Harry replied. "I've persuaded her—at least I think I have—to carry a gun inside the house and out."

"Do you think, Mr. Brock," Thahn said, "that my carrying a

gun, should it become known to the authorities, would expose Mrs. Pike to police interrogation?"

What we learn early in life is really important, Harry thought with sympathy as he listened to Thahn, realizing that the words *authorities* and *police interrogation* held more sinister implications for Thahn than they did for him.

"Do you mind if I ask if you were in the army as a young man?" Harry asked, avoiding asking which army.

Harry was watching carefully to catch, if he could, any indication that the question was resented. He saw no indication of that but something else, less easy to read. Thahn's look went inward. His face did not exactly change its expression but seemed to Harry to harden as if coping with the pain of whatever he was seeing. Then as quickly as he had left, he returned.

"I don't mind at all," he said with a flicker of a smile. "Yes, for many years. I was an infantry officer, fighting on the wrong side of a desperate war. I expected to die."

He remained silent for so long, lost again in his thoughts, that Harry said, "But you didn't."

"No, I didn't. Had it not been for Mr. Pike, I would have finally been shot, had I been lucky."

Harry regretted having wakened old and painful memories and moved on.

"You may carry a gun with no risk to you or Mrs. Pike. I will see to it that you are properly licensed to carry a concealed weapon. Do you have a gun?"

"I have a Walther P1, one of the few things I managed to salvage from the ruins of our defeat. I am sure Mr. Pike has 9mm shells. There is a P38 in his collection. Mine are too old to be reliable."

Harry was surprised at first and then was not. Beside food, what could have been more essential to a man in his position?

"I will provide you with ammunition," Harry said, "Do you agree that the less we trouble Mrs. Pike with this, the better?"

"Yes," Thahn said, "but I am afraid my wife will not be happy. The sight of the gun is sure to waken many memories."

"I am sorry," Harry said with quick concern. "Perhaps . . ."

"No," Thahn said firmly. "Some things must be done."

Harry instantly let the protest go. The *no* was clearly nonnegotiable.

Harry found Katherine in the dining room, a green bandanna tied around her head, sitting on her heels on a ragged square of canvas, picking up shards of window glass and crockery from the floor and piling them in a cardboard box, which she dragged behind her as she slid around the polished floor on her piece of canvas.

"Is this in your contract?" Harry asked from the kitchen door.

She came up in a single, smooth movement and turned to face him. She was dressed in her cut-offs and one of Harry's old blue shirts.

"Does your ass sweat?" she asked, making a face and tugging at the legs of her shorts.

"I never thought about it," he said. "Does yours?"

"Yes, and I don't like it. My underwear bunches up and shorts and slacks stick. So do skirts. It's embarrassing."

"You haven't entirely recovered from that tumor, you know," he said.

"What do you mean?" she asked, giving him a worried look.

"Well, you're talking freely about things sticking to your ass."

She grinned.

"It's not the tumor," she said. "It's the company. You have a degrading influence on me."

"I'm trying," he said.

"What do you think of the kitchen?" she asked, coming to

stand at the door with him.

Except for bullet holes in cupboard doors and the walls and the plastic duct tape over the windows and their splintered sashes, she had brought the room as close to its original condition as possible.

"It looks great," Harry said. "All we need now are the new windows and the cabinets."

He put an arm around her shoulders, and she leaned against him.

"It's a miracle we're alive," she said in a quiet voice.

"After that first burst," he said, "I don't think we were in much danger, although it did get to be a little noisy. You were great, by the way, even if you did damn near wind up my clock."

"I'm still mad at you for coming around the house that way," she said, putting her arm around his waist and giving him a squeeze. "And you're still limping."

"It's healing fine," he told her, thinking how good it would be if they could just go on standing together like this.

Ever since she had told him she was going home, he had waited with grim resignation for the day to arrive, but she had not, as far as he knew, called Minna. She had said nothing further to him about leaving. The waiting had taken its toll on him.

"Has Jim made any progress on finding Elijah?" she asked, returning to her work.

"No. The man might as well have vanished."

Harry followed her, but she warned him off.

"Back out, take off your sandals, and bang the glass slivers off them," she told him. "Talk to me from the door. The floor in here is thick with glass and china slivers. I'm picking up the big pieces before using the vacuum."

"I'm going to look into a lead in the morning," Harry said from the door, having shed his sandals and given them the mandatory whacking, "but I don't expect any good will come of it. By the way, Jim put a patrol car by the bridge."

"Good," she said, "but I've got more faith in that."

She straightened up and pointed at the shotgun lying within reach on the table. Harry started to say that he thought now would be a good time for her to leave the Hammock but found he couldn't get the words out.

"Why not keep me company for a few days?" he said.

"No," she said. "If I want company, I can visit with Tucker. I like being on my own, and no damned idiot with a BAR is going to spoil it for me."

Harry was stuck.

"Katherine," he said, feeling as if he was signing his own death warrant, "I don't think you're safe here alone."

She scrambled to her feet, turned, and planted her fists on her hips.

"Are you saying you want me to leave?"

"God, no," he replied, "but I don't want anything to happen to you."

She stared hard at him.

"Harry," she said with anger sharpening the words, "do you think I'm going to leave you while that maniac is loose?"

"Probably not," Harry replied, not sure whether he should feel pleased or miserable. Then, trying to end the stalemate, he said, "Maybe I'll try to keep him from being caught."

"That doesn't surprise me," she said, "you never did develop in moral judgment to the level of a tomcat."

28

The next morning Harry and Jim were standing in a narrow, dusty street in East Avola in front of a gray, ramshackle building, tilting slightly south, its windows boarded shut. It had once been a garage and, according to Jim, had, at some point in the recent past, been converted to a depot for stolen electronic equipment.

"The thing that gave it away," Jim said, standing with his thumbs hooked in his trouser pockets staring at the building and rocking back on his heels with a satisfied expression, "was the new roof."

"You better explain that," Harry said, chuckling at Jim's self-satisfaction.

"Look around you," Jim said. "What do you see?"

Harry glanced around at the rundown buildings, half of which had plywood nailed over the windows and the rest leaned and sagged with peeling paint and broken windows. Somewhere a loose shutter or a door was banging in the morning wind. The only other sound was the crackling of radios in the six cruisers parked at odd angles in the street.

"A movie set for a ghost town," Harry said.

"Now if the idiots who were fencing stolen goods from this place had stretched some blue builders' plastic over the part of the roof that was leaking, they might have gotten away with it. But, no, they went ahead and reroofed the whole place with top-of-the-line asphalt shingles."

"And one of your deputies, making a once-in-a-lifetime check on this street, saw the new roof and decided something didn't look right."

"Aside from the snide 'once in a lifetime' remark, you nailed it. Want to see what we found when we opened the doors?"

He was already striding up the cracked concrete driveway leading to the double doors as he spoke, and Harry followed.

"Welcome to the Second Chance Wholesale Company," Jim said, swinging open one of the doors.

Harry whistled. Inside the brightly lighted room were rows of floor to ceiling metal shelving, each side of the shelving equipped with a rolling ladder system. A dozen deputies were inventorying the yards and yards of televisions, over and under ovens, clothes dryers, computers, and stereo systems. Harry gave up making his list and just walked along the aisles with Jim and stared. Then he laughed.

"Is this outfit really called Second Chance Electronics?"

"Check the yellow pages," Jim said.

A deputy near the top of one of the ladders called, "Captain, pull that door to, will you? We just got the place cooled down."

"Air conditioning," Harry said as he and Jim left, closing the door behind them.

"Full bath with shower, galley kitchen, fully equipped office, and a bookkeeper," Jim said with satisfaction.

"This operation has been running nearly five years," Jim said.

A wide grin spread over his face. Harry had seldom seen him appear so happy.

"We have a list of every retailer who's bought from them," Jim continued. "There is going to be such unhappiness as you wouldn't believe."

They were standing on the worn cement island where gas pumps had once stood.

"I believe it," Harry said. "Now I want to spoil your fun."

"You can try," Jim replied.

"Has anyone in your department talked with Tillman Hanks, the man who owns Filigree Stock Farm in Paltrew County?"

"I never heard of Hanks," Jim said, scowling. "Why should I be interested in him?"

"It has to do with Elijah Blue," Harry said. "I don't remember whether Hanks is mentioned in Elijah's dossier or not," he added, going on to tell Jim what he had learned from Tucker about Elijah's connection with the farm. "I don't know, actually, whether Hanks is still alive or not."

"Do you think Elijah is out there?"

"It's possible, but I doubt that Hanks or whoever owns the place has knowingly been harboring a wanted man."

"I know the Paltrew County sheriff," Jim said. "I could ask him to have a look."

"It's your call, Jim," Harry said, "but I think I might have more luck getting straight answers from the Filigree staff than someone from the Paltrew Sheriff's Department."

"You're thinking what we're not supposed to think anymore," Jim said, making his unhappiness clear.

"I'm afraid so," Harry said, "and I know that I failed to get Gladys Jackson's help in locating Elijah. But she may not have known where he was and been unhappy about being asked if she did. Nevertheless, she and Rosalee Franklin told me far more than I expected."

"You're not likely to sit down and have tea with Hanks's grooms," Jim said.

"Point taken," Harry said, "but they probably will talk to me, and if you'll cut me loose, I'd like to take a shot at it."

"What if Elijah's out there?"

"Then it will get interesting very quickly."

"He's likely to know you're there before you know he is."

"Probably."

"You're going to do this whether I want you to or not."

Jim spoke it as if Harry had asked for the time.

"I'll get there without sirens and a filming crew," Harry said.

"And what does Katherine say about your going?"

Harry did not want to be asked about Katherine's reaction. For one thing, it had been in his opinion overly dramatic. For another, one of the less pointed things she had said was that he should have a brain scan because only someone with a serious mental affliction could be so stupid.

"More or less what you've said," Harry said.

"Smart woman," Jim said, calling after him as he made his escape, but Harry was already through the door.

The next morning Harry drove to the Filigree Stock Farm located in Paltrew County, southwest of Lake Okeechobee, a totally flat, sparsely populated area of huge citrus farms, cattle ranches, nature preserves, and steaming heat. He had called ahead and talked with Harkin Scropes, the Filigree stud manager, who gave him directions for reaching the ranch. It proved to be a wise decision. Harry drove the final twenty miles to the Filigree gate without seeing another person and without knowing what to look for, Harry thought he would most likely have missed it.

"Why all the mystery about the entrance?" he asked Scropes when the introductions were over.

Harkin Scropes was a tall, rangy man in his fifties whose lean, weathered face looked like rawhide. Dressed in a western shirt and boots and smelling of horses, he would have made a perfect bad man for an old-fashioned western, Harry thought, if it hadn't been for his blue eyes, which sparkled with friendliness and good humor.

"Horse thieves," he said, leaning back in a squeaky old swivel chair and lifting his feet onto his desk and crossing his ankles.

They were sitting in Scropes's office, and, although it was stuffed with the latest electronic equipment, it was furnished with two antique rolltop desks and chairs and even had a box phone on the wall with a crank and hearing piece separate from the mouthpiece.

"Are you having a joke at my expense?" Harry asked with grin.

There was no way not to like this man.

"Nope," Scropes replied. "It's the real wild west out here. "We've got cattle rustlers, horse thieves, slick traders, the whole *enchilada*. Sometimes, if you told me this was New Mexico before the railroad arrived, I'd believe it. So we don't advertise how to get in here."

"Well," Harry said, "all you're lacking is a whorehouse and a saloon. You've got all the rest."

"Who says we're lacking them?" Scropes asked with a wide grin, letting his feet drop to the floor. "Can I sell you a horse?"

"Driving in I saw a lot of top-grade stock. Do you still specialize in harness racers?"

"That's right, and we can't begin to keep up with demand. If you want your mare bred to any one of our three stallions, it's an eight-month wait."

"If I get into the business, I'll remember to get my name in early. Is Mr. Tillman Hanks still the owner?"

"Till passed five years ago. I hope you weren't counting on talking with him," Scropes said. "You might have asked when you called. Why all the mystery as to why you're here?"

"I'm working for Brandon Pike's widow," Harry said. "I suspect you've heard what happened to Brandon."

"I did. Is Mrs. Pike running the stud?"

"She is," Harry said. "Naturally, she's doing everything she can to maintain The Oaks' reputation. It's not a good idea to talk about problems in a way that might damage confidence in the business. She has a small problem she hopes to solve quietly. That's why I came up here in person rather than talking over the phone."

"What's the problem?"

"Her manager's gone missing. Does the name Elijah Blue mean anything to you?"

"I believe I've heard it somewhere, but I can't recall where. Blue was the manager?"

"That's right, and from what I've learned, his father, Homer Blue, worked as a trainer here for Mr. Hanks for years and brought the boy up in the trade."

"Now I remember. Till used to mention Homer Blue from time to time. He thought a lot of him, but that goes back a ways."

"I suppose it does," Harry agreed. "Elijah hasn't dropped in for a visit recently?"

Scropes squirmed a little, making his chair squeal, and frowned.

"That spot's a little tender," Scropes said. "We run a big outfit with a lot of men. Some are Hispanic, some are black, and the rest are white or combinations. They more or less work together, but they don't bunk together, if you take my meaning. You see, I might not know whether he's been here or not."

"I see," Harry said, "and sometimes it's best not to know everything."

"That's about the size of it," Scropes agreed, "what with the Immigration and all."

"If you were to let me talk to some of the straw bosses, who would they be?"

"I think you might have a word with Calvin Franklin."

Harry paused over the name but covered the hiatus by pulling a small notebook and pen out of a pocket and writing it down.

"And that would be all right with you?" he asked when he was finished.

"You're not involved with the police?"

"No, I'm a private investigator, going quietly about my client's business."

Scropes lifted a wireless phone off his desk and punched in a number. Harry heard a man answer.

"Cal, this is Harkin. I've got a man who'd like a word with you."

Harry could hear Franklin's voice but not what he was saying.

"No," Scropes said, "he's not the law or a bill collector. I've been talking with him a while. I see no reason not to."

Scropes listened again, nodded, and said, "He's got a car. I'll send him out," then got to his feet and motioned Harry toward one of the office windows.

"You see that road going past the corral with the sorrel mare in it? You follow that about a quarter of a mile, and you'll come on a man in a black pickup. That will be Cal Franklin. He's a good man. You can trust him."

Harry thanked Scropes and drove down a dirt track bordered on both sides with white plank fences and wide fields dotted with horses until he found the black pickup. It was parked at a crossroads, and its driver, a tall, powerfully built man Harry judged to be in his mid-thirties, was leaning against a front fender with his arms folded.

He watched Harry approach from under the brim of his low-crowned, wide-brimmed straw hat, which Harry had noted was standard wear for ranchers and farmers in Paltrew County, but made no move to greet Harry.

"Thanks for interrupting your work to talk with me," Harry said, holding out his hand. "My name's Brock, Harry Brock."

"You already know mine," Franklin said, pushing away from

the truck and shaking Harry's hand briefly. "What's on your mind?"

"Is there a chance you're related to Rosalee Franklin in Avola?"

"Nephew," Franklin answered.

"I've met your aunt. I thought I saw a resemblance."

"I don't get down to Avola much, but when I do, I stop by."

"I have a lot of respect for her," Harry said. "She's a good woman with a lot of responsibility."

"I know. I'm not married myself," Franklin said as if that explained something.

"Neither am I," Harry said. "Right now I'm looking for someone who disappeared from work a while ago, and no one seems to know where he is."

"You got a personal interest in this person?"

Harry couldn't decide whether the young man in front of him was hostile or simply suspicious and that being the case, Harry decided to stick to the truth as closely as he could without shutting Franklin down.

"I'm working for someone who does," he said.

"What's his name?"

"It's a woman, Holly Pike. She runs a stud called The Oaks in Avola. You might have heard of it."

"I mean the name of the person you're looking for."

"Elijah Blue."

"Never heard of him."

"I'm disappointed," Harry said. "He's your aunt's half brother. They're very close to one another."

"Look around you, Brock, and think carefully before you answer. Are you calling me a liar?"

Harry gambled.

"Do you know there's an APB out on Elijah for murder, aggravated assault, arson, malicious maiming of a horse, and a few other crimes? He's got to be stopped before he kills someone else. A few nights ago, he tried to kill me and the person with me. It was a near thing."

Harry didn't know exactly what Franklin had heard in that list that turned him, possibly it was the horse maiming. Whatever it was, all the aggression drained out of him.

"He's not here," Franklin said. "He was for a few days. 'Waiting for something to blow over,' he said."

"When did he leave?"

"Four or five days ago."

"Did he seem to be himself?"

"Hard to say. He never did talk much. He ate and slept and one morning I got up and he was gone."

"And you didn't know he was wanted by the police?"

Franklin shook his head. "I'd seen something on television about Brandon Pike being killed, but I didn't give it much thought. After he ran over Henry Jackson and Aunt Rosalee lost that lawsuit against him, I stopped paying attention to Pike."

"Did Elijah mention him?"

"No. I tried to talk with him about his work, but he said he had to be quiet and think. He had worked for Pike a long time. I never made the connection."

"No," Harry said. "I can see why you wouldn't, but if he comes again, don't hesitate. Call the Sheriff's Department. Elijah is not himself. Whoever he was, he's someone else now and much, much more dangerous."

"Well, you guessed right," Hodges said, reaching again toward the diminished plate of iced walnut and cherry cupcakes Katherine, who was still not speaking to Harry, had brought out to the lanai, along with a pitcher of iced tea.

Beyond the screen the locusts were fiddling full blast, their pauses filled with the high-pitched whirring of the katydids. A late sun, its power seemingly undiminished, was casting long shadows across the lawn.

"Elijah could still be out there," Jim said, scowling at Hodges's lack of constraint.

"Possibly," Harry said, "but if he is, I've misjudged Calvin Franklin."

"I wouldn't say judgment was his long suit, would you, Jim?" Katherine asked, avoiding Harry's gaze as she replenished the cupcake plate. Then, without waiting for an answer, she strode back into the kitchen.

"You want to stay at my place tonight?" Jim asked innocently.

Hodges tried to laugh with his mouth full of cupcake and created a lot of crumbs.

"There! Now look what you've done," Jim said loudly, starting to get up. "I'm sorry, Harry. I'll go get a broom and dustpan." Then, turning to Hodges again, he said, "You're a case all separate and by itself."

Untroubled by Jim's outburst, Hodges poured himself more iced tea.

"Don't even think about it," Harry said, motioning Jim back into his lounge chair. "By the time you got to the broom closet and back, the ants would have those crumbs all cleaned up. The real question is—where is Elijah now?"

"Franklin didn't know where he was going?" Jim asked.

"No," Harry said.

"Why'd he go out there in the first place?" Hodges asked.

"Looking for a place to do some thinking," Harry said, recalling Calvin Franklin's answer to that question.

"Then he came back and tried to blow Harry and Katherine's heads off," Hodges added.

"Frank, lower your voice," Jim said, throwing a glance at the kitchen door.

Then he turned to Harry and, speaking quietly, said, "Are

you worrying at all about Katherine being here alone while you're gone?"

"Yes and no," Harry said. "She refused to leave as long as Elijah is loose, and she won't follow me around. Of course, she's spending most of the day away, working for Haven House again."

"And she's got that shotgun," Frank said, "which she handles like she knew what to do with it."

"How much effort is going into finding Elijah?" Harry asked, not wanting to talk about Katherine and her shotgun.

"All the manpower we have," Jim said. "Practically all our other cases, aside from missing children, are on hold. My guess is he's either holed up somewhere or he's driving with stolen plates."

"Probably off a wrecked vehicle sitting in the yard of some body shop, waiting for insurance action," Hodges put in. "Who's going to notice they're missing?"

"Do you know what he's driving?" Harry asked.

"He *was* driving an '04 Ford pickup. How's that for conspicuous?" Hodges asked.

"Maybe that's what he's still driving," Harry said. "The bottom line here is that we're waiting until he shows up again either here or at The Oaks."

"But which place?" Jim asked, obviously frustrated.

"Elijah's not stupid," Harry said. "He knows time will run out for him. With a cruiser at my bridge and one at The Oaks' gate, I think he will go after Holly and approach from one of the drives."

No one disagreed.

29

"All right, Katherine, I made a mistake," Harry said after Jim and Hodges had left. "I should have told you where I was going, but I didn't want to worry you."

Katherine was folding clothes on the kitchen table, giving no indication she was hearing anything he was saying. Harry went to the counter, pulled open a drawer, took out a carving knife, marched back to the table, and slammed it down beside the pile of folded clothes.

"Let's get this over with," he said briskly. "Take your pound of flesh. I'm exempting my privates."

She stopped folding to look at him, her eyes like chips of emerald ice.

"You went up there to kill Elijah Blue and don't deny it."

"The question never came up. I talked with the personable Calvin Franklin and drove home, as you know," Harry said.

"You knew you might not come back," she said more quietly.

"The thought that I might die at the Filigree Stock Farm never crossed my mind," he said, "although there was a moment when I thought Franklin was going to deck me."

"That's probably true," she said, showing no sign of relenting, "but it only makes it all worse. You don't think about dying, and you don't think about the people who would be hurt if you were killed."

"The last time you drove into Avola," he said, "did you think you might be killed and how miserable everyone who loved you would be?"

"If you can't see the difference between what you did today and what I did, you're a complete fool."

"I never thought otherwise," Harry said, "but I did get you talking again."

Katherine grasped a folded towel from the pile and began beating him with it, driving him backward until his heels hit the sideboard.

"Time!" he shouted, forming a T with his hands. "Everyone go to a neutral corner!"

"I've overlooked something," Katherine said, giving him a final lick and breathing heavily. "I should have killed you years ago and gotten it over with."

With that, she marched back to the table, slammed the towel onto the pile, and carried the laundry upstairs, stamping on every tread of the stairs until she reached the top, leaving Harry staring after her open-mouthed, pondering the mystery of life.

After dinner, a truce having been negotiated and signed, they walked over to see Tucker. Sanchez and Oh, Brother! were waiting for them at the end of the farm road. As they all went toward the house together, Harry asked Katherine if she thought the two animals seemed unusually subdued.

"Is something wrong, Brother?" she asked the big mule, stroking his neck as she spoke.

Sanchez, who was leading the procession, looked back and whined. Oh, Brother! shook his head and snorted softly.

"I think it's coincidence," Katherine said, her voice lacking all conviction.

"Well, we'll find out soon enough," Harry said.

Tucker was waiting for them on the stoop with a cloth on the table, plates, tumblers, cheese and crackers, and a jug of plum brandy.

"I'm glad to see you, but the news is bad. The coyotes got into the hen run and before Sanchez and Oh, Brother! could get there and drive them off, they killed Lucinda and three other hens. Lucinda was Longstreet's favorite."

Sanchez barked.

"Oh, yes," Tucker said, "Sanchez had both of them on him at one time and was bitten in three or four places. I arrived with the shotgun just as Oh, Brother! grabbed the male with his teeth and threw him right over the henhouse. The female fled without giving me a clear shot."

"Good work," Katherine said, stooping to pat Sanchez, then turning to stroke Oh, Brother!'s nose.

"How did they get into the pen?" Harry asked while Katherine was getting boosts and bumps of appreciation from her two heroes.

"They appear to have chewed right through the chicken wire and burst in on the birds. From the feathers scattered around, I think Longstreet tried to hold them off while the hens ran for the henhouse door. They were coming out of the run with two of the dead birds when Sanchez and Oh, Brother! caught them."

"I guess you're going to need a heavier gauge wire for the run," Harry said.

"Horse high, pig tight, and bull strong," Tucker said in agreement. "Now, let's sit down and enjoy some of this plum brandy and goat cheese." He busied himself pulling out chairs, then pouring the brandy. "I've been aging this batch in a white oak cask, and I think it's about the best I've ever made. But, Katherine, I'll wait for your comments. There's no use asking Harry, he likes anything with alcohol in it."

Katherine had just escaped to the stoop and was straightening her skirt and blushing slightly.

"You can't say those two don't appreciate praise," she said, to Tucker's amusement.

Harry listened with pleasure to Katherine's laughter, which he had not heard for a while.

"By the way," Katherine said, "where's Jane Bunting and her children?"

"Gone to the wild wood," Tucker said with a sigh.

"Introducing Aurelius and Frederica to the dark side," Harry said, eliciting a sour look from Katherine.

When they were all seated, Tucker raised his glass and said, "Here's to Lucinda and her sisters."

They sipped the brandy, and Katherine declared it the best she had ever tasted.

"Then my efforts are fully rewarded," Tucker said.

The talk turned more general and gradually swung around to Elijah and Holly Pike. Harry brought Tucker up to date and skimmed quickly over his visit to the Filigree Stock Farm and his conversation with Calvin Franklin.

"Wasn't it a little reckless to go in there with no backup?" Tucker asked.

"It was way beyond reckless," Katherine said firmly.

"I'm going to take the Fifth on this," Harry said. "The subject is fraught and then some."

Tucker grinned.

"I see I've poked a stick into a yellow jacket's nest," he said. "Never mind then. We'll just agree that it was a damned fool thing to do and move on."

"That seems fair, even-handed, and respectful of all points of view," Harry replied, holding out his glass for a refill.

"Where's Elijah?" Tucker asked in an altogether different tone of voice.

"It's easier to say where he's not," Harry said, having noticed that Katherine was studying her glass, ignoring the cheese and crackers on her plate, and looking increasingly grim.

"He's not far away," Katherine said abruptly. "I imagine he's deciding whether to come back for Harry or go for Holly Pike."

Although Harry thought she was right, he did not, he found, want to expand on the subject.

"Only Elijah knows," Tucker said, paused and, turning to Harry, asked, "when after a long search you find the thing you've lost, isn't it often the case that it's been under your nose all along?"

Thinking about Katherine had taken Harry's mind off the conversation, and he only nodded and said, "There's always the chance Jim's people will find him."

"The question," Katherine asked bitterly, "is when, if ever, or only after he's killed two more people?"

The silence that had gripped the table was broken by a scrabbling sound under their feet.

"What's that?" Katherine demanded, staring at the floor.

"It's Florinda," Tucker said, helping himself to more cheese. "You're falling behind," he added, cutting Katherine another slice of the cheese and pushing the crackers toward her.

"You've named the skunk Florinda!" Katherine said, breaking into a smile.

"Actually," Tucker said, "Sanchez chose the name, saying he liked the play on flowers. Oh, Brother! enjoyed the irony but suggested Redola as being more robust, but Jane Bunting thought it demeaning, and no one wanted to argue the point with her."

The scratching and scraping increased, and a moment later, Florinda emerged from under the floor, paused to look around in a nearsighted way. Sanchez and Oh, Brother! had withdrawn to a prudent distance, and a moment later, two tiny editions of Florinda trotted into view, tails erect.

"It's best if we just sit still now," Tucker said in a conversational voice, "until she and the young ones begin to forage."

"They're delightful," Katherine said just above a whisper, watching them with a rapt expression.

A moment later Florinda waddled away toward the woods followed by the two youngsters, walking in a perfect line, leaving the faintest taint of skunk in their wake. Katherine wrinkled her nose.

"Does that get into the house?" she asked Tucker.

"I suppose it does, a little, but I find I like it. It reminds me that Florinda honored us by deciding to make her den under our house. It's something you can't buy or compel. It has to come to you."

While Tucker was speaking, Sanchez and Oh, Brother! returned to the stoop, and Katherine picked up her glass and laughed when Sanchez rubbed his nose with his paw. Harry noted gratefully that, for the moment, she looked happy.

When there was anyone around to listen, Harry unburdened himself about the paperwork the insurance companies demanded from him before initiating the payment process, deliberately delayed, in Harry's view, as a matter of policy, forcing Katherine to listen to his list of complaints before she could escape to her work at Haven House.

"Serves you right for working for them," she said, gathering her car keys and pocketbook, preparatory to making an escape.

"I'd be on food stamps without them," Harry replied.

"Not a bad idea," she said, planting a kiss on the top of his head as she left. "You could stand to lose some weight."

Harry sat for a while over his cold coffee, trying to recall what it was Tucker had said last night that he wanted to remember and couldn't. When his patience ran out, he cleared away the kitchen dishes and left for The Oaks. Before he had driven off the Hammock, his cell rang and he stopped just short of the bridge to take the call.

"It's Soñadora Asturias," she said.

"I'm glad you gave me your full name," Harry said. "I might have confused you with Soñadora O'Toole."

"Who is she?"

"An Irish girl I know, just off the boat."

"What bullshit am I hearing here?"

"I've told you before, you shouldn't be using that word," he protested and started to say more, but she interrupted.

"And you should not be telling me about this Irish girl you met on a boat."

"There is no Irish girl," Harry replied, sorry he hadn't just said, "Hello, it's nice to hear from you."

"I'm hanging up," he said. "I'll call you right back."

He did, and when she answered, she said, "Soñadora Asturias speaking."

"This is Harry Brock. Haven't we met somewhere?"

"Are you saying you don't want to talk to me?"

"No, I'm trying to make you laugh," he said. "I want to talk to you. How are you?"

"All right. Busy." She did not sound amused, and Harry began to wonder if they were at all compatible, but this errant thought was cut off by her voice. "An additional sadness to this economic mess is that spousal abuse has risen. More women are seeking protection for themselves and their children. I think in some cases, Harry, they come just for food. Also, it has become harder to raise money. For a long time now, *Salvamento* has carried a surplus, but now it is draining away."

"I'm sorry to hear it. Rowena told me their Haven House caseload has increased. Have you talked with her lately?"

"Yes. How are you?"

"Busy, like you."

He wanted to ask why she had called him but would not let

himself. He stubbornly stuck to conveying information.

"Jim Snyder hasn't been able to find Brandon Pike's killer," he said, "and I haven't been much help. But someone shot at the house while Katherine and I were inside. Whoever did it probably was the same person who killed Brandon."

"Were you and Katherine injured?" she demanded.

"No," Harry said.

"Will this person try again?"

"I don't think so. Jim's people are watching the house now."

That stretched the truth he was striving for, but he saw no point in frightening her further.

"Is it because you are working for Mrs. Pike that you were attacked?"

"I think so, but I'm sure he will soon be caught."

"Do you know who this person is?"

"I think so, yes."

"Why hasn't he been arrested?"

She was sounding increasingly anxious, and perhaps that was what he had been seeking.

"He has to be found first."

At that moment Harry remembered what Tucker had said, "When after a long search you find the thing you've lost, isn't it often the case that it's been under your nose all along?"

Where in Elijah's case would under your nose be? he asked himself.

"How is Katherine?" Soñadora asked in a quieter voice, interrupting his reflections and ending any chance that he would stop sounding like a cigar store Indian.

"She is recovering well. She's going home soon."

"You will miss her," Soñadora said.

"Minna and Thornton will be glad to have her back, Thornton especially," he said, and then took his turn at grasping the nettle. "Have you been corresponding with Pierre Robichaud?"

"Yes. Things are difficult. There has been an outbreak of measles. As usual, there are too many patients for the services."

"I'm sorry to hear that," Harry said, sounding to himself as if he was talking in a barrel.

"I help him with his Quiche occasionally," she continued, "but the costs of the telephone are prohibitive."

He thought of mentioning other options for keeping in touch but stopped himself.

"Are we going to meet any time soon?"

He regretted the question as soon as it was out of his mouth.

"It would not be wise."

"Heavens, no!" Harry said before he could stop himself, but the sarcasm was wasted on her. There were times when he wondered if they shared the same planet. Cooling down, he said, "Are you really all right?"

"Yes, Harry," she said, added something in Quiche, then said, her voice fading, *"Vaya con dios,"* and broke the connection.

Harry sat staring at the bridge for several minutes, stranded in the anomie brought on by the failure of their conversation—if that's what it was—and not only by the Quiche. She often said things to him in Quiche and refused to translate. Why had she called him? Was it anger or hopelessness that had turned him into a dry stick on hearing her voice? Try guilt, he thought. None of this trouble was her fault. How final had the *goodbye* been?

"Harry!"

The call jumped Harry out of his reverie. Corporal Fred Robbins, who had been guarding Tyce Yellen, was standing on the bridge, staring at the Rover, looking worried. "Anything wrong?" he shouted.

Harry started the Rover and drove onto the bridge, stopping beside Robbins.

"Making a phone call," he said. "Why aren't you with Yellen?"

"Reprieve," Robbins said with a grin.

"Are you missing Michelle yet?"

Robbins's face grew red.

"Truth is, I am. She grows on a person."

Harry laughed and said, "Don't they all? Thanks for looking after me. By the way, if you sit quietly and keep your eyes open, you might get a look at a panther. There's a young female that drops by now and then. You might be safer taking an interest in her."

On his way to The Oaks, Harry continued to wonder if Elijah might indeed be hiding under his nose. What, he wondered, had Tucker had in mind?

"But where could he be?" Holly asked in an irritated tone of voice.

Released from bed but restricted to walking or driving a car, she was restless and irritable. At the moment, they were in Sueño's paddock. Harry was feeding the mare an apple. Dressed in her boots and the rest of her riding gear, Holly stood with her fists on her hips, frowning at the mare. The butt of her pistol, protruding from its back holster, gave her a raffish look that Harry thought became her.

He also asked himself if she had written that note to Clarissa but killed the thought. Jones and his people had done their best to crack her resistance, but she had refused to confirm or deny the accusation. In the end, Jim called an end to the interrogations.

"There's not a scrap of evidence against her," he'd told Harry, "and no motive beyond malice. You may say revenge, but prove it."

The truth was that he had no wish to.

"No more apples," she told Harry. "I want to watch her move. Walk off and see if she follows you."

Still holding an apple, Harry set off at a good pace, and Sueño immediately followed.

"She's looking good," Holly called. "Try to make her trot."

Harry broke into a chugging jog that he knew instantly was going to leave him winded if he had to continue for more than a few minutes and immediately decided to take up running again. A moment later, he felt Sueño give him a boost with her nose.

"She wants the apple!" Holly shouted, breaking into bright laughter.

"She can have it," Harry said, slowing to a walk and dropping his arm over the mare's neck.

He gave her the apple.

"She's looking really good," Holly said, catching up with them. "Heather tells me that if her frog continues to heal, she can be ridden next week. I think I'll ride her, despite the demon Benson's *fatwa*."

Harry continued to lean against the mare as she finished the apple, thinking it would be impossible to dislike her.

"How many horse barns are there?" he asked.

"Six," Holly answered, continuing to eye the mare critically.

"What are you looking for?" Harry asked, noting that he had never known anyone who had a professional interest in animals to be sentimental about them.

"I'm looking at her coat, watching how she carries herself. Those two things will tell me a great deal about her condition, which will tell me if Parkinson's right or not about that frog healing. The heat's all gone out of the hoof and ankle. That's another positive sign."

"So, what do you think?"

"I agree with Heather," Holly said, walking around Sueño,

stroking her as she went. "This lady is almost fully recovered. She's still favoring the foot, but some of that's habit. When she forgets, she puts her full weight on it. I'm pleased."

"So am I," Harry said. "If it's all right with you, I'm going through the barns."

"You don't think Elijah's been living in one of them, do you?" she asked derisively.

"Did you ever read *The Purloined Letter*?" Harry asked.

Holly thought a minute, then said, "Poe?"

"That's right."

"It was a long time ago. I'll go with you."

"No," Harry said. "I need to do this myself."

"You're not going to find him in there, you know," she said, obviously miffed at being rebuffed.

"Probably not," Harry said, "but if you're mistaken, I don't want any distractions."

"I resent being called a *distraction!* But if you *really* think he's in there, why not call Captain Snyder and get a small army out here to search the place?"

"He hasn't got a small army, and he wouldn't send it if he had."

"Because he's as sure as I am that Elijah Blue isn't in one of those empty barns."

"Right."

At that point, Thahn, carrying a cordless phone, appeared at the paddock gate with Nip and Tuck at his heels. Seeing them, the dogs broke into a run.

"Oh, oh!" Harry said. "Stampede!"

Holly laughed, but as neither Holly nor Thahn said anything to check the dogs' charge, Nip and Tuck, barking joyously, skidded into them, almost flattening them with exuberant greetings. Finally, Holly called a halt, and both dogs sat down, panting happily, their tongues flopping out the sides of their mouths.

Despite the good cheer of their greeting, Harry noted sadly that Tuck had lost more weight.

"A call for you from Dr. Benson," Thahn said.

Holly thanked him and took the phone.

Harry started to leave, but Holly called after him.

"Take the dogs with you."

"No," Harry said. "If he's in there, I don't want him alerted."

Holding the cell to her ear, she waved both men on.

"Are the unused barns locked?" Harry asked Thahn as they walked toward the house.

"I don't think so," Thahn said. "Mr. Pike made it a policy not to lock them. He feared fire, and he feared most not being able to get the horses out. I am glad he did not see Barn One burn. Are you going into the barns?"

"All of them. I probably should have had a look before now."

Thahn was quiet for a moment and then said, "Perhaps you would like to have Buster and some of the other men make the search."

"Thanks for the suggestion, but I think I should do this myself."

"Ah," Thahn said on a darker note, "you fear a conspiracy. I had not thought of that."

"Intimidation," Harry said. "Elijah is a frightening man."

"Yes, and they must live in their community."

Harry let that go.

"Mrs. Pike thinks I'm crazy. Perhaps I am."

"If there is even the slightest chance that he is in one of the barns," Thahn said, "you are running a grave risk. I would be glad to accompany you." And then, reaching the house, he said before Harry could reply, "I have taken the precaution to carry my gun."

He pulled open one side of his house jacket, revealing his shoulder holster.

"I'm glad, Thahn," Harry said quietly, "but I don't intend to take any heroic actions. I just want to go very quietly and satisfy myself that we have no stowaways."

Harry tried to sound convincing and perhaps he was, because Thahn nodded and left him to return to the house.

30

Harry, thinking, on the one hand, that he was on a fool's errand, and on the other, that he was putting himself in a position to have his head blown off, walked quickly along the curved, white, crushed-gravel drive to the point where it left the grove of tall live oaks that gave the farm its name and led into the barn area. Stepping out of the shade and into the blazing light, he paused for a moment, letting his eyes adjust to the white glare. To his left, work on Barn One seemed to have picked up. Two front loaders were distributing lumber to the framed ends of the building.

Outside the framed area, a huge cement truck sat waiting, its mixer rolling slowly. Inside, a dozen men were nailing frames into which the cement would be poured. Beyond the construction site, the remaining five barns were arranged in a wide horseshoe, each sitting on its own grassy half acre of white, plank-fenced paddock. At both ends of the barns were large concrete rectangles with iron hitching posts where the horses could be saddled or washed and curried.

Barns Two and Three were comparatively quiet. Harry saw Buster lead a young chestnut gelding out of the barn and release him in the paddock. The horse immediately set off around the enclosure in a spirited gallop, mane and tail flowing in the wind. Buster watched him a moment and then returned to the barn. In the Barn Three paddock, two dark, very pregnant mares were standing with their heads over the fence watching the gelding.

Satisfied with what he had seen, Harry walked purposely to Barn Two, and, after talking briefly with Buster about the afternoon exercise schedule for Jack and Scotsman, he went into the makeshift office he had set up in a corner of the grain room. Turning on the computer, he spent fifteen minutes entering Buster's written reports on each of the horses into the day's report and then stapled them and put them in a file.

He walked the length of the barn, checking each of the stalls and asking questions of the men working at the endless task of keeping the stud functioning properly, after which he walked to Barn Three, forcing himself to appear relaxed, and continued his inspection. When he had worked his way to the far end of the barn and was sure he was not being observed, he stepped out the door and crossed to Barn Four, which he knew would be empty, its horses having all been put that morning into either the paddock or one of the more distant pastures.

Nevertheless, he walked through it, checking every stall and the grain room and the tack room as he went. Finding nothing out of order, he crossed quickly to Barn Five, loosening his CZ in its holster as he went. There were no windows at the ends of the barns and before opening the door, he checked to see if any of the wooden, hinged windows were propped open, hoping for a look inside. They were all closed, and with considerable reluctance, Harry eased open one of the doors.

He moved it slowly, but the grating squeal of the hinges sounded to Harry as loud as cannons firing. Certainly, no one inside could fail to hear him. He paused, not so much hesitating as allowing the adrenaline to build and the dread to spike before action burned it all away. Once the door was open, he sprinted through the opening and dropped onto one knee in the musty-smelling shadows, his gun sweeping the space in front of him.

Silence.

A rectangle of yellow light from the partially open door lay over the floor and a portion of the grain room. Harry, his eyes fully adjusted to the dusty light filtering into the barn from the narrow windows at ceiling level in the stalls, looked down the corridor, straining to hear any scuff of boot or scrape of cloth dragging against wood.

More silence, then a flurry of movement at the third stall, and a mouse skittered across the corridor and vanished under a gate. Harry relaxed slightly. Still hugging the wall, he stood up slowly. The grain room was directly across the corridor from him, its door closed. He was pressed against the tack room, three steps from its door.

Harry weighed his options and did not like them. Elijah could be in any of the stalls or in either the grain or the tack room, making it impossible to look into any of the spaces without at least momentarily having his back turned on an unexplored and deeply shadowed hiding place. Perhaps he should have accepted Thahn's offer to come with him but quickly rejected the idea. There was no reason why Thahn should put his life at risk.

Get on with it, Harry told himself. Once he had made a thorough search of the tack room, he made his way up the length of the barn, crossing and recrossing the corridor, stall to stall, until he reached the end of the barn.

"One down and one to go," he said to the mouse that had trotted out onto the last gate, nose twitching, to have a closer look at the intruder.

In the grain room of Barn Six Harry found what he was looking for, a sleeping bag, plastic spoons, emptied cans of beans and stew, bread wrappers, Subway's take-aways, and a row of empty whiskey bottles.

Harry called Jim Snyder, then waited for the Captain and Jones and his Crime Scene team to arrive.

"I don't think he's been staying here recently," Jones told Jim and Harry after his people had done their work. "Mice have gotten into the sleeping bag, and rats have chewed on the empty food boxes. I'd guess he hasn't been here for at least a week, but we've got a load of prints."

"That's it?" Jim asked.

"Our hero crapped in the corner over there," Jones replied, pointing and making a disgusted face. "We'll retrieve cells from the linings of his intestines in the feces."

"DNA?" Harry asked.

"You've got it," Jones said, shedding his plastic gloves and dropping them in a self-sealing trash container his team had brought to the scene. "Captain, you'll have a report on your desk as soon as we have the lab results."

"Make it happen fast," Jim said, "and put this place back together so that if he comes back, he won't know you've been here."

When Jones had gone, Harry asked Jim if all the barns had been examined after Barn One was torched.

"We went through all of them," Jim said.

"Barns Five and Six haven't been in use since I signed on with Holly," Harry said, looking around the room at the piled bags of stored oats and bran. "Did your people shift all these bags to see what was under them?"

"I'd have to ask Frank," Jim said. "He was in charge of the search, but I doubt it."

"Figuring no one would move a quarter of a ton of grain bags in order to hide a gas can," Harry said.

"Or cut-up newspapers," Jim concurred. "Well, I'd better have a talk with Mrs. Pike. How is she?"

As they rode in Jim's cruiser back to the house, Harry brought him up to date on Holly's condition.

"Then she's going to keep the baby," Jim said with satisfaction.

"I think so. Do you ever think of having children?"

Jim's ears lit up, and he gripped the wheel tight enough to whiten his knuckles.

"That's not a question you just ask a person and expect an answer," he said, obviously flustered.

"I didn't mean to upset you," Harry said, surprised by his friend's reaction. "I sometimes ask myself if I'd like to have any more."

"Well I don't," Jim replied. "I'm way too busy for that."

They were quiet for moment. Then Jim, getting redder, said, "Does Soñadora ever mention children to you?"

"Not recently," Harry said, trying not to sound too grim. "The last time I recall her saying anything about children, she said she thought it was a crime to bring children into a world like this."

"Kathleen wants children," Jim said as if he had revealed a secret, looking guilty and alarmed as he spoke.

Harry suppressed a grin.

"That sounds right," Harry said encouragingly. "What did you say?"

"Nothing," Jim replied.

"Why not?" Harry demanded.

"We're not married."

"But you're going to get married, aren't you?"

Of course, Harry knew perfectly well that Jim and Kathleen had been engaged for so long empires had risen and fallen. Their engagement had become the stuff of legends.

"I hope to. Yes, I certainly hope to," Jim said.

By now they were parked in front of the house, and Thahn was standing in the open front door with Nip and Tuck beside him, looking vigilant.

"I think the wheels of 'Time's winged chariot' are damned near ready to run over you," Harry said, opening his door, "and

I'm getting tired of waiting for a piece of the wedding cake."

"We're just being careful, Harry," Jim protested. "Now, let's leave it."

" 'Had I but world enough and time . . .' " Harry began, carried away by his Marvell moment, then stopped himself to watch Nip and Tuck bearing down on him. The drumming of their feet suddenly sounded to Harry like chariot wheels.

Holly, changed into a green frock and white sandals, met them in a front sitting room. She greeted them and summoned coffee, which Holly served before sitting down. Harry noted that she was not wearing her gun. Vanity? Embarrassment?

"Then one mystery is replaced with another, Captain," she said, smiling at Jim.

"You mean, where is he now?" Jim replied.

"Yes," she said, then looked at Harry. "Do you think he'll come back?"

"Possibly," Harry said, "although there wasn't much in the barn besides the sleeping bag. Something may have scared him off."

"And the place where he lived?" she asked, turning again to Jim, who was having trouble with his coffee cup and saucer. "Here," she said, "let me have that. Will you have some more?"

"No, no," he said, "but it was very good. I don't get coffee like that very often. Harry is the only man I know who makes worse tasting coffee than I do, and his is a step down from paint remover."

Harry welcomed the chance to laugh because Jim's ears were pink, and Holly had really unlocked his word hoard.

Holly also laughed.

"Put that gun back on," Harry said to Holly, getting up and spoiling the fun. "I've got the feeling that unless Elijah's decided to clear out of the county, he's not going to wait much longer before he does something."

"I agree with Harry," Jim said, following Harry's lead and becoming serious again. "I'm going to put a deputy up here nights at least for a while."

Holly had listened quietly, but once she was on her feet, she said, "If Elijah was sleeping in that barn, why didn't he try to kill me?"

"And I wonder why these dogs didn't find him?" Jim asked.

"I can answer that," Holly replied. "First, after Tuck was poisoned, I haven't let them out on their own very much, and second, they know Elijah and would not necessarily respond to his smell, even if they stumbled on it."

Jim said that sounded right, and Harry returned to her question, suspecting she would be happy to just let it go. He had come to know her well enough to know she could ask a question one moment and change her mind about having it answered in the next.

"Only Elijah knows for sure," Harry said, "but for a guess, I'd say it broke his plan when he failed to kill Katherine and me. Also, I'm all but certain that he intends to inflict as much mental pain and suffering on you as possible. And one way to do it is to hold you under the threat of death as long as he can."

"That's sick," Holly said.

"And cruel," Jim added. "Mrs. Pike, we are going to see to it that he doesn't get his way."

"I appreciate your concern, Captain," she replied, putting her hand on his arm, "but I'm not going to be that easy to kill. I'm doing everything Harry told me to do, and with one of your deputies here, we should be safe."

"I think so," Jim said, sounding supportive. As for Harry, he doubted anyone here would be safe as long as Elijah was free, but now was not the time to say so even though he had not forgotten what the BAR had done to his house.

"Are you thinking of letting the dogs stay with the deputy?" Harry asked.

"No," she said. "I want them with me. Under Thahn's supervision, they have the run of the house at night."

"Do you have fire extinguishers in the house?" Jim asked.

"Yes," she said, "Thahn sees to it that they are tested regularly and kept fully charged."

"Then I think you're doing all you can," Jim said, sounding relieved. "A deputy up here instead of at the gate should do the trick."

Following that comment, Jim said his goodbyes, and Harry left a bit later, having given Holly a report on what Buster and the rest of the men were to do during the rest of the day and promising to return tomorrow.

"How am I looking?" she asked suddenly, standing up very straight like a little girl presenting herself for approval.

"Earlier, in your jodhpurs with your Colt strapped on," Harry responded, eyeing her critically, "I thought you looked raffish. In this outfit, ravishing."

"Darling Harry," she said, beaming with pleasure. "If I weren't already pregnant, I would ask you to be the father of my children."

"I'm deeply flattered as well as honored, and would certainly be tempted," he said, "but don't you think five are enough?"

"Who's counting?" she asked, pointing at the door. "Pick up a rain check as you leave."

Harry crossed the yard to the Rover, thinking his cup was pretty nearly full.

He drove at once to the Oleander. Although he had not told anyone where he was going or why, ever since he had found Elijah's hideaway, he had been thinking about the ride linking the two properties. He had walked it once from The Oaks end and back, prompted by curiosity after learning of Brandon's relationship with Clarissa, and found that there was nothing remarkable about it, beyond the fact that it was somewhat overgrown and wet in places. But it was not under water as it had been the night of the fire when Miguel had come to see Holly.

Thinking about it now, it seemed to Harry the most accessible and at the same time safest way for Elijah to come and go. Walking up the path to the front door, Harry stopped worrying about the reception he would get from Miguel long enough to enjoy the gardens still blazing with color. It was, he thought, like walking in a painting. Then, pressing the bell, he went back to worrying about the reception he would get from Miguel.

To his surprise, Constanta opened the door.

"Mr. Brock!" she said, apparently as surprised as he. "How pleasant to see you again. Please come in."

When he stepped out of the sun's glare, Harry noted that she was wearing black shorts, although her blouse and sandals were white. Her heavy hair, however, was tied back with a black ribbon.

"It has taken me all this time to convince both Felipe and Miguel that what you proposed should be done," she told him when they were seated in the living room. "Only by demanding that the rights of the children be given first consideration was I able finally to prevail."

She paused and rang the bell that still sat on the coffee table. Her action vividly reminded Harry of his strained visit with Clarissa, and for a moment he found it easy to see Constanta as a younger version of her sister-in-law. Both were beautiful, strong women, but their personalities were so different that Harry could not maintain the fiction. Constanta had none of the tenebrous reserve with which Clarissa had confronted the world.

"Have you begun your search?" Harry asked.

"No, I arrived last night after having delivered the boys to their summer camp. Felipe slept over and then left for home early this morning.

"Excuse me," she said.

The maid had come into the room, and Constanta spoke quickly to her in Spanish.

"It is an artifact from their mother's day," she said to Harry with a slight smile, and when he was slow to respond, she said, "the Spanish. Alejandra had insisted that the children learn Spanish and compelled everyone to speak Spanish while in the house. After she died, Clarissa insisted they preserve the tradition."

"Do your children speak Spanish at home?"

"At dinner, so they do speak it, but," she added with a laugh, "I must say reluctantly."

The maid, the coffee, and Miguel arrived at the same time.

After shaking hands with Harry and refusing coffee for himself, Miguel asked, "What brings you here, Harry?"

Harry debated silently about how much he should tell them about Elijah's being a suspect in Brandon's murder and decided for safety's sake they should know at least enough to realize that he was potentially dangerous, although Harry doubted that he had any interest in members of the Cruz family.

"I came to ask your permission to explore this end of the ride between Oleander and The Oaks."

Then he gave them a quick summary of what he and the police suspected were Elijah's depredations, the arrest warrant that was out for him, and the evidence that he had spent some time sleeping in one of The Oaks' unused barns.

"Do you think he might be a danger to us?" Constanta asked.

"My guess—and it's only a guess—is that he's been using the ride to access The Oaks," Harry said. "He would probably

351

become a danger only if you or one of your people encountered him when he was coming or going."

"Since Brandon's death," Miguel said dismissively, "none of us use the ride—wait, yes, I used it the night of the fire, but I didn't see any sign of him then."

"If it's all right with you," Harry said, "I'd like to look over the ride. If he has been using it, he must have been hiding his car somewhere nearby, and it can't be on your road."

"More likely one of those old logging tracks that turn off Fullington Road," Miguel said. "Years ago they were cutting slash pine in there and trucked it out. Of course, it had to be done in the dry season."

Harry nodded.

"I'll walk it and see if anyone's been using it," he said. "How is Tyce doing?"

"He's getting grouchy," Miguel said with a grin.

"Good news," Harry said, equally pleased by the change in Miguel.

"And what about this one?" Constanta asked, pulling Miguel against her side and beaming at him.

"I think he'll do," Harry said, to ease Miguel's embarrassment at Constanta's treating him like an overgrown boy, "and he's got a sister-in-law who's spoiling him rotten."

"That is what we are for," Constanta said, "and when Tyce leaves the hospital, he is coming here to recuperate."

"Lucky him," Harry said, preparing to leave. "If you don't hear from me, you'll know I've come up dry."

Miguel, still standing, urged Harry to stay a little longer and talk with Constanta.

"She misses Felipe," he said. "Maybe you can cheer her up."

"What a thing to say!" Constanta protested, her face flaming, but Miguel's mood suddenly altered.

"Harry, do you think Blue sent that blackmail letter to my

sister-in-law?" he asked.

Harry hesitated then said, "No, I do not."

"Who did?"

"It's impossible to say."

"I've been thinking about it a lot," Miguel said, his face darkening. "Is it possible that Holly did it?"

Harry felt suddenly on very thin ice.

"*Possible*, yes, but for the rest, there is not the slightest evidence to suggest it."

"Except that she had the knowledge and the motive."

Harry experienced a thrill of fear.

"What motive?"

"Revenge, Harry, revenge!"

"Oh, Miguel!" Constanta protested. "You can't mean it!"

"Can't I?" he asked harshly.

Harry scrambled to counter the accusation, but he was too late. Miguel was already out of the room, and a moment later, the front door slammed behind him.

"Harry," Constanta said, her voice heavy with concern, "please, don't be upset. His grief at his sister's death still comes in waves that break over him in anger."

"Yes, I know," he said.

What he did not say was that Miguel was not alone in thinking Holly may have been the author of the note that led to Clarissa's suicide.

Constanta studied him for a moment, seeming to hesitate over something, and then said, "Is it at all possible . . ?"

"Of course it's possible," he said brusquely, "but it's possible you or I sent it."

"I hadn't thought of that," she said, apparently finding the idea interesting.

"Do you know where Clarissa's papers are?" Harry asked, wrenching the conversation in another direction.

"I think so," Constanta replied, seemingly as glad as he to move on. "Of course, I haven't yet been in her brokerage office, but I have talked with the president of the company. He has given me permission to go through her desk and files and remove any personal material."

She paused and gave Harry a knowing look.

"Of course, a company attorney will be looking over my shoulder, empowered to prevent anything potentially damaging to the company or in which they have a proprietary interest from leaving the office."

"Sounds right," Harry said. "From the little I know of Clarissa, I'll be surprised if you discover anything useful there."

"I agree," Constanta said. "She was ferociously compartmentalized and impenetrably private. If there is anything, it will be here, in her home."

She paused and looked again at Harry—this time wearing an entirely different expression.

"We both know why," she said.

"Yes," Harry replied, hearing neither condemnation nor approval in her voice.

He stood up, started to speak, stopped, and said, "It is one of the most extraordinary things I have ever encountered. When I read the letters, it took my breath away. I don't think I've gotten it back yet."

"*Asombroso,*" she said in a near whisper. "An act that has set them permanently apart."

"Astonishing indeed," Harry said, then added, "the English poet Byron had a long and notorious affair with his half sister Augusta Leigh. Brandon and Clarissa had melodramatic precursors."

Constanta smiled.

"When I heard of it, I found myself saying in my mind to Clarissa and meaning it literally, '*Via con dios.*' "

Harry nodded.

"Good luck with your search," he said and left reluctantly.

He would have liked to talk with Constanta longer but knew they had said all that they needed to say and was glad that they had said it.

31

After searching the ride for nearly an hour and finding an occasional boot print but no tire tracks, Harry returned to the Rover and drove out to Fullington Road. The rains could have washed away footprints, but not finding tire tracks told him that Elijah had not driven on any part of the ride. That left the old logging tracks that Miguel said ran from Fullington Road back into the pine uplands bordering the Oleander property.

Florida woods recover from fires, hurricanes, logging, and other human depredations with astonishing speed, but even the powerful combination of subtropical sun, rain, roots, and climbing vines cannot easily or entirely obliterate the devastation of trucks churning back and forth for weeks or months over a piece of unsurfaced land.

Harry had driven less than half a mile from the entrance to Oleander when he saw the first road, buried under waist-high grass, vines, and patches of saw palmetto but still visible because the scattering of palms and gums growing in the track were shorter than the surrounding trees that had not been logged off because they were of no interest to the loggers.

Harry pulled off the road and groaned out loud at he stared at the track. Was he really going to have to wade through that tangle? Images of snakes, poison ivy, briars, and thorn scrub danced in his mind. Then he suddenly broke into laughter,

"Idiot!" he said to a pileated woodpecker watching him from a cabbage palm.

"Not you, me!" he added as he pulled the Rover back onto the road.

A half mile further on, he found what he was looking for, another track, much like the first. A car or truck had bulled its way through the green tangle, leaving two puddled tracks where the tires had crushed and torn the undergrowth.

Unwilling to force the Rover through the thorns and scrub, Harry got down and, from the back, took out a pair of overalls and L.L. Bean leather top boots, pulled them on, checked his CZ, sprayed himself with Deep Woods, and waded through the ditch onto the track. He had not gone twenty-five yards before he had sweat his shirt through and begun cursing the deer flies, which seemed to be attracted by the mosquito repellant, and the small black flies that swarmed his eyes looking for a drink or a bath or a place to die.

As he got farther away from the road, the trees thickened, giving him some protection from the sun, but also killing what little breeze there was, leaving the world to the bugs, choking humidity, and the incessant sawing and fiddling to the locusts, katydids, and the occasional colony frogs that in the grip of surging passions beeped and yodeled in the shadowy canopy above Harry's head.

After twenty minutes of hard slogging, he reached the end of the track and was relieved to find there was no one there waiting for him. But someone had been there. The earth on the small hammock where the tracks ended was heavily churned by a vehicle's repeated turns.

Crushed beer cans, torn Styrofoam food containers, empty cigarette boxes, and paper napkins lay where they had been thrown. Because it had not rained for twenty-four hours, Harry concluded that some of the trash had been tossed there as recently as last night. Having made that assessment, he glanced at the sun angling through the trees, oriented himself, found where the man had left the clearing, and followed his tracks.

As Harry had suspected, they led to the ride.

"Elijah," Harry said quietly, feeling both gratified and something else that might have been sorrow, quickly suppressed. Elijah had taken pains to step out of the brush onto the ride without leaving traces of his arrival. Harry walked a short distance toward The Oaks, counting his steps as he went, then cut and peeled a stopper branch and thrust it into the mud beside the path, leaving six inches of the peeled wood thrusting up above the leaves and grass. Then he spent a few minutes studying the tracks showing in the soft earth of the ride.

Deer had crisscrossed the ground, browsing on the young shrubs that were springing up. A small herd of pigs had passed through as well, and here and there partial boot prints. Then, just as Harry was about to turn back, he saw a set of tracks that made the hair on his neck stand up and a cold hand grip his stomach. Driven deep into the ride were fresh hoof marks of the black bull. In one print the water that had run into the track was still brown, the mud not having yet settled out of it.

Harry straightened up and drew his CZ, turning slowly to scan the woods. For the first time the gun felt light and flimsy in his hand. The ten-foot-wide path that a moment before had felt spacious was suddenly alarmingly cramped and narrow as the image of the bull breaking out of the woods onto the trail in from of him and Holly crowded into his mind.

Making a serious effort to calm the pounding of his heart, Harry stopped turning and listened, trying to separate from the humming and buzzing of the insect life in the trees and grass from any sound that might reveal the passage of a heavy animal through the thick, green undergrowth.

Although he heard nothing, he was not comforted. He knew that a bull moose could tip a five-foot span of heavy antlers back on his shoulders and slip through a stand of alders without snapping a twig. Slowly and carefully, turning frequently to check the trail behind him, Harry walked back to the peeled stick and, counting his steps carefully, reentered the woods and cautiously made his way to the hammock without incident.

Nevertheless, he did not take a fully free breath until he climbed into the Rover and slammed the door shut behind him.

"When I saw where the tracks had led, I knew it was Elijah," Harry said.

"And that's why there was so little besides his sleeping bag in the barn," Hodges boomed, slapping his knee with satisfaction.

"I can't begin to guess who it would be if it isn't Blue," Jim said, tossing the pencil he had been holding onto his desk and scowling as if he'd just received discouraging news.

"For some reason," Harry said to Jim, "I don't feel any better about this than you do, but it's got to be Elijah."

"This is no time to start feeling sorry for the bad guys," Hodges protested. "We'd do better finding some way to catch the son of a bitch because if we don't, he's going to kill somebody else."

"Holly Pike," Harry said grimly.

"Right," Jim agreed, unfolding himself into an upright position and staring out the window.

"Of course he's right," Hodges insisted. "Blue is crazy as a shithouse rat."

Despite his gloomy state of mind, Harry laughed.

"Frank," Jim said, scowling. "Remember where you are."

Harry listened to Jim go on a little longer but thought his heart wasn't in it. Apparently Hodges thought so too because he sat serenely and took it all in good spirits.

"You say he's driving either an SUV or a pickup," Jim said to Harry when he grew tired of criticizing Hodges.

"That's my best guess," Harry said, "and knowing Elijah, I'll bet it's a pickup."

"Sounds right," Hodges said.

Jim nodded, picking up the phone.

"I'll put a cruiser out there right now."

When that was done he asked, "Did you see anything more in there?"

"The tracks of that damned black bull," Harry said. "He passed through less than an hour before I found his tracks."

"I'll bet that got your attention," Hodges said with a happy grin, "and you with nothing but that peashooter to stop him."

"What keeps him in there?" Jim asked.

"Food, proximity to Holly Pike's herd of Angus cattle," Harry said. "I'm guessing it's only a question of time before he goes through the fence and he and Thor start trying to kill one another."

Before Harry stopped speaking, Jim had clearly lost interest.

He interrupted Hodges, who had begun a story about a short Jersey bull his father had owned and a tall Holstein heifer, and said, "I'd like to be making some progress on finding out who put that blackmail note together and sent it to Clarissa Cruz. Have you had any new thoughts on it, Harry?"

"No," Harry said, "but the list of people who could have sent it remains limited."

He would rather have heard the story about the short bull than have to consider, as he had done many times, the possibility, or was it the probability, that Holly had concocted that deadly letter.

Hodges was sulking and said nothing. Jim stood, hands shoved into his trouser pockets, frowning at Harry but his mind obviously elsewhere.

"Do we all think that Mrs. Pike is the author?" he demanded after an extended silence.

Hodges, never staying out of sorts long, said flatly that she had to have been the one who sent it.

"Blue is out," he declared flatly. "Yellen is out, both the Cruz boys are out, and Harry damned well didn't do it. Who the hell else is left?"

"Tucker knew about Zebulon Pike's relationship with Clarissa's mother," Harry said gloomily.

Probably because the comment was so completely beside the point, both Hodges and Jim stared at him with puzzled expressions.

"Frank's father's short Jersey bull has more relevance to what we're talking about than that," Jim said, "or are you being funny?"

"Even if a little bird had whispered the truth in your ear, Jim," Harry said much too loudly, "there isn't a shred of evidence to support it. So why are we wasting our time talking about it?"

"Whoa!" Hodges said. "Don't get all aerated, Harry. The Captain and I understand."

"Frank," Jim began hurriedly, but Harry interrupted him.

"No, you don't," Harry protested. "I've worked with Holly Pike every day almost since this thing began, and I never met a woman who was trying to do the right thing more than she is. After what she's been through, most men would have thrown up their hands and quit, but she hasn't. Pregnant or not, she's gone right on keeping that place running all the while knowing that Elijah Blue, whom none of us can seem to find, is working himself up to try to kill her."

"I just asked if you think she sent that blackmail note," Jim said in a quiet voice, leaning over and dropping a hand on Harry's shoulder.

"Of course I do," Harry said, and then slumped forward, planting his hands on his knees and sighing deeply.

"Well," Hodges said in a loud but understanding voice, "she's a hell of a good-looking woman. It's easy to see how . . ."

That was as far as he got before Jim broke in with, "Frank, we'd better not go there."

But it was too late. Harry, already stressed by his outburst and in search of a way to escape his frustration, jumped to his feet.

"There's nothing going on between me and Holly Pike," he exploded. "I was just trying to . . ."

"Say that having to think something that bad about a person you like and admire cuts all the way to the bone," Jim broke in, finishing Harry's thought for him and giving his shoulder a good shake while he did it.

Harry was so surprised by Jim's comment that he forgot all about being angry.

"I wasn't suggesting that you were poking her," Hodges said, his wide face bright red.

"I'm glad to hear it," Harry said, suddenly embarrassed.

"But I'm going to have to do something about that letter," Jim said, looking worried again.

"And it will probably mean talking some more with Mrs. Pike," Hodges said gravely.

"That's if we can keep her alive," Harry said.

"Jim's assigned a night deputy at the house," Harry told Katherine as they put into the Rover the last boxes of broken glass and crockery destined for the recycle center.

"He must be very worried about her," Katherine said, pulling off her gloves and using them to wipe the sweat off her forehead.

The boxes were heavy, and the heat in the airless haze clung to her and Harry like a wet blanket.

"I wish they'd do something other than just hang there," Katherine complained in obvious irritation, staring at the brilliant white thunderheads towering in the eastern sky.

It had been one of those windless Southwest Florida days when the airless heat made moving a misery.

"Maybe tonight," Harry said, trying to sound hopeful as they walked back to the house.

"I hope you're not thinking of spending your nights there," Katherine said.

"No, I have no intention of leaving you alone here if that's what you mean," Harry told her.

They went into the cool of the kitchen, and Katherine pulled off her green bandanna and blew out her breath in relief.

"If I weren't here, would you be spending the nights at The Oaks?" she asked in a tight voice and shook out her hair.

Harry tossed his gloves onto the table and thought about the question, which had more quills than a porcupine.

"I don't answer hypothetical questions," he said, trying for a humorous evasion.

"Iced tea?" Katherine asked, already on her way to the refrigerator.

There was a lengthy pause in the conversation while Harry got the glasses and Katherine filled them. While she was doing that, he began thinking again about the possibility that Holly had sent Clarissa the blackmail note.

"Do you think it was the blackmail note that caused Clarissa to kill herself?" he asked, taking his glass to the table and sitting down.

"I think you're worrying about the possibility that Holly Pike is a murderer," Katherine replied.

"I suppose so, but would that threat have been enough to make her kill herself?"

"The question can't be answered, Harry. The most that can be said with some certainty is that if she was already in a fragile state, it might have been enough to spur her to do it. Why are you so concerned? Are you falling in love with Holly Pike?"

"No," Harry said, only half listening and imagining Holly cutting and pasting those letters onto a sheet of lined yellow paper.

The silence in the room persisted until Katherine, who seemed to be studying him, broke it.

"You're not sleeping with Soñadora, are you?" she asked.

Harry heard no invitation in the question.

"I don't think I should answer that," he said, taking a long pull on the tea.

"How about Holly Pike, then? You've got to be sleeping with someone."

That stung.

"Where is all this warmth and affection coming from?" he asked, to stop himself from saying something sharper.

She was leaning back against the counter, ankles crossed, her left arm across her waist, her right elbow resting on her left wrist, the glass of iced tea in her right hand. Harry had seen her stand in that pose, in that place, wearing the same inquisitorial expression, dozens and dozens of times over the years. The awareness hurt him as nearly every reminder of their broken marriage did.

"I'm just feeling guilty is all," she said. "I don't like it."

"One," he said forcefully, "I'm not sleeping with Soñadora as an imposed penance for sins of omission and commission, and I'm certainly not sleeping with Holly. If you recall, Holly lost her husband a few weeks ago, she nearly had a miscarriage a short way back, and I think she'd rather hang by her thumbs from one of her magisterial oaks than have sex with me."

"Are you trying to make me feel sorry for you?"

"Are you trying to look like the Statue of Liberty?" he asked her.

"I like standing like this."

"I know you do. By the way, I'm not sleeping with you either."

"No, you're not," she said, pushing away from the counter and turning to pour the remaining ice in her glass into the sink. "Did you meet all of your goals and objectives for the day?" she asked.

"You think you're funny, don't you?"

"No, but I'm hotter than Benson," she said, looking at him over her shoulder as she swung her bottom out of the room. From the foot of the stairs, she called back in a matter-of-fact voice, "Fix the drinks. After I've showered, I'll be down to make dinner."

Harry stared bleakly into his cup, which, brimming earlier in the day, was now nearly empty.

32

At two in the morning, a real Florida dam buster broke over the Hammock with wind, rain, chain lightning, and thunder, roaring and crashing as if the sky was being ripped apart. In the midst of the uproar, Katherine, illuminated by the almost constant glare of lightning and accompanied by a sonorous drum roll of thunder and rain on the roof, ran into Harry's bedroom, threw off her nightgown, and plunged into bed with him.

"I didn't know you were afraid of thunderstorms," Harry said, getting his arms around her.

If I'm dreaming, he prayed, please don't let me wake up. But while he was thinking that, he was also wondering why she was doing this and what it meant. He even wondered fleetingly if he really wanted it to happen.

"I'm not," she said, "but it's been a long time since we made love by lightning light."

"True," Harry said. "I wonder if we can remember how to do it."

"This is how we begin," she said, pressing her body against his.

It was surprising how quickly he remembered what came next.

The sun was up before they were, and they woke to the sunlight streaming across the bed and a cool breeze blowing in the windows, Harry having thrown them open when the storm was over.

"The windows are coming a little before noon, or so I was told," Katherine said over breakfast. "By the time you're home, they should be installed."

"This is Southwest Florida," Harry replied, pouring more syrup on his flapjacks. "Arrival times are fungible and almost always later rather than earlier."

Katherine had kissed Harry awake and energetically scrambled out of bed to claim the shower first, but over breakfast she had been quiet and, Harry thought, either subdued or preoccupied. Being quiet and at peace with his world himself, he was complaisant enough to believe that she was feeling the same way.

"Are we going to see Tucker after breakfast?" she asked.

"Yes, if you still want to."

"I wonder if his place escaped as easily as we did?"

"I expect so, but I'm glad we're going to see for ourselves. You know how slow he is to say he needs help."

Katherine had begun carrying dishes to the sink while Harry finished his coffee. After her first trip, she stood looking out the window at the slash of sparkling light where the Puc Puggy passed the house. A flock of large white birds with orange legs appeared over the creek and then vanished.

"The ibis are getting a late start," she said quietly.

"Like us," Harry said, coming to stand beside her.

He put his arm around her waist, but she quickly set the dishes she was still holding in the sink and, turning out of his arm, returned to the table, making no response to his comment. Second thoughts, Harry told himself with regret but let it go. What happened next between them was in her hands. Despite the pain, he found he was willing to leave it there.

★ ★ ★ ★ ★

"That old gum fell right across the hen run," Tucker said, stopping to view the damage. "It's a good thing I had Longstreet and his harem locked in the house, something I've been doing since the coyotes got in amongst them."

He and Harry and Katherine, with Oh, Brother! and Sanchez as scouts, had been looking over the wind damage, which had shredded a lot of smaller branches in his citrus grove and flattened half a dozen rows of sweet corn in the vegetable garden.

"Aside from that," Tucker said, "I think we escaped pretty easily. I'll stand that corn back up and brace it. If it lives, fine. If not, I'll replant it. That's one thing to be said for living this far south—you can plant most things almost any time of the year."

"You'll need some help getting that tree off the hen run," Katherine said.

"I'm glad you agree with me," Tucker said with a mischievous grin. "Are you volunteering?"

Harry glanced at his watch.

"We've got an hour," he said.

"You cut and I'll carry," Katherine said.

Tucker wouldn't let a power saw on the place, but he had a crosscut, the teeth on which he kept razor sharp. With a couple of ladders, he and Harry sawed off the top of the fallen tree and then worked their way, sawing off four-foot lengths of the foot-thick trunk until they were down to a stump. While they did that, to the accompaniment of a certain amount of raillery from Tucker and the cursing of man's lot from Harry, Katherine, dressed in blue shorts and a halter top, limbed out the top with a bucksaw and then dragged the branches into a pile.

"We've made a good start," Tucker said when he had laid the crosscut down beside the stump.

"I'll be back to help with the rest, but I've got to be at The Oaks soon," Harry said, wiping the sweat out of his eyes.

"And you said something about the window people coming," Tucker said, addressing Katherine. "If you don't have to rush, I can offer some cold lemonade, or I could make some tea."

"I'd love some lemonade," Katherine said.

And you'll avoid being alone with me until I leave for The Oaks, Harry thought sadly.

"Then I'll leave you to it," he said cheerfully. "I'll call you once I get Buster and his crew sorted out."

"I'm going to Haven House once the windows are in," she said.

Harry let that go.

"And you will be keeping your eyes open wherever you're going," Tucker told him.

"I don't expect anything to happen in the middle of the day," Harry replied, both his mind and his eyes on Katherine, who carefully avoided his gaze.

"Good planning, Harry," Holly said, leaning back in her chair and regarding him across her desk with a teasing smile. "You finished just in time for lunch."

Harry was just winding up his report.

"Not yet," he said. "The three heifers you bought came in an hour ago. I put them in the Barn Four paddock. They appear to be in good order, but they look pretty big not to have borne calves yet."

Holly came around the desk. She was dressed in a riding outfit and still wearing her boots. Against Benson's advice, she had ridden Sueño that morning. Harry had told her what he thought of her judgment, and she had told him that monitoring her pregnancy wasn't in his job description.

"Brandon," she said, "always urged waiting a little longer to start breeding them because it extended their productive lives. What I've read lately seems to support that view."

369

"One of them is bawling her head off," Harry said.

"Probably started her heat cycle," Holly told him. "Let's go see what's on for lunch."

"Are you going to put her into the pasture with Thor?" he asked as they went out of the room together.

At the door, Nip and Tuck met them for a crowding welcome. Harry noticed that Tuck looked thinner but said nothing to Holly. She was already worried about the dog, and Harry did not want to remind her of the dog's obvious decline.

"Not for four or five days," Holly said. "I want Heather to look at them, to make sure I don't put any diseases into the herd."

"Will she still be in heat in a week?" Harry asked, surprised to realize when he thought about it he didn't have the answer.

"She'll be in standing heat for only six to ten hours. That's when she will accept the bull."

"Then you'll have to wait, what, a month for her to come around again?"

"Around twenty days, but as she's never been bred, it could be a couple of days earlier."

Thahn met them in the hall and, after greeting Harry, told Holly that lunch was ready and asked where she wanted it served.

"My study," Holly said. "Do you mind eating off a tray, Harry?"

He said he could cope, and when they were settled and Thahn had served them, Harry said, "When I was trying to find out how Elijah had been getting into Barn Six, I saw the black bull's tracks on the Oleander ride. They were fresh. I've told Buster to warn the rest of the men to watch for him."

"Oh, shit!" Holly said, putting down her fork. "If that heifer's in heat, she'll be broadcasting on every breeze that blows over her. I thought we'd seen the last of that beast."

"I found only one set of tracks, and they were pointing away from The Oaks," Harry told her, hoping to ease her concern. "He could be miles away from here by now."

"That idiot Geoffrey Ryan was supposed to have caught that animal," she said, then shrugged and went back to eating. "I don't think an earthquake could spoil my appetite," she added around a mouthful of chicken salad.

Half an hour later, their lunch and remaining farm business finished, Harry and Holly walked out to the paddock to look at the heifers.

"Nice-looking animals," Harry said.

They were standing with their arms resting on the top plank of the white fence, each with a foot on the bottom rail.

"They are, and for the price they should be," Holly said with a grin.

Harry turned to see Thahn approaching the bottom of the fence. Holly turned and leaned her back against the fence, tilting her face up to the sun and closing her eyes.

"It's a good day, Harry," she said, "and it's good to be able to feel it."

"I'm glad for you," he said, turning back to study her, at the same time thinking that she looked as if she was at peace with herself.

A brief flash of light or something that flickered in the outside corner of his left eye made him turn his head toward Barn Six. The left half of the door swung open, and a man pointing a gun at them stood in the black rectangle.

"Down!" Harry shouted and threw himself at Holly, dragging her with him as he fell.

A shower of wood splinters and the slam of a rifle exploded around them as they thumped into the soft, grassy ground.

"Christ," Holly groaned, most of her breath knocked out of her.

"Elijah," he said, drawing his CZ. "He's in Barn Six. Stay down."

Harry squirmed his way along the fence until he could get a partial view of the barn by peering between the bottom two planks of the fence. Elijah was gone. A moment later Holly crawled up beside him, gripping her Colt.

"Where is he?" she demanded.

"He's in there with two doors to leave by," Harry said, laying down his gun and pulling out his phone to call for help, "and we can only see one."

"Then I'll cover the other door," she said, and before Harry could stop her, she was on her feet and running.

The barns stood in an arc with their paddocks pointing toward the center and toward the point at which the driveway from the house opened into the stables yard. To put Barn Five between her and Elijah's rifle, she had to run along the fence about twenty yards to reach cover.

"Shit!" Harry said, dropping the phone and grasping the CZ as he came to his feet.

He had moved quickly but not fast enough. As soon as she was up and running, her head and shoulders were visible from the Barn Six door. Guessing what Elijah would do, Harry intended to give her cover by firing into the barn, but before he squeezed off the first shot, the rifle slammed again, and Holly was knocked off her feet as if a giant fist had hit her, spun her around and flung her down like a rag doll. She gave a single cry when she struck the ground and then lay sprawled and silent, a dark stain spreading down the sleeve and back of her blouse.

Swearing with every shot, Harry fired rapidly into the place where he judged Elijah must have been standing, then dropped to the ground just as the top planks where he had been a moment before were shattered by the Browning.

"Outgunned," Harry muttered as he groped in the grass for the phone, forcing himself to make the call when what he desperately wanted to do was go to Holly.

He told the 911 duty officer what she needed to know, put a new clip into his CZ, then crawled as fast and as close to the ground as he could to where Holly was lying. There was a pulse and for that he offered up a brief prayer of thanks, also that she was unconscious, but her shoulder was a mess. Harry saw that the .30 caliber bullet had passed through one of the two-inch planks in the fence before hitting her and had left a large and ragged hole in her shoulder.

Harry was ripping his shirt into strips when Thahn arrived, crawling swiftly, his Luger in his right hand.

"How bad?" he asked.

"No exit wound," Harry said. "The bullet's still in her."

Thahn holstered his gun and set to work with the strips of Harry's shirt, skillfully padding the wound to staunch the flow of blood and wrapping it tightly with more strips passed under Holly's arm and over the wound.

"It is a good sign she is not bleeding from her mouth," Thahn said when he was finished.

"A plank slowed the bullet down," Harry said.

"I noticed," Thahn said, wriggling to Harry's side. "I called 911."

"So did I," Harry said, "but getting her to the ambulance will not be easy."

At that moment the sound of a siren tore through the silence.

"The deputy posted on the road," Harry said, "telling Blue he's coming."

Both men screwed their heads around to watch his arrival. He barreled out of the oaks and braked to a stop in a cloud of dust.

"Bad idea," Thahn said as the deputy flung open the door and sprang out of his cruiser.

Before Harry could speak, the deputy was flung backwards, his arms spread like a scarecrow, and dropped on his back just as the crash of the rifle reached Harry's ears. Before Harry had finished turning, Thahn was up and blazing away at the door.

At almost the same moment, the plank a few inches above their heads began turning into splinters, and the bark of the rifle was almost one continuous sound. Harry and Thahn planted their faces in the grass.

"What weapon is he using?" Thahn asked when the barrage stopped.

"My guess is a Browning semiautomatic."

"Old rifle," Thahn said.

"Right, but accurate and very powerful."

"How long before the ambulance arrives?" Thahn asked, looking back at Holly, who still lay silent and motionless.

"About twenty minutes."

"Can you reach them to say not to drive into the stable yard?"

"Worth a try."

"We've got Mrs. Pike down and a deputy," Harry told the dispatcher. "Warn your teams not to drive beyond the oaks in the front yard. After that, approach through the trees with caution. The shooter is in the last barn on the right. He can look right down into the stable yard. One of Mrs. Pike's employees and I are pinned down behind the paddock fence where three black heifers are penned. We're exchanging fire with the shooter."

"Mrs. Pike is still bleeding," Thahn said calmly enough, but Harry could hear the worry and shared it. "I think if this takes an hour, she will die."

"Agreed," Harry said. "And the way he shoots, if we make a run for Barn Five, he'll nail both of us."

It was almost certainly true, but Harry wanted to make the dash regardless. It was part of his adrenaline rush, part of the high that burned through him at these moments.

"It will mean leaving Mrs. Pike," Thahn said, "but we can crawl to the fence corner safely."

"Then while one of us fires into the door, the other one makes a dash for Barn Five," Harry said.

"Yes," Thahn said. "It lacks elegance, but our choices are not numerous."

"Nor attractive," Harry said, just as another swarm of bullets ripped more of the planks apart.

"We've done what we can for her," Harry said when the splinters stopped flying. "I think we'd better give your plan a try."

"I will run," Thahn said as they set off on their stomachs.

"Nope," Harry said. "You're not paid to do this."

Thahn began to protest, but Harry stopped him.

"Thahn," he said. "You've got a wife. Think of the people depending on you. No one is dependent on me, and Mrs. Pike is going to need you far more than me."

"There will be no space for error," Thahn said as they reached the corner.

"No," Harry agreed. "Just pray I don't slip on a cow flap."

The adrenaline pouring through him had brought that familiar burst of almost giddy high spirits that he always experienced in such situations.

"Or that this old Luger doesn't jam," Thahn said sardonically as he reloaded.

"Right," Harry said. "If I make it, I will find a window to shoot from. Stay low, watch carefully, and kill him if you get a chance."

"You also."

They both worked themselves into a crouching position.

"At three," Harry said. "Your count."

In his crouched position and despite his excitement, Harry became aware of joint pain and incipient muscle cramp at several points in his body, but he did not have time to reflect on their implications because Thahn said, "Three!" and Harry sprang forward and began racing for the corner of Barn Five twenty yards away.

He felt as if he was running in molasses, the distance between him and barn seemed to be increasing, and the whole scheme appeared increasingly harebrained. Behind him he could hear the steady, heavy reports of Thahn's Luger. Then the corner of the barn was finally there, and Harry, gasping, flung himself forward and skidded on the grass like a runner stealing second. The faint whisper of a lead slug passing over his head drained the last of his enthusiasm for the enterprise, and he dragged his legs out of harm's way just as pieces of wood began flying off the corner of the barn, and the slam of the Browning drowned the Luger's bark and his own curses.

As soon as Harry had caught his breath and crawled back to the corner to wave to Thahn, he let himself into the barn, entered the first box stall on his right, and edged up to the stall's window. He couldn't see Thahn or Holly, but he could see the Angus heifers crowding one another into the farthest corner of the paddock and hear them bellowing. He could also see the black rectangle of Barn Six's door, but he could not see whoever was in there or any glint of light from a gun barrel.

Peering through the dusty glass gave Harry a strange sense of detachment. The barn behind him was silent. Random rays of yellow sunlight, dancing with dust motes, reached into the gangway. One was falling across his stall, imparting a sense of extreme peace. Fighting off the delusion, Harry fixed his attention on the dark door across the stretch of grass and waited. The heifers stopped bellowing and began to graze. There was no visible movement inside Barn Six. The silence deepened, the dust danced in the barn light, the day stretched around Harry, beautiful and serene.

The knowledge that Holly Pike was slipping toward death just yards away kept him from giving way to the lassitude that was gradually replacing the adrenaline high that had surged through him as he'd made his run from the fence. His struggle was ended by the high, keening wail of sirens. Moments later, Harry glimpsed flashes of blue uniforms as the Sheriff Department's SWAT unit fanned out through the oaks.

A loudspeaker came into play.

"This is Lieutenant Bradley Mason, Tequesta County Sheriff's Department."

The voice boomed and echoed among the barns.

"Whoever is in Barn Six, lay down your weapons and come out now."

The demand went unanswered and was repeated, still nothing. Harry ducked under the window and, from the new angle, looked past the back of Barn Six into the field beyond.

"Damn!" he said, watching Elijah Blue, carrying the Browning in both hands, a small backpack bouncing on his left shoulder, racing for the woods. An instant later he plunged into the bushes and vanished. Harry pulled out his cell.

33

Harry and Thahn had reached Holly first. To Harry's relief, she was still breathing. Only moments later, a medical team unceremoniously rousted them and went to work on her. Another team was working on the downed deputy. Working swiftly to stabilize her and deal with the wound, they moved her onto a collapsed gurney and lifted her into the ambulance.

"They're good," Jim said, joining Harry and Thahn as the last two members of the team jumped into the ambulance and shouted, "Go!"

"One hopes better than good," Thahn said quietly, pausing to watch the ambulance pull away before leaving for the house.

"I've made a call," Jim said when Thahn had left. "We'll have bloodhounds on that trail within the hour."

"He'll have reached his truck before then," Harry said.

"We've got patrols all over this area," Jim protested. "They'll stop every pickup truck on the road. If he's driving, I don't see how we can miss him. If he isn't, the dogs will find him."

"Sounds likely," Harry said, trying to sound hopeful.

"Holly is okay," Harry told Katherine when he finished describing the encounter with Elijah.

He had called her as soon as he had spoken with the surgeon who operated on Holly. "She's still under anesthetic," he continued, "and in possession of a new shoulder joint. The old one was shattered."

"What about her baby?" Katherine asked.

"The surgeon said the fetus had come through safely."

Harry gave a short laugh.

"I don't know how they got everyone into the OR," he said. "From one of the nurses, I learned there were an anesthesiologist, an obstetrician, a neonatologist, the surgeon, and the support team, all crowding her."

"Holly was lucky," Katherine said somberly. "I've heard that pregnant women having major surgery frequently go into premature labor."

"Unfortunately, the deputy didn't make it," he said, knowing that if he didn't tell her, she would learn about it elsewhere and haul him through a thorn bush for not having told her.

"I'm sorry," she said. "It could just as easily have been you."

It had been a long and very rugged afternoon. Harry was tired. The dogs had lost Elijah in a creek. The road patrols had not apprehended him. Despite the efforts by a lot of people, there had been no resolution, and the struggle would continue.

"It looks as if I'll be managing The Oaks for while longer," he said, not wanting to discuss his mortality and already beginning to think of the work waiting to be done.

"Being sarcastic isn't acceptable, Harry," she said.

He heard the pain in her voice and realized she had misunderstood him, but before he could respond, she severed the connection.

Driving back to the Hammock, he had a call from Soñadora.

"You have not been hurt," she said. "Were you at The Oaks when the shootings occurred?"

"I was there, and I'm all right," he said. "Where did you hear about it?"

"An hour ago, the radio reported a shooting at The Oaks and said a deputy had been shot and Mrs. Pike hospitalized. I tried to call you, but I could get only your voice mail."

"I was at the hospital," Harry said, "waiting for Holly to come out of the operating room. My phone was shut off."

"The report said the assailant escaped, and the police are looking for a black man by the name of Elijah Blue. How is Mrs. Pike?"

"She's going to be all right, according to the doctors. She was shot in the shoulder."

The words brought back the memory of her running and being suddenly knocked off her feet and slammed into the ground by the impact of the bullet.

"A policeman was killed?"

"Yes," Harry said, struggling to throw off the renewed pain of the events. "I don't think I can say anything more about it right now."

"No," she said quickly. "Tell me again that you are all right."

"Yes, I am." He hesitated, and when she started to say goodbye, he thanked her, adding, "I haven't called you because . . ."

"I know," she said. "It is my doing. Goodbye."

So Harry carried that home with him. Katherine met him at the lanai door and said, "Get in here. You must be exhausted," and grasped him by the arm to hurry him into the house.

"Unless you feel you have to," she said when he came downstairs from having a shower, "I don't want to talk about the shootings." She thrust a large gin and tonic into his hands. "Here," she said. "Let's go onto the lanai. There's enough breeze to make it bearable. Dinner's coming. I decided to roast a chicken. Everything's just about done, but first we're going to have a drink. Two if that feels right. Come on. Don't dawdle."

"Katherine," he said finally, having been dragged to one of the lanai chairs and pushed into it and unable to constrain himself, "what in hell are you doing?"

"Acting like an idiot?"

"I wouldn't say . . ."

He was looking up at her, wondering with considerable uneasiness if this presaged something seriously unpleasant. She was half bent over him, her face pink, either, he thought, because she's been cooking or because she's really angry and hiding it.

"I think maybe I am."

She retrieved her drink from the kitchen and came back and sat down beside him.

"Elijah got away. Now what?"

"First thing tomorrow," Harry said, deciding to just go along, "I'm having heavy locks put on all the barn doors, and when the grooms are not working in a barn, it's going to be locked."

"What about the windows?"

"They're too high to reach from the ground without a ladder."

"And then?"

"Then we wait for Jim and his people to find Elijah, and if whoever finds him doesn't shoot him, we let the state put him away."

"And you're not going to be involved in the process."

Actually, he thought he knew where Elijah might be hiding and intended to see if he was right, but he had no intention of telling Katherine his plans. He knew where that would lead.

"Until Holly comes home, I've got enough work for three of me."

"Then that's a no."

"This whole thing is drawing to a close," he said, expressing his torn feelings about how she had acted at breakfast more than about the hunt for Elijah.

The next morning Harry was obliged to appear in court to give evidence for the state in a delayed hit and run case in which he had done work for the victim's husband. After that, he stopped at the hospital to see Holly, who was still too heavily sedated to communicate. The duty nurse, however, told Harry that she was doing as well as could be expected.

Harry, having to settle for that cold comfort, finally reached The Oaks at noon. Giving in to Thahn's insistence that he eat, Harry allowed himself to be shepherded by Thahn and the two dogs into Holly's study where, while waiting for his lunch to arrive, he gave Thahn as full an account of Holly's condition as he could.

"Of course, there is no way to know when she will be home," Thahn said.

"Normally, they'd have her up and out of there probably too quickly," Harry said, "but because she's pregnant, I think they're going to be very careful with her."

"Good," Thahn added. "With one arm out of action, she will not be able to ride a horse."

His relief was evident in both his voice and his expression.

"I wouldn't put a lot of money on it," Harry said, unable to resist.

"I will be very firm," Thahn said, either missing or dismissing the joke.

While he ate, Harry talked with Thahn about the arrangements that had been made to cope with the house in Holly's absence.

"I have been given a message for you," Thahn said, taking a memo pad from his jacket pocket and consulting it. "It came this morning from Mrs. Cruz."

For a moment, Harry was stymied. Then he remembered. Constanta.

"She wishes to consult with you before calling her lawyer."

He tore off the page and handed it to Harry, who was already speculating on what Constanta had found.

"She left this number. Please use the phone on the desk if you wish to call now. And one more thing, Mr. Brock, it would be a great favor to me if you would take the dogs with you on your rounds. I am without time, and they should be given a run."

Harry guessed that just dealing with Holly's telephone calls would have kept him busy. Her computer had signaled the arrival of a message several times while they had been in the room.

"Okay," Harry said and asked, "are you responding to the e-mail?"

"On this address I do," he said a bit grimly, nodding at the computer on the desk. "It is only business here. I have turned off her personal computer and her other electronic devices."

While Harry was calling Constanta, Thahn gathered up Harry's tray, told the dogs to stay with Harry, then left.

"I have found a signed, dated, and notarized letter from Brandon to Clarissa," Constanta said, her voice climbing with excitement, "giving her unqualified ownership of Oleander, land, buildings, stock, everything."

"Did you find anything else with the letter?" Harry asked, mentally crossing his fingers.

"Yes," she said, "a deed, with Brandon Pike's, Clarissa's, and the names of the witnesses on it, also. It's stamped, signed, and dated. It was in the envelope with the letter. What should I do?"

"First, congratulations," Harry said, surprised by how pleased he was with the news. "You must call your lawyer and give him the names of some people to contact as soon as possible. Are you ready? Good. First, Gus Shriver, Brandon's lawyer at Brisket, Shriver, Polyphemus, & Thrale. Next, Jeff Smolkin, Holly's lawyer. Let the lawyer make the calls. Fax him copies of the documents you have. Any questions?"

"No. I think everything's clear. Will you be surprised if I say

I'm very relieved?"

"Not at all. Were you concerned that Holly might not extend the lease?"

Harry found, allowing himself now to consider the question, that he had no idea what Holly would have done about the lease. The doubt troubled him.

"Perhaps I shouldn't have been, but I was. I have felt for a long time that there was something not right about Clarissa's relationship with Mrs. Pike."

Harry wanted to say that a wife knows when her husband is sleeping with another woman, but instead he asked if she had any idea why Clarissa had kept the deed a secret.

"Because she could," Constanta said with bitter emphasis, "and because she was probably terrified that revealing the truth would give rise to questions."

Harry did not have to ask what those questions were.

"It's history now," he said. "Have you told Miguel?"

"Yes, I called him just before I called you. You know, it's odd. He was much more excited over the fact he was bringing Tyce Yellen home today than he was over the news that Oleander was ours."

"Sometimes," Harry said, "when we want a thing so much and the possibility of not getting it is just too painful, we fool ourselves into thinking we don't care if we get it or not."

"He's very complex," she said. Then, brightening again, added, "Thank you for urging me to make this search."

"You're welcome, very welcome. It's wonderful news, but don't let anyone except your lawyer put a hand on that deed."

34

Harry put down the phone and stood for a moment, staring out at the fields and wood beyond. It was a rare, blustery day with fleets of broken clouds scudding across the sky, bringing at erratic intervals tiny showers, many of which evaporated in fragmented rainbows before reaching the ground. Thinking about Constanta's discovery of the deed led him to wonder what Holly would make of Brandon's gift to Clarissa. Then he shook off the speculation, tinged as it was with an autumnal melancholy, and called on the dogs to follow him.

Harry had made a call that morning, and was happy to find the handyman he had contacted installing hinges and locks on the barn doors. He had reached Barn Four. Buster, his shirttail half out of his trousers and his shirt front soaked through with sweat, came out of Barn Three and hurried toward Harry.

"How is Mrs. Pike?" he demanded, pulling off his hat and banging it against his leg, the chopped hay clinging to it. "I can't get nothing out of that Thahn worth hearing."

"I can't tell you much, Buster," Harry said. "She was doing well this morning. I think she's got to be in some pain, but it's being controlled. They'll probably keep her for a few days, just to be sure she's all right. What have you been doing?"

Buster grinned, displaying two of his gold teeth and dropping his hat back on his head.

"Me, Tyrone, and Duncan been currying that Jack," he said cheerfully. "Leastwise, we been trying to. So far, he's kicked his hay rack off the wall and boosted me into a corner."

"That wound on his hip closing any?"

"It's slow. He chews on it, you know, pulled all them stitches out twice. The vet, she's some worked up, but I think the infection's keeping out of it."

"That's good news."

"I believe so."

Buster took off his hat again and this time waved it toward Barn Four.

"We locking these barns before we leave?" he asked.

"More than that," Harry said, nodding. "Make sure they're kept locked unless you or one of the men are working in them, and I'd like it better if none of you is working alone."

Buster hung his head and kicked at the dirt with the toe of his boot.

"This Elijah's doing?" he asked quietly, examining his hat.

"Yesterday, I saw him running into the woods," Harry said with equal lack of emphasis. "His back was to me, but I'm fairly sure that's who it was."

"Lord God," Buster said, looking up and finding Harry's eyes, "what twisted his head into that kind of knot?"

"We may find out, but I wouldn't bet on it," Harry said. "Don't take any chances with him, Buster. Keep the barns locked when no one's in them, and if he shows up, call 911, then run like hell for the house."

With that, Harry snapped his fingers at the dogs, which fell in beside him. Buster turned back to his work with Jack, who throughout his talk with Harry had been squealing as if he was trying to kill Duncan and Tyrone; Harry, however, had learned enough about the stallion to know Jack was just amusing himself.

Making a quick circle of each of the remaining barns and finding nothing, Harry set out at a brisk walk for the Oleander ride. If the police had not caught Elijah, he had decided, it was because the man hadn't gone anywhere. As for why the dogs had failed to locate him, the answer seemed obvious. He had broken his trail by getting into his truck and driving just far enough to escape them, then diving back into the woods for cover, successfully dodging the cruisers Jim had dispatched to Fullington Road.

After leaving Buster, Harry let the dogs run, and they took advantage of their freedom by galloping in long loops around him as he made his inspection of the barns. He paused briefly at the paddock where the heifers were held and noted that the animal in heat was repeatedly riding the two other cows.

He thought briefly of the black bull but quickly put him out of his mind. He would be miles away by now.

Once he had returned past Barn Two, Harry whistled in the dogs. With Nip on his left and Tuck on his right, he strode through the oak grove to the head of the Oleander ride.

"Stay close," he said, starting down the drive, which where he had entered was quite dry and open. But before he had gone a quarter of a mile, the ground under his feet softened, and he slowed his progress, studying the grassy ride for boot prints. The dogs, drawn by new and intriguing smells, began to wander out to the sides of the trail. Harry was not paying much attention to them until a young rabbit sprang out of the grass and sprinted between his feet.

Nip and Tuck saw the rabbit at the same moment and bounded after it in roaring pursuit. The rabbit made a dodge to the right and then to the left, but the dogs, tearing up the grass as they switched directions, hung on its tail. Harry shouted at the dogs to stop just as the rabbit decided things were getting serious and bolted into the brush beside the trail.

"Now look what you've done," he told them when he had one on each side of him again. "Between your barking and my shouting, everyone in the woods knows we're here."

Nevertheless, Harry continued to move along the ride toward Oleander, studying the ground as he went. He did not know the ride well enough to have any clear idea where he was in relation to the Cruzes' house, but as a rough estimate, he guessed that he was nearly halfway there. He had seen plenty of old boot prints but nothing fresh. Harry felt a sprinkle of water on his face and looked up. A small, dark cloud was skittering over, spitting rain as it passed.

He stopped and wondered whether he had made a mistake. Even if Elijah had hidden himself on one of the half dozen overgrown logging roads leading off Fullington Road, he wouldn't necessarily have come out to the ride. What was there to bring him out here?

"Unless," Harry said quietly to the dogs, "he planned to come back to kill me."

He had no sooner finished speaking than both dogs growled. Harry looked up and saw Elijah step into the ride twenty feet in front of him, holding his Browning halfway to his shoulder, the barrel pointed at Harry.

Once over the shock by his sudden arrival, Harry was startled by Elijah's ravaged face, deep-sunken eyes, and gaunt frame from which his stained and torn red T-shirt and tattered trousers, ripped at the knees, hung off him like rags on a scarecrow. He was bearded and dirty, and even from twenty feet Harry could smell the reek of sweat and worse.

"You too smart for your own good," Elijah said with a death-head's grin.

Having recognized Elijah, the dogs relaxed and sat down beside Harry, their tongues lolling.

"I'm surprised to see that Tuck dog still walking," Elijah said, losing his grin and stepping slowly toward the small group in front of him.

Harry said nothing, but he was thinking hard. He had one chance and only one. He would fall to his left, draw the CZ as he went down, and fire. If he failed to get the first shot off before he landed, Elijah would kill him. He would wait as long as he could, hoping for something to break Elijah's concentration.

"Pike's wife wasn't so lucky," Elijah said, stopping again.

"She's in some pain," Harry said as casually as he could, "but she'll recover."

Elijah's face contracted into a scowl of fury.

"I saw her go down," he shouted. "You playing with me?"

The dogs came onto their feet, growling, their eyes fixed on Elijah.

"You set them down," the man said, "or I'll blow them to hell."

"Sit," Harry said sharply.

Still growling, the dogs obeyed.

"The bitch is dead," Elijah said.

"She's in the hospital," Harry said with studied calm. "Your bullet went through a plank on the fence before it hit her. It broke her shoulder and tore her up some, but she's got a new shoulder. She and the baby will be all right."

Elijah's face worked.

"Then I'll have to kill her all over again," he said, the grin returning.

The dogs stood together, their eyes fixed on something beyond Elijah. For the first instant since Elijah had appeared, Harry took his eyes off him and looked down the ride. Fifty feet beyond Elijah, the ride turned sharply to the right.

"What they looking at?" Elijah demanded.

"I don't see anything," Harry said, then stiffened. "The bull."

The freakish wind might have kept their smell from him or it might not. He came around the corner with his head up, trotting purposefully. He came on possibly twice his length, slowed, then stopped, slashing his horns from right to left, a deep rumble building in his chest. At the same time, he began rocking back and forth as he pawed the ground, his hooves tearing up grassy sods and hurling them behind him. Then his head dropped and his tail came up.

"He's coming," Harry shouted.

At the same moment, the dogs leaped away, running directly at the bull.

"What . . ." Elijah shouted and glanced behind him.

Harry fell sideways, freeing the CZ as he went down, and shot Elijah as he continued to turn toward the bull, cursing and raising his rifle. He stumbled forward as if a giant hand had slapped him on the back, then he pitched forward, struck the ground heavily, and did not move.

"Nip! Tuck!" Harry shouted, "Stop!"

It was too late. The animals came together. The bull hooked left as he always did and caught Tuck, staggering as he twisted away from the thrust, and tossed him like a rag out of the ride. Harry groaned when he saw the bull's left horn, running red with Tuck's blood.

Nip had dodged the horns and fastened his jaws on the bull's ear, and the bull, roaring with rage and pain, broke his charge, trying repeatedly to trap Nip under his forehead and crush him into the ground, trampling the ground into a muddy circle of torn earth and grass in his efforts to free himself from the dog's grip.

Harry scrambled to his feet, ran to the fallen Elijah, and yanked the Browning free.

"Nip! Drop it!" he shouted.

The big dog waited until the bull had swung him off his feet again and fell away at the end of the swing. The bull instantly turned and lunged at him, but Nip jumped back from the enraged beast, keeping just out of reach of the scything horns. Still holding the Browning in his left hand, Harry moved quickly to place himself directly behind Nip.

The bull, noticing Harry's approach, threw up his head, shaking his horns at this new threat, preparing to charge. At that moment Harry raised the CZ, aiming for the bull's forehead, and fired. His shot was a little high, and the bullet struck the boss of the bull's horns. The huge animal took a single step backward, tried to bellow, and, groaning, slowly collapsed onto the ground, neck thrust out, his chin plowing into the mud.

"Out cold," Harry said, stroking Nip's head.

The dog, panting from his exertions, cocked his head at the fallen warrior, barked once, and began wagging his stub tail. Together, they went back to Elijah. Very cautiously, Harry bent and pressed his finger under Elijah's ear, waited, and shook his head.

"He's gone," he said to Nip, who was pressed against his leg. "Let's find Tuck."

Nip found Tuck, lying fifteen feet from the ride behind a head-high clump of stopper bushes.

A long, ragged tear in the animal's side where the horn had driven through to his heart had ceased to bleed.

"He was probably dead before he hit the ground," Harry said to Nip, who was standing over his companion, lying stretched out in the tall grass as if he was resting.

"Your mistress can add this to her heartache," Harry added.

Nip nosed his companion, whined once, and then moved back beside Harry.

"He was slowly dying," Harry said because Nip was looking at him, ears cocked. "That's why the bull caught him. It's probably better this way."

While Harry put his CZ back in its holster and took out his cell phone, Nip moved to stand over Tuck.

Once Harry had spoken to Jim Snyder, he called Nip and pushed through the bushes to the ride. Elijah still lay where he had fallen, but the bull was gone. His tracks, sunk into the soft earth, led up the center of the ride, moving steadily in the direction of The Oaks.

"Guess where he's going," Harry said.

Whatever Harry felt about killing Elijah, it lay too deep to be available to him at the moment. He deliberately returned to stand over Elijah's body and study him. From its point of entry, Harry guessed that the bullet had exploded through to the man's heart, killing him instantly. He probably owed the bull his life, and the one emotion he registered was relief that he had not killed the animal.

35

Once Harry finished telling Jim's people what they needed to know about Elijah's death, he walked back to The Oaks, accompanied by Hodges, who, having quizzed him closely about how he felt, all the while studying Harry as if he expected him to explode or collapse, clapped him on the back as they walked up the ride and regaled him with a long, scrofulous account of his latest pig hunt, in which one man had his hat shot off, another was run over by the swamp buggy, and a third had his camouflage trousers ripped off by an enraged boar that resented being shot at.

"I have absolutely decided," Hodges said, concluding his account as they came out of the ride into the oaks, "that moonshine and pig hunts are a bad mix. The only good thing about this one was that I didn't have to attend no funeral when it was over, although when Philly got home without his trousers, his wife pretty near killed him."

It finally dawned on Harry that Hodges's long and trying tale had been intended to keep his mind off the shooting.

"Thanks, Frank," he said when the sergeant had clapped him on the back again before veering off toward his cruiser.

"Anytime," Hodges said, moving away in his rolling gait. "You're a better listener than the Captain."

Harry found he wanted to laugh at that but couldn't and was surprised by it. When he stepped out of the trees into the stable yard, Buster saw him and came toward him at a trot.

"You all right?" he asked, shaking Harry's hand.

"I'm fine. Everything all right here?"

"Well, there's something . . ." He stopped and looked at Nip. "Where's Tuck?"

"The bull got him," Harry said, keeping a tight grip on his emotions, which had begun to stir. "Have you seen it?"

"Oh, yes," Buster replied. "Just step this way. You won't believe it."

Buster walked Harry along the paddock fences until they could see the Barn Five paddock clearly.

"This here's as far as we better go just now," he said, beginning to show signs of concern. "Climb up onto this gate with me."

Harry did as he was asked, and, gaining some elevation, he could see into the paddock where the Angus heifers were pastured. At that moment a black head with significant horns rose up from the clustered group of black bodies.

"That's three times he's serviced her in the last hour."

Harry managed to laugh.

"How did he get in there?"

"After he'd chased us all into the barn," Buster said with a touch of awe in his voice, "that black devil jumped over that five-barred gate like he had wings."

"*Amor vincet omnia*," Harry said.

"What?" Buster asked.

"In the game of life, sex trumps gates."

On his way to see Holly, he called Katherine and told her that Elijah was dead. He did not elaborate and begged off explaining because he was driving. Then he called Soñadora, telling himself that if she heard from someone else that Elijah had been killed, she would worry about him.

"Are you driving?" she asked as soon as she answered. "I

hear road noises."

"Yes. There's something I want . . ."

"You know it is dangerous what you are doing," she insisted.

"Elijah Blue is dead," he said, talking over her.

"Are you all right?"

When he told her that he was, exceeding the facts somewhat, she said, "Good. Now stop talking before you cause an accident."

Harry threw his cell onto the seat beside him and swore. She was the most aggravating woman he had ever known. Putting his cell in his pocket, he began rehearsing how he was going to tell Holly that Elijah was dead without saying he had shot him. He did not explore why he didn't want her to know he had been the shooter, although if he had been asked, he would have said that he didn't want to upset her.

"You're dressed!" Harry said when he entered her room and found her sitting in a chair beside the metal bedside table, looking at a magazine and turning the pages with her left hand.

Her right arm was in an elaborate blue brace that held it bent at the elbow and locked in place in front of her.

"Would you rather I weren't?" she asked, looking up him with dark-rimmed eyes.

"I refuse to answer on the grounds, etc.," he said. "How's the shoulder?"

"Sore as hell."

"I believe it. I saw the wound. Do you remember being shot?"

"Absolutely. You're looking pretty bad yourself. What is it?"

"Elijah Blue is dead," he told her.

"Well, Hallelujah!" she said, breaking into a broad grin. "Who got the son of a bitch?"

Harry paused, not because he was worried any longer about upsetting her, but because he didn't want to think of himself as having "got" Elijah. Yes, the man was a killer and had to be stopped, but . . .

"Harry!" Holly said, looking worried.

"I shot him, Holly," he said quietly, "but I didn't 'get' him."

"You mean you're not going to have him mounted."

Harry felt his face stiffen.

"Let's drop this," he said. "The man's dead."

"Tell me," she said seriously.

It took him a minute to sort through his feelings and get them into some kind of order. "Before I decide whether or not I'm going there, I've got some bad news. Tuck is dead."

She sat looking at him in silence, tears welled and ran down her face.

"I'm sorry," he said.

"How did it happen?" she asked.

"He and Nip attacked the bull, and it killed Tuck. Nip is fine."

She sank into the chair, her head tipped back, her eyes squeezed shut.

"Oh, God," she said, her voice breaking. "I knew he was dying, but I didn't want him to go this way."

It's not really possible to hug a person sitting down with her arm in a brace, but Harry came as close to doing it as he could.

"It happened so fast, I don't think he had time to suffer," Harry told her, reaching out to the box of tissues on the table and starting to dab her eyes.

"Stop it," she said, knocking his hand away.

By now she was crying all out and making sounds that wrenched Harry's heart. So he didn't let go of her. He just held her tighter. After a bit, she grew quiet, and Harry went back to drying her eyes.

"Thanks," she said at last. "That's enough," and pushed him away.

"Okay," he said and picked up the other folding chair and set it beside hers.

She blew her nose, holding the tissue in one hand. It wasn't altogether successful.

"Oh, shit," she said, struggling with the tissue.

"Are you going to let me help?" Harry asked.

He did without waiting for an answer.

"Do you do bedpans?" she asked when he was finished.

"Reluctantly," he said and quickly told her more about Elijah, the bull, and the dogs.

"There's one more thing," he said when he was finished with the account. "I don't know whether you're going to think it's bad news or not."

He stopped and waited until she demanded he go on.

"The bull is in the paddock with the Angus heifers and the one in heat has had her prayers answered."

Holly gave a shout that was half laughter and half protest.

"How did he get in there?"

"He jumped the fence."

"How are you going to get him out?"

"Don't look at me."

Harry returned to the Hammock to find Katherine sitting on the lanai, wearing her traveling clothes, her bags beside her. She was reading, and when Harry pulled open the screen door, she closed her book, stood up, and with a smile said, "Just in time to say goodbye."

She looked at her watch.

"I've got just about enough time to return my car, catch the shuttle, and make my flight."

He stepped inside and stood looking at her, trying to gauge her mood. His stomach had already fallen into his shoes, and he saw no reason to give it any more attention. There were levels of misery that required no support.

"What brought this on?" he asked, unable to say anything more appropriate.

"I said I'd leave after the windows were installed and that I wouldn't leave you alone with Elijah on the loose. The windows are in and Elijah's dead. Both conditions are met."

"Why are you angry?"

Her smile hadn't slipped, but her voice was sharp as a sliver of flint.

"Where did Elijah die?"

Harry decided to get this over with and try to work with what was left, not that he expected much to be left standing. Dust and ashes would about sum it up.

"On the ride between The Oaks and Oleander."

"How did he die?"

"I shot him."

"Congratulations. One giant step toward making the world safe for everybody."

Harry had expected worse, but her sarcasm still hurt.

"How close were you to being killed?" she demanded harshly.

"What if I just told you what happened?"

"All right."

He told her. When he was finished, she bent and pushed her book into a pocket on her carry-on case. Then she stood up, pulled down the jacket on her blue suit, and, stepping forward, hugged him, pressing her face against his.

"You idiot," she said softly. "I'm glad you're all right."

"I'd be a lot better if you'd unpack these bags," he said, hugging her as hard as he dared.

"Nope," she said, leaning back in his arms and then kissing him.

"For all the old reasons?" he asked.

"I can't take it, Harry. It's bad enough when I'm in Georgia," she said, her smile slipping. "Here, waiting for the call that will tell me you're dead, is more than I can bear."

In all the years they had been together, man and wife, she had never stopped trying to make him find some other work, and he had never stopped refusing.

"I love you, Katherine," he said.

"I know," she said, "and I love you, but it's not enough. Goodbye, Harry. Thank you for taking me in and helping me to get well. I'm very grateful."

With that, she picked up her bags and pushed open the lanai door.

"Say goodbye to Tucker for me," she said, letting the screen door slam behind her. Then she paused and said over her shoulder, "Harry, if you change your mind, you know where to reach me."

He thought it best to say nothing and felt a large piece of his life being wrenched out of him as she drove away. The white dust blown up by her car drifted over the Puc Puggy and vanished in the sunlight. He stood staring through the screen until he heard the rattle of the loose plank in the bridge. As the silence flowed back, he forced himself to walk into the deserted kitchen, feeling the emptiness of the house expand around him.

36

"Did you part on good terms?" Tucker asked Harry the next morning as he and Harry, working off short ladders, were stapling squares of aluminum hurricane fence across the top of the hen run. Harry, using a three-foot crowbar, stretched the wire taut as Tucker drove in the staples.

"Well, she left," Harry said, still feeling too bruised to allow for much generosity of spirit. "That pretty much sums up the parting."

Harry had not slept much, and breakfast had tasted like wet cardboard.

"Katherine probably feels as bad as you do," Tucker said.

Harry leaned into the crowbar with a grunt of effort rather than say that her feeling bad didn't help the situation.

"Slack off a bit," Tucker warned. "The frame is starting to give."

"It's all such a damned waste," Harry said, easing the strain he was putting on the wire.

He would have said more except that knowing how Tucker felt about Katherine made him censor himself. She was the daughter he'd never had, and his protectiveness ran deep.

"What can't be changed must be endured," Tucker said. "You and Katherine are like the two robins pulling on that worm. Neither is going to give up, and neither is going to learn anything."

"That made me feel a lot better," Harry said sourly.

"No extra charge," the old farmer said.

"What about those coyotes?" Harry asked, changing the subject.

"They've been sneaking around," Tucker said, pausing to mop his face with his bandanna, "mostly after dark."

He chuckled and leaned against the section of fence that was stapled.

"You've noticed the smell of skunk is fairly strong," Tucker said.

"Worse than that," Harry complained. "It's almost strong enough to make my eyes water."

"Night before last, Florinda and her youngsters were out here in the run—I hadn't yet stapled that back section on— digging for worms. The hen manure attracts them, or so it seems. Anyway, the coyotes came into the run, thinking, most likely, that they might find a way into the henhouse from this side. They know the hens go in and out and probably intended to learn how they did it."

In spite of his troubles, Harry had become interested in the story and asked why the coyotes would risk getting sprayed.

"There was enough moon showing to satisfy Oh, Brother! and, from what he said, he was out for a little walk before sleeping—he likes that moonlight walk and usually has a final look around to see if everything's all right before going to bed. Sanchez used to go with him, but he doesn't see at night as well as he used to and lets Oh, Brother! make the rounds alone now."

"So Oh, Brother! saw what happened?" Harry asked, trying to hurry Tucker along.

"Yes, but I still don't know whether it was carelessness on the coyotes' part, a lapse in judgment that led them into the run while the skunks were there, or an unusually strong attack of chicken fever. Whatever it was, no sooner had they trotted in

401

than Florinda and her young ones sprayed them."

Tucker stopped to laugh, and Harry managed a chuckle. Tucker went back to driving in the staples, leaving Harry to brood as he stretched the wire.

"Have I told you that Constanta found a letter from Brandon to Clarissa, giving her the deed to Oleander?"

"No, and I'm glad to hear it," Tucker said, driving in the last staple. "What does Holly say about it?"

"I haven't asked."

Harry helped Tucker gather up his tools, turning over in his mind why he hadn't spoken to her about the discovery.

"I know Jim's talked to her again about the blackmail letter," Harry said, "pretty much failing to get any helpful response. He's thinking over whether or not to press the issue."

"Of course. I've asked you before, but do you now think Holly wrote it?" Tucker asked.

While looking for an answer, Harry hung the hammers and the wire cutters on the barn wall and stood the crowbar in its barrel with the long-handled shovels and the rakes.

"I have no way of knowing," he said as he and Tucker left the barn, pausing to stand in the sunlight filling the barn door and feeling dissatisfied with his answer.

"No," Tucker replied, lifting his face into the sun and closing his eyes, "I suppose not, but who else could have sent it might help."

"As you know," Harry said, "it's a short list."

"And Elijah's dead."

"And you and I didn't write it."

Tucker smiled.

"And neither did Jim Snyder or either of the Cruz brothers."

Harry was getting more and more uncomfortable, but he said, "Neither did Tyce Yellen."

"No," Tucker said. "When's he leaving the hospital?"

"Miguel took him home yesterday. He's going to stay at Oleander until he's well enough to go back to work."

"Occasionally, things work out well. I won't mention silver linings."

"You know what you just did," Harry said.

"No," Tucker said, opening his eyes and looking at Harry with apparent surprise.

"Yes, you do. You eliminated everyone on the short list except Holly, then tried to change the subject."

"Oh, did I? Here come Sanchez and Oh, Brother! They've been in the citrus grove. Have I told you the latest about Jane Bunting's saving the woodchuck cubs?"

Harry gave up.

When Harry got home, he made a pretense of sweeping off the lanai, a daily task because of the pollen that filtered through the screen, leaving a dusting of pale green on the floor. The task only made Harry feel worse because Katherine was the one who had taken over the job while she was with him. Then he thought he might put back the section of the wisteria that the wind had pulled down in the last thunderstorm.

But while collecting his hammer and garden twine and a knife from the kitchen drawer where they didn't belong but where they more or less lived, he suddenly stopped and put everything back in the drawer and closed it.

"I've got to do it," he told the mockingbird, perched in the sagging wisteria, watching him through the open window.

Straightening his back, he marched to the phone and punched in a number.

"*Salvamento.*"

"It's the first time I've spoken to a building."

"Are you at home?"

"Yes."

403

"Are you alone?"

"Yes."

"Is Katherine at Haven House?"

"No. Can we stop this anytime soon?"

"I'm busy."

"So am I. I called to tell you that Katherine has gone."

He suddenly felt like an idiot. Why was he doing this to himself?

"Thank you. Perhaps we can talk later," she said.

"All right. Goodbye."

Once off the line, his feelings of loss and humiliation were quickly morphing into depression, and he decided the best way to cope was to go to The Oaks and begin dealing with the bull. He was pretty sure Buster wouldn't have gone near the beast.

As Harry had expected, the bull was still in the paddock with the heifers.

"We've been keeping back from him," Buster said.

He and Harry were looking at the backs of the cattle from behind the fence of Barn Four, trying not to be seen.

"He and those heifers need hay and grain," Harry said. "The grass in the paddock's about gone."

"He jumped into that paddock," Buster said, regarding Harry with a solemn expression. "He can jump out."

"You're right," Harry agreed, "but I think he's right where he wants to be. Let's get the tractor and find out."

"I'm driving," Buster said, "you can ride on the trailer."

"In case he jumps."

"That's right."

The bed of the trailer was only about two and half feet off the ground and designed to be loaded and unloaded easily by hand. As Harry rode on the trailer, standing behind Buster and holding onto the tractor seat for balance, he felt less and less sanguine about his situation the closer they came to the Barn Five paddock.

"Pull up as close as you can to the hay rack," he shouted to Buster over the tractor's din. "We'll cut the wires on the bales and throw the hay into the rack and pour the grain on the ground."

"What if he jumps?" Buster shouted back.

"I'll go over the fence the other way. You get the tractor out of here as fast as you can and come back with a truck."

Buster shook his head but kept on driving. Harry noticed he was not having any trouble concentrating as the tractor approached the fence, especially when the heifers and the black bull came trotting across the paddock toward them.

When the tractor stopped, Buster jumped off the seat onto the trailer and said, "Dump the grain first. They going to want the grain more than the hay. Might keep him occupied."

"Here goes," Harry said, grasping the sack and clambering up onto the fence.

The bull stopped ten feet from where Harry was stranded on the fence, unfastening the twist of wire closing the sack, staring back at the bull. Twice in as many days was twice too many, Harry thought, the breath in his chest getting tight as he studied the powerful animal, his head thrown up, the horns curving out and up from his head, one still stained with Tuck's blood.

"Don't be waiting for no introduction," Buster said, working swiftly below Harry with the wire cutters and trying to keep his eye on the bull between the planks at the same time.

"Right," Harry said, forcing himself to look away from those huge dark eyes and get to the business of pouring out the grain.

Once the grain began to pour from the sack, the heifers, who had held back in deference to the bull, now shouldered forward. The bull dropped his head, shaking his horns and rumbling quietly as if communing with his inner self, but then, seeing the grain being swept up by the three eager and efficient heifers, he totted forward and joined the feast. By then, Buster had pitched the opened bales into the rack and was peering at the four animals.

"You ever see the beat of that?" he enquired, joining Harry on the fence.

"Love has tamed the savage breast," Harry said, allowing himself to laugh, finding his breathing had returned to normal.

"More likely the grain did it," Buster replied. "But it's about gone. What say we leave?"

"Done," Harry said. "I'm going to the house to call Geoffrey Ryan and tell him to come and collect his bull."

Between the demands of Jim Snyder's department and the Assistant District Attorney's Office, both of which were occupied with closing the various cases involving Brandon Pike's murder and what followed, as well as his ongoing work at The Oaks, Harry was kept busy. Holly came home, but her activities were limited, and her temper sharpened as time passed and Esther Benson refused to give her more freedom. Tyce Yellen, under Miguel's care, recovered rapidly and most days was able to spend some time with Harry catching up with the work going forward on the farm. The painters finished work on Barn One and departed, leaving Harry the task of supervising the return of Jack and the other displaced horses to the new barn.

It was as well Harry had work to occupy him because nights and when he was not busy, his mind invariably turned to grim reflections on the barrenness of his life. He missed Katherine, but he was, to some degree, resigned to that loss and found that, having long ago made peace with himself over his decision to let her go, it was a pain he could live with.

What increasingly disrupted his peace of mind was his inability to come to terms with the unfinished business between himself and Soñadora. The absence of resolution became, in ways he did not understand, mingled with his more general and strengthening sense of emptiness, loneliness, and the pointlessness of his life.

Call her, one of his voices told him, but it was drowned in his resistance, resentment, and the powerful conviction that she was finished with him. And how could he blame her after treating her the way he had before and after Katherine's arrival on the Hammock? He couldn't. The fault was his, and he must live with it.

The problem was that he didn't seem able to do that simple thing.

37

Then one night when he was sitting at his kitchen table, staring out the window at the moon, his dinner uneaten in front of him, feeling more than ordinarily sorry for himself, the phone rang.

"Why haven't you called me?" she said.

Harry was not much worse or better than most men, and his first impulse was to be angry and to let her know it. Fortunately, he was feeling sufficiently miserable to be grateful just to hear her voice and he said, "I didn't think you wanted me to."

The lameness of the response gave some indication of just how far down the well he had tumbled.

"I am sorry, Harry," Soñadora said. "I was unpleasant. Will you accept my apology?"

Whatever anger he had been feeling was washed away by her appeal.

"Only if you will have dinner with me," he said, trying to retain some self-respect.

"Where?" she asked suspiciously.

"Here, with me. I make a fierce shrimp salad."

She laughed, frightening Harry because he had braced himself for a refusal and dreaded what might follow a laugh.

"A wild animal is said to be fierce," she said, her voice breaking up. "How could a salad be fierce?"

"You can only find out by eating one with me."

"All right. Tomorrow night? Can you pick me up at six? When

408

you get here, just bark," and she hung up, laughing again.

When Harry, still dazed, glanced out the window, he was astonished to see how beautiful the moon was.

As Harry turned into the *Salvamento* driveway, Soñadora came out the front door, carrying a brightly colored cloth bag slung over her shoulder. She was dressed in a plum-colored skirt, a collarless dark orange top with three-quarter-length sleeves, and matching sandals. Her black hair was plaited and wound around her head. For a moment, Harry just sat, watching her, thinking how lovely she was.

"What's in the bag?" he asked after handing her into the Rover.

"You should not ask, but I will tell you anyway as you are a *gringo* with no finesse," she retorted. "It is dungarees and a shirt with collar and sleeves because you might force me to stroll in the woods again. I will wear Minna's sneakers."

"You walk in the woods and stroll on a boulevard," he replied, backing into the street.

"Do you know how rude you are?"

She spoke as he had with no trace of humor.

"And you are far more beautiful than is fair."

"I am not beautiful, but what is not fair?"

"It makes it very difficult for me to keep my eyes on the road."

She blushed and could not suppress the laugh that followed it.

"*Idiota,*" she said.

She must be, he realized, enjoying herself. Otherwise, she would not have called him an idiot.

Once they reached the Hammock, she asked if they could take a walk. Because it was growing dark, they walked on the road toward Tucker's place, the evening star dodging in and out

409

of the gaps in the trees beside the creek. As they watched, four small, shining black heads drifted into the bright spot on the dark water.

"What are they?" Soñadora asked.

At the sound of her voice, all the heads vanished, only to re-appear closer to shore.

"Otters," Harry said. "The mother and three young ones. Their den is under the bridge."

Satisfied that she knew what was making the racket, the mother resumed her path down the creek, dutifully followed by her cubs.

"Wonderful," Soñadora whispered as they swam out of sight.

Before Harry could answer, they were surrounded by a deep, throaty sound, resembling the purring of a giant cat.

"Are we in danger?" Soñadora asked, moving back a little from the water.

"No," Harry said, taking her hand, "it's Benjamin, the alligator. Let's stand a minute more. We might see him."

"Why does he make that strange noise?"

"He is telling all the female alligators that he's open for business."

"You're taking me for a nincompoop!" she said, freeing her hand and giving him a push.

"I'm serious," he said, laughing. "Where did you learn the word *nincompoop?*"

"Two of my people were arguing in Spanish and one called the other a nincompoop. I thought it was a very funny word. And also it is suitable for you."

Just then, silent as the otters, a long, thick black body drifted into view.

"There he is," Harry said quietly.

"That's a tree," she said.

"Watch."

Benjamin slowly turned his length, swirling the water with his bulk, to face upstream. Then he began to rumble again. The water along his sides rippled into tiny, glittering waves, agitated by the vibration of the huge animal's body.

"He is a giant creature," Soñadora said in an awed voice.

"And he's still growing," Harry said.

They watched until the alligator let himself drift out of their sight with the current. Then they walked back to the house. They walked mostly in silence, listening and looking at the teeming night world.

"I might not have walked on the road in the darkness if I had known Benjamin lived so close by," she said as they crossed the lawn, "but I would not have missed seeing him and hearing his love song."

"I like it best when there's moonlight," Harry said.

"One sees better," she replied and hurried off to change out of her walking clothes.

When she came back, she helped Harry finish putting their dinner on the table and while Harry poured the wine, she made the coffee. "The moon is in the window again," she said before sitting down. "It was here the last time."

"Yes, it was," Harry said, holding her chair. "I remember that very well."

"A good memory?" she asked him, and when he said it was, she said, "For me too."

"I found the salad delicious but lacking in ferocity," she told him when she poured their coffee.

"*Ferocity!*" he said. "I'm impressed. Perhaps next time we'll make the salad together."

That was followed by an awkward silence. When she had sat down again, she said, staring at her coffee cup, "I do not have to go home tonight or be back early. Gabriela will open *Salvamento.*"

When she raised her eyes to meet his, Harry saw the effort she was making and the fear of rejection lurking in their dark depths.

"You have made me the happiest man in Tequesta County," he said, reaching across the table to put his hand over hers.

"You would be happier if it were Katherine who was here," she said. "Is it not true?"

"I won't answer that question," Harry said, "but I want you to know this—she is not here. If I were willing to give up my work, which I'm not, I could have our marriage back, but she will not have me back, ever, unless I do."

"Do you still love her?"

Harry hesitated and decided to be honest. There was too much at stake not to be.

"Yes. I think I'll always love her, but I won't be with her, and I won't cling to her as I have in the past." He paused, then decided to make a clean breast of it. "You see, when she came here ill, I told myself as I always have when she's here that she had come back for good. For a while I allowed myself to believe it. I was afraid to talk with you about it because if I had, I would probably have been forced to see what I was doing. I deliberately deceived myself and in the process hurt you. I am terribly sorry for that."

"Do you regret that she is gone?" she asked quietly.

"No. I regret that it took me so long to understand that she and I were never going to be together again. And if I am to have any happiness, real happiness, I must be honest with myself and with you."

He stopped talking, half certain that she would ask him to take her home, and that would end their relationship. He found it hard to face.

"Do you want me to be a part of your new life?" she asked.

"Yes," he said, determined to see this through.

412

Quite suddenly, she smiled.

"Dishes first, bed second," she said, pushing back her chair.

Sometime after midnight, she told him she loved him. They slept, and when they woke, made love again with a pale pink dawn light falling over them and the bed. Their passion spent, she fell forward onto his chest, her face buried in his neck, her shining black hair spilling over his shoulders like a fall of water.

"If I tell you I love you," he whispered in her ear, "can you believe me?"

"Yes," she said, "I will believe you."

"I love you," he said.

"Then we are one," she answered and covered his face with kisses.

They had finished breakfast when she told him. They were standing together at the sink. She was washing the dishes, and he was drying them. After she had passed him the last dish and wiped her hands, she turned to him, waited until he had hung up the cloth, and then put her arms around him.

"Harry," she said, "I have something to tell you, and before I do, you must understand that when I made the plan, I could not have known how things are now between us. Please say you know."

"All right," he said, embracing her but dreading what was coming because he thought he knew.

"I am going back to Guatemala. I will be gone six months. I have promised, and I must go."

Then she waited.

"It's Pierre Robichaud, isn't it? You're going back because he needs you."

"Please don't say that, Harry, not that way."

"Then tell me I'm wrong."

"You are wrong. I am going back for me, not him. I have lost my way here, Harry. I no longer feel I'm needed at *Salvamento.*

413

It runs without me."

"Guatemala has run without you for some time."

"It's very hard for me to explain," she said with increasing urgency. "I will go there and work very hard. At the end of six months, I am certain that I will know what to do."

"Marry Pierre Robichaud," Harry said bitterly.

"I could almost be his mother, Harry!" she cried, shaking him. "And he is a priest!"

"Your mother married one."

"She never married. Besides, do you think I can ever be like my mother?" she demanded, her voice edged with anger.

"No," he said, aware he should leave it there but driven to go on. "But I will tell you what I do think. This young man has taken your father's place. He's become your father as a young man. You're already sympathetic, drawn to help him, and you've probably idealized him. I think there's a strong chance that once you begin to work with him, you will fall in love with him, and I will lose you forever."

She waited until he had finished and then took his face in her hands.

"Never," she said. "Never, Harry. I love you. I have loved you for years. I could never do what you have said."

"And I love you," he said. "Are you sure you have to go?"

"What I have worked for here has been accomplished. I cannot do more for *Salvamento*," she said sadly, dropping her hands. "It has been my life, and now it no longer needs me. I am empty, Harry. I must learn how to fill myself again. Please. Try to understand."

For him, the worst part of her plea was that he did understand. Her work had sustained her all the years he had known her. Hers had been a solitary life of almost total dedication to the victims of human trafficking, abuse, and despair. If she had lost that work. . . . He knew all there was to know about the salt losing its savor. If it had happened to her, then he had no choice but to support her in her efforts to fill that emptiness.

"Why Guatemala?" he asked, erasing all anger from his voice.

"Harry, I am a stranger here. I must go back to my people. Once there, perhaps I can recover whatever it is that I have lost."

"All right," he said. "If you have to do it, then go. I'll be here, but are you sure you need to go back? I'm here now. Rowena Farnham is here, and there are others."

"I know," she said, "but I made promises, and I made them when I was certain I had lost you. They are promises I must keep."

He would not argue. He was in no position to argue because he knew she had made the promises after she learned that he had brought Katherine to the Hammock without telling her.

"When are you going?" he asked, trying to sound practical. "What about your plane fare?"

"I have the ticket, Harry," she told him. She hesitated. "I am leaving this afternoon."

That was a blow, but he absorbed it without comment.

"I'll drive you to the airport."

"No, Harry," she said, clinging to him. "I want to leave alone from *Salvamento* to the airport. Will you let me do that?"

Of course, he said yes. They took a final walk with her wearing Minna's sneakers and one of his long-sleeved shirts. He drove her to *Salvamento*. Her plane departed on time, and Harry began the work of believing that she would return.

38

A week later, Harry, Holly, Yellen, and Buster were in Barn One, watching Jack go through his usual squealing and slashing routine while being carded and brushed, preparatory to being put in his paddock. Holly was out of her frame and wearing her arm in a blue canvas sling. Tyce was thoroughly enjoying the show but still at some distance from riding the stallion. His clothes still hung off him like rags on a scarecrow.

"His hip looks good, Buster," he said, dodging close to Jack for a closer look.

"Watch yourself, man," Buster said, scowling at Tyce. "None of us want you back in the hospital."

"A real pain in the ass," Tyce said fondly to Jack, giving the animal a slap on his side, then dancing away from a flying rear hoof.

"Has anybody been riding him while I've been gone?" Holly asked Buster.

"I have," Harry said, "almost every day."

Everybody looked at him, including Buster, who said after a pause, "Every day. Saw it with my own two eyes."

"I take it the answer is no!" Holly said, looking put out. "Why didn't you or one of the other men exercise him?"

"We all thought of doing it," Buster said, "but decided that what with that cut in his hip that took its time about healing, we'd all just hold off on putting a saddle on his back."

"We really were concerned about that gash, Mrs. Pike,"

Tyrone said, stepping back to knock the hair and dirt out of his currycomb with the back of his brush. "I'll ride him if you want me to. Course, I ain't as good as you and Tyce, but he'll probably put up with me."

"Somebody other than me is going to explain it to his wife," Carlyle said from the other side of the horse.

"Explain what?" Holly asked.

Harry managed to keep his face straight.

"How come we're bringing Tyrone home in a basket."

"Very funny, Carlyle," Holly said, but she managed to laugh with the rest.

When Jack was finally delivered to his paddock, and Tyce had gone to his office to catch up on the work Harry had left for him, Harry and Holly walked back to the house.

It was a brilliant, clear morning with the thunderheads already building in the east, bringing with them the promise of a blistering afternoon. The katydids and the locusts were already tuning up, and Nip was hurrying ahead, his eyes on the shade under the oaks.

"How did Ryan get that bull out of Number Five paddock?" she asked.

"His people backed their cattle van up to the gate and teased the heifers into the van with grain. Once they were loaded, the bull followed, tame as a kitten. He's really smitten with that Angus heifer."

"Maybe there are miracles," she said and gave his arm a shake. "You know, I don't want to go into the house. Can you stay long enough to walk down to see Sueño?"

"Of course. How's Nip taking the loss of Tuck?" he asked when Holly came out of the house with Nip and passed him an onion sack bulging with half a dozen winesaps.

"He misses him," she said as they went on toward Sueño's pasture. "I miss him if it comes to that. Speaking of losses, how

417

are you getting along?"

"Scraping by," he said.

Neither Katherine nor Soñadora had called or written. He thought they might as well have vanished off the earth. It was not a pleasant feeling, and he did not want to talk about it.

"Did Katherine have easy pregnancies?" she asked as though it was a question that logically followed his response.

Harry thought that was an odd question but decided to answer without complicating things.

"She wasn't chased by a wild bull or shot," he said. "So, compared to yours so far, I suppose they were."

"Very funny. You ought to take that act on stage."

"Ouch," Harry said, feeding Sueño an apple.

The horse no longer had her limp and had even galloped toward them when Holly whistled her in.

"Sorry," Holly said, without convincing Harry she was at all sorry. "Jim Snyder and that Millard Jones"—she colored slightly mentioning his name—"have been treating me very badly since I came home from the hospital."

"Women usually like Millard," Harry said, trying to sound sympathetic.

The pink in her cheeks brightened.

"Well, yes," she said, looking quickly away, "and probably in another situation . . ." she left the thought uncompleted, "but he and his people have been a nuisance."

When she turned back to Harry, a frown had replaced the blush. Harry did not have to ask what the trouble was about. There had scarcely been a day since he learned of the blackmail letter that Harry had not asked himself if she had written it.

"What does Jeff Smolkin tell you?" he asked, knowing the answer but not wanting to say so.

"He keeps telling me to say I didn't write it and stick to the story." She paused. "I don't know why he keeps calling it a story. I don't think that's being very supportive."

"And you've followed his advice?"

Now they were leaning against the fence looking from one another to Sueño, who, resigned to the end of the apples, was grazing near them.

"Wouldn't you?" she said.

There was harshness in her voice that Harry had not heard before.

"That depends," he said.

"On whether or not you'd written it?" she asked.

"Something like that," he said.

Her smile when it came was one Harry couldn't read.

ABOUT THE AUTHOR

Kinley Roby lives in Virginia with his wife, author and editor Mary Linn Roby.